Hanging Softly i

Hanging Softly in the Night:
A Detective Nick Larson Novel

by Maria Elena Alonso-Sierra

Hanging Softly in the Night: A Detective Nick Larson Novel
©2020 by Maria Elena Alonso-Sierra
ISBN-13: 978-0-9862095-4-3
ISBN-10: 0-9862095-4-6

Cover design by Scott Carpenter
Formatting by Anessa Books

Other Titles By
Maria Elena Alonso-Sierra

A Small Note from the Author

The Sixteenth Police Precinct in New York City does not exist. Neither do the characters who work in it. Everything is imagination and creation.

New York City is, well, New York.

Acronyms, however, are part and parcel of police work and report writing. It is a type of shorthand used because the names they replace are entirely too long to keep rewriting. Some may already be familiar to the reader, others not so much. So, in order to facilitate things, below is the list of acronyms used in the novel and their meanings.

ABFO – American Board of Forensic Odontology ruler used in investigations

AEW – All Elite Wrestling

AF – idiomatic expression meaning "As F*ck"

AFIS – Automated Fingerprint Identification System

ASL – American Sign Language

ATI – All Things Internet

BOLO – Be on the Lookout

CCTV – Closed Circuit Television

DA – District Attorney

DAS – Domain Awareness System

DB – Dead Body(ies)

DIY – Do-It-Yourself

DMSO – Dimethyl sulfoxide

DMV – Department of Motor Vehicles

DNA – Deoxyribonucleic acid

DUMBO – Down Under the Manhattan Bridge Overpass

EMS – Emergency Medical Services

EMT – Emergency Medical Technician

FID –Forensic Investigations Division

GC-MS – Gas chromatography-mass spectrometry

GMOs – Genetically Modified Organisms

HEA – Happily Ever After

HIPAA – Health Insurance Portability and Accountability Act

HR – Human Resources

IIT – Irresistible Impulse Test

IND – Independent Subway System subway line

IoT – Internet of Things

IRT – Interborough Rapid Transit Company subway line

IT – Information Technology

LIE – Long Island Expressway

LIRR – Long Island Rail Road

MASPEC – Mass Spectrometer

ME – Medical Examiner

MIA – Missing in Action

MJ – marijuana

MMA – Mixed Martial Arts

MO – modus operandi

MOD – Manner of death

Nixle – Real-time alert system used by law enforcement to inform communities on public safety and emergency issues

NYPD – New York City Police Department

OCD – Obsessive-Compulsive Disorder

OCME – Office of Chief Medical Examiner

PBA – Police Benevolent Association (union)

PCL-R – Hare Psychopathy Checklist – Revised

PCR – Polymerase Chain Reaction

PDQ – Pretty Damn Quick

PIO – Public Information Officer

PT – Personal Time

PTO – Personal Time Off

RTCC – Real Time Crime Center

SAT – Scholastic Assessment Test

SCME – Suffolk County Medical Examiner

SNL – *Saturday Night Live* (TV comedy show)

SOS – Morse Code distress signal

STIF – Scandinavian Therapy Industry Franchisees (I made this one up)

TOD – Time of death

TXA – Tranexamic Acid

VPN – Virtual Private Network

WWE – World Wrestling Entertainment

Now I lay me down to sleep,
I pray the Lord my soul to keep...

The New England Primer based on Joseph Addison's essay in
The Spectator 1711.

CHAPTER ONE

Monday, January 6

THE SCENT OF decaying flesh, human excrement, and hopelessness assailed Detective Nick Larson as he stood at the entrance of the elegant foyer of the Upper East Side brownstone.

Nick's nostrils flared in offense. He gagged. Death was a smell he never got used to.

"Ah, shit."

The vapor from Nick's words hung in the frigid January air. Another body. Just what the department needed after a week from hell. Definitely not what Nick needed, not after barely two hours of sleep.

He grabbed a couple of booties from the box laid next to the doorway, covered his shoes, and stepped inside the foyer, followed closely by Vic Sacco, his partner for close to six years.

Sacco coughed. "A bit early for the dead to be so..."

"Pungent?" Nick interjected. His face was probably an unhealthy shade of white already. He felt clammy, his skin tight with an inner cold that had nothing to do with the outside temperature. "Should have brought my car, not hitched a ride in yours," Nick muttered, covering his nostrils as best he could.

Sacco patted Nick's shoulder in commiseration. He was used to Nick's squeamishness every time a dead body turned up. The smell from decomposition always did Nick in, the reason he usually stowed a small bottle of Febreze in his car trunk to spray on the cheap dust masks he kept there. Without it now, Nick would probably dry-heave throughout the entire investigation, or run to throw up someplace where he wouldn't contaminate the scene.

Sacco passed him by, widening the front door. The gap acted like a vacuum cleaner, with the noxious air slicing the men as it escaped. Larson panted through his mouth, his teeth a pithy barrier against the miasma rushing at him in the sudden crosscurrent.

Somewhere inside the foyer a "Goddamn it!" exploded simultaneously with Nick's.

"Close the damn door." The yell came from Tish Ramos, NYPD's Forensic Investigations Division guru, who kept tagging evidence a few feet away. "It's twelve fucking degrees out there."

Sacco ignored the order.

"Ramos, I don't care if it's fifty below," Sacco said. "It's either blue balls or my clothes smelling like shit all day. Guess which I prefer?" His bull-like head jerked in Larson's direction. "Besides, Larson here is about to puke all over your crime scene. I doubt your shift supervisor will like it."

Tish Ramos methodically closed the evidence paper bag, labeled it, and turned her attention to the men. Her eyes captured Nick's six-foot image in a swift up and down. He knew he looked like a recently crumpled paper bag, skewed tie and all, black hair combed with impatient fingers to give it some sort of order, his angular face already displaying the usual five o'clock shadow. He hadn't had time to shave or dress neatly, as was his habit. After shift, he'd fallen face down on his couch and hadn't moved until the call had come through twenty minutes ago. For once, he'd been grateful for the call. It had interrupted a recent, recurring nightmare.

"What are you doing here?" Ramos asked. "You're not on call and this isn't a domestic."

"Another flu casualty," Nick croaked, gagged, and rubbed his eyes. He watched as one of the most meticulous women in their Forensic Investigations Division neatly deposited evidence into what the department euphemistically called doggy bags. As usual, Ramos looked sterile, dressed sterile, and breathed sterile.

"Captain's tired of juggling the domino meltdown with personnel calling in sick," Nick told her. "We're it for a while, unless we fold. Not that I mind, but why the personal touch here, Ramos? The call came in as suicide."

"The first responder thought so—at first." Ramos uncurled from her crouch, all five foot two of her, and gestured toward the rear of the townhouse. "Stan worked with me on a similar, supposed suicide about two months ago. When he saw the victim, his instinct kicked in. She is too neat. No evidence of thrashing. No rope burns."

Nick stared at Ramos, hoping for a denial and knowing he wouldn't get one.

Thrashing.

Rope burns.

Ramos stared back. Regret was there in her chocolate eyes, underscored with a wallop of pity. Nick recognized the look, having known Ramos for three years now, ever since she'd come on board FID. She knew there was only one type of incident that affected Nick after the death of Angela, his ex-wife. Only one. The main reason Nick's captain avoided giving him suicides for the moment. That is, until Nick got his shit back together.

"Hanging." Nick's voice sounded rough.

Ramos nodded.

Sacco cursed.

"Who called it in?" Nick asked. Anything to delay the inevitable.

Ramos's chin jerked toward the uniform. Nick recognized him. Stan Horowitz had fifteen years under his belt and was a staple at the Sixteenth Precinct. Always dependable, detail oriented, and, especially, experienced.

Horowitz studied his clipboard and, without prompting, began giving details.

"911 called in the possible 10-29 at oh four hundred from a neighbor across the backyard," he said. "Witness is a Pradeep Mansoor. His bedroom gives him a bird's eye view of the crime scene. Called it in after he realized what he was looking at."

"Witness coming or going?" Nick asked.

"Yoga before work," Horowitz replied.

"Bet you the sight fucked up his Pranayama," Ramos commented and immediately held up a hand. "And before you give me your usual wise-ass quip, Sacco, that's a Yogi term for breathing exercises. Expand your vocabulary."

Nick's lip twitched. Sacco blew Ramos a kiss.

"Let's start canvassing the area, Stan." Nick turned to Horowitz. "Have two uniforms roadmap the street and get statements. I'll set up an interview with the witness later."

Horowitz extended his clipboard. Nick wrote down the contact info on his flip notebook.

"What about the victim, Ramos?" Sacco asked. "ID?"

"License identifies her as an Isabel Creasy and, without a prelim from OCME, there's practically zilch as to exact cause of death, except the obvious," Ramos said, reaching the threshold of the attached sunroom at the rear of the brownstone. "Eyeballing it, the victim was probably drugged and placed in the noose like a rag doll. Cursory exam on the neck doesn't show signs of excessive trauma. Totes will tell us more once he gets the victim on the slab."

Christopher Millsap, affectionately known as Totes, was medical examiner for New York's finest. Several years ago, some wise-ass had come up with a brilliant syllogism after a fire on the D line. Amid the chaos on the scene, where sixteen people had been trampled and seven had died from smoke inhalation, the Office of Chief Medical Examiner had toted body bags to the morgue for hours until the scene had been cleared. To everyone's misfortune, though, whoever had come up with the affectionate moniker had made it stick, which had truly pissed off Millsap. And you don't piss off Christopher Millsap, ME. Soon after, Totes returned the favor by baptizing everyone in the precinct with ridiculous nicknames. Now, when anyone was pissed, they used the nicknames to piss everyone else off. Just a wonderful tit-for-tat, piss-off game at the Sixteenth.

Ramos paused on the threshold and looked at Nick. "Ready?"

Nick's body tautened. Past whispered conversations teased the recesses of his mind.

Come to me, Nicky. Save me.

You don't want to be saved, Angie. You want to rip and drag me to your level. I'm tired of this shit. Go bleed someone else.

His stomach heaved, and he broke out in a sweat despite the cold settling through the dark paneled hallway. He clenched his jaw and his fists. He was Angela's legacy: a pathetic mirror of himself, corroded by guilt and scarred by recrimination. Pathetic, he knew, but he was powerless to stop it for the moment.

Ramos stepped through the open French doors into the sunroom.

"It's hotter than hell in here," Sacco said, taking stock of the room as he stepped inside. Within seconds, he opened his coat and flapped it.

"Thermostat set at ninety-two," Ramos answered.

"For whose benefit? The plants or the victim?" Nick asked.

Ramos smiled. "Watch out where you step. Floor's slippery."

Nick entered the pentagonal sunroom. Breathed minimally. Gagged some more. Concentrated on a visual catalog of the area. During daylight, the room would absorb light through huge rectangular panels of tempered glass. Now, brightness from environmentally correct light bulbs bounced around generously, spotlighting expensive rattan furniture and tropical plants in an attempt at faux cheer. But the imitation sunshine failed to dispel the smell of tragedy or camouflage the body of a petite woman, dressed in a peach spaghetti-strapped nightgown, hanging in the middle of this greenhouse like meat in a butcher's freezer.

"Ramos," Nick's chin jerked toward the body, his voice hoarse. "You're all goddamn consideration." Unreasonable demand, he knew.

"Hey, take your frustration out on someone else," Ramos's eyes reproved. "Totes hasn't arrived yet."

Nick's bile rose. He tasted the acid on his tongue, and his throat muscles convulsed as his eyes locked on the woman's body. It was rocking gently from the breeze generated by an overhead fan and further helped by the soft hand of the rotating earth. Nick wished, and not for the first time, he hadn't hitched a ride with Sacco. His partner didn't even carry a jar of Vicks Vaporub. The menthol would at least camouflage the smell.

Concentrate on the room, damn it, not the body.

Nick turned. He surveyed the glass enclosure, delaying and preparing. The sunroom used space and light effectively, especially in a backyard as big as a thimble and surrounded by canyons of brick and steel. The townhomes and apartment buildings in this part of town were notoriously joined like Siamese twins, and every backyard watched a mirror image of itself barely ten feet away. *No privacy.* He'd rather hide within the solid walls of his apartment than be exposed like this, with spying or curious eyes lurking ten feet away behind tasteful window treatments.

Nick squinted, focused. "Son of a bitch." The witness was glued to his window, his silhouette creating a ghostly dark image against the brightness behind.

"Horowitz."

The officer's head popped around the doorway. "Yes, Lieutenant?"

"Get a uniform to the witness's apartment. Now, Horowitz. Have him close the damn blinds, or whatever the hell else the man has on those windows. I want him blind to what is happening in this crime scene."

Horowitz nodded and was about to disappear when Nick stopped him. "Have the uniform go through his phone. Confiscate it if you find any photos or videos."

"He's probably tweeted the fucking universe already." Ramos's words dripped with an angry cynicism.

"Ramos, buck up," Sacco said. "Live video, emojis, hashtags, podcasts, and selfies are the fare du jour."

"More like the bane of our existence," Nick said, making a mental note to check for postings later. He simply didn't understand the hedonist (or narcissist society, take your pick) through which the world muddled, with phones as an added extra appendage, its regurgitated contents more valuable than privacy or morality. There was no filter for the violent, coarse, or vulgar. Like Angela's suicide...

"By the way, first unit found a suicide letter." Ramos's tone suggested she wasn't buying it. She gestured, palms up, to the limp body. "First. Tell me what you see."

Nick tried to keep his composure but failed miserably, his mind substituting twisted memories for reality. His eyes registered the victim's curtain of blond hair, but his brain superimposed shoulder-length chestnut hair over it. Hazel eyes, bulging with fear and strangulation, replaced the closed eyelids of this dead woman. A small mouth, howling like Edvard Munch's *The Scream*, replaced the almost peaceful lips on the now-waxy face of the woman a few feet away.

His stomach burned. His mind supplied the acid.

Nicky, I need you.

You don't need, Angie. You butcher.

If you don't come back, I'll kill myself. I swear it, Nicky. I'll kill myself.

Nick clenched his jaw. This moment proved Life was a bitch with an agenda, eager to screw him at every opportunity. His body shuddered. He wondered for the thousandth time if he'd ever be normal again.

He needed a drink.

He needed his Febreze.

He gagged.

"Here, buddy." Ramos banged a plastic Ziploc bag onto Nick's chest. "Heave away. Just make sure to lock it tight after you're done."

Sacco chuckled. "Always prepared. You're anal, Ramos."

Ramos smiled sweetly. "You bet your tight ass, Sacco. You boys screw up my crime scene and it's my butt that'll get chewed." She eyed Nick, who was winning the battle with his stomach and his ghosts, and nodded. "Now stop wasting my time and get your butts in gear. I need input."

Nick concentrated. The real victim came into focus. She hung like a potted plant from a crude noose hooked from the slanting ceiling. Her feet limply pointed to a dining room chair placed four inches below her purpling toes. There was no sign of struggle, no evidence of that primitive instinct of survival that rears up as air is choked off. No wonder Ramos was suspicious.

Both he and Sacco put on their latex gloves.

"Unless that rope has retractable properties we don't know of," Sacco said, pointing to the gap between the victim's feet and the chair. "Someone helped her."

Nick studied the woman's bare arms. "Definitely not a do-it-yourselfer. She doesn't have the upper body strength to hang like a monkey, place that rope around her neck, and then drop."

"Damn uncomfortable way to commit suicide, not to mention unreliable," Sacco agreed.

Nick turned to Ramos. "Any evidence of scraping?"

"The chair?" Ramos shook her head. "That thing hasn't moved a millimeter since it was placed there. She doesn't have scratches around her neck, either."

Nick looked at his partner. Suicides by hanging were never static. Momentum, jerking, and thrashing always dispersed or overturned anything within a radius of several inches. More importantly, people jumped from their temporary platforms, not hanged themselves above them.

Ramos pointed. "Take a look."

Sacco held the wobbly ladder Ramos had placed next to the body. Nick climbed.

"The plastic protecting the metal on that hook is ripped," Ramos continued. "Bet the victim was roped first, the cord later looped through and pulled, using the thing as a fulcrum. Lab will determine if there are traces of plastic on the rope itself. After she was hanged, the rest of the room was staged."

Nick studied the area to which Ramos had pointed. The hook was the type used to hang heavy objects, like boats or bicycles in storage or garage areas. The plastic protector at the well was ripped, the plastic twisted, as if someone had squeezed in opposite motions, like a mop.

"Could the damage have been done previously?" Nick stepped off the ladder and held it as his partner climbed to take a look. Staff from the medical examiner's office began parading into the room, two of them rolling a gurney between them, mumbling excuses for their late arrival.

"Don't think so," Ramos said, acknowledging the newcomers with a bob of her head. "No other hook sports the same damage."

"You take that side," Nick said to Sacco as he stepped down.

Both men roamed the area, weaving around the furniture and the techs in the area. Nick studied the wells of all the other hooks dotting the rafters, saw signs of water damage on some, discoloration from iron rub-off on others, but nothing similar to what had happened to the victim's hook. He caught Sacco's attention, but his partner shook his head. He'd found nothing.

"Oh, and that's not the best," Ramos said, understanding the silent communication between the men. "Look at the left front leg of the chair, near the floor."

Nick inched closer and crouched carefully. There was a clear, doughnut-like ring circling its base. "Is that ice?" His tone was incredulous.

"Ice," Ramos confirmed.

They stared at each other, wondering how the hell ice had wrapped itself around a suicide's chair, in a room steaming worse than a decaying tropical hothouse.

"This has got to be someone's idea of a joke," Nick said, still incredulous.

"How'd the ice get there?" Sacco asked.

Ramos gave Sacco "The Look," the one that said his question didn't deserve consideration or an answer from her.

"I've been working here for half an hour. The house was toasty until you clowns tilted the temperature to freezing. How on earth could ice form at the base of that chair? You're the genius detective. You tell me."

Nick interrupted before the banter between these two got out of hand. "Outage?"

Millsap maneuvered around the growing number of live bodies filling the area and headed straight for the body, spouting apologies for the bitch traffic on Thirty-Fourth.

"Possible, but doubtful," Ramos said. "Even if Con Ed short-circuited around the area, there is simply no time for bodily fluids to congeal that quickly."

Nick made a notation to contact Con Edison for electrical outages nearby. "When was TOD?"

"By my thermometer," Millsap told the room in general, knowing everyone would pay attention to his voice. "She's been gone for several hours." He took the liver probe out of the victim and swabbed at the growing perspiration on his brow with a forearm. "But then, here in the room from Amazon hell, her body temp read will be off. Will let you know later."

Ramos crooked her finger so the men would follow her. They stepped into the colder foyer. "Even if there were power hiccups," Ramos continued, "cursory glance doesn't show any environmental particles inside the ice. As a matter of fact, the material is too clear." She walked to her evidence collection kit, bent, and retrieved a sheet of paper cradled inside a plastic evidence bag.

Nick reached out. "Is that the suicide note?"

"Read it and weep." Ramos relinquished the plastic baggie.

Lies. All liers.
time to sleep.

"Cheerful," Sacco said. "And can't spell worth shit."

Nick shook his head.

"It was taped on the outside of the closed doorway." Ramos picked her camera and showed the men the digital photograph she'd taken earlier. "I'm hoping for some fingerprint evidence on it."

"Print the plant pot by the body, as well." The overflowing basket with blossoms of what looked to Nick like impatiens had been carefully retrieved from its hook, placed neatly on an end table at the edge of the sunroom nearest the victim, and replaced by another, more macabre showpiece.

"Telling me my job, GQ?" Ramos quipped. Her mouth jerked a bit upward.

Nick smiled. "Me? Never, Kit Kat. A man knows when to stop imminent castration."

"Such cloying sweetness," said Sacco. "Don't make me puke. We all know you are neither sweet, tasty, nor soft, Ramos."

"Ah, there's the rub. Wouldn't *you* like to know?" Ramos said.

"Oh, yes, he would," Millsap said, jerking his chin toward Sacco while zipping the victim into her temporary travel bag. "Everyone's betting on when you'll finally do the horizontal dance. I have twenty bucks in the office pool."

Nick choked. Sacco turned an unhealthy shade of red. Ramos made as if she hadn't heard a thing, and continued to uncap an evidence jar from her pocket. She crouched to grab the ice.

"Gotta keep bagging, boys. Later."

Nick's eyes followed her. Through the open doorway, activity continued at a respectful decibel in deference to the victim. Flashes from cameras cataloguing everything at the scene lit the area from time to time. The body was bagged and ready to go.

They would be processing the scene for hours. And it wasn't even six o'clock in the morning yet.

CHAPTER TWO

THE STEAMING MANHATTAN streets swirled subway exhaust and cab fumes around Nick and Sacco as they rushed to the car.

"I think my eyebrows just froze," Sacco said, jumping into the passenger seat.

Nick slammed the car door against the cold, took a sip of the cappuccino he'd picked up at the hospital's cafeteria, and sighed. God, he was tired—bone tired, soul tired. They'd worked fifteen hours without a single break yesterday. They needed downtime to make some headway on the piles of paperwork mounting back at the precinct. FID was still processing this morning's crime scene, and he needed to start the Creasy case binder.

Nick grimaced as he took another fortifying gulp of caffeine. He hated to create these books of death. They sketched the violent aftermath suffered by the victims, rather than celebrated the vibrancy of their lives. By week's end, he'd be sifting through pages of reports, adding more as the investigation progressed, while stocking it with photographs of death and dissection. It always depressed him.

And he still had to survive the autopsy.

He took a longer sip of his coffee.

"Damn, but this hits the spot," he said, appreciating how the warmth expanded from his stomach and shredded some of the tiredness. "If the situation at work stays like this for a few more days, I'll be dead and no longer tired."

Yesterday, two more detectives had succumbed to the flu and four were still out sick. Some had dragged their butts into work before they'd been given a clean bill of health, only to be sent back home after coughing and puking several times. The captain's tobacco was seriously chewed from all the stress. Everyone else who was still healthy enough to walk without falling on their faces was spread all over the area, with debriefings coming in at any hour of the day.

"At least we wouldn't give a shit," Sacco said and leaned his head back. "What a damn day."

And it's only eleven thirty of this wonder a.m.

Nick started the car and drove up Sixty-First, heading for the precinct. Despite the closed windows, the chaotic noise of New York filtered in, the typical pedestrian masses of humanity, cabs, buses, and cyclists getting in his way. A faint fog hugged the air in this frigid January morning, as heat from every pore of humans, asphalt, and concrete dissipated upward.

Nick ticked away his mental list of things to do. Apart from starting more reports, they needed to set interviews with the latest victim's friends, relatives. Reinterview the witness. Maybe grab some lunch while briefing the captain on everything, including the domestic they'd just worked.

"That was some little Puerto Rican spitfire the EMS dropped off with her skewered boyfriend at NY Presbyterian," Sacco said, as if reading his mind.

Nick remembered the woman they'd interviewed on that last domestic. She'd had hematomas all over her face and a few fractures, but she'd gotten even with her latest boyfriend the moment she'd rammed a fork through his testicles.

"Wonder what he'll think when the surgeon informs him that, a few more millimeters in either direction, he would've been singing soprano...permanently," Sacco said.

Nick's voice turned hard. "Son of a bitch deserved it."

He swerved the car to avoid an idiot messenger on a bicycle and slammed the horn to release some frustration. He rushed down Second Avenue, evaded a taxi by millimeters, and gravitated through the traffic disgorging from the Fifty-Ninth Street Bridge, cutting across several pissed-off drivers. He braked for a light and rushed straight into more traffic.

"Wanna stop by Laura's place?" Sacco asked.

Laura Howard's high-end bakery, Les Gâteaux Riches, was close by. Nick and Sacco had met her when they'd arrested her close to a year ago. She'd been the primary suspect of her husband's brutal murder and would have gone down as guilty if Nick's gut hadn't raised five-alarm warnings that Laura wasn't the murderer. The latter, and a thumbprint found on the bedroom's surveillance camera, had led them to a twin sister Laura never knew existed. And it was that print that had exonerated Laura.

Despite the conflict of interest and internal warnings, Nick had fallen hard for Laura Howard. Fallen for those dark chocolate eyes that always brought to mind liquid hot fudge. And no matter what mood Laura was in, Nick always drowned in her eyes...had since she'd sat across him in interrogation, disbelief, horror, and pain etched on her face.

Nick shook his head and accelerated.

Sacco stared at his partner. "When are you two going to stop pussyfooting around each other?"

"It's too soon for her."

Sacco huffed. "Bull. It's been, what? Close to a year already since we cleared her of murder? And she was separated from the bastard husband before that."

Sacco's eyes rounded when he saw Nick's clenched jaw.

"Shit. Don't tell me Angela is still pulling your strings from beyond the fucking grave? After what she did to you?"

Nick's expression hardened. Before Angela's suicide four months ago, he'd been thinking about approaching Laura. Have a few dates, see how things would pan out. He'd thought he could have had a chance at a normal life once more. Not that a detective's life was ever normal, but many of his colleagues and friends had made a go of it. They had husbands, wives, children. Family. Warmth to offer and receive, not anger at the degree he now offered.

You're a selfish bastard, Nicky.

Yeah, Angie. So selfish that I'm the one listening to your bullshit instead of your latest boyfriend.

It's all your fault! I need—

Shit! Spare me the broken record. You need, you want, you demand. You, you, you. And I'm the stupid prick that, despite our divorce, keeps putting you back together.

Come back to me, Nicky. I love you.

Bull, Angie. You don't love me. You love your booze, your pills, your clinging needs, and your highs.

Please, Nicky. I promise I'll be good. Come back. I don't know how to live without you.

Christ! I'm hanging up. We'll talk when you're sober.

I swear, Nicky, I'll kill myself.

Go ahead. See if I care.

The sad part of it all was that Nick had cared, but Angela had cried wolf so many times, had staged her attempted suicides so often, and had manipulated his pity for so many years that he'd gotten vaccinated to her demands. And that last time? That last time she'd miscalculated, too drunk to see the truth in Nick's eyes as she hurled invectives and curses through the phone. She had been too confident she could still manipulate the situation, him. She'd always hated it when he didn't succumb to her suffocating needs. But she'd been too drunk to lift the belt she'd staged around her throat for his benefit. Too drunk to realize that the chair she'd climbed on was wobblier than she was. Too drunk to understand the image she saw on that FaceTime call was an electronic one of Nick rather than a face-to-face encounter. In the end, she'd fulfilled her prior empty promises. And Nick, realizing what she had done, had arrived too late to save her.

"Save it." Nick's voice turned hard. "Laura's got enough on her plate with the appeal next week. She's a mess. I'm not going to add to that shit."

"What is her sister claiming this time?"

"Her new lawyer said she was not in her right mind during the killing and that she confessed under duress."

"You've got to be shitting me. Insanity plea now?"

"Yeah," Nick said. "The legal blah-blah is that the system had failed to appoint a mental health professional to assess the accused at the time of the murder." Sandra's new attorney now wanted an IIT, together with the M'Naghten Rule test, done. Duress and distress, and an abusive childhood, where Sandra Ward had been deprived of nurture, should have been indicators to her previous public defender to provide her with a better defense. Or so Sandra's new lawyer claimed.

"Laura is afraid her twin may get what she wants, a mistrial, so she can present the new evidence, and get a transfer to a minimum-security psychiatric facility."

Both men fell silent. Sandra Ward, Laura's estranged twin sister, was as nasty as they came. She'd chopped and skewered

Orlando Howard without turning a hair. And all so her long-lost sister could see what she was capable of doing. Basically, screw you, screw your comfy life, screw your peace and sanity. And, oh, you're the one the cops will drag to jail and charge with the murder. Have a nice life.

Thank God, Nick had doubted, and they'd found proof Laura had not committed the crime.

IN one of the back rooms at Les Gâteaux Riches, Laura Howard sat at her prep table and slowly blew into the piping. The sugar mix she'd attached at its end started to inflate. Like a master glass blower, she rotated the piping between her fingers as the pliable mass grew from parison, to bubble, to a translucent sphere. The end product, once she shaped it with the wooden ladle and her hands to create her sugary forms, would resemble a magnificent soap bubble. Sweet and fragile. Too fragile. That was why she was making extras for the cake she'd be decorating later. The three-tier engagement cake would eventually look as if different-sized colored bubbles were overflowing from an imitation iron-clawed tub, cascading down from its edge to the imitation tile floor. Her clients had emphasized more than once they were into frothy things: baths, champagne, foam. Thank God they hadn't gone into much more detail. Laura's imagination had filled in the rest as to why they had this particular love of things bubbly.

Oftentimes, clients, in their enthusiasm, didn't realize she really, really didn't want to know the ins and outs of their relationships, but it was part of what made her cakes special. Her designs were customized for originality based on what they told her. The care she took making their celebratory cakes always remained special and unique. That was why clients came back. That was why her business flourished.

Until she'd been charged with murder.

Until her previous unbeknownst twin sister, Sandra Ward, had almost destroyed her business. Her life.

She'd definitely destroyed Laura's peace.

If it hadn't been for Nick...

A tremor spread throughout all her extremities and she stopped. With infinite care, she placed piping and bubble on the table near the heat lamp to keep the sugar from crystallizing. She rubbed the fatigue from her face. She couldn't afford to break the fragile shapes she was creating, not because she couldn't afford the cost of the sugar, but because she couldn't waste any more time. These fragile shapes took the patience of Job to make, and were so brittle, a whisper could shatter them.

And she had a deadline.

She paced the room, stretching her spine, arching her back to release the knots in her muscles. Somehow, she couldn't settle down after the image of her sister and Nick had vandalized her thoughts. Usually, concentrating on shaping these forms would transport her into what she described her creative zone, where nothing would distract her and where time was irrelevant.

Not now.

She wondered if she would ever be able to revert back to when there had not been a Sandra Ward to mess up her life. A time where she'd never met her late husband.

A time where she wouldn't have to relive nightmares about Orlando's murder.

But then, she would never have met Nick. And that had made her life the richer...and extremely complicated.

Laura bent to touch her toes. Maybe if she got her circulation going and stretched her muscles, she could shake loose the thoughts of the woman who had been separated from her by birth and fate. If only she could understand why Sandra Ward had crashed back into her life, maybe Laura could eventually forgive why she'd tried to destroy it and still harped on ruining it.

And then there was Nick. Couldn't he see they were perfect for each other? Granted, their relationship would be different from their previous fiascos but, after all, they were two marked souls, cracked by the very people who were supposed to keep the porcelain of their love buffed, shiny, and intact. This time around, however, would be different. Laura was convinced of it. Their relationship would be stronger, healthier, deeper, and that much the richer exactly *because* of what they'd endured in the past.

Real expectations, not fairy-tale ones.

Unfortunately, to date, Nick wasn't committing. She wasn't, either. Both wanted to, but were still behaving like skittish horses, dancing around the trainer, wanting the sugar offered, but afraid to grab and hold. It was ridiculous, this waiting for the other to take the plunge first.

A soft knock interrupted her mental diatribe.

"Are you almost done?"

Erin Devreaux, her partner and friend from culinary school, poked her head into the room. Round faced, with early graying hair and a motherly air about her, her partner was soft-spoken, with a gift at working sugar paste into the most beautiful flowers not created by nature. She had the patience of a saint and ran her life in sloth-like motion. Deadlines never fazed her. Only one thing had shaken Erin Devreaux, and that had been the murder of Laura's husband a year ago, and the fact her partner had been dragged to jail, charged with the crime. And even then, during that horrible debacle, Erin had kept everyone grounded and calm.

Laura didn't know if she, and their business, could have survived without Erin.

"I'm working on the last one." She moved her head and heard muscles pop. "Took a short break."

Erin, iPad in hand, entered the room and closed the door softly, turning to face her.

Laura glanced at her friend's face and saw it was flushed. "What's wrong?"

"This has got to stop, Laura. It's got to stop."

Laura's stomach and mind clenched. Somehow, she knew what had upset Erin. It had been a constant barrage since last year, with measures and countermeasures to quash the chaos thrown at them.

They always ended one step behind.

Erin turned the iPad to face Laura. The screen showed a small window with ratings of their shop, Les Gâteaux Riches, through the Google search engine. For a moment, pride overtook concern as Laura knew what her clients would see once they opened her home page. Her webmaster had created a beautiful design, reflective of her and Erin's tastes and goals for the business. User friendly for the technology challenged, as Laura was, displaying their cake designs in full glory, their bios, events, testimonials, products.

Well, the testimonials, "melts in your mouth," "rich flavors to die for," and "innovative designs to please the imagination," together with any possibility of a write-up on the page, had been deleted. And the events calendar had also been scrapped from the web page, especially after Sandra, prior to her arrest, had gone to one, posed as her, and ruined the cake for the couple whose heart had been set on her design.

Now, both she and Erin stayed until her clients came into the venue, saw their product, and oohed and aahed over their creations, security on alert until they left the premises.

Erin tapped the screen with a force unusual for her. "Look at the ratings."

The five-star ranking on the site had dropped dramatically to a two star.

"What the hell?"

Erin jabbed at the screen with uncharacteristic impatience when the window didn't change quickly enough.

"Come on. Come on. Come ON."

The page opened.

Laura was shocked. It was as if nasty internet trolls, about which many of her colleagues had complained, had taken over the comments section. Laura had known, through her webmaster's previous warnings, what to expect once they'd opened their doors to the public. Some comments about the business would be generated by a robot program meant to spam sites with negativity. They'd flagged some, and their webmaster had blocked them. Others would be paid miscreants, choosing sites at random to criticize. No one could fix that. And many others would come from nasty people with too much time on their hands, who happened to get up on the wrong side of the bed and decided to take it out on whatever business they happened to target. It was the reality of doing business in Manhattan, of exposing product on the internet. After all, Laura and Erin would never please one hundred percent of the clientele passing through their doors. Overall, however, they hoped the positive would always supersede the negative. They'd shrug off the rest.

And, for close to five years, customer satisfaction had slanted in their favor.

That had changed the moment Laura had been charged with murder.

They'd clawed their way back up the rankings when she had been exonerated of the crime.

But suffered the moment Sandra Ward began targeting Laura's business.

Which had changed in their favor the instant their webmaster started blocking IP addresses preying on their reputation. But the internet had more holes than termite-ridden wood through which Sandra could climb back through in order to harass and destroy her business, despite a restraining order, a conviction, and an incarceration. Despite monitored email accounts and a lack of cell phones in jail, Sandra always found a way, a dupe, a lawyer, someone else's friend or lover who would post for her, create profile pages for her, and do the dirty work for her.

It was a constant struggle.

Laura thought they'd finally gotten the upper hand. She'd thought, since they hadn't had any attacks directed at them for three months, that things were under control.

She'd thought wrong.

"Who the hell is cheekiefelon at whatever the hell address that is?" Erin asked.

Damn it. "Another pseudonym, probably. Or Sandra conned one of her cellmates to post for her."

Laura scrolled down slowly as she scanned the postings, all of them untrue.

> *cheekiefelon@...*
> *My sister is LGBT. Laura Howard, owner,*
> *REFUSED to fill order for engagement party.*
> *Disgusting!*
>
> *Lahar12@...*
> *What a bitch. Bigot!! I'm canceling my order.*
>
> *IamThinker3000@...*
> *Owners like Laura Howard suck.*
> *#boycottGateauxRiches*
>
> *cheekiefelon@...*
> *Heard cakes not THAT good.*
>
> *oopintszNOT@...*

Ate one of Howard's cakes at a wedding. Portions were raw. Waste of the bridegroom's money.

Papitsrice19@...

Hear ya, oopintszNOT@ Bought a purse cake for my girlfriend.

Found fondant thick and rubbery. Left it

untouched. Told her never again from Gateaux Riches.

oopintszNOT@...

Agree. Cakes look really beautiful. When you taste them, they're awful.

Should be called Shit Gateaux.

106Jadix@...

Mouse droppings on top of the buttercream when delivered.

Reported the business to the Health Department. If there

had been a zero star on Yelp, I'd have given it.

And those were the nicer posts, Laura saw, scrolling and reading faster through the vitriol.

"What are we going to do?" Erin's eyes misted. "None of that is true, but we've had two cancellations today, and there are whispers the NY Wine Trade Fest convention is considering using someone else."

"Did you call Mac?" Laura asked, referring to their IT webmaster.

Erin nodded, but she didn't look happy. "He will try to get to this today, but he's swamped with work. Besides, this goes beyond his skills. He suggested we hire a specialist to plug all the holes." She leaned closer. "There's also talk among the employees. I overheard Alexis saying she's outta here soon. Told Paki she has a few things lined up already."

And so she would, thought Laura. Some of their employees were sought after by the competition because they were the best in the business. Others left to open their own shops. Name of the game. This, however, was new ground.

Laura sat at her workstation and handed the iPad back.

"I'll make copies of all that to drop at our lawyer's as soon as I'm done here." She looked at Erin, feeling a soul-rending sadness. "I'll have him draw the papers for the sale, as well."

"No, Laura."

"It's for the best, Erin. You know that."

With hunched shoulders, Erin left the room.

Laura picked up the piping and bubble, checked for softness with her fingers. Satisfied the material was still malleable, she continued working the sugar until the shape and translucency were up to her standards.

Things were coming to a head, and she had to make a decision. She'd thought more time would be allotted her. Now, her hand had been forced to initiate plan A. And if Sandra got a mistrial next week...well...God help them all.

CHAPTER THREE

NICK BACKED UP his unmarked onto the wide sidewalk fronting the precinct, next to a cruiser, fatigue heavy on his back. Inside the steel-and-glass building housing his home away from home, Nick scanned the office. The usual beehive of noise was somehow muted.

"How many down today, Horowitz?" Nick asked.

Horowitz lifted two fingers from the keyboard. "Captain chewed through the previous cigar," he added. "Working on a new one."

"We're screwed," Sacco said.

A rookie patrolman, looking harassed, shoved some message slips into Sacco's hand and kept on walking out the door. Nick and Sacco continued to their own cubicles without breaking stride.

"Totes scheduled the autopsy of the victim for five this p.m.," Sacco said, reading one of the messages. He handed Nick the slip and dropped into his office space across from Nick.

Great. Just in time to spoil dinner.

Nick laid his notebook on the desk and grabbed an empty three-ring binder from the bookshelf. He booted up his computer, sat down, and began to type his notes on the summary report. By the time Josh Carpenter, one of their crime techs, appeared, Nick was almost done with the scene report.

"Here you go," Carpenter said, extending a manila folder to him. His skin had a greenish undertone to it.

"How are you feeling?"

The disgust on his face could have been from the memory of the miserable week he'd spent with the flu or from the fact he was still nauseous. Nick thought it might be the latter.

"So, so." His small frame shuddered. "At least the scene today was a clean one. If not, you'd have had company puking."

No crime scene is ever clean. But Carpenter had a point. Apart from the actual area where the victim had been hanged, the house was in pristine order.

"Impressions?" Nick asked as he opened the folder and spread out the photos in an array.

"Either the woman was a neat freak or she had just recently cleaned house. I would go with the latter. Third floor looked empty and unused." Carpenter pointed to three photos on Nick's desk. "Second floor seemed to have been recently half-emptied. Several boxes, labeled and sealed, were stacked in the unused bedroom. Looked like she was getting ready to move."

Nick nodded. "The closet was almost empty, just minimal clothes and shoes. Bathroom was about the same. Only bare essentials."

"Same for the kitchen and living room," Carpenter said.

Nick glanced at the photographs. Everything tidy. Nothing out of place. If he didn't know better, it was almost surreal, as if the victim had come home, deposited everything in its place, and gone calmly downstairs to end her life.

Not much to go on to solve the case.

"Thanks." Nick waved Carpenter out. "Go veg at your desk. You look like you're about to drop."

Carpenter didn't need any prodding. Seconds later, however, he reappeared. "Almost forgot. Captain wants debriefing in half an hour," he said and vanished.

Moving his head in an arc, Nick released some of the tension gripping his neck as he continued the binder's preparation. He separated some of the crime scene photos for the case whiteboard and stuffed the remainder inside sheet protectors. He reread his notes and added more particulars to the scene report, uploaded the DMV photo of the victim into his computer file, and sent everything to the printer.

On his way to the briefing room, Nick noticed the office had perked up in noise and people. The ranks were filling up once more, although some looked as if they needed a few more days of downtime. But cops were, well, cops. Sick or dying, they'd feel guilty not dragging their asses to work. Not to mention the delayed, crushing paperwork they'd have to deal with later.

He dropped the binder on the table and glanced at the case file number. He wrote that, the victim's name, and a small timeline of the crime on the board. He stepped back and scrutinized the information. Who the hell was he kidding? They had shit info on the victim and the crime. Nick remembered the silent house, which spoke of emptiness, despite the "H&G" decorative perfection on the lower level. He wondered about the victim's life before some callous bastard wielding a rope had arrived to snuff it. Nick's eyes roamed the precinct floor, with its crammed spaces, decrepit desks, washed-out paint, glass enclosures, and people coming and going all day. The usual daily grind. Had the victim's life been ordinary? How had she landed on this murderer's radar? Was it a crime of passion? Opportunity? Were their impressions mistaken and had Isabel Creasy taken her own life? With more questions than answers, Nick stepped outside to fetch the victim's DMV photo and, by the time he'd clipped it next to the information he'd written, Sacco, Horowitz, and Carpenter had joined him.

Ramos came in seconds later, settled herself next to Carpenter, and stared at the board.

"She looks so staged," she said, pointing her chin at one photo. "Almost as if she'd been lovingly posed for Carpenter's camera."

"If that is the case," Nick said. "We have one sick son of a bitch to catch."

"Then let's catch the bastard," Captain Jared Kravitz said as he strode in. Short, stocky, with a buzz cut that showed more white than black, the captain was a thirty-year veteran of the NYPD. Dressed in a suit ten years old in fashion, and a stomach too rounded to allow for the jacket to close, he dragged a chair back and sat. He took the battered cigar out of his mouth and placed it on top of his notepad.

"What have we got?"

Nick averted his eyes from the tobacco, which resembled a wilted plant with roots ravaged by the captain's stained teeth. As the best indicator of the captain's mood, the poor thing radiated a continuous SOS.

"Not much to go on," Ramos commented. "At least not yet."

Kravitz stared at the photos of the woman, then looked at Nick.

"Heard you didn't lose it at the scene." His glance was a mix between concern and approval. "How're the sessions going?"

Nick didn't appreciate the reminder. He understood why his presence at the department's shrink's office was required. Departmental policy and bureaucratic bullshit. But without the shrink's clearance, the captain would not return Nick to homicide, and that made him feel, somehow, incomplete.

"Maybe you can tell Kilcrease to hurry my release," Nick said.

The captain stared at him for a few moments more. "Let's see," he said. "In the meantime, what's happening with this new victim?"

Horowitz took that as his cue to begin.

"Call came in through 911 dispatch. Neighbor called it in. Name of the victim is Isabel Creasy, thirty-one, recently divorced. Lived in the unit alone. Uniforms are still canvassing the area, and we'll follow up with statements. Two neighbors have agreed to come by the station this afternoon to give us info."

"What about the eyewitness?" asked Kravitz.

Nick shook his head. "Not much on that score. Initial interview confirmed what was given to 911. Mr. Mansoor was doing his morning yoga before work when he noticed the victim through his living room window."

"He has a clear view of the victim's premises and the crime scene?" asked Kravitz.

"Too much," murmured Nick and Sacco at the same time.

Horowitz continued. "Didn't know her except by sight. Claims she liked to entertain and her backyard was always full of people. Complained about the noise level several times. We're looking into those reports."

"Did the man see anyone?"

"No," Sacco said. "Pleasantly quiet for a while, according to his statement. Said the parties have been nonexistent for four or five months." Sacco turned to Horowitz. "Does that coincide with the finalization of the divorce?"

Horowitz nodded after looking at his notes and doing quick mental math.

"The only reason Mr. Mansoor was up and saw the victim was that he works in international banking," Sacco continued. "That makes for odd working hours."

Nick looked at the captain. "Without his 911, we may not have known about this for days."

"Or until the stench had overpowered the neighbors," Ramos added. "In between the toasty room and the weather forecast calling for high fifties by tomorrow night, people would have noticed. Even New Yorkers."

"Follow-up interview with the witness?" Kravitz asked.

"Already set up," Nick replied. "But I think it's a dead end."

"What about electronics?" Kravitz asked.

"IT has her computer. No cell phone that we could find," Carpenter said. "We're compiling a list of friends, acquaintances, and work contacts from whatever she has on her cloud. You should have the victim's photos uploaded to your case file soon. We're also rummaging around all her social media, dating sites, checking for anything out of place. We should have a list and other info compiled by tomorrow morning after warrant OK."

"And we've got nada on trace evidence. Not yet," Ramos chimed in. She went into a detailed description of the crime scene for the captain. "Apart from that ice and the fluids under her, the scene was pristine. No suspicious garbage, castoffs. Nothing in the house or basement that pointed to the rope as a weapon of opportunity. Nothing out of place. No blood anywhere. Processing fingerprints through AFIS as we speak, but no hits yet. Tox is pending on samples from autopsy. Trace is working on the rope and whatever else Totes picks up from the body."

"ME has set autopsy for this afternoon." Nick chimed in. "Hopefully he can add to what we have."

"Which is bupkis for now," Captain Kravitz said and picked up his cigar. He resumed the chomping torture. "Let's hope we can wrap up this one quickly, guys. By the way," Kravitz zeroed his gaze on Nick and Sacco. "What's the deal on that domestic?"

"We drew the shit straw when the spitfire decided to assault her heavy-fisted boyfriend in our jurisdiction," Sacco said. "If not, it would have been the Thirty-Second's case."

"The man, a Ramón Otero, is a dishwasher over at El Rio Lindo on Thirty-Eighth and Third," Nick added and gave a rundown of the assault. "Both Otero and his soon-to-be ex-girlfriend, Miriam Pagán, are currently being treated for their injuries. Woman wants to put his sorry ass in jail. We're waiting for the skewered boyfriend to surface from the anesthesia to see if he wants to press charges. Uniforms on both. She'll be booked once she's discharged. He'll be as well."

"Where do these two clowns live?"

Nick scanned his notes. "They shared an apartment on West 143rd, between Bradhurst and Douglass."

"I'll place a call to the Thirty-Second. They need to take over this one. We're already understaffed and overworked."

"The original assault took place at their apartment, according to Ms. Pagán," Nick said. "It's their jurisdiction. And she is pressing charges. They'll need to get crime scene techs over there."

The captain jotted down some notes before dismissing everyone. "Back to work, guys. Keep me posted if anything new pops up."

Nick cleared everything from the whiteboard and retreated to his desk. Five minutes later, Sacco took a seat next to Nick.

"Just got off the phone with the victim's ex. Works at a place called TeC4M, a telemarketing support firm, near Battery Park. Said if we wanted to talk to him, he'd be available after two at his office." Sacco took a bite of a PowerBar, chewed it halfway, and swallowed it with a gulp of root beer.

"Can't understand why you like that pissy drink," Nick said. "Hate the shit."

Sacco smiled. "Tickles the puke reflexes?"

"Like the smell of a DB. What did you tell the man?"

"Advised him we'd be there by three and not to go anywhere."

Nick rinsed his mouth with a Coke he'd grabbed from the vending machine a while back. Warm fizz. He threw the practically full bottle in the garbage pail.

"What's his excuse for not seeing us earlier?"

"Meeting all morning," Sacco said and kept on chewing. "Super busy. Time is money bullshit. Said he doesn't know anything and claims we'd be wasting our time."

"We both know he meant we're wasting his," Nick said.

Sacco smirked. They knew the type.

"Told me he hasn't seen the victim since she served him divorce papers. Emphasized he spent the night at his Tribeca apartment and was chaperoned by his latest..."

"Did he take the time to tell you the reason for the breakup?"

"Unbelievably, yes. A real bleeding heart, that one." Sacco cleared his throat in preparation to imitate the ex-husband. "And, I quote: Too needy...suffocated me. Couldn't be my own man. Wanted space. Separation five months ago was the best thing ever."

When Nick's computer pinged, he reached for the keyboard and mouse. He saw that, true to their word, the IT department had uploaded all photographs from the victim's laptop. He searched through those first.

"We've got her cell photos from the cloud," Nick said.

Sacco stood behind as Nick began to scroll down photo after photo of the woman.

"Selfies and mostly selfies," Sacco said. "Incredible."

What is it with this society, Nick thought, where ninety percent of its members were into this narcissistic rendezvous with themselves? He kept rummaging down the folder, looking at previews of this woman's life. Selfies in coffee shops, in Central Park, at the movies, watching plays, at home, in the bathroom, at restaurants. A few photos from work, or so Nick assumed. A lifetime presented in small flashes of pictorial history.

Normal people on display, not realizing bad shit happened to nice people.

"Unfreakingbelievable," Nick whispered. "Her entire life in the ether for every pervert to see. No one should do this kind of shit."

"We're cops." Sacco patted him on the shoulder. "We don't even put our names on our mailboxes."

Nick clicked through a dozen more photos. Paused. Two or three poses of the woman caught his attention. His eyes moved to the dates. About four months ago, right after the divorce. He refocused on the victim. There was something about her bearing, which brought to mind a sense of...what exactly? He scrutinized Isabel Creasy's face. Her expression seemed almost forlorn and, at the same time appeared to telegraph a need for approval, for love. *Look at me,* she seemed to be saying. *I matter. I yearn. I'm available, sexy. Like me?*

Please like me.

Love me.

Vulnerability on stage.

Nick didn't know why he thought that.

"How many of these are there?" Sacco squinted at the folder.

"Too many."

"Well, we'd better hurry," Sacco said after a brief glance at his wristwatch. "Traffic to Wall is a bitch at this hour."

Nick thought a few minutes' delay now would not be worth a blink in this poor woman's eternity. For Isabel Creasy, earthly delays wouldn't affect her forever time clock anymore.

"Meet you by the car in five."

CHAPTER FOUR

THE DRIVE TO Wall was tedious, long, and annoying.

Once at their destination, Nick placed the parking placard on the dashboard, an advantage of the shield, and rode up with Sacco to the ex-husband's work floor.

The elevators opened to a wide lobby, swanky in impression and decoration. The telemarketing support firm was one whose name Nick didn't recognize but, by the real estate they currently rented, had to be one of the Fortune 500 giants out there, or someone close to their profit margins. Then again, it could be window dressing bullshit.

"May I help you?"

A receptionist, young, dressed in New York chic perfection, approached. Although a robotic smile plastered her lips, her eyes telegraphed their presence was considered an unexpected nuisance.

Nick almost looked around for a "No Soliciting" sign. Instead, he tapped the shield pinned on his left suit pocket.

"NYPD to see Mr. David Creasy."

That stopped the woman, who, in an impressive millisecond, replaced her initial shock with ingrained and rote customer-service training.

"Certainly," she pointed to her left. "Does he know you're visiting?"

Nick and Sacco exchanged glances. Sacco's smirk said it all.

"He's expecting us," Nick answered without satisfying the sparkle of curiosity in the woman's eyes.

Glass doors slid open into a buzzing work area as long as a basketball court and twice the width, with tables spanning the entire length and breadth of the space. To the front and sides of each employee work area, a translucent Plexiglas privacy shield fenced every workspace. Floating over several cubicles, colorful banners stamped with employee-exceeding-quota braggadocio occasionally undulated from the circulating heated air.

They continued toward a bank of windows cutting an L into the floor's horizon. Curious, Nick scanned the cubicles surrounding him. Many held personalized touches dropped here and there around two computer screens on opposing ends, each touching the Plexiglas boundary with a keyboard marking the center. One screen was lit with alerts, flashing like schizophrenic traffic signals in haphazard green, yellows, and reds. The other had prewritten conversations for employees to rattle to the customer.

Everyone penned for utmost production. Very *Animal Farm.*

"That's David." The receptionist pointed to a cubicle a few feet to the left.

The man caged within the cubicle was slim, dressed in casual clothes, and carried an earpiece as a permanent fixture to his head. His color codex screen was green, and his voice held a persuasive tone, luring in the caller to buy more product.

"Mr. Creasy," Nick began, but the man raised a finger in an emphatic, silencing gesture.

Nick and Sacco waited while the man typed furiously. A new screen popped on the right computer screen, and he launched into another diatribe.

"Is he reading from a teleprompter?" Sacco was unbelieving.

"Close enough," Nick whispered.

The green shifted to yellow, then red. Creasy hung up in disgust.

"Thank you for seeing us," Nick began, introducing himself and Sacco. He scanned the room. "Is there somewhere more private where we can talk?"

Creasy, despite his obvious frustration, nodded. He did something quickly on the keyboard and turned to them.

"We can use the gathering room," he said.

They followed the man to a glass-enclosed area only a few yards to the left. Before the door had closed and Nick could offer his condolences, Creasy turned to them.

"This isn't some sort of joke, is it?"

"Your ex-wife was found hanging in your sunroom early this morning, Mr. Creasy." Nick didn't dial down the brutality of his statement. "So, no, it isn't."

Creasy sat, like a balloon deflating. "I mean, really? Isabel?"

"Afraid so."

"It's just that she doesn't have the ovaries to commit suicide."

A revealing comment, if Nick ever heard one, and a testament to the man's view of the woman who no longer graced this earth. But the man's impressions did corroborate their own at the crime scene...that the body had possibly been staged.

"Why would you think your wife could not take her own life?" Nick asked.

"Ex. And Isabel is a mousy thing." He stopped for a moment, as if digesting the fact his ex was no more. "I told your partner she is...was needy. Super clingy. Doesn't have much confidence in herself and is always looking for approval, you know."

No. Nick didn't know.

"Pissed the hell out of me all the time. I couldn't breathe. Always asking if I loved her, that she loved me, blah, blah."

Creasy glanced at both men, as if they would empathize with his masculine plight.

Nick and Sacco waited.

"I need my space, you know," Creasy continued, a bit deflated by their lack of engagement. "This job takes all my juice. Can't have her hanging on me twenty-four hours a day, or interrupting me at work. Our shifts are a bitch, fluid, depending on need, or commission, and stressful enough. After a while, it grates, you know, the lack of confidence, the clinginess. Who the hell wants someone sharing your space who thinks like a deer caught in the crosshairs? I couldn't take it anymore. So, I bailed."

What a humanitarian. "Was she seeing anyone?" Nick asked.

"Wouldn't that have made my life easier? But, no."

"Any incidents of depression?" Sacco asked. "Divorces can be hard on people. Did she ever speak to you about suicide?"

"Isabel? Nah. She is...was terrified of death. And I mean, phobic about it. I'm into eating healthy, exercising, you know? But Isabel took it to a whole new level. Vitamins for everything...moisturizers, the latest in anti-aging products, probiotics, protein shakes, bars, no GMOs, or whatever bullshit acronym is the new trend. Our grocery bill was ridiculous. It milked a third of my budget."

Nick stared without comment.

"So, no," Creasy answered, now more nervous. "Isabel wasn't thinking about suicide. At least, I don't think so." He glanced at both men. "Have you talked to M-Li Watson yet? She's Isabel's best friend. Knows her better than anyone. She owns a high-end beauty salon on East Fifty-Ninth, between Madison and Lex."

Nick and Sacco opened their notepads and wrote down the information.

"Our investigation and interviews are at the initial stage," Nick said. "Would you happen to have Ms. Watson's telephone numbers? It would save us precious time."

"Sure." Creasy slipped a smartphone out of his pocket and scanned through the contacts. "M-Li's business is The Ultra Pampered Girl," Creasy said. He saw Nick writing Emily and waved his hand in dismissal. "No. No. That's not how you spell it. It's capital M-dash-L-i. She's Asian American."

He rattled off both business address and phone numbers, including the personal one. "Isabel went there religiously to do her hair and nails," he finished.

"Did Isabel work?"

The man nodded. "She was a beauty consultant for one of the major cosmetic firms at Saks."

"Would you happen to have those contacts as well?"

A few seconds later, Nick and Sacco had a work phone and a supervisor's name.

"To the best of your knowledge, was she having problems with anyone at work or within her circle of friends?"

Creasy shrugged. "After we separated, I cut the umbilical. Didn't talk except through our divorce lawyers. M-Li would know that shit better than me."

"Were you aware your ex-wife was moving out of the brownstone?" Nick asked, thinking about the boxes.

"Lease was up, so yeah." A bit of vindictiveness shone from his eyes. "Paid the last half of my rent for that fucker in December. She milked me for that, too, the..." He stopped, possibly realizing how he sounded.

"If you should think of anything else, however trivial," Nick took out a business card and gave it to the man. "Please give me a call. Any information helps."

Not bothering to offer any condolences, Nick and Sacco left the way they'd come without waiting for an escort.

The cold, amplified by the wind crashing through the artificial canyons of lower Manhattan, beat Nick into a protective ball within his winter coat. The inside of the car wasn't any warmer, but, at least, the wind didn't slice his skin into pieces. Nick could kill for a bracing cup of caffeine right now.

"Well, that was a real loving relationship," Sacco blurted.

"And a total waste of time. No love lost, at least not by him." Nick started the car. The heater coughed a blast of cold air before raising the heat level. "Rather nice of him not to refer to her as the bitch."

"I think he believed we might arrest him if he finished the sentence."

"That makes him an asshole, not a killer," Nick said, pulling into traffic. He braked and honked simultaneously as he rounded the corner. He hated lower Manhattan. A contortionist had better chances of twisting his body into a knot than a person getting out of the area without hassle. He swerved, evading jaywalkers, and drove up William.

"But we'll see. Let's find out what this M-Li friend has to say about the not-so-grief-stricken ex. See if we can interview her now." As Nick cut west at Liberty and hooked a right on Trinity, he saw the dashboard clock and realized they wouldn't have enough time to interview the victim's friend, not before five.

"Scrap that. See if she can come to the station tonight. Totes will not be happy if we're late for the autopsy."

Nick slogged through the ever-increasing traffic, and delays, and listened to Sacco speak with M-Li Watson.

"She's working until eight tonight and can't reshuffle her schedule," Sacco said, pressing a finger against the mic of his phone. "Asked if we could be at her salon around eightish, after she closes shop."

"No problem," Nick said. What would another four hours, added to their current twelve-hour shift, matter?

Sacco confirmed the appointment and turned to Nick.

"The news seemed to hit her hard. She was crying by the time I hung up."

At least someone is grieving for the poor woman.

"Text Totes that we're on our way."

DESPITE the traffic gods screwing with every shortcut Nick took, they made it to the medical examiner's office two minutes before five.

The hallway to the dissecting room was no warmer than the air outside, and the smell no better than usual, but the cold temperature always helped tone down the odor on Nick's get-ready-to-puke meter.

"Now that is consideration," Sacco said, pointing to the items on a small table next to the swinging doors. Two surgical masks, a tiny jar of Vicks Vaporub, and a small bottle of Febreze aerosol, were arranged on top.

"I'm not begrudging it one bit. Thank you, Totes," Nick said and grabbed the jar before Sacco could snatch it.

He scooped a fingerful of the Vicks, handed it to his partner, and swabbed the paste under and a bit into his nostrils. Camphor and eucalyptus rammed through Nick's nasal passages and rushed into his brain. He breathed deeply several times, saturating his nasal airways with the scent, and sprayed some of the air freshener on a mask. He placed that tightly against his face, and followed Sacco into the room.

Millsap, dressed antiseptically for those who would not have to worry about infections ever again, was bent over the victim, inspecting her naked body carefully, while his assistant took photographic record of everything. Paper envelopes of different sizes were already sealed and catalogued on top of a metal tray next to where Millsap stood, including some sealed swabs.

Another autopsy, two tables to the right, was underway, as well. The drone of the assistant medical examiner's voice dictating the condition of the victim's innards into a digital recorder, catalogued the injuries of what sounded like a hit and run.

Nick avoided looking that way and breathed in shallow bursts.

"Afternoon, boys." Millsap raised the victim's right arm, inspecting the skin for residue or bruising. "My wife would kill for skin like this."

"Is that a metaphor for no bruising?" Nick asked.

"Not even a scab."

Millsap placed the arm on the table with the gentleness oftentimes reserved for infants or women. Nick knew Totes always treated his clients that way. Constantly reminded his assistants and detectives that the victims on his slab deserved consideration in death since, most of the time, they'd been dealt brutality in life.

Nothing wrong with a respectful final send-off.

"So, what is she telling you?"

Millsap's surgical mask twitched, as if a smile had tugged it. His eyes said as much.

"This woman took very good care of herself, at least outwardly. Skin shows no sun damage, with no sunspots or scars, except for the appendix which was removed years ago. Fingernails and toes manicured to perfection. Natural hair, not tinted."

"Ex said she never skipped going to the beauty salon," Sacco volunteered.

"And she was a cosmetic specialist at Saks, as well," Nick added.

"Makes sense," Millsap said and continued his inspection. "Results like hers come in two-hundred-a-pop serum bottles. Or it could just be her DNA."

Millsap looked about done with the outer inspection of the body. The next step would be the examination of the organs.

"Now for the million-dollar question," Nick asked, swallowing several times. "Based on this preliminary inspection...suicide or homicide?"

"This, gentlemen, is in no way a suicide, in my professional experience." Millsap pointed to the victim. "Not violent at any level. Fists are unclenched. No sign the ligature shifted from jerking. Knot of rope is a bit higher than normal in the occipital region."

"The knot isn't on opposing sides?" Nick asked, remembering Angela's suicide. Unfortunately for him, he'd become an unwilling expert on hanging deaths since then.

"No. She couldn't have done this had she committed suicide. It's atypical." Millsap pointed to the victim's throat next. "The normal asphyxial signs, in this case the stretching of her neck, petechial hemorrhages on facial skin and eyes, are present. Neck grooved deeply from ligature. Liver mortis indicated she hanged around six to seven hours max before we found her. X-rays discarded cervical fracture." He nodded toward Sacco. "Thought I'd keep the medical jargon to a minimum for your sake. Is that glaze over your eyes?"

"Very funny, Millsap."

"Please tell me she fought against being hanged like a pig for slaughter," Nick asked.

Millsap turned to face them. "That, gentlemen, is the mystery of the day and one for us to solve. She suffocated from her own body weight, but there are no signs of any struggle anywhere on her body. None. No scratches. No foreign material under her nails. No fibers from the rope in either hand. No crescentic nail marks around her throat to indicate either attempted strangulation by persons unknown or through her visceral reaction to tear at the ligature that's suffocating. That is, before confusion sets in."

Christ. Nick remembered Angela's frantic tugging moments before blood flow was cut from reaching her brain. The awareness in her eyes, the terror of what had happened instants before the phone crashed on the floor and the FaceTime feed was cut off. An image that would take years to forget. If he ever could.

"You saw the crime scene," Nick said. "Her clothing was not torn or disarranged, either. We didn't see any signs of struggle at all."

"I remember."

"Ramos swears she was staged," Sacco supplied.

"Until I open the victim, my first conclusion is to concur with her assessment. My bet is the woman was drugged until unconscious, placed in the noose, lifted, and left to die. There is no bruising around the axillae, so she wasn't held first, with the rope placed around her neck later. I'll check under the dermis for evidence of that once I open her up."

"The hook showed signs of rope drag," Nick said.

Millsap glanced at him. "Upward or downward?"

"Up. We'll know more after Ramos checks it out."

"That screams homicide, not suicide."

"Christ." Nick didn't like the look in Millsap's eyes.

"Tox will have the blood samples after I finish. Asked them to run a complete panel."

"Trace evidence?" Nick asked.

"None that I can see now. Swabs, rope, and clothing will be in Ramos's hand same time frame. Let's hope she finds something."

"Meaning there's nothing," Nick supplied.

"And that means we're fucked," Sacco replied.

Millsap recorded his findings, took up the scalpel, and started the Y incision. Nick blurred his eyesight. Made whatever came next in the autopsy less gruesome.

CHAPTER FIVE

NICK FLIPPED THE cap on his beer and took several satisfying swallows. Sacco had dropped him off at his apartment a bit before seven. After autopsy, they'd needed to shower away the stink of death, change clothes, and interview Isabel Creasy's best friend. Nick hoped she would add to their victimology because, as of now, they didn't have much to go on.

No acquaintances.

No enemies.

No suspects.

Zilch.

Just a jerk ex-husband, a best friend, and some photos on a computer.

He placed the beer inside the refrigerator for later consumption. He was about to return to the bedroom and pick up his tie when a soft knock, followed by *Nick, it's Laura,* pivoted him. Before he reached the front door, three more staccato raps sounded.

Nick unlocked and opened his door as he finished buttoning his freshly laundered shirt.

"Can I talk to you?" Laura asked, looking uncomfortable, indecisive, squeezing a manila envelope against her chest. "I know you are busy..."

For a moment, Nick stood rooted like a star-struck teenager facing a Venus in the flesh. God, but she was beautiful...so physically yummy he wanted to delve into her body like he'd dug into her cakes. He remembered the first time he'd sampled one of her creations. In gratitude for all they'd done, Laura had baked a cake for the precinct. For the first time, Nick understood compulsion. A slice hadn't satisfied. It would be the same with her. And the need was bad. He understood that if he sampled Laura, the woman who made his blood zing, the hunger for her would continue until it consumed him.

"I'm sorry to bother you. I saw your lights on when I got home."

Laura lived in the building across from where he lived on West Thirtieth. About seven months ago, his super had been notified two apartments across the way were for rent. Seeking a good recommendation, the man had asked if Nick knew anyone dependable for the rentals. Nick had jumped at the chance. He knew Laura was looking for a place of her own. After her husband's murder, Laura had opened her previous apartment doors to Goodwill and her church's charity services and had donated everything inside. Her personal papers and her pastry equipment had been packed and placed in a storage facility and she'd moved into Erin's place. But her business partner's apartment was small, and Laura had felt like the third wheel she was, sleeping on the sofa and affording Erin, her husband, Gabe, and their two-year-old no privacy.

Once the building's management had approved Laura's application, Nick had been happy at her proximity, at their growing bond, hoping an intimate relationship could pan out soon.

But, first, some things had to be exorcized. And he was almost done.

"It's no bother," Nick said and stood aside for her to step through.

Laura sidled past him into the living room as he closed the door.

"Sacco is picking me up for an interview about a murder case in a minute or so," Nick said, walking toward his bedroom. "Mind if I keep preparing?"

"I'm so sorry. I didn't mean to interrupt." She turned, ready to retreat.

Nick sighed. "Laura, stop."

He took her hand and gently pulled her to the kitchen counter. He felt a slight tremor tickle his palm, knew what it meant, recognized a yearning that matched his. But he left it, for the moment, at that—a stolen touch. "I'm glad for the company. Can I offer you anything? Water? Beer?"

Laura sniffed the air, inhaling the heavy citrus fragrance that mingled with that of men's cologne. "I'll have some of the lemonade, if there's any left."

"That's not lemonade, it's me."

Laura waited for Nick to expand his comment, but he wasn't about to tell her that lemon juice was the only way to rid your skin and hair from the clinging smell of death. He sat on a stool and waited for her to explain what was wrong, because there was something wrong. He felt it. Saw it. She was edgy, her beautiful eyes unfocused, as if carrying on an internal debate with herself.

"Laura?"

"Oh, right. Sorry." Her eyes focused. She placed the manila envelope on the counter and slid it to him. "These are for you."

"And they are?"

"More evidence of harassment and stalking by Sandra...for your case file."

Nick didn't reply. It seemed psycho sister would never outgrow her destruction phase. He opened the envelope and scanned the comments.

"Son of a bitch."

Laura smirked. "My lawyer's expletives were much more colorful."

"I thought we'd finally gotten her activities stopped." Nick rammed the papers back inside the envelope. "They're supposed to monitor this shit in jail."

Laura shrugged, as if uncaring, but her eyes misted. "So the prison system should. But that's not reality, is it?" She breathed deeply. "Sandra probably conned someone outside the prison to post for her. Or something worse."

Nick didn't even want to think about the unpleasant methods Sandra might have used to get what she wanted. He looked at the kitchen clock and cursed mentally. His partner would arrive at any moment. Typical. His need to comfort Laura was now intense. Another example of the universe bitch-slapping him awake, reminding him, *Tough shit, buddy. Duty calls.*

"Let me get a tie. I'll be right back."

Nick rushed to his bed, picked up the tie he'd chosen earlier, and tied it on his way back. As he pulled the knot upward, Laura's next comment stopped him cold.

"I'm selling my share of the business to Erin."

Nick recovered and continued fixing his tie. "Isn't this rather sudden?"

Laura cocked her head, her lips spreading in a sad smile. "No, it isn't. I've mentioned the possibility once or twice."

"As a hypothetical," Nick said. "Not a definite."

"This," Laura said, pointing to the manila envelope, "is not fair to me. But it's more unfair to Erin. Can't allow what we've built together to be destroyed. Once I'm out of the picture, the business will recover, stay profitable. She is so talented. She'll pull through. And Gabe will help."

"You should give yourself more time to think about this."

"The moment for thought is over. I have to take action. The quicker I get out of the way, the better."

As she approached, the sadness in Laura's eyes almost dropped Nick to his knees. She swatted his hands away from his tie, and began to finish what he'd started.

"There is a very good possibility Sandra will get away with what she wants—a transfer to a psychiatric facility. Personally, I think she belongs there. But, as a psychopath who looks like me, dresses like me, walks like me, and even altered her appearance to resemble me almost exactly, down to the thumb wound she inflicted..."

Laura turned her thumb to reveal the scar there. When about eight years old, she'd had an accident where the knife she had been using to cut a bagel had slipped, slicing her thumb deeply. That scar had been her saving grace, the evidence that had exonerated her from her husband's murder. But once Sandra had found out about it, she'd ripped her own skin to imitate Laura's old wound.

She gave the tie one last tug, adjusted Nick's shirt collar, smoothed his shirt, and stepped back.

"There," she said, an approving gleam in her eyes, which turned serious a second later. "She's dangerous."

"We can protect..."

"No." Her head moved in echo of her denial. "There is no protection from this, except for what I'm doing...and need to do. Can you take care of my plants for a couple of days?"

"Your plants."

"I usually don't ask, but I can't let this business opportunity slide. It's out of town."

She reached into her jeans pocket and slid out a key, took Nick's hand, and pressed it on his palm.

Nick stared at the silver key, its head covered in blue plastic, the word *Home* filigreed in bold black. There was a shitload of meaning with this gesture. Of: *I'm taking the first step. Will you accept?*

He fisted the key within his hand.

"Okay. Not a problem."

"Should be back in three or four days. Depends. If it's a bother, I could ask Erin—"

Nick stared.

"What is it that you're really trying to tell me?"

Laura gulped. "I'm thinking about leaving New York altogether."

"You're leaving." A dry statement, said as if in a trance. Nick felt as if his feet had been swiped off the floor.

Laura nodded.

"To your parents?"

"I can't. I can't drop them in the hell I'm living." Laura's breath hitched. "I'm only considering... Well, one thing can... I'd stay if..." Her eyes transmitted the message left in the silence.

Shock glued Nick to the floor. His breath seemed to disappear. The echo of Angela's voice reverberated inside his brain...*Whatever, Nicky. Whatever you want me to do. I need you.*

Nick saw Laura understood his barely concealed reaction and the memory behind it accurately. Her arms moved toward him. Stopped. Instead, she tucked her hands inside her jeans' back pockets.

"I know I may be treading quicksand." Her gaze changed from hesitant, to determined, and her body braced as if waiting for a blow. "I love you. There. I said it." She shrugged in inevitability. "I'm hopelessly in love with you. Can't help it. But this," she pointed to the manila envelope, "changed things. I can't live in this emotional merry-go-round anymore. I can't have the people I care for affected by this over and over. I need to disappear, to go somewhere no one knows me, where my deranged sister can't get at me." She lifted her chin in resolve. "But I'd take my chances if we're together. Do we have a future? Can we?"

Nick wanted to tell Laura her timing sucked. That she couldn't drop this bomb on him just before his partner came to pick him up. That he wanted to cuff her to his bed and not let her go until she came to her senses. But the only thing he said was "When?"

"Don't know exactly," Laura sighed. "Depends on what I accomplish on this trip."

Nick's cell vibrated. He slid it out of his pocket and saw Sacco's text claiming he was almost there.

"Shit. Listen, I have..."

Laura placed soft fingers on his lips.

"I know. Work beckons."

Then, this woman who could change the essence of his life, did something she'd never done before. Something Nick had wanted to do for forever. Laura cradled Nick's face, leaned forward, and kissed him with a devastating softness and a depth of feeling unlike any he had experienced before.

Laura backed a few paces.

"I know I've thrown a lot at you. But think about it. Be careful at work, please."

She pivoted and let herself out quietly.

A minute after Laura's exit, Nick still stared at the door, wondering how a kiss could breathe such warmth into his scarred soul.

THE Bedford Hills Correctional Facility's common room was abuzz with conversation clusters.

Sandra Ward sat in a corner, unconcerned and, frankly, a bit bored. The snippets of conversations reaching her simply rehashed the obvious event of the evening, and the newspaper she was reading had not produced articles about her main focus of attention—her sister or the detective who'd so callously placed her behind bars.

"They're taking her body to the morgue later tonight," one of the inmates to her right said.

Sandra used her nail to separate the pages stuck together and turned to the obituary section. She would have preferred getting her hands on a computer, but she was banned from them since last week. Scanning the contents on the page, she focused on the announcement of a ballerina's death at the ripe age of seventy-eight. At least the woman had had a life in a career she loved. A lifetime ago (when was it, when she'd been six?) Sandra had had dreams of dancing in a colorful, frilly tutu, twirling like a top across a bright stage in pink toe shoes. Claps of adoration and awe would have followed her spinning form and overpowered the music surrounding her. But since her druggie bitch mother had kept *her* instead of her twin sister, dear Mom had prepped her for those johns who were more interested in spreading young legs and penetrating young, tight flesh. Guaranteed retirement money coming in for her mother's fixes and sagging skin.

"That was seriously screwed up."

"Didn't know allergies could kill you."

Sandra's eyes dropped to another obit, this time about a young man who'd OD'd from the latest cocktail of opioids. The family was devastated, it seemed. Sandra wished this new fentanyl mix had been available years back. Getting rid of Ramona Ward would have been easier and faster.

"Did anyone know?"

"Don't think even Sonia knew."

"I say good riddance to the bitch."

Sandra's lips twitched. That last comment would be from the lifer, Vanessa something or other. A kindred spirit, as crimes would have it. Vanessa had been convicted for slicing and dicing her pimp and the younger ass he was humping. All because the man had screwed her on the meth promised.

Men. Don't know shit about priorities.

"Ah, come on, Vanessa."

Sandra collapsed the corner of the paper just enough to see Vanessa's profile.

"Don't you 'Oh, Vanessa' me. Sonia...was...a...bitch. Don't care who hears me." Vanessa turned her face up and yelled. "You hear me? Sonia was a bitch." Vanessa looked around the gathered group. "A bitch and a snitch. How many of us she got in trouble?"

Sandra went back to perusing the obits. Suck-up Sonia was the name all the inmates in the ward had baptized her with. More like parasitic vermin, Sandra thought, always sniffing into what wasn't her business, looking over shoulders, trading information with guards for perks.

Someone from the group whispered, "Think someone got even, finally?"

Sandra smiled. Last week Sonia had found Sandra using someone else's time on the computer. She had reported the transgression to the bleeding heart teacher from Vassar who thought that, by giving up her time to teach a computer course in prison, she'd somehow maintain recidivism to a minimum. People like the teacher believed the Oprah-like sob stories out there, convinced a good majority of women inside this prison had been shafted by society's neglect, abuse, repression, or oppression.

What an ignorant ass.

But that report had gotten Sandra off the computer, something she desperately needed to keep tabs on her twin. Or to keep tabs on her latest scheme. Or continue her campaign of ruining her twin's good life. And no one fucked with Sandra's plans. She'd shown remorse and repentance to the proper authorities, accepted her punishment, and dealt with Sonia the way she'd dealt with all the Sonias in her life.

Good riddance.

CHAPTER SIX

THE ULTRA PAMPERED Girl's storefront was understated for this area of town. Nick assumed the owner was going for classy, with simple display windows flanking the entrance, each latticed in uneven grids of wood. Above the door, the salon's name was written in elegant script. Nothing else obstructed the view of a potential customer looking in, where they would see the same clean lines continued within the shop all the way to the back wall.

Sacco knocked on the locked door, while Nick held his shield close to the glass for easy identification.

A woman who was in her late twenties or early thirties, stood from behind the receptionist's desk and approached. Slim, dressed in black slacks and a white blouse, her hair was cropped in a pixie cut, its color matching the magenta, blue, and black striations of her nails.

"Please come in. M-Li is waiting for you." With her psychedelic vampire fingernails, she pointed to the back of the shop.

"Can I offer you anything? Coconut water? Our special blend of pomegranate rose?"

"No, thank you, Miss...?" Nick asked.

"Oh. Sorry. Galina. Galina Breshnevskaya."

Nick and Sacco took out notepads and asked for the spelling.

"We're all shocked, really shocked about this," Galina said and started leading them to the back. The place was a beehive of activity, with everyone who worked there sweeping, cleaning, and organizing workspaces for the following morning. The perfume of essential oils permeated the area, a trademark of every New Age business. Nick didn't believe in the latest trend that touted the merits of aromatherapy, which claimed to always invigorate, de-stress, and even detox the body. Despite that, he rather enjoyed stepping into these scented areas. To him, they simply smelled good.

In any case, it beat, hands down, the smells of the station and the morgue.

"Isabel was so sweet, and funny," Galina interrupted his thoughts, veering around a manicure station. "We just don't understand why she would do something like this."

"Were you close?" Sacco asked.

"We weren't best buds. Not like she was with M-Li." Galina stopped and played with the top crescent moon diamond clip that bordered her right ear from top to lobe. "I did her nails on occasion, when M-Li wasn't available. But we all knew her. And she was getting her life back in order. She was really looking forward to that." Galina's gaze shifted to the front window.

Nick saw the attempt at holding back emotion, her reluctance to show how the news had affected her. She was not as successful at keeping the roughness out of her voice.

"I just don't get people," she whispered and stared at Nick first, then Sacco. "How can you do that to yourself?"

Nick didn't have an answer. He didn't think anyone had an answer to that question, let alone the possibility Isabel Creasy may have come to a violent end by another's hand.

"How often did she come by?" Nick asked.

"Oh, man, she didn't miss a beat on that score. Was here on the dot every Friday at six. Said the pampering kept her sane." Her body hiccupped to the realization of her words. "Oh."

Galina pointed to Isabel Creasy's best friend near the back of the shop and left them to their own devices. She was sniffing loudly before she'd fully turned back to her post.

Nick and Sacco continued in the direction they'd been pointed.

Separated by white curtains whose material looked like silk to Nick, the pedicure area resembled a fancy day spa more than a nail salon. The chairs were lushly padded, made to wrap and cushion a body in a cocoon of softness. Each station was separated by a white paper latticed privacy screen, increasing the sense of seclusion for the customers, as though they were the only people in the world, cared for by a pedicurist, expert in beautifying and relaxing the customer in all her, or his, every need.

Nick's thought flashed to Laura. She'd like this pampering. And she could use a bit of de-stressing in her life at this moment.

"Again, do I really need to confiscate your cell phone tomorrow like you're a ten-year-old?" M-Li's voice, soft timbred though berating in tone, carried all the way to where they stood.

Nick looked at Sacco. His partner raised an eyebrow, his eyes reflecting what was on Nick's mind. They were witnessing a little ass kicking by the boss.

Creasy's best friend was truly small in stature, around five foot two or three, as she stood face to chest with her employee. A long, thick braid, almost bluish black in its tonality, was draped over her shoulder and fell to waist level. Both women wore the same black slacks and white blouse ensembles Nick had seen on Galina and every other staff member they'd passed. Must be a signature uniform of some sort.

"But..." the employee began.

M-Li interrupted. "What are my three rules?"

When the woman did not answer immediately, M-Li Watson repeated the question, this time with an added emphasis to the words and waited.

"To pamper the customer," the employee said. "To make reality disappear. To give superior service."

"For that hour, that customer is your world. You do *not* look at your messages. You do *not* answer your phone. You're *not* there for anyone except that client."

"But..."

"No buts. Galina mans the front desk for that very reason. If there's an emergency, she knows what to do. This is the second complaint I've received, from different clients no less. If you need to speak with your significant other, or mother, or whoever tagged you on Facebook, or pinged you on Instagram, you take a break *before* you greet that client, or *after* you finish. That cell is to be on silent at *all* times. This is your last warning."

"Yes, Ms. Watson," the woman agreed, albeit reluctantly.

Nick cleared his throat. M-Li gave them a cursory once-over, acknowledged them with a nod, and turned her attention back to the other woman. "Go get those foot basins disinfected and ready for tomorrow. Then take inventory of nail polish, scrubs, and masks. Let me know what needs to be replaced."

Chastised, the woman excused herself and went about her business.

"Detectives?"

At their nod, M-Li picked up a vinyl cash pouch and pointed to a back curtain. "Do you mind if we talk in my office?"

"Lead the way, please," Nick said.

M-Li took them up a ridiculously narrow metal spiral staircase, starting at street level, opposite the restroom. Upstairs, the area was an open warehouse, as deep and wide as the floor below. The walls were brick lined all the way to the end, where floor-to-ceiling glass panels displayed the view of the avenue and city buildings across and below. To the right of them, the area was full of inventory boxes sectioned off by wooden tables, spare equipment, and extra privacy screens. Letter-sized white paper, with hand-printed information about inventory content, hung from the tiled ceiling to identify batch. On the left, they passed an area set up as a break lounge, with sofas, recliners, a small TV, a multifunction table, and kitchen counter with espresso machine, microwave, a small refrigerator, and a sink. Close to the window, they now approached an L-shaped wooden desktop with aluminum T-brackets for legs. A computer screen and other personal and business necessities to make that space M-Li's own cluttered the top. In front of the desk stood two chairs, and to the left of those, four file cabinets pressed against the wall. To complete the personal touch, a Chinese silk print and family photos decorated the wall behind the desk.

"Sorry about what you heard," M-Li said and sat at her desk, placing the vinyl pouch in front of her. She pointed to the two chairs, which they took. "Dependable employees are hard to come by, I'm sad to say."

"We get it," Nick said, thinking of Laura and how that topic always came up whenever she discussed her own employees.

M-Li shifted her gaze to a framed photograph near her keyboard. She picked it up, her eyes tearing. "This...hurts. It's totally surreal." She looked at them, tears trailing over her cheeks. She brushed them away with her knuckles. "I'm expecting her to call at any moment, bragging about the great massage she received, or what she bought for her new place..."

Nick stretched his hand and M-Li relinquished the photo. It was taken at Central Park, at the Bethesda Terrace and Fountain at the end of the Mall. Both women were younger, in a foolish mood it seemed, making faces at the camera, their fingers stretched out in a V for victory near their eyes, very like the habit Japanese teenage girls have when taking photographs.

"My husband took that before our engagement party."

"How long ago was that?" Nick asked.

"Six years ago. We got married five months later." She accepted the photo back. "Isabel hadn't met the jerk yet."

"You mean Mr. Creasy?" Sacco asked.

"Major asshole. She thought she'd found her HEA…"

"HEA?" Nick interrupted.

"Yeah, her happily ever after. Told her he wasn't the right match, but Isabel was so in love. So sure she'd make it work."

"What can you tell us about her husband?"

"Idiot comes to mind. Self-centered bastard is more accurate. Has delusions of grandeur."

"Such as?" Nick asked.

"Thinks he's going to be the next Zuckerberg or some such bull. Spends practically all his waking hours trying to outsell Mary Kay herself in that shit job of his. The rest of the time, he lives above his means, wants to show off to anyone who'd slightly connect him with the right people. When they lived at the brownstone, he entertained constantly, inviting only those he deemed would advance his career. And if he wasn't throwing extravagant parties at the house, he would wine and dine people at trendy restaurants." M-Li shook her head, her eyes sad. "Poor Isabel. She worked her butt off for that bastard."

"How so?" Nick asked. This visual of the conjugal situation was in complete contrast to the ex-husband's view of things. He also made a mental note about how M-Li Watson had not mentioned the ex by name, not even once.

"Isabel is…shit …was constantly working overtime hours to make ends meet. They barely spent time together. No private couple time, unless you call the occasional thirty-second bang nurturing a marital relationship."

Sacco cleared his throat. Nick caught the small twitch to Sacco's lips in his peripheral vision.

"What about friends?"

M-Li shook her head. "More acquaintances than friends. Always like that, even when we were roomies way back when. I am...was her only friend. She was a tad shy, especially with strangers. And that bastard always surrounded her with strangers. It started taking its toll, especially after wasting four years with that control freak. Her self-esteem began to erode, she was indecisive, always second-guessing herself, thinking she wasn't good enough, pretty enough."

"Would that have driven her to suicide, you think?" Sacco asked.

M-Li's face changed dramatically.

"*Ne-ver*. Is that what that bastard told you?"

"Actually, he was shocked by the news," Nick answered. "Said she was afraid of death. Is that correct?"

"She almost drowned in a lake when she was a kid. Death terrorized her."

More so the asphyxiating death she'd had. No, hanging would not have been her chosen method of suicide. This smelled more and more like a homicide.

Shit.

"Miss Breshnevskaya said she was getting her life back together?"

M-Li nodded, her braid moving up and down with the force.

"We were her support group, almost her weekly therapy sessions. So were her weekly massages at Deep Tissue and Hot Stones. She always said we all were her de-stressers. That we kept up her morale and sanity, especially after the separation and divorce."

She saw their expressions and blurted. "Okay, she was a bit lonely and depressed at first, but she rallied. She found a really cute, affordable place in Queens last month, somewhat of a schlep from work, but what New Yorker doesn't?"

"You said she had trouble making ends meet. Did she have a second job?"

"No. But she was working on a private product line for my business. You know, polish, scrubs, creams? We were her constant guinea pigs. Did you know she had a chemistry degree?"

Nick shook his head.

"Her goal was to have her own beauty product line so she could sell in QVC and other online retailers. That was her dream job. Told me she had other ideas for the massage industry. Some hush-hush thing she didn't want to discuss, at least, not yet."

"Through work?" Nick asked.

"Hell, no. They could claim proprietary rights on her work, even when she made sure there were no clauses specific to exclusivity of ideas while in their employ in the contract she signed."

"When was she planning to move to her new place?" Sacco asked.

"This week. She was almost done moving the smaller stuff from the brownstone. Lease was up. I was going to help empty the old place this weekend while the movers moved the heavier furniture."

Sniffing once more, M-Li opened the top drawer and took out a key. "This opens her apartment. We traded in case of emergencies." She rattled off the Queens address. "My home keys are hanging from a holder near the entrance door. Can I get them back?" She choked. Her eyes misted and she blinked repeatedly, trying not to cry.

"That will be no problem." Nick said.

"She had her life ahead of her." It was said softly but with an underlying wail.

"Any boyfriends, lovers, or new significant other?" Nick asked.

The question threw her. She became thoughtful, searching back through memories, comments.

"Funny thing that. She was a bit cagey on that subject lately, but when I asked about it, she would blush, smile in an *I've-got-a-hell-of-a-secret* way, and change the subject. Then, about two weeks ago, she stopped talking about dates altogether. Seemed upset." She paused. "No. Not upset. More disappointed and a bit disgusted."

Nick made a note. Maybe the photos from her cloud could give them a rundown of places she'd been with those mystery dates, especially the one she'd reacted to negatively.

"Did she have any unusual habits? Vices?"

"Not really. Isabel was, if not anything else, predictable. Fridays were her days off. She went at eleven sharp for her deep tissue massage with EriK, that's EriK with a capital K at the end," M-Li said, watching them jot down the information. "Afterward, she spent two hours at a laboratory, one that specializes in renting space for inventors and grantees. Shopped a bit, and was sitting at her pedicure station promptly at six. All other days, she worked from nine to eight weekdays, fewer hours on weekends. Do you have her work number?"

"Yes, thank you. Did she have any family here?"

"Oh, God, her parents." And, with that said, she started to cry in earnest.

Nick stood and grabbed a paper napkin next to the coffee machine. He handed it to M-Li, sat, and waited for the grief to abate.

After a while, M-Li's emotions settled.

"She's from Montana," she said. "I'll have to call..."

"Why don't you let us handle that?" Nick said with pity. "Do you have their number? It would expedite things."

While M-Li looked through her phone contacts, Nick asked, "Are you from New York?"

"My family is from California. Isabel and I were two homesick girls trying to make it in the Big Apple." She looked at the photograph of her friend on the desk. "I made it. She was about to make it. Maybe that's why we bonded so well."

She turned her phone around for them to see the names and numbers of Isabel Creasy's parents. Nick jotted the information, then stood. Sacco took his cue from him.

"We will need a list of your employees, the ones who had contact with Mrs. Creasy."

"Let me print that for you." She booted her computer, quickly scanned for the appropriate file, and had an Excel spreadsheet of employees with addresses and phone numbers printed within two minutes. She took a highlighter from the pen cup and highlighted two names there.

"Galina and Leticia were the ones who had the most contact with her. Everyone else pitched in on the occasions where we couldn't make it."

"Who's this Leticia Millian?"

"She's our waxing expert. Did upper lip and bikini wax for Isabel. She's off today."

Nick took the paper, folded it, and placed it inside his notebook.

"Thank you, Mrs. Watson," Nick said and shook hands. He took out a card and handed it to her. "We'll contact you if we have other questions. Please call me if you can think of anything else."

"This is probably going to sound like a broken record, but, Detective Larson, I know Isabel. There's just no way she would do something like this to herself. She just wouldn't."

"We're just starting our investigation," Nick said as gently as he could. He couldn't divulge anything else. "We'll let you know our findings."

"Can I see her?"

An image of Isabel Creasy's body at autopsy came to mind. Not an image he would want M-Li to live with.

"Why don't you help the family organize funeral arrangements first?" he said, hoping she would get the silent message from his voice. "Then see her there. Say goodbye there. I'll let you know when the medical examiner's office releases the body. We'll need a mortuary's name by then."

Nick turned and walked to the back of the shop, Sacco not far behind.

As they climbed down the staircase, the echoes of M-Li's weeping followed them all the way to the first floor.

CHAPTER SEVEN

NICK SLID OUT into the night behind his partner. They'd parked the car about two blocks away from the salon. The city, usually vibrant in its nightly colors and sounds, seemed more muted because of the hour and the cold. Everyone with brains was already at home, or inside warm restaurants, or finishing up errands at supersonic speeds. What few pedestrians were about, were cocooned inside their jackets, their only thought to reach their warm apartments as quickly as possible.

"Quite a different take on the marriage, wasn't it?" Nick said to Sacco. "Did you notice she didn't mention his name even once?"

They stopped at the corner of Fifty-Ninth and waited for the light to change.

"We're going to have to wade through a boatload of shit to get to the truth of what was really going on in that relationship," Sacco said.

"Maybe the massage therapist, this EriK with a capital K, will give us something." Nick shook his head. "Shit. Where do people come up with these asinine names?"

Sacco smiled. "We, my friend, are not trendy, according to my niece. We are not relevant AF."

"Your niece," Nick said, glancing at Sacco, "is turning as foul mouthed as you."

"It's every New Yorker's right."

"Rebecca must be having a cow."

Sacco's grin turned wider. "My sister doesn't take after anyone in the family, sad to say."

Nick glanced at his partner. "Wants to improve the stock?"

Sacco laughed. "Afraid that's a losing battle."

They crossed the street. Nick concentrated on zigzagging around cars stuck in the middle of the intersection while avoiding pedestrians pushing through like flotsam in a culvert. He rapped on the hood of an overly enthusiastic cabbie, which had wanted to push him out of the way with his bumper, and jostled through onto the sidewalk.

Sacco caught up with him. They got into the car several minutes later.

"Home or precinct?"

Nick debated. They'd passed shift limits hours ago. They needed to add all this information to their case notes. They needed sleep. They needed to set up more interviews, look through the photographs, check with IT if they'd gotten anything from the victim's computer. They needed to verify if Ramos had anything back from trace, or if she'd discovered something they'd overlooked. But with sleep came new perspectives, new angles they could discuss about solving this case. And if more crap didn't pile up on them, they were looking forward to the same shit day tomorrow.

"Home." Nick said. "We're not on call tonight." *As if that had mattered for the past weeks.* "If Dispatch needs us, they'll call."

Sacco headed west on Fifty-Seventh and took a left on Ninth.

"I saw Laura crossing the street when I pulled up to your place earlier. Anything I should know about?" Sacco asked, as they waited for the light to change. He turned to Nick and did a Groucho Marx impression with his eyebrows. "Anything juicy, finally?"

Sacco waited.

Nick didn't reply.

"Nothing?" Sacco said, with a hopeful nudge to his voice.

Nick kept silent, staring ahead as the traffic brushed by them and around them, the continual flashes from cars and buses braking here and there resembling red Christmas lights on an asphalt backdrop.

"The timing in my world just sucks," Nick finally said.

"O...K?"

"Laura decided to sell."

Sacco waited for the punch line. Nick knew his partner was expecting something he'd not heard before. The selling of Laura's business had been a frequent topic of discussion and argument ever since Sandra Ward had started, in very creative ways, planning the destruction of Laura's business. But Laura always changed her mind.

"She's looking for business possibilities outside the tri-state area."

"Ouch." Sacco's glance was quick as he drove around a merging city bus. "Although that's not a complete shocker, knowing who's been stalking her for a year. But I figured she'd move to the suburbs, never out of state. Hearing that must have kind of sucked."

"Ya think?"

"Don't worry, buddy." Sacco's words held a hint of cheer. "Laura always changes her mind."

"Not this time. Last straw came today," Nick said. "Miss Ward was able to get her paws on a useful dupe and plastered the Yelp comment section of Laura's business with negative reviews. Nasty reviews." He rattled some of the juicier samples to his partner.

"Damn. Hadn't her webmaster gotten control of that shit?"

"Controlling the web is like trying to control bacteria," Nick said. "You burn its ass on one side of the Petri dish, but it ambushes you on the other." Nick breathed deeply and rubbed his face. Even his skin pores were tired. He needed four hours of uninterrupted sleep, at least. He hoped he'd be lucky tonight.

"The lies are starting to destroy years of great work and Laura is thinking of her partner, of Erin's future."

Sacco whistled.

Nick nodded, caught sight of the Los Madriles tapas bar sign to his left. Home was around the corner and he'd be hugging his pillow soon.

"Laura went to her lawyer this afternoon to finalize everything and show him what Sandra had done."

"Can't wait to hear the choice comments from Stef Masiani on this new shit."

Nick thought about the prosecutor in Sandra Ward's case. Unhappy would not capture Masiani's mood once she found out about this latest incident and how Sandra Ward had beaten the system yet again. Knowing Masiani, she would slap malicious intent, and a few other choice words, to the slew of charges against Sandra Ward, hoping it would throw the insanity plea out the window and keep her locked tight at Bedford Hills.

Nick wasn't so sure she'd succeed.

"Understatement of the year and more paperwork to add to the files."

"As if we didn't have enough shit to handle."

Sacco turned on Nick's street and braked in front of his apartment building, leaving the car running, waiting for his partner to hustle out. But Nick didn't move. He stared at the *Psychic Reader* neon sign gracing the first-floor apartment window of his building. A gaudy hand blinked its reddish-pink neon garishness front and center. Lorena Garcia, his very colorful neighbor, who thought she'd soon be the next Walter Mercado or the *Long Island Medium*, would turn the neon monstrosity off at ten o'clock sharp. George Lenning, the neighbor with the annoying yappy terrier on the second floor, was freezing his ass off while he smoked on the stoop. Five months ago, Nick had had to break up a major shouting match between George and his newly acquired significant other. It would have ended in each party pummeling the other if Nick hadn't threatened to arrest them right then and there. But what almost got their ass dragged to the precinct was the motive behind them going after each other in the first place. The little lady hadn't wanted her dog exposed to George's secondhand smoke. Not her lungs, mind you, but the freaking dog's. Should have booked them both for mere stupidity.

"Laura fessed up," Nick blurted. Seconds later, with a more unbelieving tone, "Damn, but that woman can kiss."

"Well, fuck. It's about time," Sacco said. "She's got more balls than you, dude. Still horny?"

"Christ, Vic."

"Come on. It's obvious, isn't it?" Sacco put the car in Park and turned to face his partner. "She's looking for a way out of leaving."

Nick nodded, thinking about Laura's words. The key she'd shared. Now it was his turn at bat. She wanted to hear his words. He wanted to say them.

"So, you told her you're crazy about her, too, right?"

Nick remained silent. He'd been an asshole for not saying them.

"You didn't?" It was an angry statement. "Shit, Nick. Not all women are Angela."

"Lay off, Vic." Nick understood, better than anyone, he'd been avoiding women and their motivations. He'd been painting them with the same brushstrokes his ex-wife had patterned for him years ago. But he'd broken that mold with Laura. But damn, Laura had picked a shitty time to tell him, with half his foot out the door to interview people for Creasy's case. Another time? He'd probably have dragged her to bed and made love to her until they were both sore.

Shit. They needed time to sort things out. And circumstances were not giving it to them.

"What's with the indecisive wussness all of a sudden? Never thought I'd see the day. Damn it, talk to her. You're both adults, experienced in personal bullshit and tragedy. Work it out."

"Look who's talking. The person who sniffs around but never commits."

Sacco was offended. "Tish and I are playing a game. She knows it. I know it. It'll be explosive once we go for each other. But we will. You, on the other hand, are letting the past screw your future."

Before Sacco could continue, Nick got out, braced against the cold, and slammed the car door. He flipped his partner the finger, climbed the steps fronting the four-storied building he called home, and ignored his neighbor's trembling "Hello."

Two minutes later, and keeping thoughts of Laura at bay with routine, Nick exchanged his suit and tie for matching sweatpants and sweatshirt, then grabbed the open beer from the refrigerator, took a deep swallow and flopped on the sofa. He placed his notes by the now-sweating beer bottle and flipped to a new page on the writing pad he always kept on the coffee table.

He scribbled his impressions about the latest interview. Like a shorthand version of free writing, Nick jotted words, connections, interpretations about the victim and the case. The center of the page had a huge circle encapsulating the victim's name. On the left hand side, he'd attached several connecting lines and smaller oblongs to it. One had M-Li's name written inside it. The other elliptical shapes would remain blank pieces of the puzzle until he could fill them up with names and his impressions after interviews. On the opposite side of Isabel Creasy's name, he'd done the same thing, this time with the victim's husband's name written there. He leaned back and studied the scribbles, lines, and bubbles that resembled a malformed insect created by a psychotic Mother Nature. Even this distorted, the page was similar to his revisiting a crime scene so it could talk to him. By the time he finished his beer, he had emptied his brain.

He scanned through Isabel Creasy's descriptors first:

Intelligent. Shy. Chemist. Depressed (doctor? support group?)?? Friendly, but not many friends.

Check selfies dates. Something off—saw neediness there, like husband claimed. Temporary? Due to divorce? Protected by friends.

Responsible worker?? Dating? Pissed someone off? Someone pissed her?—see M-Li's comments on interview. New apt—need to get FID involved. Scared of death. (Suicide—improbable by method used. Killed—definitely—my gut, Totes's, and everyone else). Why set up as suicide? Why the note? Hush-hush project. Secrets????

Her ex-husband's list was a bit terse:

Self-absorbed. Uncaring. Moved on. New live-in: possible threat? Asshole. Show-off. Screw it...Yes, Asshole. Workaholic. Corporate chain climber. Opportunistic. Doesn't believe wife committed suicide. On that score, we agree.

M-Li's were straightforward:

Real friend. Knows for years. Protective. Doesn't like husband much. Avoided acknowledging him as human being or by name. Filled gaps on victimology (see case notes). Need shock to pass before reinterview.

Nick yawned. His body and brain were now screaming for sleep. He reached for his cell and dialed Ramos, who answered with her usual no-nonsense what's up.

"I have the key to the hanging victim's new apartment. How soon can you get your team over there?"

"Give me a sec." Nick heard some paper rustling. "Carpenter is available tomorrow in the a.m. I'll pick up the key tomorrow on my way to the office. Where's the place?"

Nick gave her the information and hung up. Jotting with even quicker strokes, he created a list of names at the bottom of the page. Once more, using his notes as reference, he used his cell and dialed the numbers of Isabel Creasy's supervisor, the massage therapist, and the lab director. He left a message for all to return his call early tomorrow morning to set up interviews, and gave the precinct number.

He stood, stretched. He grabbed the empty beer bottle, rinsed it at the kitchen sink, and dropped it inside the small recycle bin he kept underneath. He dragged his feet to his bed, let his body slide face down onto it, and immediately fell asleep.

Not even the constant wails of fire engines responding to calls managed to slither in and disturb his dreamless sleep.

CHAPTER EIGHT

Tuesday, January 7

AT SIX THE next morning, Nick was sitting at his desk, having eaten a stale bagel with cream cheese for breakfast. He was entering last night's notes and impressions into the computer's case file when Ramos strode in.

"Have that key for me?"

Nick pointed to the desk where he'd dropped it next to the ripped-up page he'd doodled on last night.

She scooped up the key and tossed it in the air while she read Nick's notes upside down. Ramos chuckled at Nick's written impressions of witnesses and perpetrators.

"Asshole?"

"Don't ask," Nick said, returning her smile.

Ramos did a quick scan of Nick's face. "You look rested for a change."

"Slept like the dead for the first time in a week or two."

"No calls from Dispatch?"

"None," he answered, not adding his sleep hadn't been interrupted by nightmares, or dreams full of recriminations or regrets. "A small wow moment that Sutton and Beekman were at a crime lull last night."

"That you know of." Ramos checked the other side of his doodled page. "But the cold probably kept the crazies inside their hidey-holes, snuggled to their paper padding and cardboard planks inside the IND and the IRT."

"Hey, I'm not complaining. Tonight will be a different animal, though. The thaw will bring out the usual predators, drug dealers, burglars, junkies, and overall idiots who prowl our streets," Nick added. This morning, the local weatherman had cheerfully predicted a high of fifty-nine degrees by late afternoon.

Ramos tapped a section with comments about Isabel Creasy. "She was a chemist?"

"That's what M-Li Watson said. I'm waiting to hear back from the lab director. See what she can tell us about the creams and other beauty stuff Ms. Creasy was creating."

"Heard the flu recoveries are starting to trickle our way," Ramos said. "Oh, and Horowitz said the death desk from the *Post* called. Usual shorthand on this?"

"Yeah. Don't have anything yet to add, anyway."

Ramos nodded, a bit pensive. "We need normal soon. Those days without Carpenter and the others were a bitch."

"Speaking of," Nick said. "Remind Carpenter to give me a copy of his sketch of the apartment and contents as soon as he gets back. I'll need a visual of the place."

"You're not going to be there?" The remark came out surprised.

"Have an appointment with Kilcrease at nine. Couldn't get out of it."

"Ah," she said. "Sacco your point man?"

"Don't sound so pleased."

"Bah. Opportunity wasted. I'm stuck in the lab today." She pointed to the sheet. "And you gave me a few things to ponder. Let me know what the lab director tells you."

"Want to tag along?" It wouldn't be a bad idea if Ramos accompanied them to the interview. She understood the jargon and could add to his impressions, take what she needed for analysis.

"Always said you were a perceptive animal," she answered, looking pleased, and slapped the desktop. "Later."

For the next hour, Nick kept adding information to his case binder. The office took on a constant murmuring, reminiscent of the sound of industriousness inside a hive. Things were starting to get back to normal.

He made a copy of the suicide note and his malformed diagram, then separated those for the debriefing later. The lab director, as well as the victim's boss from Saks, had set up appointments for later in the afternoon. Tish Ramos had made room in her schedule to go with them to interview the lab director. The EriK with a capital K, however, was nowhere to be found yet. Nick had left two messages on his phone already, and one at his place of work. Maybe a surprise visit to the spa was in order. Maybe dragging his ass to the precinct would be more effective.

He checked his watch and saw it was time to exit for his appointment. He grabbed notebook, shield, gun, and coat, together with a small manila envelope stuffed with photocopies of the fork-stabbing case yesterday.

"This," Nick said, dropping the envelope next to the overstuffed inbox on Horowitz's desk, "is for Detective Barrios from the Thirty-Second. He'll be picking this up sometime today."

"They're grabbing the case?" asked Horowitz.

Nick nodded. "Captain there owed ours a favor."

"God knows we need the help."

Nick glanced around, saw some desks manned by officers and detectives for the first time in weeks. "Things improving?"

"One new casualty today. Three bodies back, and they look healthier than they looked a week ago."

"Puke green definitely doesn't complement the ratty brown of the walls here."

Horowitz had a good chuckle at that. "Captain's cigar looks less ragged, too."

"Did Ramos get back to you on the death desk request?"

"Gave the PIO the redacted info. She'll spread it around all the media outlets, as is, for now. No need for them to know that Mrs. Creasy's death just didn't look right."

"Who's at the media desk right now?"

"Anton Cardoso, but I haven't seen him in about a week. Probably camping out on Fifth. New president throws out better chum."

"Keep curious eyes away from my desk, just in case. Spread the word."

"Will do, Lieutenant. Off to see Kilcrease?"

Nick nodded, ill humor draping him. There just wasn't any way to keep a damn secret in this office.

By the time Nick arrived at the psychiatrist's office building, three avenues down from the precinct, the remnant cold had whipped his face and ears to a painful burn. He thawed on the way up the elevator and entered the doctor's reception room feeling less hypothermic. Before he could knock on the small frosted glass pane dividing waiting room from the office, one of the secretaries opened it.

"Hi, Detective. The doctor just got in. He'll be with you in a sec."

Nick acknowledged with a nod, took off his coat, and sat. He hoped he wouldn't have a long wait.

Minutes later, he was ushered to the doctor's somewhat cozy office, one side fitted with two cushiony love seats arranged in an L-ruler formation. Across from the sofas, a big mahogany desk was covered with haphazardly arranged mounds of papers, textbooks, and patient files. Behind the desk area, the wall was covered with shelves, books, framed diplomas, and quiet landscape photographs from exotic places. The doctor himself had taken those during his numerous vacations to islands Nick hadn't even known existed on this planet. The doctor called them his serenity focal points.

Nick didn't doubt the need for them. The doctor dealt with his share of lunatics in this office, needing, like an infant sometimes, to focus on something other than the boatload of distressing stimuli generated by the mentally disturbed, depressed, grief-stricken, angry, and psychotic.

"Good morning, Lieutenant."

Nick turned toward the voice of the man who held the power to return him to homicide full time.

For such a big name, Maximilian Kilcrease, MD, was rather small in stature, head reaching about Nick's shoulder. He moved at the pace of a starfish and had the buggy eyes of a sloth. With his thinning, silver-gray hair and soft voice, people were often deceived and thought of him as a pushover. However, Dr. Kilcrease was anything but. His demeanor hid from new patients the astuteness of his scrutiny and the razor-sharp mind behind watery brown eyes framed by old-style, plastic-frame glasses. His soft baritone had a steel edge to it, which, when necessary, brooked no argument. Or, oftentimes, the bass tonality of it lulled, soothed, and hypnotized.

"Nippy today," Kilcrease said, pointing to one of the seats. Nick took the hint and settled on the stiff sofa. The cushions were deceptive. Another stratagem of the good doctor: Keep the patient uncomfortable, alert, and on edge.

"Enough to freeze Satan's privates," Nick agreed.

The doctor grinned, retrieved the perpetual handkerchief out of his shirt pocket, and dabbed at his eyes. He sat in slow motion, crossed his legs, rested the notebook he carried to all his sessions on his knee, clicked the pen twice, and fixed his laser eyes on Nick.

"Heard about the suicide. Why don't you tell me about it?"

Nick's face showed his cynicism. He was sure the good doctor already knew all the details of the hanging, supplied by his captain. What Kilcrease was really interested in was Nick's reactions to it.

"I didn't puke."

Kilcrease lowered his face and stared at Nick over the eyeglass frames.

"Felt like it, but you know how my stomach protests around DBs."

Kilcrease kept staring.

Nick gave up the charade. He had the secondary crime scene to investigate, plus all the interviews he'd set up for the afternoon.

He needed Dr. Kilcrease to finally give the green light.

"For a minute there, I thought it was Angela's face instead of the victim's."

"Understandable." The doctor raised his head and pushed the glasses up his nose. "What exactly reared up at the sight of the hanging woman?"

"Just the memory of Angela. Her last insults, the last plea." Nick's eyes unfocused, zeroing on the memory. "My anger at her. The regret. The feeling of failure. It didn't last long. I was more worried about not throwing up on the crime scene."

"So was Ramos, I heard."

Nick thought the good doctor was very well informed indeed.

"I'm more interested in your reactions to those memories."

"It was more like an echo, this time," Nick said. "Surprising when it reaches you so clearly; amazing when it doesn't affect you, except as a somewhat painful recollection. Roils the self-doubt for a moment. Briefly makes you feel like you're shit." Nick looked at the doctor, his gaze unwavering. "Then it was gone. The victim took precedence. The case needed solving."

Kilcrease took a long moment to study Nick, his face, his posture, listening to the murmurs of what was left unsaid. He nodded at some internal comments, wrote something on the pad. His gaze returned to Nick's face and he asked very casually, "How's Laura?"

"What does Laura have to do with you clearing me for full duty?" Nick asked, his demeanor shifting.

"Nothing, actually. Just indulging in personal curiosity." Kilcrease clicked his pen twice and placed it inside his front pocket.

Nick stared. The good doctor never indulged in personal curiosity unless there was a shitload of professional inquiry underlying the questions. But, what the hell. Maybe it would be good to talk around the issue.

"She's leaving the area."

"Manhattan?"

Nick shook his head. "The state. Further complicated things yesterday by confirming what I knew already..."

"Love?"

"Yeah," Nick said, the wonder of the feeling and the kiss still at the forefront. "Hinted at staying if I reciprocate."

"And did you? Verbally?"

"No." His voice turned rough. "It wasn't the time. She landed that doozy a moment before I had to do interviews on this new case."

"Will there be a time?" Kilcrease asked. "Or will you let her go?"

Nick's face showed his conflict.

"Did she tell you where she's looking for business opportunities?"

"No, and I didn't ask. I don't have the right to prevent her leaving if she can create a new life elsewhere, safe from..."

"Psycho sister," Kilcrease interrupted, no underlying humor in his eyes.

The change in expression didn't throw off Nick. Kilcrease had dealt with Sandra Ward when administering the prelim psychological profile of her for the DA's office.

"Very sick woman. Nevertheless..."

"Come on, Kilcrease," Nick said. "You damn well know I communicate well with cops, but not with others. Laura hasn't dealt with the reality of a cop's life, except briefly on the receiving end. To tell you the truth, I'm bowled over she still wants to hang around me after what happened a year ago. However, committing and living with a cop...well, let's say my silences with Angela while I processed the day, trying not to take my frustration out on her, despite her constant need and invectiveness, fucked up my marriage."

"Compartmentalizing is difficult for anyone," Kilcrease said, commiserating. "It's hard not to taint the good around you with the ugliness you see every day. The worst thing you guys have to deal with."

Nick nodded. Kilcrease understood only too well. He dealt with the aftermath of cops not coping on a daily basis.

"Angela resented that no end," Nick said.

"Angela had her own issues, unique and separate from yours."

"Yeah, well, I don't know if Laura can cope with my shit on top of hers. She might not even want to cope with it. Wouldn't blame her."

"Laura, from what you tell me, is different. Stronger."

"Doesn't matter. What does, bottom line, is regrets. I don't want her to have any around me or of me."

Kilcrease took a moment to wipe his teary eyes with the handkerchief. "Damn allergies," he complained and dropped his glasses back on his nose. "The possibility of regrets in the distant future should not stop you from pursuing what seems to be a good match. Or is it something else?"

Nick paused. "I'm not sure I'll be able to protect Laura," he finally said.

The men stared at each other.

"Now that's refreshingly honest," Kilcrease said. "Help me here a sec, though. Protect her... how?" He studied Nick for a long time in silence. "From you?"

Nick's face turned hard. Kilcrease understood another side to some cops. An uglier side.

"Never. And you know that."

"Then what? Still believe Laura will change the moment you open up to her?" Kilcrease asked. "That she'll turn into another Angela?"

"It's happened before," Nick said, his tone a touch bitter, thinking of Angela's transformation the moment after they'd said their I dos. "But, no. Not Laura."

"And..."

"And, what? Screw my instincts and grab happiness by the balls despite all the bullshit? Sorry, Doc. No can do."

"So basically you don't want to invest in you both."

"God. You have no clue how much I want that. Need it. But next week," Nick leaned forward to make his point, "there's a good chance that crazy sister of hers will get transferred to a low-security mental institution, unless we get a hard-ass judge who won't overturn her sentence on appeal. But, if that happens, how can I protect Laura from a woman who looks, breathes, talks, dresses, and imitates her to perfection? A woman who can con another lawyer, manipulate another corrections officer, or scam another health professional to help her with her cause? How can I protect Laura from that if I tell her I'm crazy shit in love with her and make her stay?"

"Now, Detective, you can't protect everyone from life. You, better than anyone else, know that. So be honest. What is really preventing your commitment? You are over Angela. You've been over her for years. What screwed you up was her suicide. That shocked the crap out of you. But your issue has been more about regret than loss. And," Kilcrease lifted a hand to stop Nick from interrupting. "I think you've processed that successfully. As a matter of fact, I'll be releasing you from purgatory this afternoon. However, speaking as your friend, you need to kick-start yourself out of the limbo you've been parked in since your divorce. You need to live, Lieutenant, despite the fears."

"Sorry, Doc. Guess I'm not on board with that scenario," Nick said, his voice low. "Because all I know, right now, is that if she's my next 911, I don't think I'll be able to survive it."

Kilcrease, for once, had no comment.

CHAPTER NINE

AFTER LEAVING KILCREASE'S office, Nick was in a bizarre mood, despite the good news from the doctor. Damn the shrink. Got under his skin every time they spoke. On purpose, too, needing to get to the bottom of a cop's psyche, or some such crap. But Kilcrease was good. Probably why the good doctor earned the bigger paycheck. Still, it had done him good to talk about what worried him. About committing to another woman.

Stepping outside the building, Nick hunched inside his coat like a turtle hiding from attack. Shortly, he was back at the precinct and into warmer air. Inside, Nick booted his computer and took off his coat, thinking that the doctor was right—he needed to get beyond his past, not wallow in this half-assed, halfway-bull world of indecisions and silences. His anger at Angie had to stop coloring his love life...period. He couldn't permit his ex to taint a viable, positive future with another woman. His guilt at not being able to save Angie was unproductive. Angie had made her decisions. *She* had created her own monster, one that had eventually devoured her. And one thing he'd learned from his years as a detective—some people were not salvageable, despite every effort. Angela, to his misfortune, had been one of those.

"I need to kick my own butt into gear," he mumbled.

Nick knew he and Laura could have a very satisfying relationship. And he wanted one, badly. Laura understood a bit about his own demons, having had a crazy ex herself, not to mention the pathological sister. Bottom line, though, Nick needed Laura, wanted her depth of emotion, her maturity, her gentleness, and her courage. He scoffed, his lower body reacting to the thought of Laura and reminding him that all that nicety and new millennial PC-ness was bullshit.

Let's get real here, Larson, my boy. You're always horny around Laura, wanting her naked, in bed, while sweat-drenching the sheets until exhaustion.

It was high time to stop the juvenile bullshit and the fear. As soon as Laura returned, he would lay everything on the table and let things roll on their own.

He rang Sacco, asked if he needed help at the victim's apartment. His partner advised him to stay put, that the scene was more than properly covered, and to expect him at the office sooner rather than later.

Nick reached for the keyboard and spent the next two hours catching up on paperwork, setting up interviews, and adding to the case notes of pending cases he and Sacco had.

He was as frustrated as a fish in a bowl.

"You've got the I-can't-believe-this-shit look on your face," Sacco said by way of greeting and dropped hand-drawn diagrams in front of Nick.

"People," Nick said, pointing to the paperwork. "Just people, what they do, say. The vitriol. The nastiness. The lack of humanity and the endless hours we spend on this shit. Anyway, anything of note at the apartment?"

"Nah." Sacco pulled up the chair next to the bookcase and dragged it next to Nick. "She hadn't settled in yet."

Evidence limbo. Life all but erased from one home and nothing imprinted on the other.

"Just what we need to solve this case."

"The apartment is also miniscule in comparison to the brownstone," Sacco continued. "She either downsized considerably, or never collected much stuff." He shifted in his chair. "Although, I must admit, the place has a better feel—it's cozier, homier, despite the clutter of unopened boxes, disorganized furniture, and clothing still draped over chairs. Carpenter found samples of the product line the victim was creating in the living room, as well as some used ones in the bathroom."

"Testing the product, probably."

"Ramos should be able to tell if anything hinky was in these things once she analyzes them."

Nick studied the diagram. The doorway to the victim's new apartment opened into a small foyer that gave way to an open living room, divided from the dining space and kitchen by a wall. According to the sketch, the victim seemed to have set up a small table at the edge of the living room, facing some windows.

"What the hell does this chicken scratch say?"

Sacco glanced at what Nick pointed at.

"Temporary office. That's where she set up her desktop and inventory. Techs are bringing everything in. Carpenter took the desktop and a small book with IDs and passwords to IT. They'll be looking through those when they can. They're a lot backed up, like us."

Nick nodded and mentally walked through the apartment by way of the diagram. From the kitchen, a small hallway led to the bedroom and the bathroom. All the little rectangles were boxes and furniture, evidence of the clutter spread haphazardly around the area. It was a stark testament to a woman who, according to her friend, had wanted to renew her life and had failed through the murderous action of another's hand.

"Did you check these?" Nick pointed to the small rectangles.

"Mixed bag of things." Sacco took out his notes. "Jewelry, neatly labeled. Diplomas, graduation photos, textbooks, packed underwear, shoes, purses, and a binder with articles of incorporation...an LLC."

"So, she was serious about opening her own business. Any personal photographs?"

"Two or three," Sacco said. "But she seems to follow today's generation, with most photographs either on the phone or the computer."

Nick glanced at the bathroom sketch and saw an asterisk next to a bathroom cabinet. "What is this?"

Sacco began to laugh. "You'll have to ask Carpenter."

"Who needs to ask me what?" The young tech handed a bundle to Nick. "Sorry. The photograph copies are grainy, but I knew you wanted to see something more recognizable than my scene sketches. I'll get the digital ones processed later in the week."

Nick flipped through the photographs until he came across the ones of the bathroom and its contents. The area had been completely decorated with a beach motif. Towels, shower curtain, and bathroom accessories were all adorned with starfish and seashells. Even the only print decorating the wall was that of a parrotfish.

"Color scheme in there was pastels. Typical tropical blues, pinks, and whites," Carpenter supplied, since the photographs were black and white copies.

"You think the frigid weather outside influenced her choice of theme and colors?" Nick asked, amused. Even with the forecast set to defrost concrete today, the cold outside tenaciously clawed and bit people, refusing to go away. It had been a bitch of a winter.

"Wouldn't surprise me," Carpenter said. "I have visions of hot beaches every time the cold smacks me."

Nick looked at the other photos of the bathroom. Organized and neat, each drawer designated for a specific purpose: feminine hygiene products—lower right. Bathroom necessities—lower left. Beauty products—second drawer on right. Dentistry—upper right. Cleaning supplies, beneath sink.

Nick stared at the last photo. It was a close-up of the contents inside one drawer. A really good close-up of K-Y jelly, condoms (in all flavors and textures, it seemed), and several vibrators of different shapes and sizes.

"Is this what I think it is?" Nick pointed to what looked like a G-string with a battery pack on the back.

Sacco laughed.

"C-string vibrating underwear." Carpenter looked at the men, very serious. "Guaranteed hands-free pleasure anywhere, or your money back."

"It's sick the amount of garbage you gather on crime scenes, PC," Nick said, reverting to Totes's nickname for Carpenter. "You really need to get out more."

"My girlfriend prefers me in," Carpenter said with a grin.

Sacco's belly laugh exploded around them.

"Get out, Carpenter," Nick said, shaking his head. "Make sure the evidence reaches Ramos today."

"Won't she be delighted," Sacco said, his grin stretching as Carpenter left the office.

"Wishful thinking?" Nick asked.

"Hey," Sacco swatted Nick's shoulder. "Never hurts to hope."

Nick stared at the last photo and shook his head. "This type of technology will soon make us damn obsolete," he said.

"Nah. Only for the lonely and alone."

Nick stared at his partner. Funny he should pick up on the lonely factor.

"Let's mosey on out of here," Nick said.

"What's the agenda?" Sacco asked as he followed Nick to the elevators.

"Work supervisor first. Ramos will meet us at the research lab later. She's picking up the warrant. And last is a meet with invisible EriK of the effing capital K."

Sacco's laugh accompanied them all the way inside the car. There, Nick directed the blast of heat toward his hands and face and headed to their next appointment.

"How was the session with Kilcrease?"

"Same bull," Nick said and left it at that, maneuvering through traffic. "But I'll be getting a signed report card this afternoon."

"About time," Sacco said.

After parking close to Madison, Nick and Sacco dodged delivery vans, taxis, cars, delivery people on bikes, and the frustrated pedestrians rushing around for a quick lunch. Everyone pushed aggressively past shoppers and tourist cliques that blocked the sidewalks, either gawking at the sights, posing for selfies, group shots, or panoramic views of the local sights. Sometimes Nick envied them their glitzy view of New York. For him, however, New York was not always glamour and beauty. Reality had a habit of always body-slamming him.

By the time they reached Fifth and Fiftieth, New Yorkers were out en masse. The sun had finally clobbered the cold into submission. And after the frigid weather of two days ago, the high thirties felt like a damn heatwave.

Inside the posh retail store, they followed the directions Isabel Creasy's supervisor had given them. In the basement, the woman was already waiting next to the entrance to a salon-cum-spa business. Nick studied the woman who was pacing with typical New York impatience as they approached. Her garments screamed designer coordinates. So did the shoes and makeup she wore. She was reed thin and decked out in model perfection, her black hair coiffed in a French twist, a few wisps of hair strategically loosened to give her face a more casual look. She wore a black skirt and blouse ensemble, accentuating her figure to an almost emaciated slimness. The only hint of color came from the red lipstick, the matching earrings and bracelet she wore. To complete the ensemble, a red-hued scarf artfully surrounded her throat and shoulder.

"The woman needs a few good steaks," Sacco observed under his breath.

Nick agreed, but said nothing. He understood healthy, but this was taking it to a whole new level. Personally, he preferred a woman with a bit more flesh and curves. A woman like Laura.

"This is a real tragedy," the woman, introducing herself as Alina Doering, said. She pointed to an elevator bank and headed that way. Pushing the Up arrow more times than was necessary, she turned to the men.

"Isabel was one of our best assets. She's been top board for ten consecutive months, and she was about to break a record after the holidays."

"Top board?" Nick asked as the elevator doors closed. Alina Doering alternately tapped the tenth-floor and close-door buttons in staccato impatience, even after the elevator slid upward.

"Our store is all about diversity and self-empowerment," Ms. Doering said, veering left toward her office after stepping off the elevator. "Those employees on our leader board who've topped performed with clients are posted there on a monthly basis. Sometimes names climb or fall from their positions, but Isabel has been a constant this year."

She led the men into a small office with no windows. To Nick it looked like a refurbished closet. She sat facing the men.

"Dying so suddenly," Doering said, her eyes concerned and earnest. "It's unbelievable. So young. Was it a heart attack?"

Nick wasn't about to get into the details. "You mentioned Mrs. Creasy was an asset. Can you expand on that?"

"She made over five thousand dollars in commission sales for the company in December," Doering said. "Her own record for this month was on its way to exceed that."

"Motivated employee," Nick commented.

"You have no idea. After the separation...you know about the divorce, right?"

Nick nodded.

"It was as if a flashbulb had exploded with brightness inside her. Oh, don't get me wrong. She was punctual, courteous, and enthusiastic about work. She loved demonstrating our top-of-the-line cosmetic products, giving clients her expert suggestions on each. She catered to the clients' demands and dermatological needs. Isabel was good, but mostly because her sales correlated with the total overtime hours she worked."

"So, what changed?" Sacco asked.

"Divorce. After her husband left, she became a different person, more relaxed, focused. She became the poster woman for what our company expects to be the perfect salesperson. Isabel engaged people in a most nonconfrontational way, which, in turn, brought in more sales. Clients began asking for her specifically. She reveled in that. Began creating an impressive client following," Doering said.

Nick and Sacco looked at each other.

"Did anyone here object to her rise in the company's good graces?" Nick asked.

Doering stared, first at Nick, then at Sacco. "You mean could anyone here wish her harm?"

"Competitiveness is a strong motivator for people to do crazy things," Nick replied. "Not to speak of personality clashes."

"Competition is encouraged, but we take pride in our employee diversity, and demand that all respect each other. Dissension is considered inexcusable behavior and our company strongly frowns on that. There's room for everyone to shine in our organization."

"So," Sacco said. "HR had no complaints lodged either by Mrs. Creasy or against her?"

From Sacco's tone, Nick knew his partner hadn't bought the jealousy factor not rearing up.

"None that were brought to my attention."

Nick made some quick notes. "I saw that you offer customers a salon spa experience. Did Mrs. Creasy ever use the facilities?"

"Not for lack of my trying," Doering said, the first sign of disapproval on her face.

"Does your company demand its employees use the retailers it sponsors?" Sacco asked.

"No, but we are an example-based company. We encourage our employees to buy our exclusive clothing lines, at a discount, of course, and to use them, our fragrances and cosmetics, including any other services we provide. That way there's truth in advertising. Clients see the quality of our products, hear about them and, therefore, buy them."

"And why did Mrs. Creasy refuse?" Nick asked.

"Isabel is very faithful to her friend M-Li. I couldn't get her to change once she was gainfully employed here."

"What about the spa services," Nick continued. "Did she ever use those?"

"On occasion...that I know of. She used someone else uptown. Recommended them every once in a while, but I wasn't interested."

"Did Mrs. Creasy ever speak about working on her own beauty product line?"

A penny, dropped a mile away, would have been heard in the silence that followed.

"No." Terse. The woman looked like she'd swallowed vinegar. "No, we were not aware of that."

"Is there a way we could see her locker space or workstation? Speak with co-workers?"

"Certainly." Doering stood. "Follow me."

For the next hour, Nick and Sacco asked questions, received impressions, but no one had anything negative to say about Isabel. The victim seemed to have been well liked. No one knew her well, except for the day-to-day exposure of work. From all they heard, Isabel Creasy basically went to work, blabbed pleasantries, didn't share much of herself to anyone, and didn't reciprocate by befriending co-workers, except at the most rudimentary level. Frustrated, Nick concluded the interviews. There was nothing more to add to their victimology profile, no more clarity about possible motives to dispatch the victim. At least, not in this venue.

"If this Doering woman had given us another royal we, I would have puked," Sacco said as soon as they hit the street.

"The dichotomy of the age—the ones who blindly embrace company policy while at work, but who probably rail against the injustices of capitalist business giants to friends."

"While indulging in the commissions. I'm sure her dismay at the victim's death is the loss of future earnings to the company."

"Well, five grand clear profit in beauty products sales is nothing to sneer at. I'm sure Mrs. Creasy got a lot of brownie points for her department with that."

Back in the car, Nick pointed it toward the Hudson, navigating them through the mess of Fifty-Third Street traffic.

"What's wrong with this picture?" Nick asked, knowing his partner was on the same wavelength. "Either Isabel Creasy was the incarnation of Mother Teresa..."

"Or someone is lying through their teeth," Sacco finished. "But I didn't get the impression anyone was."

"How can a person be at work every day and not spill a comment about how pissed she was at her husband, or rail at her situation, or share joys and likes? No opinions, no personal interchanges. Just...existing." He cursed under his breath. "Shit. How can a person be so...so...beige?"

The bottleneck on Fifty-Third eased a bit as he neared Eleventh Avenue. He made a left there and headed toward the Hudson Yards area, near Chelsea, where the lab was located.

"It's more like invisible to me," Sacco said.

Nick thought about that. "Not invisible. Insignificant. No impact on life or on others whatsoever except in a tepid way."

"Except for her friend and her ex. Those had very strong emotional connections to the victim, even if they were opposite."

"I think the emotional connection is a violent reaction to each other. But those two had no motive to get rid of Isabel Creasy. The husband went his merry way and got himself a new girlfriend and a new life. M-Li Watson has her business and her husband. It gets us nowhere."

The Lincoln Tunnel inflow bottlenecked them again. By the time Nick saw the turnoff at Twenty-Third, he was cussing.

"Do you remember the photograph Isabel Creasy took of herself in her bathroom? The one that we were looking at briefly yesterday?" Nick realized now that the background in the image was the same as Carpenter's photos in the victim's bathroom.

Sacco nodded, as he scanned the street for the lab's address.

"Did you get the feeling she was desperate to be noticed?" Nick asked.

Sacco stopped his scan of the street to stare at Nick. "What do you mean?"

"My gut..."

Sacco groaned. "Fuck, not your gut again."

"I don't know, Vic. Who the hell takes a picture of herself facing the mirror, striking what she deems a sexy pose that looks more pathetic and a cry for help than seductive? When I looked at it, I couldn't help but feel sorry for her, at her small, pathetic move to show people she's desirable, vibrant, important. What I got from it was a desperate attempt for any man to notice her. The photo was taken to provoke a response. I'm wondering whose response did she want?" Nick paused. "And who reacted?"

"There's Ramos," Sacco said. Ramos and two techs were talking and shuffling in front of a nondescript entrance to an old concrete building in the middle of the street. Nick double-parked the car and got out.

"Do you think that's what may have gotten her killed?" Sacco asked, at the same moment Ramos approached.

"Hell, I don't know. Saw the dates on the photos. They were taken after her divorce. Maybe it was depression talking. A little self-pity."

"Serious faces mean serious conversations," Ramos said.

Sacco pointed at Nick. "Thinks we may have a "going nowhere" case here sooner rather than later. His gut."

"Ooh," Ramos practically purred. "I want dibs on that, Larson."

"Later. Let's get out of the cold."

The lab entrance had no reception and no elevators, just a stairwell facing the doorway. Nick surmised that, in the past, the owner had sectioned off the empty factory's open floor plan, converting it into these thin claustrophobic entrances to maximize rental profitability. The walls were painted an old, dismal gray and had scuff marks and dirty spots near the vinyl baseboards.

"Well, this is cheerful," Ramos said.

"And smells rancid," Nick commented.

"Since they deal with various chemicals up there, that's what you're smelling," Ramos said, and started up the stairs.

The lab entrance was on the fourth floor, where the landlord had been more generous with space. It was still a small area, but wider than the entrance, with doors to interior rooms facing each other on opposite walls. Windowless, the occupants had tried to make things cheerful by painting each wall a different shade of ochre. A poor ficus, going bald from the lack of sun or water, stood in a corner, while smaller plants were spread around the area. Large framed museum prints were hung strategically to focus the eye on more color. A wood desk, with filing cabinets surrounding it, hugged the middle of the area. Two chairs faced the somewhat cluttered desk.

When they stepped in, Nick felt the place shrink. He was not claustrophobic, but he wanted to bolt and get some fresh air. He never understood how anyone could work in such enclosed quarters day in and day out.

He approached the woman sitting at the desk and introduced himself and the rest of the officers. From the engraved desk tag, she was the office manager, a Rachel Brennan.

"I was shocked, really, when you called me, Detective. Isabel was such a nice woman. Hard-working. Professional. Such a shame."

Nick and Sacco exchanged glances. Sacco's eyebrows lifted.

"Did you know her well?" Nick asked.

"Not really. I'm mostly at my desk. The lab is pretty busy lately with inventors and grantees coming and going, working on their projects. I have to juggle an inordinate amount of times and dates, protocols, plus the phones, and all the other clerical work here, so it limits my interchange with our clients. But Isabel always greeted me with a smile."

"How often was she here?"

"Every Friday on the dot," Ms. Brennan said. "Never missed her scheduled time. Always here five minutes before and left on time."

"Were there any issues with the other inventors or grantees that you know of?" Sacco asked.

"Not really. Ms. Leitelt, the lab director, will probably know better than me. She's expecting you." The woman stepped to the right, knocked on a secondary door there, heard the command to enter, opened the door, and ushered them inside. "Detective Larson to see you, Bonita."

Nick saw that this room was practically a twin to the previous one, except it was painted in shades of contrasting, soft greens.

What it didn't have was plants. Instead, every corner of the room had standing lamps in them. Plaques and diplomas covered one wall, and open bookshelves arrayed another.

"Detectives."

Bonita Leitelt was, if anything else, a surprise. Almost as tall as Nick, with lustrous ebony skin and green eyes pinched at the corners, her exotic features should have been plastered on glamour magazines rather than wallowing in a sunless room, her statuesque body covered with a lab coat over normal clothing.

Nick nodded to Ramos, who stepped forward with the warrant. Bonita Leitelt took the paper.

"This is so out of my comfort zone," she said and shuffled the warrant from hand to hand.

Nick supposed the lab director had never dealt with warrants allowing search and seizure of property. These things always unnerved normal people.

"The warrant allows possession of Mrs. Creasy's notes, computer disks, and whatever prototypes she was working on," Nick said. "We'll try not to disturb any of your clients in the process."

"This is such a shame, especially when Isabel was almost at a breakthrough." She shook her head. "We'll cooperate with you as much as we can, but I have to warn you to keep any disturbances to a minimum. Those that are working at this hour don't need disruptions of any kind. Distractions will mess up results. Thankfully, not many of our clients are here today," Leitelt said.

"What was Mrs. Creasy working on?" Nick asked, curious.

She motioned them to follow her. She crossed the office manager's area and opened the door directly opposite to her office. The area was five times what they had left behind. Lab tables, decked with all types of equipment, were arrayed in six long columns, filling the entire width of the space. Overhead, fluorescent lights set the place ablaze with faux sunshine. True to her word, only three people were in the room, working on different, and what looked to Nick, very complicated and expensive equipment.

"She was attempting to excite certain fibroblasts, the specialized cells for the biosynthesis of the hyaluronan-rich matrix in the dense facial tissues." At Nick's blank stare, she grinned and continued. "In any case, she wanted to test the absorbability of therapeutic materials into the dermis and what materials and percentages were optimum."

"Wound healing and regeneration?" Ramos asked, more excited than usual.

"Yes, that was her goal, as well as to expand the scope of its use."

"What was she using for the absorption method?"

"That was proprietary material and we are not privy to that," Leitelt said. "But I'm assuming she was using DMSO. TXA could be another possibility. Maybe Laurocapram? I don't really know, nor did she volunteer information. Inventors keep things very close to their vest. Her notes should have it, as well as the abstract in the grant application. Here you go."

They stopped at the back of the lab, where vertical filing cabinets covered the space wall to wall. Leitelt slid a master key from an extendable key ring at her waist and opened the cabinet. She pointed to a thick binder and product sealed in plastic bags behind it.

"Everything is there, neatly catalogued."

Ramos nodded to her team and they began extracting the evidence.

"What are the possibilities of theft of material by other inventors here?" Nick asked.

"None," Leitelt replied. "There are protocols. I log everyone in, or Rachel does if I'm not available." She pointed to a binder on top of the filing cabinets. "They can access their materials only after they log in and I unlock the cabinet. See those buzzers under each workstation? Once finished for the day, they buzz me or Rachel, and we go through the entire process again, but in reverse."

"Are there any other keys to access materials and notes?" Sacco asked.

"None. Just the two of us."

"How about access to experiment results on those?" Nick pointed to all the equipment.

"Same protocol. Once the client has printed a copy of his results, and we've verified the printing, whether it's on the mass spec, PCR, and others, we clear that data for next client use. That way there is no way anyone can see the results of the others, or duplicate them, or mess up their own results."

Nick made a note and, without looking up, asked, "Ever tempted?"

"Don't insult me, Detective," she said, rather amused by the question. "I have three patents and two more pending. Besides, I am bonded for this position. If I do something that stupid, who do you think will be suspected first?"

"Have to ask," Nick said, no apology in his tone. "Any altercations with other inventors or grantees that you know of?"

"No. We run a lab here, not a social network. Apart from the typical pleasantries of 'how are you?' and 'nice day,' we don't mingle. Isabel was serious about her work. Very focused. She didn't want to waste her time or money on small talk. She came and went during her allotted time and that was it, I'm afraid."

"We're done here," Ramos told Nick at the same time handing Leitelt a copy of the evidence sheet with the items taken. With a "catch you later" wave, she headed for the exit with her techs once the lab manager had signed.

Nick knew they had crashed into another dead end here.

"If you can remember anything else," he said, handing over his card. "Please let us know. Maybe other clients can help give more information."

Leitelt flipped the card several times. "I doubt it, but I'll ask around. Like I said before, Detective, our clients are extremely focused on their own work here, not on someone else's. But I'll call if I find any other information."

Nick thanked her and followed Ramos out into the somewhat warmer afternoon.

The way things were developing, Nick thought, disgusted, the case might soon wind up in ice instead of the cold.

CHAPTER TEN

As soon as Nick and Sacco stepped inside the Deep Tissue and Hot Stones spa, the noisy ruckus of New York came to an abrupt halt. Insulated glass muted and isolated the racket of vibrant life outside and replaced it with soft New Age sounds and melodies of waterfalls on the inside. Fragrances imbued the air, as well, very reminiscent of M-Li Watson's salon, meant to relax the customers before they were serviced, Nick presumed.

Well, that hadn't come out right.

Reception was on the small side, displaying a two-level Formica desk in a J pattern, with marketing materials strategically scattered on top for customers to use and take. The company's logo and name were set in bold letters on the wall behind two smiling receptionists. To the right of the desk, an engraved plate indicated the closed access to the manager's office. To the right, comfortable chairs were arranged around end tables and more shelves displayed the spa's product line with a wall waterfall bubbling nearby. Beside the door marked "Spa Entrance", a small tray cradled two tall containers filled with different-colored liquids that stood next to a water cooler. Small drinking cups, arranged in a half moon, were set upside down for the clientele to use. Nick saw customers, as they waited for their appointments, already taking advantage of those exotic refreshments touted to cleanse body and mind. Others lounged about, either reading the latest gossip from pop culture magazines or ignoring everything and everyone, except for their smartphones.

The area was a complete opposite to the claustrophobic lab they'd just left.

"May I help you?"

Nick turned to the receptionist, whose smile seemed frozen on her face. He showed his shield and nodded to Sacco's, who'd taken his out as well.

"Detective Larson and Detective Sacco to see EriK Wexler," Nick said.

That didn't settle well with the woman, nor with the other receptionist, or with the waiting clients. Nick sensed the air shift, attention zeroing in on them and what would be said next.

The woman rushed around the desk with impressive speed. She tried to block the customers' view of their next exchange with her body—at least, as much as her height would allow. Nick did not remark he was a foot taller and much wider. The clients would not miss a thing.

"Do you have an appointment?" Her voice was hushed, with an underlying tinge of nervousness. Was that due to her attitude around cops in general or to management disliking surprise visits?

"Is he available?" Nick asked, not lowering his voice or worrying about clients' sensibilities.

"EriK," undue emphasis on the K, "is with a client right now. Can I set up a more convenient time later?"

"We'll wait," Nick said, further raising the woman's anxiety level. Without a word, she turned to the other receptionist and transmitted a this-is-an-emergency gaze. In an instant, the second woman picked up the phone, dialed, and with a few hushed words, alerted what Nick presumed was the manager to their presence.

Code speak, emergency relayed within the span of less than twenty seconds.

Impressive.

The door to the manager's office opened, and a man between his fourth and fifth decade approached. Bearded and a bit bulgy around the waist, with hair dyed too black to look natural, he substituted for the receptionist in stance and position, pointing to his office, as if trying to herd them into his pen.

Nick smiled but didn't budge. Neither did Sacco.

"May I assist you, officers?" the man asked.

Nick repeated his request.

The manager sized them up, very much how they would assess a person of interest. "What's EriK's schedule?" he asked one of the receptionists.

After a few clicks, Nick and everyone else knew EriK was working with his last client. The manager gave instructions for him to pass by the office before leaving.

"Please," the manager said and pointed to his office once again. It was more a plea than a request. Nick and Sacco obliged. No need to ruin the man's day by acting the unreasonable, obstinate New York cop.

"Can we offer you some refreshment, Detectives?"

Nick refused. Sacco didn't. "I'll take some of the flavored water you serve. Any will do."

Nick shook his head.

"What?" Sacco shrugged. "I'm parched."

The manager returned a few seconds later. "Our coconut fragrance water is very refreshing and good for the kidneys."

Sacco gulped down the drink in two seconds.

So much for spitting on a fire in order to extinguish it, Nick thought, knowing Sacco would be clamoring for more thirst-quenching water soon. He was a sucker for those types of drinks.

"I'm sorry, Detectives," the manager leaned into them even before taking his own seat. "This is a high-end, service-oriented business. Had you called ahead of time, we would have accommodated you without disturbing our clients."

"And since we've left several messages, none of which were answered, we thought a more personal touch was called for," Nick answered. "We're running an investigation..."

But the man interrupted.

"Your call was probably referred to our corporate office. They handle all complaints. But first, a formal, written grievance must be lodged. The attorneys..."

Nick and Sacco exchanged glances.

Now this is interesting. Nick made a note to do a background on the business.

"Do you mean to tell us," Sacco said, "that customers can't complain in person?"

"Or can't get their grievances heard and resolved at the place where you rendered services?" Nick added.

The man's nervousness was evident in his failed attempt at a laugh.

"No, no. Our customer service is one of the best for spas nationwide, and our reviews reflect that. But there is always a client who messes up their appointment, gets charged, and needs to be reminded of our appointment policies. Others say they haven't received their full-time's worth, which needs to be verified by the login system. A few complain the product used made their dermatological issues worse, despite our careful inquiries about allergies in the forms they fill out before any service is given. There are also disclaimers signed. Corporate investigates all. Some are real, others mainly want to milk the company of money."

"Are those the only nature of complaints?" Nick asked, fixing his eyes on the manager.

Clearly, the man was uncomfortable discussing the issue. "The industry has been under...scrutiny since this #MeToo movement exploded months ago."

Sacco interrupted. "Isn't there a court case pending somewhere in the south? A spa franchise was sued for alleged inappropriate touching of a client by one of their employees?"

The manager nodded. "Yes. But here at our spa, we have been extremely careful about the issue. Regardless, we've had to retrain our employees, set new parameters, and protocols. Extra costs and pressures on our massage therapists and estheticians are now intense. How can they work at their best when the difference between great service or an accusation of wrongdoing is razor-thin? I'm telling you, this doesn't happen in Europe."

"Have any complaints been lodged against EriK Wexler?" Nick asked.

"None." The manager was emphatic.

Well, shit. Another marvelous and perfect employee of the month. It was time to do a thorough background check on everyone surrounding Isabel Creasy, including one on the victim herself.

"As a matter of fact," Nick paused as he caught the manager trying to read his notes upside down. He shifted his notebook. "We want to ask Mr. Wexler some questions about one of your clients, a Mrs. Isabel Creasy. She came here every Friday."

"Mrs. Creasy is one of our most loyal customers. Don't tell me she's lodged a complaint?" The man sounded disappointed, as if someone he was fond of had just thrown him off the pedestal.

"Actually, she's dead."

In the shocked silence that followed, the back door to the manager's office was flung wide and a young man, not older than thirty, barged in, brandishing a note in the air.

Nick stared. As a police officer, and later as a homicide detective, he had been exposed to all types of New York characters before, but Nick felt as if he'd stepped into an absurd reality TV show with this one. The man was about five-nine, five-ten, give or take, slim, long necked, with a neutral look to his features. He was wearing the uniform of the spa—black, baggy sweatpants and a T-shirt with the company logo near the left shoulder. The fitted shirt highlighted sleek musculature underneath, reminiscent of the build of a swimmer or a martial arts aficionado who'd been working out pressing weights. But what was worth the admission ticket were the earlobes and hair. The former had gaping holes, stretched big enough for Nick's captain's cigar to go through, and stiffened into shape by what looked like decorative grommets. The hair? Well, the hair was something Nick couldn't quite understand. It was almost as if this EriK had tried to fashion a man bun on top of his head that, unfortunately, had transformed into a frizzed-out, deep purple, green, and pink fuzzy pom-pom instead. He knew, by Sacco's choked chortle, that his partner was trying not to react.

"What now, Cy?" Irritation raised the timbre of a voice too husky to be normal. It was almost as if the vocal cords had been damaged. "I have an appointment in Brooklyn in an hour, and I've got to catch the D before rush hour. If not, I'm screwed."

"EriK. These are..." The manager began, but was interrupted.

"Is this about that Noemi customer again? She's never going to get the best of the deep tissue unless she loses weight."

"EriK..."

"I've got to push through three layers of fat as it is before I can safely reach her muscle. If I do what I need to do, she'll have bruises all over her body and we'd be staring at a lawsuit. We've got to stop being politic."

"EriK," the manager stressed, louder.

"That, or you assign her to someone who doesn't give a shit. I'm outta here." And with that, EriK Wexler pivoted.

Nick stood. "Mr. Wexler," he said in his best cop voice.

Nick's tone aborted the exit.

"I'm Detective Larson and this is Detective Sacco. NYPD. We need to ask you a few questions about your customer Isabel Creasy."

"What about her?" The tone was dismissive.

"She's..." the manager started but couldn't continue. He cleared his throat.

"Dead," Nick supplied.

The reaction that followed startled everyone around.

"What assholes, all of you. This is what you consider payback for last week? Well, your sense of humor sucks." His gaze switched from Nick to Sacco. "Who put you up to this, eh? Cy here? Amanda?"

"Last I checked," Nick said, looking at the young man with some scorn. Both he and Sacco showed their shields. "Today is not April Fool's Day. We found Mrs. Creasy dead in her brownstone yesterday morning. Apparent suicide."

"What?"

"What you heard," Sacco said.

"But that's impossible," EriK stammered, realizing this was not a sick prank. "She was here last Friday. She was happy."

"Mr. Wexler, please sit down." Nick gestured to the chair he'd recently vacated. "We need to ask you some questions."

The man was now visibly shaken and sweating as he took the seat, his eyes round in shock. He stared from Nick to Sacco fingering his right earlobe to the point where Nick thought he'd stretch the lobe beyond the grommet's use.

"How was Mrs. Creasy when you saw her last? Was she nervous, upset?" Nick asked.

"She was fine," Wexler emphasized. "She came in at her usual time." He checked with his manager, who nodded in agreement. "Isabel complained about her neck and shoulders being tighter than usual. Asked for specific attention to those areas at the session since she'd been working extra hours sitting at the lab."

"Had she complained about anything else?"

"No. Isabel was the quiet client. Didn't talk at all during her sessions."

"Unlike others, who tell you their life's story within fifteen minutes," the manager added.

Wexler smiled. "Isabel apologized the first time I saw her, telling me not to take it as a personal insult if she didn't chat. She wanted to enjoy the complete relaxation experience, concentrating on the soothing music and the de-knotting of her stressed muscles. I didn't care one way or another."

"So, you know nothing about her at all?" Sacco asked.

"I wouldn't say that," Wexler said. "She's been coming here for close to two years. And we started to chat before the session and after." He looked at his manager. "Not enough to cut into her spa time."

"Our customers receive a fifty-minute massage or facial," the manager explained. "That gives our cosmeticians and massage therapists ten minutes to escort the customer in and out and prepare the room for the next person."

"Did she appear depressed during her last session?" Nick asked.

"Are you freaking kidding me?" Wexler moved forward in his chair, as if to emphasize the next words. "She was moving to a new place in Queens and was really excited about it."

"Detectives," the office manager interjected. "Despite the fact that Mrs. Creasy was a very private person, anyone could tell she was not happy when she first started coming here. But lately, everyone here saw a change. She became more open, and she was smiling all the time."

"Yeah," Wexler said. "She'd finally gotten rid of that prick of a husband."

Well, Nick thought, everyone except the husband agreed on his personality.

"Remember the day her divorce was finalized, Cy?" Wexler said. "She broke down right after the session and couldn't stop crying."

"Shocked the shit out of us. Gave her my office until she got her composure back," the manager smiled with a tinge of sadness.

"She was extremely embarrassed. Kept repeating she didn't know why she was crying because she was so happy."

"Any change when you saw her last?"

There was a small knock on the door and one of the receptionists appeared, excused the interruption, but explained she really needed the manager's assistance.

The manager excused himself and walked out.

Wexler scooted out of the chair in seconds, grabbed the knob, and pressed his back against any intruders.

"Cy would have my scalp if he knew," Wexler whispered. "But I was seeing Isabel outside of work."

Nick and Sacco's attention grew keener.

"Personal? Business?" Nick asked.

"Both?" Sacco chimed in.

"Isabel was working on a line of cosmetics and creams."

"We know," Nick said and waited.

Wexler said nothing for a minute, listening. Satisfied he wouldn't be interrupted yet, he continued.

"Cy can't know this, if not, the spa could claim proprietary ownership on this."

Or you'd be out on your ass lickety-split.

"I've been working with Isabel on my end, and so has M-Li. You know M-Li, right?"

"Yes."

"Well, for about four months now, I've been helping Isabel create a holistic approach to a massage cream, something I could use with my personal clients. Certain floral and spice oils have different therapeutic effects on the skin and, if absorbed, can be beneficial to the body as well. Isabel had come up with a formula. Gave me the prototype the week before last. I've been using it for about a week on myself and on her. It's been working beyond our expectations."

Experimenting on themselves. Could that have caused an imbalance of some sort that pushed the victim over the edge toward suicide? Could they be wrong?

"Don't you need FDA approval before using that stuff on anyone?" Sacco asked.

"Not when all the ingredients are natural. That was the key. And Isabel hated any type of animal testing."

Nick needed to check with Ramos on that one.

"What about Friday. Was anything off?"

Wexler opened his mouth but shut it immediately. "Now that you mention it," he said after a few seconds' thought, "she seemed a bit upset. You could see it in her eyes. Her body was stiffer than usual and her facial muscles were tight. I asked her about it, but she just shook her head. Said she'd take care of it."

Wexler glanced from Nick to Sacco. "Maybe her husband was giving her shit again."

"Why would he?" Nick asked, interested.

Wexler scoffed. "Are you kidding me? That jerk is all about money, money, and more money. Before the divorce, with no serious money to her name, she was practically invisible to the shit. If he found out about what she had been working on since before the divorce was final, which, by the way, if successfully marketed could potentially make millions, exponentially...her ex might have started sniffing around her again to get a piece of the pie."

"We'll check that out," Nick said.

Wexler's watch beeped an alarm. He cursed. "I'm sorry, but I have a client waiting."

"We know. In Brooklyn." Nick slid out a card and handed it to him. "If you think of anything else, any quirks that weren't normal, a conversation, anything, even if you think it's trivial...call us."

Wexler took the card absently, already with phone in hand, thumb searching his client's contact number.

Nick and Sacco left Wexler to his excuses and walked out of the spa.

"Well, we've got squat out of this," Sacco said, snapping his seat belt in place.

Nick, frustrated, pointed the car toward the precinct and roared out of his parking spot, missing the bumper of a taxi by millimeters.

CHAPTER ELEVEN

Wednesday, January 8

MICAELA LATIMER SAT staring at her social media page, tears running down her cheeks.

She was in shock. The co-worker, who had promised not to post the office Christmas party video, had done it anyway.

It had been going viral, unbeknownst to her, for several hours.

Through her tears, Micaela scrolled down, scanning the comments to this latest fiasco. Some people had responded with *Don't pay attention*, or with *Whoever posted this is a total dickhead*. Others had been supportive of her drunken behavior, posting *I still like you*, *This will pass*, or *Delete it and unfriend the jerk*. Others had sent hugging emojis or *I support you* GIFs. But the great majority had liked the video, poking fun at her obvious, out-in-the-open attraction to one of her co-workers. She'd never said anything about how she felt, but with several drinks and little food to counteract the effects, her inhibitions had dissolved and she'd pranced around the woman, her twerking movements overtly sexual as she urged her co-worker to join in the lewd dance.

The distaste etched on the woman's face had been magnified several times as the camera zoomed in to capture it. Watching the disgust was debasing, more so with everyone gathered around, egging Micaela on and encouraging her to do more outrageous things. The worst, though, was the laughter. How could people be so insensitive? So awful? Why didn't those who called themselves her friends at work STOP her?

She scrambled through the barrage of new comments popping up, with more and more people viewing and sharing them on their pages. The consequences proved devastating. People started unfriending her in waves, leaving insulting comments in their wake.

She desperately clicked and changed windows to report this to the powers that be on her social media page. She also blocked the asshole who'd posted. And as she kept up with the horrible notifications coming her way, a little voice reminded her this might be social media karma. How many times had she participated in poking fun and leaving nasty comments on other videos, not feeling a wink of guilt about it?

Too many to count.

But hadn't that been the lure? No ramifications. No blame. Impersonal interchanges. Ethernet anonymity.

Not anymore. To say the barbs now directed at her were appalling and lacerating was to diminish their effect. Her life was being torn apart.

Misery tore at her gut.

Desperation invaded after she realized this post would probably cost her her job.

She couldn't take it anymore.

Fingers flew over the phone keys. There was only one person who'd understand her despair, who'd empathized with her insecurities and struggles for months. Someone who'd wanted to resolve things for her and with her.

Today 12:15 A.M.

Hi.

Are you there?

Hello!!

?

Why aren't you answering me?

....

Hi.

I thought you had unfriended me. 🙁

Why?

A video was posted of the office Xmas party, with me drunk shitless. I can't take it.

That sucks.

I feel so battered. Do you??
Hello?

....
I don't want to dump on you.
Been a very bad day 4 me 2.

I've been dumped on already today.
The video has been doing the
rounds for HOURS!!! My family
is going to have a fit.

You never said you had a family...
....
....
....
....
Here?

No. In Omaha. OMG. What can I tell them?
They're already so ashamed of me.

🙁
No one should be ashamed of you!!!!

But the video is awful!&! And I couldn't get*
to it in time to delete it. And the person
who posted it is not taking it down!!!!

That's sick. Report him.

I DID! Media admins haven't blocked him yet.
I'm MISERABLE!

Me 2. ☹

Micaela's fingers paused. She couldn't see through the tears. More awful comments kept popping up in her notifications—the tags, comments, and shares kept multiplying. Then the worst happened. An email notification from her parents flashed on screen.

OMG. My parents sent me a message
What am I going to tell them?

The truth?

They're ashamed of me enough already.

My mom refused to see me today.
Said to the nurse I wasn't her son.
The only person she loved, her daughter, was dead.

OMG! How cruel!
</3

Said it to my face before the nurse pulled me aside.
Apologized for her. Told me her pain was getting worse.
A change in meds again tomorrow.
What about me? What about my feelings?
How can she hate me so much?
I know I wasn't the favorite, but...
....
....
....

Honestly, been thinking more and more about what we discussed doing together. I can't take it anymore.
Let's go for it.

Why not? My life sucks. And I may not have a job tomorrow. The company I work for is very conservative. Other employees have been dismissed for this type of behavior.
I can't believe this person would do THIS to ME.
Said he would never post it.

I've told you before, never trust the assholes.
Bottom line, everyone is a lier. They are all liers.

The nasty comments kept coming in.

Her computer pinged an email notification. It was her employer.

Micaela came to a decision, dried her eyes, and messaged her address.

Come on over.

CHAPTER TWELVE

LATE IN THE evening, Nick closed the inner entry door to his apartment building and headed for the mailboxes at the rear of the hallway. His body vibrated from the cold assaulting the city once more. Thrown into the mix tonight was the bonus of gusts worthy of the Antarctic. Nick could usually deal with it, but his exhaustion made it difficult to take today. It had been one of those days where shit kept happening and nothing could get done except them running around like chickens with their heads cut off—even when the precinct was now working at cruising speed and almost everyone had returned to man their stations.

But New York was New York. Nothing stopped it from pulsing and vibrating, not from the good or the bad.

It hadn't taken a second after they'd stepped into their offices that Nick and Sacco had been assigned to a botched robbery at a chic boutique on Thirty-Third and Third. The perpetrator, a teen looking for quick cash and an even quicker getaway, had gotten his clock cleaned by the two women in the shop. As soon as the punk had jabbed the knife their way, the two women had beaten the crap out of the kid, each using an arm of the mannequin they'd been dressing. After verifying with the EMTs the robber had only suffered minor cuts and bruises, a possible concussion from falling to the ground and hitting his head while evading the women, and a definite broken wrist, Nick had watched the security video while Sacco spoke with the victims. By the time he joined his partner, Sacco had calmed the ladies, who'd been very worried they'd be hauled to jail for assault. Nick had assured them they wouldn't be charged, that the video had corroborated their statements of self-defense, and had warned them not to risk their health in the future. Better to lose money than their lives.

What Nick left unsaid was that the punk, on his next robbery, would bring a gun instead of a knife, and he'd shoot first and rob later.

They hadn't even driven a block away, when they'd received their next call: an accident involving a child, burned by scalding liquid. He and Sacco had reached Morgan Stanley Children's to learn the child was in critical condition, the mother hysterical, and Nick hoped the kid would survive. But it had been an ugly hour, especially when the questioning for possible abuse began. The father, who'd arrived at the hospital almost as hysterical as the mother, had had to be restrained by the accompanying officer and some orderlies before doing something stupid, like hitting Nick or Sacco in his blind despair. But the questions, unfortunately, had needed to be asked. Nick had made a note to obtain hospital or pediatric records, and had left with a bad taste in his mouth.

Now that he was finally home, he wanted nothing better than to get into his warm apartment, take a shower, and chill for a bit. He rifled through his mail and discarded the junk mail inside the recycling bin parked next to the mailboxes. But he'd barely reached his doorway when Lorena Garcia, his colorful neighbor from across the way, made an entrance. She must have been listening because she opened the door the moment he placed key to lock. And, as usual, what an entrance it was, very à la crazy *Sunset Boulevard* silent actress sort of way, her psychedelic-colored caftan open full and wide, her earrings, bracelets, and bangles tinkling like Christmas ornaments. She held the door open while she scanned the building's entrance and Nick.

"Doing retro today?" Nick asked, a smile conquering his partially frozen face. The warm blast as he opened his apartment door thawed him a bit more.

"You like, *muñeco*?" Lorena did a quick pirouette, arms akimbo. "eBay." She scanned the front stoop of the building, saw there was no one there, and dropped the act.

"Definitely suits you." Nick said.

She shrugged. "You know how it is. Gotta look the part."

"Ruben, I presume?" The old man was one of her ten best repeat customers. Nick had met him a while back. The gentleman came to consult Lorena once a month like clockwork. Boasted he couldn't live without her horoscope guidance, even when he'd been doing a good job of living without Lorena's recommendations for the past seventy-two years. What Nick really suspected was

Ruben's visits had more to do with infatuation and companionship than counsel.

Lorena laughed. "Bullseye. Besides, he's an Aries, *muñeco*. Have to hold back his impulsive nature." Lorena cleaned the edges of her lips with thumb and forefinger. She cocked her head, considering Nick. "You look like the trash compactor gave you a once-over today."

"Long day," Nick said, and knew it was going to be an even longer night. He'd transferred a shitload of work to his department's system account to look over, fill out, and correct.

The buzzer rang inside Lorena's apartment. She saw her customer peeking through the area of nonfrosted glass at the building's entrance and waved to the old gentleman, who looked more shriveled than usual. The cold would do that to you, Nick thought.

"You'd better let him in," Nick said. "He looks about ready to become an ice sculpture."

"Be a dear and hold my door open for me?" Lorena said as she rushed to let Ruben in. Nick held the door while Lorena fussed over Ruben, who could barely whisper his greeting from the cold.

"Go ahead, honey, and get warm," she said, as she steered him inside her apartment.

Nick turned to go inside his own when Lorena detained him.

"Listen," she said, her face serious. "Do you know where Laura is today? I went over to her apartment, but she didn't answer."

Damn. Laura's plants. He was supposed to have watered them last night. Now, he'd have to brave the bitch cold again. But he'd promised.

"She's traveling. Why?"

Lorena lowered her voice, her expression earnest. "If you talk to her, tell her I worked on her horoscope today. It's been nagging me for days."

"Come on, Lorena. Really?"

"Now, *muñeco*, don't get all huffy and puffy and your usual skeptical self. She's going to get some unwanted news from a letter, or something else soon. The cards say she needs to be extra careful for a while."

Nick stared.

Lorena patted his cheek like a fond grandmother does, despite her being nine years his junior. "Not everything is a show," she said for his ears alone. "Besides," she said from her doorway. "Gotta protect your beautiful Scorpio love interest. Never seen such high percentage of compatibility between two people before."

She winked at him and closed the door.

Well, hell.

LAURA had been working on the four-tiered cake for close to two hours. Actually, a day and a half so that the ganache would firm and lock in the rum soak by the time she'd have to frost the cake. She knew this presentation would seal the deal that had begun months after she'd seen the advertisement for a creative baker and silent partner in a new business venture in Suwanee, Georgia. Laura never understood why the idea to start afresh down here, incognito, had grabbed hold, and as she rotated the lazy Susan to check for imperfections or gaps in the frosting, she paused to swipe the sweat beading on her forehead.

Who the hell was she fooling? After the first barrage of negative comments on the review sites and her web page, the idea had sprouted, teasing and tantalizing her like fresh water to a castaway. When she realized she might have to sell her portion of the business to Erin in order to save it from her sister's destructive claws, her brain erupted with possibilities, germinating ideas as if it were on steroids. That same afternoon, she'd bought a disposable cell with cash and set up talks. Only the fiasco of Sandra Ward had made her rethink many things, including executing this, her plan B. She knew that if her twin got her way and was transferred to a psychiatric hospital, Sandra would find a way to escape. And then, where would Laura be?

Once she'd taken the first step to contact her possible new partner, ideas burgeoned, turning full-fledged OCD after rifling through a travel magazine at the dentist's office. The article had displayed photographs of Tuscany and this wonderful farmhouse on the outskirts of Montecatini, where the repast table had been decorated with foliage and flowers from the region. She remembered vividly there had been a tart of some sort next to the decorations, where some of the latter had fallen delicately on the pie. The image had triggered a new, creative spate of decorations, cake flavors, Genoise recipes, and other frostings. She wanted fresh, zing, something to overwhelm the palate, using flowers, spices, fruits, and even candied vegetables for decorations.

The visual end result had been a fabulous smorgasbord of color and textures.

The taste? An orgasm of pleasure, Erin would have said.

Wait until I get back to town. I'll introduce Nick to a different smorgasbord of pleasure.

She sighed.

No.

No.

And NO.

No thinking of Nick right now. If she did, she might not conclude this deal. As it was, she'd almost caved into scrapping her plans the night of the kiss. But the Yelp comments disaster reminded her to stay the course. Even if she and Nick became a couple, she needed to work. She needed this plan B, regardless if she stayed in New York. Her mother's favorite advice was that life's unexpected circumstances always bit you in the ass. So, preparation was key. Laura took that to heart. If all went well, she would become a silent partner in this new venture, under her new persona, L. Hoffster.

Laura swiped a fingerful of frosting before placing the now-empty bowl and spatula in the sink. She licked her finger clean and savored. Damn, but she had outdone herself this time.

"An orgasm of flavor indeed, Erin, my friend," she said out loud to no one in particular. The room was empty. "Created by the new L. Hoffster, idiot at large."

Laura retrieved the cookie sheet with her chocolate creations and prepared to decorate. Honestly. Of all the names she could have come up with, she'd thought of only her maiden name. Not very original. Super lame, if anyone asked her. But it had been her only recourse. She still had her old IDs, and, if she ever needed to disappear, legally, well, that was her only option. For how long she'd remain incognito? God only knew. Nowadays, interconnectivity made disappearing without a trace practically impossible. One crumb easily led to another, lighting the path to your whereabouts as the outrageous floats on Fat Tuesday lit the way down Bourbon Street to revelers. It had taken an inordinate amount of time and effort to plan and think outside the box so as not to create an obvious crumb trail for Sandra to follow. Laura was going so far as to pay for this partnership with a certified check from an account she'd had before her disastrous marriage. It somewhat guaranteed there'd be no paper trail from New York to follow. No electronic trail, either, since she wouldn't open a new account here bearing her name. She'd use the new business.

No telephone trail either, since the phone was disposable and replenished with a money order from the post office.

Laura sighed. All these Gordian knots simply to throw Sandra off her trail. She hoped her sister would never, in a million years, unravel it all.

Maybe not even Nick could, either.

"Darn it all. Not again."

Ok. Let's get real here.

Nick could, she thought. His bloodhound detective nose and gut would lead him to her. He'd be super pissed, though, not to mention sorely disappointed in her for not confiding in him. But what were her choices after the incident in her apartment the night she prepared for her trip? Someone on behalf of *dear sister* had slipped a handwritten note under her door, despite restraining orders and the fact her latest address was a secret. If her sister could find her in a city of whatever million it was now...well, it was frightening. And somehow, deep down, Laura knew her sister would get her way—too many bleeding-heart judges sat on the New York Court of Appeals bench. Sandra's lawyer seemed to have found one, and the judge might rule in her sister's favor. If that happened, Laura might have to disappear where not even Nick could find her.

She cleaned the cake platter of stray material, making sure the presentation was perfect. Up to now, her potential, new partner had been impressed with her ideas, her knowledge. After this visual and taste presentation, there would be no doubt about bringing her on board. Laura knew this new venture would be a moneymaker, once the business took off. It would also mean her financial freedom.

Once she got back to the city, she'd notify her lawyer and the DA, who were pissed off enough at this never-ending saga, about how to tackle this new confetti piece amid the ton of garbage already in her sister's files. Hopefully the DA could use the letter as a weapon to keep Sandra locked up.

Laura glanced at the clock. She needed to get this decoration down, right now, so tomorrow she'd be free to implement her contingent plan C, which had coalesced the moment she'd decided to take a chance with Nick. Not only that, but he would be the only soul privy to what it was.

Laura shuddered. She hoped daydreaming about him would mitigate the pain. In the meantime...

Let's see what happens when I get back.

Peeling from the parchment paper the raspberry-flavored chocolate tears she'd made yesterday, Laura alternated chocolate and candied baby's breath blooms into a cascading pattern. She wasn't going to worry about plan C at the moment. After all, as Margaret Mitchell had said in *Gone with the Wind*, tomorrow was another day.

NICK had the final orchid under the tap in the sink. He never understood why people kept plants, let alone such delicate ones, but Laura loved her orchids. He only hoped he wasn't drowning the poor things with all this cold water.

He pivoted to the freezer and grabbed several ice cubes. Laura had explained the heat in the apartment dried the roots too quickly and the ice would melt slowly, keeping them moist.

He distributed the remaining ice on the watered plants and reached for Laura's key where he'd dumped it on the kitchen counter. He paused and stared. A half-opened sheet of paper had been discarded there. And because his neighbor had mentioned a letter, and Laura had conveniently left this out for him to notice, curiosity took over. He dried the moisture from his hands on his sweatpants and opened it. The word *sister* jumped off the page.

Nick's stomach did a flip.

No fucking way.

He jammed Laura's key in his sweatpants pocket and read.

Hi, sister dear.

And here you thought you'd finally gotten rid of me.

Tsk. Tsk.

But that's okay. Soon I'll be able to get the help I've always needed. I'll need all the support I can get and I know you will support me. After all, we're family, right? I'll soon get healthy and whole. I'll be able to live a normal life...like yours. Maybe I can even take up baking at the psychiatric hospital and eventually help with your business?

Wouldn't that be lovely?

Keep in touch. I know I will.

Oh, and say hi to that dreamboat detective who's by your side. If you don't get into his pants soon, your loss. I wouldn't dream of not getting inside his pants.

With all my sisterly love,

Sandra

P. S. Sorry about the hand delivery. I was in a rush.

The bitch, as Elton John had so succinctly put it, was back, and in rare form. Son of a bitch.

CHAPTER THIRTEEN

Friday, January 10

"YOU KNOW, YOU'VE been in a piss-poor mood for the past two days."

Nick saw something square skid across the conference table. He looked at the small thing wrapped in gold foil. "What the hell's this?"

Sacco smiled and got up from his chair. He'd seen Ramos on her way into debriefing and opened the door. "Dark chocolate. It'll sweeten you up."

Nick hurled the chocolate back at his partner, who caught it like a major leaguer. "You're an asshole, Vic."

Sacco unwrapped the piece and popped it into his mouth. "No bigger than you, buddy."

"Lay off."

"You've got your gonads into a knot and there's nothing you can do about the situation until she gets back."

Sacco was right. There was nothing he could do until Laura returned. But Nick was furious. And worried. He couldn't reach Laura. Had been trying for two days. He'd even had Carpenter trace her cell phone, but the signal had turned up in New York, in her apartment. He'd gone over that evening to find the blasted thing on her nightstand. Why had she left it there? Where the hell was she? And was she all right?

Ramos breezed through the open door. She glanced at each man, her eyebrows quirked. "Cat fighting so early, ladies?"

"Fuck off, Ramos," Nick said as viciously as he felt.

"Temper, temper." She lifted a hand to stop Nick's next explosion. "Before you chew my butt off—"

"Tiny, tiny butt," quipped Sacco.

"Preliminary lab reports came in on your suicide." She dumped both her case binder and an evidence bag with some sort of lavender-colored mold sealed inside it on the table. She opened the binder. "Stomach contents show she ate Caesar salad, red wine, strawberries, and chocolate, not necessarily in that order."

"Celebrating freedom, no doubt," Sacco said.

"Alcohol content in her blood was a bit high—"

"How high?" Nick asked.

"Enough for a buzz. About two or three glasses."

"Shit. Did she offer herself up for a sacrifice?" Nick asked. "I've never seen such degree of passivity going to an execution."

He knew his face reflected frustration and incredulity.

"According to Totes," Ramos continued, "the larynx was forty-percent crushed, hyoid bone barely fractured, and trauma to the surrounding epidermis minimal."

"Meaning?" Nick asked.

"Meaning," Millsap offered from the door, "she slowly asphyxiated and didn't even twitch with discomfort." He strode to an empty chair and flopped his binder on the table. He looked like he'd been up for seventy-two hours.

Ramos nodded in acknowledgement. She flipped to another page on her file.

"The ice doughnut we found on the floor was your basic, heavily chlorinated New York Water Management-grade water, with traces of fluorination, plus added bodily fluids expelled by the victim at time of death. It came from that." She pointed to the evidence bag on the table. "Found it in Creasy's freezer."

"What the hell is that?" Sacco asked.

"Your generic silicone, oval soap mold. When I bagged it, the mold had five of the six compartments half-filled. Comparison in diatoms between what I recovered on the floor and the ice inside that thing is still not in."

"Prints?" Nick asked.

"Will dust, but don't hold your breath," Ramos said.

Both Nick and Sacco grunted in irritation.

"Oh, it gets better, boys. There were minute rock particles frozen within the ice. Beats me where those came from, but we're still checking. That scraps the mold being used for designer ice."

"What about the chair?" Nick asked.

"Nada. Standard oak, with round 0.2-millimeter-thick Teflon casters. Legs were a bit off."

"What do you mean a bit off?" Sacco asked.

"Off-kilter. One leg was shorter than the rest."

"The one with the ice-donut necklace, you mean?" Nick asked.

Ramos nodded. "All chair surfaces were clean as a whistle."

"How clean?" Nick asked.

"Wiped-down clean."

"Shit. We're dying here," Sacco complained.

"Sorry. Can't invent data that's not there. How about on your end?"

"Zip-a-Dee-Doo-Dah," Nick said. "What about drugs?"

"Waiting on Totes for that one." Ramos nodded toward Millsap.

"How long will that take, Doc?" asked Nick.

"Too long," Captain Kravitz said from the doorway.

Nick thought things were looking brighter for the Sixteenth if the captain was sans cigar. That meant the stress level bordered on back to normal.

"This flu thing has decimated all departments," Millsap agreed. "We're going slower than the LIE at rush hour. Rule of thumb? Add three more weeks on top of the usual pileup."

"How can there be squat on this one?" Sacco asked no one in particular.

"I don't know," Nick said. "We're missing something. I can feel it."

"Woo-hoo," Ramos quipped, a twinkle in her eye. "Nick's gut rears up. Can't wait to hear this."

"Well," said Millsap. "He's not the only one. This case has been bothering the shit out of me. Despite the fact suicide of females by hanging has been inching upward in our fair city since 2000, something had to have incapacitated her to the point where there was no reaction during strangulation. But nothing's come up in the muscle tissue or organ samples under the scope." Millsap opened his binder and checked his notes. "The initial lab reports came back normal, too, which left me totally dissatisfied. So I took her out of storage, reswabbed, took hair and more vitreous fluid, and sent everything back to toxicology, including more organ tissue. Told them to rush an expanded drug panel on everything this time. And I mean expanded."

"I started background checks on everyone involved," Nick said, annoyed. "This goody-two-shoes image just rubs me the wrong way. No one is that neutral or good."

"What about cross-check of MO?" Kravitz asked.

"As soon as I come back from court, I'll start a quick search through the boroughs. Maybe something will pop up."

"So, we've got nothing on the investigative end, and Millsap won't rule homicide or suicide until he gets more info. That's our impasse?" Captain Kravitz asked.

Everyone nodded.

"OK. Executive decision. Gut or no gut, we're putting this one on the back burner for now. When something concrete comes back from the labs, we'll jump back on it. Everyone onboard?"

Nick agreed. So did the others.

Still.

"What's going on with the boutique robbery?" asked Kravitz.

"Idiot wanted to sue," Nick replied. "But his public defender mentioned his aggression was caught on the surveillance tape. They'll probably plead."

"Good."

A plea meant less paperwork and time for all involved.

"What about the scalded victim?"

"Called the hospital this morning," Sacco said. "Child's still critical."

"No evidence of abuse, prior or current," Nick added, anticipating Kravitz's next question.

"Verified?"

Nick nodded. "Looks like an unfortunate accident."

Kravitz huffed. "Court?"

"We're scheduled for today," Ramos said.

"Definite?"

"Definite," said Nick. "Gave Aaniyah Foster a buzz this a.m. to confirm. She said, and I quote, 'If the fucker doesn't disrupt the morning session like he did yesterday with his bullshit drama, I'll wrap up today,' unquote. So, yeah, she'll make sure we testify today."

Kravitz turned his attention to Millsap. "What's the status on the floater?"

Millsap sighed. "Too decomposed and too many critter bites. Verified vertebra was broken between the C3-C4."

"A jumper?" asked Nick. A ferry had churned up the body topside between the Brooklyn Bridge and Pier 36 several days ago.

"No way of knowing. Referred the body to forensic anthropology." Millsap closed the binder with a snap. "If this is all, guys, I have four patients waiting for me."

"And I have a ton of work to process on the bar shooting on First before I hit court," Ramos added.

Everybody took that as his cue to scatter.

Nick grabbed a soda on the way back to his desk and checked his watch. If he hustled, he could explore for similarities to his Creasy investigation on the Real Time Crime Center system and get back to the new cases given to them this morning.

He opened the search engine on his computer, added all the keywords he could think of, including an all-boroughs search, and let loose the hunt. Let technology do the grunt work for a change.

He was about to dial Carpenter for IT news about the Creasy case when Horowitz stopped at his desk.

"What's up, Sergeant?"

"There is a Mrs. Millian here to see you. No appointment, but said she's here about the Isabel Creasy investigation."

Nick glanced at the computer screen and saw there was still time left before court.

"Bring her in, Stan, and let Sacco know she's here. He's in the break room."

Not long after Horowitz left to fetch the woman, Sacco arrived, munching his favorite PowerBar.

"Think we'll get anything new?" he asked.

"Let's see. But I'm not betting on it," Nick said.

As Sacco crumpled the empty foil, Horowitz ushered in a woman in her thirties, short and stocky, with night-black hair and eyes. She was gripping a folder-sized purse in both hands, pressing it against her stomach, her left elbow cradling a folded camel-colored coat. She was wearing the uniform of M-Li's salon, the black pants and white shirt, the ensemble looking almost starched from the stiff manner in which she held herself. The woman's body language screamed reluctance at being there.

"Thank you for coming, Mrs. Millian." Nick walked to meet her, hand outstretched, his voice soft and modulated to help ease her nervousness. He gestured to the chair next to his desk, which Sacco had pulled away for her to access comfortably.

A strong grip shook his before Millian settled at the edge of the chair.

"This is all so appalling," she whispered, the tone holding vestiges of the horror she'd probably felt upon hearing the news. "We're still in shock, and M-Li is inconsolable."

Nick nodded. There wasn't a day that passed where M-Li hadn't called, asking about the release of her friend's body. And every day she received the same response, with M-Li breaking down after Nick's negative, disconsolate she could not arrange the funeral of her friend yet.

Nick and Sacco sat.

"What can you tell us about Mrs. Creasy?" Nick asked.

Leticia Millian gulped. "She was such a nice woman. Quiet. Never missed an appointment."

Nick exchanged a quick, knowing look with Sacco.

"What exactly do you do at the salon?" his partner asked.

"I'm a depilatory specialist. I use various methods to make sure excess body hair is removed."

"Did you see Mrs. Creasy every week?" Sacco asked.

She shook her head. "No. When sugaring, the results last longer."

"Sugaring?" Nick asked.

"Hair removal paste made from sugar. Less uncomfortable than wax and gentler on the skin."

"How often did Mrs. Creasy use your services?" Nick asked.

"She had very fine hair, so most of the time she'd come in every two weeks, unless there was a special occasion."

"Such as?"

"An important dinner with her ex-husband's associates." She thought a bit. "Sporadic vacations. She came in once for an anniversary dinner." The woman's mouth pursed. "To my mind, that was a waste. They separated a week later."

"Were those appointments separate from her usual Friday routine?" Nick asked.

Leticia Millian shook her head. "She would extend her spa time on those days. She'd usually see me earlier, or after her nail treatment."

"When did you see her last?" Sacco asked.

"She came in on that Friday, before..." She gulped, eyes tearing. "Well, you know."

Nick waited in silence, allowing her to rein in her emotions.

"That day," Leticia Millian continued, "she only needed upper lip."

"Was anything off about her?" Nick asked. "Did she seem depressed or anxious to you?"

"That's what's so bizarre about this," she said, her tone a bit incredulous. "Isabel usually didn't say much. She was my silent one, unlike other customers who can't seem to shut up. But I could tell by her eyes whether she was sad or depressed. Isabel had been nothing but happy, especially since the divorce."

"But?" Nick asked. He sensed there was one there.

"She was angry." Her tone marked her continuing surprise. "When I came into the room to check the temperature of the sugar mix, she was ramming her phone into her purse."

Nick glanced at Sacco. Maybe, maybe this could be their break in the case.

"Why was she upset? Did she tell you?" Sacco asked.

"No. But, honestly, it blew me away because I'd never seen her like that. I asked if everything was okay, but she shrugged it off. I had to make a joke about the fact she kept pursing her lips, you know, like when you suck on something sour? Told her she would ruin my expert application if she kept doing that. She laughed a bit and relaxed. But you could tell whatever she'd seen or heard on that phone had upset her." She shook her head. "The strangest part, though, was her muttering."

"Muttering?" Nick asked.

"She kept going on and on about 'not with my stuff you don't.' She didn't say much else once I started her lip treatment. By the end of her mani/pedi appointment, she seemed relaxed, planning the final move with M-Li."

She looked from Nick to Sacco. "Does that help any?"

"Anything at this point is helpful," Nick said.

A catchy tune filled the silence. Face flushing, Leticia Millian opened her purse and fished out her cell. A quick glance and a faster swipe muted the ringing. "I'm so sorry," she said and rose. "I have to leave. My shift starts soon."

Nick and Sacco stood as well.

"We really appreciate your coming, Mrs. Millian," Nick said. "If you remember anything else, give us a call." Nick handed over his card and escorted her to Horowitz's station by the elevator. But before the sergeant could escort her into it, she turned to Nick.

"Of everyone we see at the salon, Isabel would have been the last person I'd think would commit suicide." Her eyes were a mixture of pain and curiosity. "Do angry people commit suicide, Detective?"

Nick had been asked many variations on the same theme for years, and he didn't have a patent answer.

"I honestly can't answer that question, Mrs. Millian. No one truly knows the mindset of a person seconds before they decide to take their life."

Nick watched as Horowitz escorted her into the elevator. However, the moment the doors closed, he reached for the phone on the sergeant's desk and dialed Carpenter's extension.

"Please tell me you have something on Creasy's computer and phone."

"We haven't gotten to the computer and cloud info, yet," Carpenter's cheerful voice greeted him. "Captain shifted priority to the bar shoot-out yesterday. I'm drowning in postings."

"Carpenter, I need her phone records and her browsing history PDQ. I just finished speaking with a witness and she said Creasy was angry on Friday after receiving a phone text or a call."

"Really?"

"Come on, Carpenter. Work your wiz magic for me. This may be the break we've been looking for."

"You paying me overtime?"

"In your dreams, wiz kid, in your dreams. But find something for me. Soon. Consider this putting you on notice."

"Can you at least limit the search parameters for me? Anything that I should be concentrating on?"

Nick thought back to the conversation. "Anything work related—tampering of product, misuse, hell, even product theft. Look for a break in the norm."

"Can't promise I'll get to it today, but I'll squeeze some of it either tomorrow or the day after."

Nick thanked him and walked over to Sacco.

"You think someone messed with her product line?" Sacco asked.

Nick smiled. His partner knew him so well.

"Kind of logical, if you think about it. What was the only constant in her life, almost like true passion?"

"Her work," Sacco said without hesitation.

"The question is what happened that pissed her off to the extent where she jumped out of character."

"Did Carpenter have anything?"

"Captain shifted his priorities, but said he'd get to it tomorrow or the day after. Shit."

Shit was right. They had nothing. He hoped to hell Carpenter could come up with something.

In the meantime, they had a court case to catch.

CHAPTER FOURTEEN

NICK AND SACCO dragged their butts into the precinct a little after six that afternoon. True to her word, Aaniyah Foster had gotten to their testimony as soon as lunch break was over and, by the time Tish Ramos had finished presenting her evidence, the perv's lawyer had requested a private conference to rethink a plea bargain to a possible lesser charge. By the look on Foster's face, though, Nick knew she had the accused by the balls and would not back down from what she wanted—the maximum sentence.

Nick flung his coat onto a chair, placed his folded suit jacket on top, and fired up his computer. He groaned when he saw the number of cases popping borough-wide from his search.

"Sacco," Nick yelled.

A couple of seconds later, Sacco materialized.

"You won't believe the number of cases the RTCC is barfing out. Christ, we'll be at this longer than a trip to Mars."

"You've got to be shitting me," Sacco said after a double take at the results. "Fifty-three suicides by hanging this year?"

"That's Manhattan only, buddy. It hasn't compiled the Bronx, Queens, or Brooklyn yet."

"Damn."

Nick took pen and paper and jotted down ten case numbers. He then wrote down the next ten on another paper.

"Here," he handed the second set of numbers to Sacco. "Let's start with these. If we can't find anything on them, we'll hit the next set."

Sacco left and Nick opened another window, input the first case number, and began to read.

As time passed and Nick got into more cases similar to Creasy's mode of demise, details of death from desperate souls who'd thought their lives were not worth living clogged his brain. The first two were drug-abuse-induced suicides. The third one was from an Asian woman who'd been smuggled into the country and forced into prostitution for an Asian gang in Chinatown. She'd taken the pants belt from her last john and latched it around her neck and a doorknob, saying a desperate sayonara to the world. One of the three cases had a suicide note in the file, nothing like the one found at the Creasy brownstone. The others had left nothing except their lifeless bodies dangling from a hastily crafted noose. The file he was currently perusing presented the death of two runaways who'd thought they were the twenty-first century's version of Romeo and Juliet. Street life had probably become too horrible to bear, so they'd jumped, hand in hand from a beam in an abandoned warehouse drug den bordering the FDR.

Nick pressed his palms against his eyes. Effing depressing, he thought. What the hell dampened, even destroyed, the visceral instinct to live in these people? As an NYPD homicide detective, he'd seen others in the same position, with uglier stories to their names, who had survived and thrived. And yet, the suicides prevailed.

He opened the fifth file. After reading through the incident report, he turned his attention to the ME's.

No apparent reaction to suffocation.

Well, that was interesting. He kept reading.

No struggle evident or signs of strangulation by parties unknown. Additional neck pattern suggestive of prior trauma, but inconclusive. No fibers found on necrosed tissue. No drugs in system.

So why had it been labeled a suicide? He circled the case number he'd jotted down on his pad with a red pen and searched through the evidence list for a suicide note. He would need to jog Totes's memory on this one.

"Hi."

Soft. Unmistakable.

Laura.

Nick glanced back and saw her a few feet away. Relief and anger slammed his gut. He closed his eyes and counted to five. He wanted to vent and yell at her. Grab her by the shoulders and scream to all who could hear about what the freaking A was she thinking when she disappeared for four fucking days.

"Nick?"

He heard the indecisiveness in her tone. He opened his eyes and, this time, took his time surveying her. The ready, frustrated anger, which had welled up at the sound of her voice, diminished. She looked like he did after a week of intense investigation—exhausted, beat-up, and trying to hold it together.

"Hi, back."

He stood and stopped mere inches from her.

"I'm really, really pissed at you," he said. Anger and frustration simmered underneath his best cop voice. "Why the hell did you stay incommunicado?" He combed her hair back over her ear. "And what is with this new do?"

He felt her slight shiver.

"It's a long story," she answered. "One that I owe you. Can you take time for a quick dinner?"

He studied her. "Does this have to do with the letter you received from dear sister?"

Nick saw another tremor, while distaste curled down her lips. Her eyes, though, held the unsettled look of one who is trying to ward off fear, weariness, and frustration. Weariness won.

"Saw it, did you?" Her fingers repeated the combing he'd previously done to her hair, as one does when not yet accustomed to a new coiffure.

"Really want me to answer that?"

She shook her head. "It's one of those obvious duh moments with you, Detective."

"Hey, hey," Sacco's voice reached them a few seconds before he came into view. "The prodigal daughter returns."

Sacco leaned in and gave her a quick peck on the cheek. Did a double take as he leaned back.

"Wowsa. What's with the new look?"

"Strategy," said Laura.

Nick saw Sacco's knowing look. "Speaking of family," Sacco turned to Nick. "I'm headed over to Rebecca's for dinner."

"Spaghetti and meatballs?"

Sacco licked his lips. "You know it."

Nick smiled. Sacco's sister made marinara from scratch once a month. The meatballs were also homemade and slowly marinated in the sauce for hours. Complement that with freshly made pasta and baked bread dripping with garlic butter and, well, you had a true gastronomic delight for a meal.

"Any luck with the files?" he asked.

"Depressing shit," Sacco said, slipping his coat on. "And no, nothing. Not yet. Six down. Will get on with the rest tomorrow."

With a final salute, he left.

Nick looked at his watch. Barely eight.

"Unless dispatch calls, I'm also done here for the night. Why don't we grab some Chinese takeout from Yao's Garden and go to your place? We can talk there."

Laura nodded.

He shut down his computer, grabbed notepad, suit jacket and coat, and steered Laura out of his office.

Nick had the restaurant on speed dial, since it was the cuisine of choice for the times when he worked late, odd-hour meals at brainstorming sessions with Sacco and Ramos, or the times he didn't want to cook. After a quick phone call to place their order, Nick drove crosstown with minimal traffic delays. The ride was silent, almost as if they'd arrived at the consensus not to discuss anything yet.

Or maybe it was a tacit delay so they could mull over how to tackle the eight-hundred-pound gorilla in the car.

More like an eight-ton elephant.

Nick rammed the brakes as a cabbie swerved in front of him to make a lightning turn on Thirty-Third. A few minutes later, he dropped Laura at Yao's, giving her two twenties to cover the meal. He hunted for a nearby parking space next. At this time of night, there wouldn't be a problem finding a spot close to the apartment on the wrong side of the alternate-street parking zone. He squeezed into a space half a block from their apartments, secured the car, and jogged to Yao's halfway up the block.

Laura was waiting for him by the door, food ready and cradled in one arm.

After saying a quick hello to the restaurant's owner and his wife, Nick grabbed the bag and led Laura out of the place. The hike back to her apartment was short and brisk.

Unlike his smaller apartment building, where neighbors were overly friendly, or plain nosy, Laura's building was larger and totally opposite in dynamics. Everyone there kept to himself. Barely anyone knew his or her neighbor, apart from the occasional nod as one passed by. Heading to her apartment, the only thing Nick heard was muted conversations or television program noises filtering through closed doors. A strong odor of cooked cabbage competed with the rancid odor of the refuse chute next to the elevator. He wrinkled his nose. Other than that, the echo of their footsteps was the only thing bouncing around the thin hallway.

"Please, don't mind the mess," Laura said, opening the door.

Nick nodded, doubting the apartment was anything but as neat as he'd left it a couple of days ago. What he did notice was that she'd left her suitcase, unopened, next to the living room couch, a few feet from her bedroom entrance. Her traveling canvas bag was on top of the coffee table. That meant she'd arrived from her trip and simply dropped things before going to the precinct.

Nick strode to the round dining room table and dropped the food on top.

"What would you..."

Nick didn't let her finish. He grabbed and pulled her into a tight embrace. He ignored the surprised yelp and the initial stiffness in her body, a stiffness that subsided the longer he held her. But after a minute or two, he captured her lips and dove into the kiss, sating his thirst for her. Over and over, he shifted and changed his mouth over hers in decadent exploration. Her arms circled his waist, pulling him into her body, while her mouth took and gave equally, with matching enthusiasm.

They came up for air what seemed like an eternity later.

Stared at each other.

Smiled.

"So...are we an item now?" Laura asked.

"Oh, be quiet."

Nick dipped his head once more and delved into the wonder that was this woman. God, the more he took, the more he wanted. He started to walk her backwards toward the convenience of a comfortable bed a few yards away. He was horny as hell, and his kisses took on a more aggressive note. Small tendrils of the anger and frustration he'd felt these past days surfaced. He became more aggressive, impatient. Lifted her. Laura whimpered. Nick didn't quite know if it was from passion or discomfort.

The moment of déjà vu slammed him better than a cold shower. What the hell was he doing? This wasn't the way he wanted to make love to Laura the first time around. This felt too reminiscent of an Angie 2.0, after she'd pissed him off royally. Sex had inevitably followed, but sex that was too urgent, too rough, too close to a slam-bang-thank-you-ma'am union that would hardly be satisfying. Well, physically, it would be for a whopping ten seconds. Emotionally? Not even close. Laura deserved better, especially when Nick knew the history behind the murdered ex-husband. Laura had not taken out a restraining order on him for the heck of it. The bastard had been abusive.

Nick pressed his forehead against hers and breathed deeply.

Counted to ten.

Then counted to twenty.

This wasn't the right moment. Their first time shouldn't be a reminder to Laura that Nick could be the same type of prick her ex-husband had been. He wanted to take his time to wine and dine her, seduce her, and get each other into such a burn that it would take them all night to extinguish the need.

No past habits or vices to mar the event.

A fresh start.

And, to tell the truth, he was tired, Laura looked exhausted, and he was starving.

"Let me just get one thing clear, right now, before we eat. Don't," Nick cleared his throat. "Don't you ever do this to me again."

Laura leaned into him for a second.

"The kiss or the disappearance?"

"What? Turning into a wise-ass like Sacco?"

"He does sort of rub off on you," she said.

He cupped her cheeks, lifting her face.

"Doesn't change things. I'm still very pissed at you. You have no clue the control... I really want to shake some sense into you right now." *Or take out my frustrations on you with sex.*

Her expression changed. "I'm sorry, Nick. Really."

"I'm a cop, Laura. Don't forget that. Speaking strictly as a cop, what you did was stupid and dangerous, especially with your sisterly issues."

"I know, but..."

"You should have called me," Nick interrupted. "Should have let me know you'd received that letter." He closed his eyes and released her. "Damn it. Do you have any idea what I've gone through once I discovered your sister's letter? How worried I was when I couldn't reach you? Imagine my shock when Carpenter told me your phone was pinging locally, in your apartment."

"Carpenter did that?" Her surprise showed.

"Yes, as a favor. I was afraid the creep who'd hand delivered the message from your psychotic sister had ambushed you the day you left."

"Oh."

He grabbed her shoulders.

"A few days ago, I told Kilcrease one of the reasons I was hesitant about getting involved was that I didn't want you to be my next 911 call. When I couldn't reach you..."

Nick watched as the instant of comprehension, horror, and pain widened her eyes.

"Oh, Nick." Tears welled. He thumbed them away.

"Don't do this to me again, okay? Especially now that we've jumped into the hot tub together."

Laura chuckled.

"How about we eat? You're about to fall down. And you have to tell me what the hell is going on before you collapse."

He went to the table and started taking out the containers from the bag. Laura brought utensils, bowls, and paper plates. They served themselves and heated everything in the microwave.

"Why did you leave without a phone?" Nick asked, digging into the hot-and-sour soup he'd ordered.

"I didn't."

Nick stared. "Well, I'll be damned. You have a burner phone."

Laura nodded. "And I don't want that number popping up in anyone's caller ID."

"Not even mine." Nick supplied, finishing his tepid soup and reaching for the spareribs. "Were you planning on telling me?"

"Yes, as soon as I got back. Didn't take into consideration the nasty letter surprise from Sandra." She pushed aside the half-eaten soup and took a bite of the fried rice. "But that validated my plans. I've been doing the right things in preparation."

Nick placed the now-stripped bone down slowly and studied her face as he licked his fingers.

"You're planning to disappear," he said, not as a question but as a statement.

"I must say, Detective, you are quick. That's the plan, but as a last resort."

"That's why the makeover, too."

She nodded.

"Gotta hand it to you," he said and took a healthy bite of the fried rice. "Whatever that is." He pointed to her hair with the empty fork. "It looks good on you."

"It's called a blunt cut bob with highlights."

Nick's expression said it all.

"Okay, okay. Men are not into this. Neither am I. I only know because the beautician went on and on about how nice it looked, especially after I had done the keratin treatment and the highlights. I only wanted to look different from Sandra. I may even invest in wigs, just to throw her off my style."

Nick thought the latter might be a better idea than having to go through this rigmarole every time Sandra found out Laura had changed her appearance so she could copy it. The woman was nuts.

"What else did you do?"

Laura told him about the new business partnership, how she had planned her identity to remain as anonymous as today's technology allowed, and her success. She told him about her new product line and how it had clinched the deal.

"The lawyer started the paperwork to sell Erin my half of the business. Once that is finished, I'm not planning to open another bakery in New York. It'll look like I'm living off the sale. However, on the sideline, I'll be working behind the scenes at the new business from home, creating new flavors for batters and frostings. Experimenting with new cake shapes and designs. I'll be free from the day-to-day running of the business end at the new bakery, and will only need to make the trip there every so often to train the employees on the new methods. Unless I have to disappear."

"Doesn't bode well for a future together," Nick said.

"It's simply a contingency plan."

Nick grabbed another sparerib and bit hard into it. That sister had turned into the bane of their existence.

"But that's not my ace in the hole."

Now, he was curious.

Laura cleaned her fingers very carefully and lifted her hair above and behind her ears. She turned her head right then left.

"Are those tattoos behind your ears?" Nick's tone was totally incredulous.

"You like?"

"Sexy. But I'm sure you didn't get inked to get a rise out of me."

Laura smiled at the double entendre.

"You know," Nick said. "The moment she finds out what you've done, Sandra will have it done to herself."

"She can copy the design all she wants, if she ever finds out about it, but she won't be able to duplicate it perfectly. She definitely won't know the meaning behind the wing pattern, either. And *that* is the key."

That intrigued him even more. He cleaned his hands, took his chair, and plopped it beside her to see the design up close.

It was a small, beautifully crafted butterfly in iridescent blues, blacks, and reds. Delicate in design, the insect had been drawn in profile with antenna, head, thorax, and one wing visible. He turned her head to see the other side. It was the same tattoo, but executed as a mirror image of the other. If you could flatten Laura's head and neck, the image of a whole butterfly would emerge.

"Did it hurt much?" he asked, touching the skin, the trauma to the skin still visible. He kissed the spot.

"Yeah," she said, shivering at his touch.

Her tone of voice, however, told him she didn't want to discuss the process at all.

"Okay, it's a pretty design but easily duplicated. You said there's a message, but I don't see anything, anywhere."

"Oh, it's there. Look closer."

He studied the tattoo once more, searching the coloring, the shapes, and lastly, following the wing design in black.

"Sorry. I don't see anything."

Laura sighed, as if happy he'd not seen anything. She turned her body sideways on the chair.

"If you look closer, at the bottom of the wing here on my right side there are two letters." She pointed with her finger so he could focus on the right place.

"What am I looking for?"

"An I and a D. They are visible if read from right to left. The black line designs on the wings branch out from them."

Now that she had pointed out the spot, Nick could actually see the elegantly scripted letters. They were very cleverly camouflaged into the image.

She shifted to the other side. "Now look here. The D and the I are visible from left to right."

He searched and found what she'd described.

She faced him.

"ID...DI," she said, marking in staccato taps the letters with her fingers. She was excited by a cleverness to which only she was privy.

Unfortunately, whatever meaning was attached to the letters did a flyby over his head. He was at a complete loss.

"Sorry, honey, I'm totally in the dark here."

"No one knows the meaning behind the letters, except me. No one else will ever know, except you." She emphasized the initials once more with her forefingers.

"ID...DI," she repeated, leaned very close to his ear, and whispered the meaning.

To say that Nick was shocked was the understatement of the year.

"And that," Laura said, satisfaction oozing from her voice. "Is my ace in the hole."

CHAPTER FIFTEEN

Tuesday, January 14

THINGS HAD BEEN extremely busy at the precinct for the past three days, much to Nick's chagrin. Manhattan, being the bitch that she was, kept regurgitating new cases, just to be ornery. Fortunately, the weeks from flu hell had passed and the precinct was humming at its usual throttle. Unfortunately, that meant Nick and everyone else in the department remained up to their ears in work, thanks to the city that never sleeps.

It also meant no Laura.

He was getting grumpy.

Thankfully, Laura had been busy with Les Gâteaux Riches, the selling of her portion of the business to her partner, and her newest venture. Most days, they'd kept in touch by phone. Yesterday, they'd made plans for tonight. And, boy, did he have plans.

"Well, don't you have a spring to your step?" commented Ramos when he stepped into her lab. "Despite our recent carnival hours."

"We're not on call tonight," Nick answered.

"Hot date with Laura?"

"Shut up." Nick sat down, but the pleased smile didn't leave his face. Mentally, he crossed his fingers. With luck, this promised to be one hell of an evening, barring no screwups.

"About time you committed," she said. Her smile crinkled her eyes. "But there goes the office pool we were planning."

"You'd have all lost your pants to Sacco."

Ramos guffawed. "Inside information is a bitch."

Nick waited until she'd catalogued the evidence she was working on, and handed her a copy of the incident report he was interested in.

"Do you, by any chance, remember this case? The RTCC spit it out four days ago. I know it's five months back, but can you tell me anything about it?"

Ramos took the paper and skimmed over the information there.

"Ah, the Victor Hugo case."

Nick stared at her. "Victor Hugo?"

"Be still, my beating heart. You? Miss a detail?" Ramos flicked the paper in her hand. She pointed to the name on the case file's top corner.

Nick stared. There it was, bold as brass and written in a clear hand. He hadn't bothered with that information at the time, wanting to get to the meat of the case. Too many similar cases being spit out of the system to keep up with names. Not until it was necessary.

"You've got to be shitting me."

"Scout's honor. We thought it was a fake, too. Turns out it wasn't. Born and registered with it. We found him in a chair facing his computer, with a garbage bag wrapped around his head. Very properly sealed with duct tape, I might add. Prints on tape matched the victim's. There was a somewhat suicide note."

"What the heck does a somewhat suicide note mean?" Nick asked.

"His computer screen was flashing it over and over. Hey, Carpenter..."

Carpenter, who'd just arrived with a binder that looked heavier than him, stopped midstride.

"What did I do?"

Ramos laughed. "Not a thing. Remember that Victor Hugo case?"

"The farewell dude?"

"That's the one. Nick wants to know about it."

Carpenter placed his burden on the table. "The man must've been bipolar or something. He'd written 'farewell' and 'master' all over his social media and on small Post-it notes pasted everywhere in the apartment. At one chat room, he said his master had told him to say farewell. Seriously fucked up."

"Yeah." Ramos looked at Nick. "According to Totes, the man offed himself. Case closed. Why do you ask?"

"Something Millsap wrote caught my eye. Reminded me of the Creasy case."

"Gut flaring?" Ramos asked, seriously.

Nick grimaced. Ever since the Sandra Ward case, his intuition about investigations had taken on legendary proportions. Everyone now in the precinct always spoke about his gut in awed reverence. He wished he could live it down.

"Won't know until after I talk to Totes about it."

"Well, get in line," Ramos said. She handed back the report and pointed to what she was doing. "I'm working on one out of five homicides borough-wide last night. Totes and his staff will be up to their eyeballs with bodies for a couple of days."

Great, Nick thought. Another delay. But he'd be damned if he went to Millsap's office with so much Eau of DB around.

"Can you tell me what you remember about this scene?" Nick rattled the paper in his hand. "Read part of the medical examiner's report. Said no drugs, and no reaction to the suffocation. Weird pattern around neck under the duct tape that Totes couldn't quite recognize. Also saw the crime scene photos. For a man sealing his head tighter than vacuum-packed food, there was no last attempt at ripping the sucker from his face."

Ramos gave some serious consideration before answering him.

"I don't know about this one, Nick." She pointed to the report. "He'd been juicing for a while by the time we found him."

Carpenter's face showed his disgust. It had also turned a murky shade of pale. "God, Ramos. Don't remind me."

"How long?"

"Definitely more than forty-eight hours." She nodded to the paper in his hand. "Check Totes's estimate. A co-worker had called the police about the man when he hadn't shown up to work after a long weekend. Told us his colleague had been acting stranger than usual and was afraid he'd done something stupid. This Hugo guy could have swallowed several happy pills to take off the edge before placing that plastic over his head and then metabolized the product before we got to him."

Nick nodded. Sometimes that was the only way the suicide could get the guts to end it all, especially by self-suffocation.

"But Totes could tell you more," Ramos said.

"Thanks. I'll give him a call."

Nick walked back to the office, very dissatisfied. He stood contemplating the rotation and case roster while ingesting caffeine and sugar by way of a soda. The Creasy case had been delegated to fifth position next to his and Sacco's name. He picked up the dry eraser and wiped the scalded child victim from the board. He and Sacco had closed the case two days ago, evidence box sealed and transferred to the department's paper morgue. Nick erased the jumper, as well. The captain had pleaded with the good citizens of the tri-state area to come forward with any information on this John Doe. After the composite sketch of the victim's face (supplied by the forensic anthropology team) hit the media channels, a very distraught girlfriend had called to identify the victim as one Noonan Hadi from Brooklyn. Turned out his forthcoming extraction by ICE for overstaying his visa by more than seven years had been the stressor. Shame the man had achieved in death what he had not in life—permanent legal residence on US soil.

These were the extreme measures people took to solve their issues that never made sense to Nick.

Familiar footfalls interrupted his thoughts. Only one person could pound the floor with such verve, in heels more fitting to a pole dancer than a prosecutor. He looked down the hall and sighed. Aaniyah Foster approached at her usual New Yorker high-speed stride. Nick always wondered if there was some sort of purposeful metaphor in her choice of footwear. To Nick, every footstep telegraphed the woman wearing them would grind anyone to a bloody pulp in court.

"Ah, shit," was all Nick said after scrutinizing her face.

"And it's only Tuesday," Foster said. "Glad I caught you."

"Please tell me it's good news."

"Depends on the topic. Good, if you count that Judge Taylor gave the diddler the maximum. The man gave quite a show after the sentence was gaveled in today. It finally dawned on the creep his lovely virgin ass would do the rounds at Rikers this evening."

Her orthodontic smile widened. "Karma is a bitch without anesthetics, baby."

"Foster, you are downright scary."

She shrugged. "Not as scary as that psycho sister Jonas will be facing tomorrow at appeals. Have a minute?"

Nick gestured to the conference room. Once inside, they sat, Aaniyah Foster expelling a grateful sigh.

"Laura get in touch?"

She nodded. "Last week. Friday. Dropped off at the office the latest chapter in this ongoing penny dreadful."

"How on earth does that bitch do it?" Nick's hands speared his hair in frustration as he leaned back in his chair. "Every time we clobber Sandra, thinking she's finally under control and tucked away forever, she springs up somewhere else, like a damn Whac-a-Mole."

"That's why I stopped by." Her milk-chocolate eyes held no humor as she leaned forward. "Nick, Jonas and I spoke. He's not introducing that letter into his oral arguments tomorrow at the Second. I agree."

His eyes and jaw hardened. Before he spoke, she lifted a hand in a pacifying gesture.

"Hear me out, please."

"Aaniyah, she knows where Laura lives."

"I know." For a moment her face reflected weariness at having to deal with this unending saga. "But we'd be beating a dead horse, and you know it. This is appeals, after all. Judge won't allow anything except the record of the prior proceedings."

Nick's face said it all.

"Ok, ok," she conceded. "Laura's order of protection expires in four years. The only thing I can do is issue a violation of the court order and file a contempt of court. That doesn't get us anywhere. Sandra is not up for parole. Now, if she were, this would seal her stay in prison. I'd rather keep this as my trump card for future use, especially if she gets a favorable ruling at appeals. The letter is handwritten, undated, and sprinkled with Sandra's prints."

Nick stood, his chair slamming against the wall. F-bombs, the last louder than the previous, bounced around the room as he paced his frustration.

"That's not all," she said in between his curses, her voice all sympathy.

Nick stopped, stared, cursed one last time, and sat.

"Had a long conversation with Kilcrease today, too."

"Screw my day more, why don't you?"

Foster's laugh caught him by surprise. "Told me to tell you it's about time. You and Laura? Finally?"

"Crap." The twinkle in her eye irritated Nick. "No keeping anything private in this precinct."

She wiggled one finger at him. "Are you serious? We're worse than Twitter with personal gossip."

True, Nick thought. With each other. With outsiders, cops were more silent than a pharaoh's tomb.

"Wipe that deprecating smile from your sexy lips," she said, smiling. "Fess up."

"Yeah. Got a hot date with her tonight."

"Good for you. And her. God knows you both need a break."

"Thanks," Nick said and meant it. "What did Kilcrease say?" *Might as well get the bad news out in the open.*

"He concluded this was blatant manipulation on Sandra's part. The good doctor believes she wrote the letter to get us to react without pause or thought. As a matter of fact, he swears Sandra is counting on it. So do I. If you read the letter again, carefully, you'll see. That woman is scary smart."

Nick leaned back, digesting this last bit of info.

"I'll be right back," he said and left the conference room. He reached for the file that was never far from his desk, returned, and reread Sandra's letter at the top of the pile. As he did, he tried to control the knee-jerk reaction at finding this at Laura's and the cynicism evoked by the words written. There was a threatening undertone to it, but then he knew who'd written the thing. But going over it once more, if he were a judge or a defense attorney for Sandra, he would welcome such a letter. It projected regret, a hunger for absolution, some remorse, and even a slight hope at redemption. Superficial, but it was there.

"Son of a bitch."

Foster nodded. "Kilcrease's exact words. He's impressed and pissed. But he is also pleased. This has opened the door for him and another psychiatrist to interview her. The guilty plea last time precluded evaluation on everyone's part. We'll have time to rethink strategy and get more ammunition if the psych ward doesn't want to keep her penned."

"Jesus, Aaniyah." Nick's horrified whisper hung in the air for a moment. His thoughts reverted to Laura, and how she had concocted her crazy plan. It *was* brilliant, though. Never in a million years would he have come up with *that* solution.

"Listen, we'll jump across that river if we ever get to it. In the meantime, I'm keeping this letter as possible future ammo," Aaniyah's voice interrupted. "Kilcrease is hoping that, no matter how disciplined she is with regard to her getting-out-of-jail-free card, she'll eventually lose her temper and do something to land her back in prison."

"At what time is the case being heard?"

"The docket has it for ten," she said, leaned forward and studied his face. "You can't be serious about schlepping to Albany tomorrow?"

"Nah. Why give Sandra the pleasure of seeing me there? She doesn't need much to bloat her grandiose sense of self. Besides I have plans for tonight."

Foster laughed. "I bet."

She slapped the table, picked up her purse and briefcase from the floor, and stood. For the first time Nick noticed she hadn't even taken off her coat.

"I'm out of here. Meeting my staff at Rudy's for a drink."

"Celebrating one down?"

Foster smiled.

"Enjoy," he said. "One less outgoing in our revolving door system is always cause to celebrate."

"In my opinion, I'd rather be earning combat pay."

Nick nodded. "So should we all. Our clown mayor, governor, and idiot lawmakers block us at every turn. And it's getting worse. Can't wait for the mayor's sorry ass to go."

Foster grimaced. "Hurrah for term limits. Anyway, this girl is not giving more personal time to the system. Let's get the heck out of here to enjoy our night."

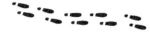

"COME ON," Arjen cajoled. "Let's do it."

The silence at the other end of the phone reflected his friend's uncertainty. Russ hadn't been too convinced about this latest scheme. When things came down to the wire, his friend always chickened out. He was a real wuss. Mad lame.

"I don't know," Russ said, his voice fidgety even over the phone. "Snopes debunked that story. It's not real. My mom heard about it and would not believe for a minute that we're missing. My ass would be skinned the moment we return."

"Yeah, I know it was a bogus game. But brilliant AF. And we *can* make it real. We can start a trend, go viral even."

"I don't know."

"You are beyond lame," Arjen said, frustration eating at him. "Loser."

"I'm not." The outrage was in the answer.

"Loser, loser," Arjen kept chanting, knowing the word irritated his friend no end.

"FU," Russ screamed into the phone. "I have soccer practice in thirty. You and your scheme are seriously messed up. Besides, to disappear for forty-eight hours, you have to plan it well. You've got shit for brains and no plan."

And with that rejoinder, Russ hung up.

Arjen threw his phone on top of the bed. He hated to admit it, but Russ was right. He had no plan. But ever since he'd read the magazine article from the UK about this 48-Hour Facebook Challenge, his imagination had geared into overtime. He needed to leave the house. It was suffocating him, especially after his ball-buster of a stepfather had discovered his stash and gotten all over his face last night.

Arjen picked up his pillow and punched it in a savage, staccato rhythm, wishing it were his stepfather's face.

Grounded. Laughable. And for what? Some weed? Seriously? His stepfather should open his fat-ass eyes and look around Long Island. Heroin still reigned, Calvin Klein was getting more popular, and supplies of crystal meth or prescription drug pills were in abundance everywhere. You just had to follow your nose to the friendly neighborhood MS-13 gang member in school, or your average rich kid who'd raided his parents' medicine cabinet. Arjen knew anyone could buy anything from Suffolk County's version of Walgreens on wheels.

He was also super pissed. Someone had ratted him out and he would bet it had been the nerd next door. He'd been spreading salt on the driveway and sidewalk, like a good mamma's boy, when Arjen had passed him by, smoking the joint he'd scored. The day after, his mom and the asshole had raided his room.

One day, he'd get even.

But back to his current pain in the butt. Who the hell did the asshole think he was, trying to impose parental rights? Just because he was banging Arjen's mother didn't mean he was a father figure. Besides, if his stepfather only knew he didn't have exclusivity rights to his wife's vagina, he'd be singing a different tune. Granted, his mother was very careful at keeping her extracurricular activities secret. Always had been very careful not to spoil her comfortable life and her status within the community.

He walked downstairs and opened the refrigerator, took out a beer, and swallowed several gulps. Another rule his parental units didn't know he broke constantly.

Anyway, it wouldn't matter if they found out. His mother made excuses for him regularly. Chucked it as harmless teenage rebellion every time he was caught.

His Apple watch buzzed as he took another gulp. He rinsed the bottle and dropped it in the recycling bin under the sink. He opened his mother's text message and read the short note.

Running late. Traffic backed up on Sunrise. Accident?
He's coming today at 3-ish. Let him in, offer a soda.
Sent him txt about delay, don't know if he saw msg.
You can visit your friend Russ after I come home. Be
back before stepfather @ 8-ish. Set Crock-Pot to warm.
Don't borrow any more trouble.
xoxo

Arjen deleted the message and checked his watch's calendar. Yep. The fourteenth. Like clockwork. Once a month this dude showed up at their house for his mother's relaxation session. A chuckle escaped him. Loved his mother's euphemisms. As though it was yoga or some such bull. But he knew better. More like sex release therapy by any other name. He'd caught them at it the day he'd skipped school several months back. Not that they'd noticed.

They'd been too busy to realize he was home. And what he'd heard wasn't like the muted sounds his mother and stepfather made nightly, thinking him asleep. The moans, sighs, and screams this dude had been extracting from his mother were IMAX surround sound material. After that eye-opener, he occasionally skipped school on the fourteenth to see if they were at it again and, sure enough, BANG-O, like monkeys. Even funnier...his mother didn't know that during their last session he'd been in the basement jerking off while listening to their groping therapy.

He raided the pantry and scampered back up to his room with a popcorn bag. Grabbing a handful to munch, he scooped up his phone and flopped on the bed. As he chewed, he thumbed through his social media pages, shifting from window to window, comment to comment, reply to reply. The latter ones ranged from really sympathetic, *OMG, your stepfather sucks*, to those not sympathetic at all, *Tired of your bleating, you cushy-life bastard.*

He posted angry and turd emojis to those who could not relate, then proceeded to bleach them from his friends' list.

Why wasn't everyone sympathetic to his plight? He was reduced to walking because his stepfather took his car to work and would continue to do so until the punishment was over. Usually his mom would drive stepdad to the LIRR. But, because of the debacle with the MJ, he was wheelless. He didn't even have the option to Uber—he had no cash with him after buying his last stash, and he couldn't plastic anything. The parental units had reduced him to depending on friends, which was embarrassing AF.

Arjen started pacing and opened his favorite venting app, SuckOpedia, where anyone could post anything about his sucky life.

Thumbs flew over the digital keyboard.

Ballistic mode! Caged. Need OUT of HERE. Someone pls shoot me.

He paced and paced, more agitated by the moment. He had to get out of this place. His thoughts reverted to his conversation with Russ, the plan he wanted to implement.

He cursed, needing to find someone who would be willing to stash him for forty-eight hours and not snitch on him. Some place where he would be safe for that amount of time, and where he could monitor the comments and tweets.

But if he posted his desires, someone would blab about his plans. Positive. And he wouldn't put it past Russ to implode and spill the beans to his overbearing mom.

The doorbell rang, interrupting his internal harangue.

The creep had arrived.

The creep.

Arjen's eyes widened in an instant eureka. What if? His mother wanted him out of the house today until the session with the creep was over. But what if he doubled back, came in stealth-like, similar to how he'd done it before, to take a picture or video of the activity going on? Bet they wouldn't notice. And even if they did, Arjen didn't give a shit. He could use the evidence to put his plan into action. And once he got what he wanted, he'd delete everything.

The melodic chime of the doorbell bounced all over the house once more.

Arjen smiled.

This might work. This might work very well.

He stashed the phone in his back pocket and, while whistling "Flex" by Element One, went downstairs to answer the door.

CHAPTER SIXTEEN

Wednesday, January 15
THE CELL PHONE startled Nick awake.

Disoriented for an instant, he reached over to grab the ever-annoying thing, and bumped into a warm body.

His confusion disappeared.

Laura.

He fumbled for and found his phone. Before swiping to answer, he kissed her nape and tried to convey the depth of pleasure and love with which she had filled his life that evening.

"Larson."

"Sorry, Nick," Sacco's tired voice filled the waves. "They've given us a case."

Nick rubbed his face, hoping it would dispel the sleepiness.

"Where?"

Laura began to stir. Nick nibbled her shoulder and sat up.

"Fifty-Third and First. Ramos warned you'd better be prepared."

Oh, shit. That meant the murder scene was reeking of the dead.

"She already there?"

"On her way. But first responder on scene sent word of situation." Sacco paused. "I would offer to pick you up but your protective stash is in your car."

Laura clicked on the bedside lamp.

"Right." Nick squinted at the phone. Four fifteen in the freaking a.m. Why was it that most of the times they landed a homicide it was at this wonderful witching hour? "I need to go to my place and get ready."

Laughter filled his eardrum. "Say hi to Laura for me."

"Screw you."

"You wish." And without waiting for Nick's rejoinder, Sacco hung up.

"Was that Sacco?" the sleepy voice behind him preceded the arms around his waist.

"Yeah." He turned his head to look at her as she knelt behind him. "New case. Welcome to my world."

In a shy move, she leaned forward a bit and played with his lips in a long, soft kiss. "Go get the bad guys. Just be careful."

He turned slightly, anchored her head with his hand, and deepened the next kiss.

"Tonight?"

"Tonight." She smiled.

They exited the bed on opposite sides, Nick to find his clothes and slip into them, and Laura to wrap a robe around her naked body.

"Coffee?" she asked.

"Don't bother." Nick squeezed into his shoes. "I'll grab something after I leave the scene." *If I can hold anything down after this crime scene.*

She helped him into his coat and slipped her arms around his waist.

He folded her within his embrace, his face dropping into the crook of her shoulder. They stayed that way for a few minutes, each inhaling the essence of the other. Basking in the feel of each other.

He squeezed her as goodbye and left the apartment.

Outside, the cold slapped Nick fully awake. He crossed the street, now quiet and empty in that somnolent half sleep typical of the city at that hour. He bounded up the steps, slipped through the entrance door, keyed the inner foyer, and was about to slip into his place when he heard the building door open. He caught sight of his neighbor, Lorena, her shocking pink coat acting much like her neon sign did as it overlooked the street.

"*Muñeco*," she whispered, following that greeting with a whistle. "Late date?"

"Fun night?" was his rejoinder.

She smiled and salsa stepped to her door while humming a peppy tune. "What a night. El Timbal has never been this packed with dancers. And I mean dancers. Didn't lack a partner. Unfortunately, they threw us out."

"The sun *is* almost out."

He waited until she opened her door. Usually, if he bumped into her at this late hour, he ensured she was safe inside her apartment before he left.

She turned and scrutinized him for an instant.

"You look...well used."

And with that comment, she closed her door, the lyrics of "Macho Man" receding in laughter.

He closed his own door and rushed into the bathroom with a smile on his face.

By the time Nick double-parked behind one of the two squad cars on the street, the city was spurting awake in fits and starts. Delivery trucks blocked lanes, basement steel doors gaped like monster maws in the middle of sidewalks, and citizens, oblivious to everything, including the garbage mounds barring their way, jaywalked or cycled to their destinations at different speeds. Others rushed to subway stations while sipping their fancy Frapuccinos, thumbs scrolling through messages on their phones. Others, with a fixed, glazed gaze locked in drive position, simply ignored the surrounding humanity, especially the homeless who dotted the landscape.

Nick grabbed a mask from his car's trunk, sprayed it with his lavender-scented odor eliminator, and slipped his travel-size jar of menthol in his jacket pocket.

The crime scene was in an older, four-story, brick-façade building, which stood at the corner, with windows overlooking First Avenue. Typical of such premises, the entrance into the apartments was sandwiched between businesses, this time a copy center and a pizza joint. The fire escape ladders zigzagged across the wall on the building's street side.

Nick scooted underneath the barrier tape and nodded to the officer in charge of the perimeter.

"Where to?"

"Fourth floor, sir." The man pointed to another officer by the elevator.

He reached the fourth floor and followed the hushed conversation to his left. When he saw Sacco and Horowitz standing by the closed door with masks already in place, Nick knew it was going to be a bad one.

"Okay," Nick greeted the men. The air nearing the victim's apartment had turned unhealthy. He swiped a bit of the ointment under his nose before putting the mask in place.

"Give me the abridged version. I'll see for myself in a minute."

Horowitz spoke first. "Possible murder/suicide. Victims are Jessica Waitre, female, Caucasian, aged twenty-five, and a Desha Adnet, male, Middle Eastern or Indian, aged twenty-seven."

"Have you gone in yet?" Nick asked his partner.

Sacco shook his head. "Waiting for you."

First impressions. Nick extended the ointment jar to the men. Sacco reached for it, swabbed, and handed it to Horowitz. After dabbing his upper lip with a few specks of menthol, Horowitz gave it back.

"Ramos in there?"

"Arrived half hour ago. Still waiting for Totes and his crew," said Sacco.

"Heard over radio there's a major pileup at the Lincoln Tunnel," Horowitz said. "One dead, several injured. Jaws of Life involved. Assistant ME coming over here instead."

"Who called this in?" Nick asked.

"A Mr. and Mrs. Kyriakou. Piros and Ione, respectively. The 911 came in at two ten this morning. We were dispatched and arrived at two twenty-one. We met the witnesses who claimed neighbors started noticing a funky odor in the hallway a day or so ago," Horowitz stated. "Didn't think much about it because the building's super is on vacation and the garbage's been piling up in the basement and around garbage chutes on each floor since he left."

"Doesn't say much about the replacement sent by the management office," Sacco said.

"Why the call?" Nick asked.

"According to the husband, their dog went ballistic in front of the victims' door early this a.m. When occupants didn't answer the knock, they thought maybe something was amiss, especially after they got a whiff of the stench filtering under the door. We verified there was indeed some sort of smell coming from the apartment, knocked, but also received no answer. Dispatch sent a uniform to get the super pro tempore, a Geraldo Fontinela, who lives across town, according to the information supplied by the management office. He arrived around three forty-seven. As soon as he opened the door, we knew we had a crime scene. I asked Davis to secure the perimeter, stepped into the foyer and discerned the situation in the living room. I backed up and called it in. No one has gone in or out until FID arrived."

"Get two more uniforms and have them canvas for initial statements. Where are the witnesses?"

"End-of-hallway apartment," Horowitz said, pointing. "4D."

"Super?"

"Downstairs, basement office."

"I'll speak to them later." Nick looked at Sacco while they put on booties. "Ready?"

"Hope you are."

Nick snapped his gloves in place and opened the door.

To say that the fetid air slapped him like a living force was an understatement. Nick's stomach heaved. Sacco closed the door behind him. Breathing took on a minimalistic quality.

Nick paused a moment to scan the crime scene as he stood with Sacco in a rectangle-shaped foyer no bigger than an end table. The inside apartment was typical of the buildings in the area: short on square footage but ample in rent. The forensic team, which roamed around like ants collecting food, had turned on every possible light in the apartment and had cracked open the latticed windows overlooking First Avenue. The ever-growing morning light outside wasn't dispelling the drabness inside. The furniture, drapes, and doodads that decorated the place looked secondhand or rented. On Nick's left, the miniscule galley kitchen, divided from the rest of the open area by a wall, separated the dining room and living room. There, the furniture gave function to each zone. Close to the kitchen's wall stood a round dining set more apropos to a dollhouse than an apartment. The back of the love seat next to it was the boundary of the living room, with the sofa creating a ninety-degree angle to its partner, its back and side touching walls. There was a television, at least a seventy-inch flat screen, Nick gauged, hanging from the wall a few feet directly opposite the sofa. No skimpiness on the tech, he thought. An industrial-looking entertainment stand complemented the television and held a DVR, Blu-ray box, and whatever cable or gaming systems these people used. To the right, the small hallway opened the way to the bedrooms and bathroom.

A small cyclone, however, seemed to have swirled through the area of the living room. Tidy it was not. Neither was the body in its final sleep.

Carpenter, taking photos from as many angles as possible in front of the body, came round the love seat in their direction. The rank air swirled. Nick opened his mouth and breathed in shallow spurts.

"Hey," Carpenter acknowledged Nick and Sacco with the greeting. "Mind moving? Need to get pics from this angle."

"Where's Ramos?"

Carpenter nodded to the hallway opening. "In the bedroom with the other body."

Nick and Sacco followed the marked, safe path to the other side of the love seat and concentrated on the victim.

The body lay slightly angled to the right, half on and half off the love seat, the rope around the neck keeping the victim's bottom from reaching the carpet by about a few inches. That same rope had been double looped around his neck and, in turn, was connected to the middle of another rope, the latter having its ends securely anchored at both ends to the love seat legs. That had created the upside-down-V pattern Nick had seen from the doorway, a pattern formed the moment the man had decided to end his life.

The body, in its bloated splendor, came into focus.

"Man," was all Sacco said.

Nick studied the face, the neck skin folded over the rope, almost hiding it. The victim's blue-black tongue protruded slightly from an open mouth, as though he was gasping for oxygen. There was some evidence of blood from the nose and ear that joined the trail of dried saliva that had spilled over.

"He definitely did not go easy," Nick said.

Nick considered the victim's body for a few moments, following the position of the legs on the carpeted floor. They were stretched straight. Nick's eyes shifted to the coffee table, overturned a few inches away from the man's feet, the contents on it—magazines, fake plant, open beer bottles, tortilla chips, and a salsa container—thrown in no apparent pattern all across the carpet.

"Last throes?" Sacco speculated to Nick, pointing to the mess surrounding the overturned coffee table.

"Possibility."

Nick studied the man's hands next, fallen after rigor halfway down the love seat, palms up almost in supplication. He anchored his mask deeper into his nose and leaned forward. He gulped. Getting so close to the body was always a bad idea, but it needed to be done. Lividity had settled, and blood had pooled in the tips of the fingers, so the man had not been moved. Totes would later determine if there were any injuries there from the victim's effort to relieve his asphyxia. Nick wasn't going to bother examining the neck for the same obvious reasons.

He straightened quickly.

"Let's have a look at the other victim."

Again, walking within the marked area, Nick veered to the back bedroom. On the way there, his brain catalogued a small, rectangular room to his left. Desk, recliner, bookshelves, and computer indicated the room's use. Carpenter and two other techs were now all over the contents there.

The master bedroom looked bigger than it was because of the light filtering in and the sparse, smallish furniture. The stench here, thankfully, had been greatly relieved by the fact Ramos had opened the windows wider than the living room ones. The wintry air circulated in from one area to the other, taking the smell in tow.

"Step lightly, gentlemen," Ramos said from her kneeling position on the floor next to the victim. "I haven't catalogued everything yet." She pointed the way with her finger. "Go through there."

Nick and Sacco obliged, standing a foot away from the dead woman.

The victim was hanging from a heavy-duty, multifunction doorway exercise pull-up bar, set high on the bathroom entrance frame. She looked her youth, was about five-four, a bit heavyset, her waist-length hair, catching some of the incoming breeze, floated next to her body like seaweed in tidal water. She was naked, except for a thong, and looked peaceful, almost as if she'd fallen asleep in the noose. Her extremities showed blood pooling, so she'd died in place, her toes pointing to a colorful towel crumpled inches away.

"What's under the towel?" Nick asked, pointing to the floor.

"Zip," Ramos answered. She cut two pieces of tape with her scissors and stuck them on top of her glove for easy retrieval.

"No shit?" Sacco asked.

Nick scanned the immediate area, but didn't see a footstool anywhere near the woman's feet, or in the vicinity of the bed, or in the thimble-sized bathroom. The bed itself, and the end table next to it, were too far away for her to have jumped from there to the position she was in at the moment. That scrapped the suicide theory. The rope would have had to be much longer, and the victim would have ended up in a completely different position if she'd launched herself from that distance. And that trick might not have worked from where she was hanging. It was a matter of physics. Force and mass would have ripped the doorframe where the exercise rod was positioned. She'd have ended on the floor with a sore neck and an even sorer butt.

"So we're working on two assumptions: Either she was an unwilling participant to her hanging..." Nick began.

"Making it murder by boyfriend," Sacco added, and angled his head toward the living room.

"Which, by the way, the crime scene here does not corroborate," Ramos answered.

"Or someone placed her there like a ham to dry, with her full cooperation," Nick finished.

"Suicide pact?" Sacco suggested.

"For her, suicide by proxy, at least," Nick answered. "Note?"

"Nope," Ramos said. "But that doesn't mean squat. They could have left something in the computer. Besides, I haven't finished." She took a paper evidence bag, flicked it open, and carefully covered the victim's left hand. She held it in place, ripped free one of the strips from her glove, and sealed the bag snug against the wrist, without touching the tape to the skin.

"There are no marks that I can see on the fingers," Ramos said. "No obvious defensive wounds, if this were leaning towards murder. No struggle that I can see from any of the evidence as yet, at least not from my cursory check. No obvious hematomas visible, especially antemortem ones that always show through. Totes will need to look for subcutaneous hematomas, if she was held in place for a short time before death."

"She could have been dropped before creating any," Nick suggested.

"Totes will verify either way." Ramos picked up her camera and snapped several photos of the victim's right hand and covered it as meticulously as she'd done with the victim's left hand.

Nick studied the dead woman once more. Again, the scene was too static. Had the boyfriend held the body just low enough for her to lose consciousness and then released her? Had he choked her beforehand and, once the woman was unconscious or dead, hanged her there? Was this, as Sacco had suggested, a suicide pact? Why such contrast between the two victims' death scene? The man had not gone easy. Could it have been he'd had suicide remorse, kicking out when he realized what was happening? Yet, by the position of the body, the victim would have had space and time to reverse his decision, if that had been the case. Or had he drugged himself to the point where his reactions would not allow his saving?

"What's wrong with this picture?" Nick said to no one in particular.

Ramos looked up, her gaze knowing.

"Reminds you, huh?"

"Yeah," Nick said. His gut was churning, and not from the DB smell.

"Shit," Sacco said and scrubbed his blond fuzz with his palm.

The possibility was mind-blowing. Nick knew this could turn into a bad nightmare, if their supposition proved true.

"I want to check out the other body again," Nick said.

Ramos held up a plastic bag. "You need one of these? You're turning a little green there."

Nick held up the menthol jar. "No. I'm good."

"Glad your stomach and brain are under control," Ramos said, grabbing a bigger evidence bag. She reached for the towel. "Welcome back."

"Thanks go to an all-night dose of Lauracillin," Sacco said. "Guaranteed to cure all prior Angie cooties."

Ramos laughed. Nick flicked his middle finger at both and went into the living room.

The body was still in place, with no assistant medical examiner in sight yet. Good. Nick grabbed Carpenter as he scooted past.

"Did you measure the distances yet?" he asked, and pointed to the victim's legs, the overturned table, and the scattered contents.

Carpenter shook his head. "Took the photos with the ABFO scale, but I need to finish cataloguing contents in the office first. Will start the sketch and measurements before the assistant ME shows up."

"Let me borrow your folding ruler for a bit."

"You need the entire scene sketched?"

"No. I only want measurements between the overturned table, the items on the carpet, and the victim."

Carpenter went to his kit near the doorway and took out a yellow folded ruler. "Let me do it."

Nick dabbed a bit more menthol under his nose, and crouched down by the victim's feet, his notebook open, already sketching what was before him. Sacco was doing the same.

"What do you want measured?" asked Carpenter.

Nick tapped the areas in his notebook.

Opening the ruler, Carpenter made quick work of what Nick needed. In less than five minutes, Nick had the measurements between the victim's feet and overturned table, from the edge of said table to each scattered item on the carpet, distance between each, and depth, breadth, and height of the overturned table.

Sacco scribbled everything Carpenter rattled off, as well.

"Guess we'll do a mock-up later?" Sacco asked.

Nick nodded. "Let's go talk to the witnesses."

They discarded their booties and gloves in a bag next to the doorway. Nick nodded to Horowitz and headed to the end of the hallway, taking off his mask and stuffing it inside his jacket pocket.

Nearing the door, an incessant, high-pitched barking greeted them.

"Both witnesses in there?" Nick asked, his voice at a par with the barking.

"Yes, sir."

Nick was reaching for the door when the officer warned. "Be careful, Lieutenant. The mutt likes to nip at the ankles if he's let loose."

Great.

Nick knocked. The barking became a crescendo of hysteria. He opened the door a crack and tried to call at a decibel that competed with the dog's growing one.

"Mr. and Mrs. Kyriakou?"

A gray-and-white Shih Tzu mix, with a pug nose, calculating dark eyes, and angry teeth, tried to shove the door wider. Nick's grip on the door didn't budge.

"Pip," a woman's voice said in a somewhat admonishing tone. "Be nice."

"Pip," a louder male voice.

The dog paid no attention, his barking and growling increasing, and his efforts to widen the door more desperate.

Nick glanced at Sacco, whose expression reflected his own of *Can you believe this shit?*

"Sir...Ma'am," Nick said, this time with a warning. "This is Detective Larson. I need to speak to you about what happened in apartment 4G. Please control your dog; if not I'll be forced to call animal control."

A male hand grabbed the dog's collar and dragged the wriggling mass of fury back. Nick counted to five and opened the door wider.

Husband and wife stood side by side in the foyer. The man looked like he'd slept in his clothes and been dragged out two seconds after he'd fallen asleep. His wife had put on an earth-tone caftan lounger that clashed with the neon-blue sneakers she wore. The dog was under control and now lay quiet in her arms, staring suspiciously at them.

"He's so upset," the woman said, stroking the dog from head to butt. The animal began to close his eyes in ecstasy. If it had been a cat, it would have been purring like the engine of an expensive sports car. "Please come in."

She nodded to the men to follow her into the living room, her husband in her wake.

This apartment was much more spacious than the one they'd been in, Nick observed, with a separate area for a formal dining room and kitchen to their left. The furniture was top of the line, every sitting area covered in vinyl for protection against the dog, Nick presumed. The walls were littered with mementoes and photographs of family, Greek landscapes, and lithographs. Curio cabinets were also filled with bric-a-brac figurines, statuettes, and urns. It looked like a home, well lived-in. The kitchen was wider than in the victims' apartment and updated. A hallway to the right provided access to bedrooms and bathrooms, he guessed.

"This has been very traumatic," the woman said. She visibly shuddered. "To think..."

Her husband stroked her back similarly to the way she was caressing the dog.

"Ma'am. Sir. Why don't you have a seat?" Nick asked and waited for them to do so. The husband gestured for them to take the seats opposite the sofa.

Nick and Sacco thanked them.

"I'm sorry for what you've been through this morning," Nick said. "And thank you for your cooperation."

"Crime and homelessness we can deal with," the husband said, squeezing the tiredness out of his eyes. "Hell, we deal with it every day."

"The city's a dump and going downhill by the minute. A total disaster," the wife complained.

"But you're ready for crime, you know? Out there," the man pointed somewhere in the vicinity of his living room window. "You never expect violence in here. Not here..." He looked at Nick. "Was it murder?"

"We don't know," Nick said. Not that he was going to tell them, either. "It's too early in the investigation. Have you lived in the area long?"

"Since we opened the restaurant ten years ago," the husband said. "We own the Taverna Delphi a couple of blocks away." He looked at his wife. "Maybe we should close for today."

This time around, the wife offered comfort to the husband by stroking his arm.

"Piros stays until closing and comes home after midnight," she said, picking up the conversation. "I help greet, seat, and keep an eye on waiters and cashier, or take orders if needed. Well, except Sundays. That's my day off. We got home today at around two."

"Were you both acquainted with the victims?"

"Ione more than me," the husband stated and then nodded to his wife.

"More than anyone else here in the building, anyway," she said. "Typically, with the others, we only nod, or say hello when we bump into each other. But, usually, we all go our separate ways."

"The building's had a high turnover in renters in the past few years," the husband said. "Not much time to know anyone with the constant flow of new faces."

"But Jessie was friendlier than most," said the wife. "She adored Pip. Bought him treats, sometimes accompanied me on our walks, even doggie-sat when I had my knee issues. I can't process..." At her shudder, the dog opened his eyes and whined. "Shh, it's okay, baby. It's okay."

More stroking.

"You called this in around two this morning, is that correct?" Nick asked.

Their heads bobbed up and down. "One of the servers was sick yesterday and, of course, the restaurant was busier than usual. It's like the curse of the full moon, you know? All the crazies get crazier? Well, diners also know when a restaurant is short-handed. Never fails. So we had double duty. Came home at about that time."

"Usually, Pip doesn't bother to get up from his bed when we come in that late," the woman added. "But he's been a bit agitated these past two days."

Some recollection changed her expression. She closed her eyes, shuddered a bit, and snuggled the dog.

Nick and Sacco waited for whatever memory had hit her to fade.

"You said your dog had been agitated. How?" Nick prompted.

"He'd been tugging his leash more, wanting to linger around Jessie's door. Smelling the area as if he wanted to do his thing right in front. Yesterday afternoon he was dragging his butt, almost fighting me when we walked past their apartment. Even started to scratch and bark at the door. But I needed to rush back to the restaurant, so on my way back I carried him home from the elevator."

"What happened when you arrived this morning?" Sacco asked.

"As soon as I opened the door," the husband said, "the damned dog scooted right past us. He zeroed in on Jessie's door, sat across from it, and bayed as if his heart was being ripped apart."

The woman shuddered.

"It was the creepiest thing I've ever heard," the husband continued. "Frankly, if I never hear it again, I'll be happy." He rubbed his arms as if trying to prevent goosebumps from popping up. "I can still hear it."

"Was that what prompted you to call this in?" Sacco asked.

"That and the smell," the husband said. "When I picked the dog up to muffle him, I got a whiff of the smell. Asked Ione about it and she recognized it, too. Rotted meat has a particular scent. That's when we knocked and knocked, but when we got no answer, we figured something was wrong."

"Why assume that? They could have made a spur-of-the-moment decision to go on a short trip," Nick said.

"No. Jessie would have let us know. She always worries someone might try to break in, always fretting about how her bedroom window faces the fire escape. Whenever we leave the area, we let each other know. Keep an eye out on things."

"And she hadn't said anything?"

The woman shook her head. "That's why we came back home and dialed 911."

"When was the last time you saw either victim?" Nick asked.

"Let's see...what day is this?" the woman asked, her eyes apologetic. Nick saw she was still rattled. When Sacco supplied the answer, the woman continued.

"That's right. Saw them Monday...around sixish."

"Them?"

"Yes. Jessie and Desh came home together, which is bizarre because their work schedules don't really coincide."

"Can you walk us through what you saw?" Nick asked.

"I came home as usual. Poor Pip was about bursting. Right, sweetie pie?" She nuzzled the dog, which licked her nose and mouth with delicate delight.

Nick waited a moment before asking, "Where were the victims?"

"Coming up on the elevator. I was waiting for it and heard the arguing. Well, Desh seemed more upset and louder. Took them by surprise when the elevator opened and they saw me. Desh was embarrassed, and Jessie looked like she'd been crying."

"Did they argue much?" Sacco asked.

"Not really. Not at first. But lately..."

"What did they argue about?" Nick asked.

"Honestly? About stupid things," the husband said. "Fought about greenhouse gases."

"Plastic straws," the wife added.

"Pro-choice."

"Too much sugar."

"The environment."

"How we will all be dead in ten years if we don't change." The husband finished. "Ridiculous millennials. Too much time on their hands."

"Who was for what?" Nick asked.

"Jessie was much more into all this global apocalyptic thing," the wife said.

"Turning into an unthinking ditz more like," the husband retorted.

"Now, Piro..."

"It's true, Io. Remember when she tried to make us change things at the restaurant?" the husband said, shaking his head. He looked directly at Nick. "Here she was, a twenty-something woman, with practically no life experience and no idea how to run a business, let alone wipe her ass well, telling me to replace paper napkins with reusable cotton, and to chuck out our Styrofoam takeout containers. That I should invest in fans. Raise the temperature of my air conditioning. Do you know how hot the kitchen gets? I'd have no chefs and no assistants within two seconds." He shook his head. "Reduce carbon footprints, my ass. The operating costs would be so high we'd be out of business within a month. Our profit margins are already minimal, sometimes in the pennies with all the additional restrictions, regulations, and taxes the City slaps on us for the privilege of running a restaurant in the city." He shook his head again. "Ridiculous millennials."

"Was that what they were arguing about when you saw them, Mrs. Kyriakou?"

"Actually, no. Lately, Desh was upset Jessie was spending too much time on social media."

"I think he was jealous," the husband said. "Stopped by the restaurant last week before we opened for dinner and asked if anyone had been hanging around Jessie."

"I didn't know that," the wife said, surprised.

"Couldn't have answered him anyway. I'm barely at home and have no time to babysit his girlfriend, her friends, or her moves. And you only see her sporadically."

"Getting back to Monday," Nick interrupted. "What were they arguing about?"

"I've never seen Desh so angry. Practically screaming."

"About?" Nick asked.

"Some Thor download. Jessie had done it without his consent and he was livid she'd placed their identities at risk."

A what download? Nick looked at Sacco, who shrugged.

"Desh did say she had been invited months ago to a chat room from a sub-read it group," the wife added. "Honestly, Detective, I usually side with Jessie, but this time, I had to agree with Desh. She's been changing. Afraid of everything. Focused only on the negative impact humans were having on the Earth. That not enough people were 'up' with the world."

Oh, damn. Reddit. Now he understood the previous Thor reference. *Dark web shit. Not good.*

"Whatever that 'up' means," the husband scoffed. "Reminded her that if New York was really going to end up underwater in ten years like she believed, then why did these filthy rich millionaires and billionaires keep buying beachfront property in the Hamptons and at Martha's Vineyard?"

"Did she say anything else?"

"Oh, yes," said Mrs. Kyriakou. "Complained her world was full of ifs and what was the use of living if everything was being poisoned. Saw no future. Our walks with Pip became more like therapy sessions in the past few weeks. Her fear and anxiety were getting out of hand. Hysteria, almost. I told her she needed to seek help about it. That's not any way to live. She could do something unhealthy if she kept that up."

"Did you see them after your walk on Monday?" Nick asked.

"Only Desh. He slammed his way out of the apartment when I got home with Pip and didn't say anything. Just got in the elevator and left."

"Do you know if they had enemies? People who didn't like them here in the building or at work?"

"Not that we know of," the wife answered. "We're so busy with the restaurant and, on my day off, I'm running around doing errands. Our grandchildren visit me that day, too, and we hang around town, as they say."

Nick reached into his coat pocket and took out a card. "If you think of anything else, remember anyone suspicious around the neighborhood, give me a call."

He handed the card to the man and stood. Sacco did as well.

As soon as they stepped outside into the hallway, Nick turned to Sacco. "Did you get the reference?"

"Yeah." Sacco's tone was not a happy one.

"Let's go see the super."

"He won't have much to say if he's a replacement," Sacco said.

An arrow, pointing right as they stepped off the elevator, directed them to the manager's office.

The basement of the building looked similar to the one in Nick's and thousands of other building basements around the city—cement floors, cement walls, painted an unremarkable slate gray so that scuff marks, dirt, or spills would be less noticeable.

"Ah, basement perfume," Sacco said.

"In serious need of an air freshener," Nick said, as they zigged and zagged the length of the building. Even when recently replaced with trash compactors, too many years of furnace garbage burning had become part of the air molecules surrounding the place. Very similar to getting stuck in traffic after a garbage truck had rumbled through.

Nick knocked on the super's door and walked in. The office was a converted closet, with file cabinets pressed against one wall and a desk against the opposite. A space of about two feet separated the furniture, just enough for one person to sit, which was where they found Fontineli, leaning back, eyes closed, hands wrapped around a steaming coffee cup. The man looked like he'd ingested something sour that was not working well through his body.

Nick and Sacco identified themselves and showed their shields.

"I don't know how I can help you, Detectives," Fontineli said, his Adam's apple made more prominent by his constant, excessive swallowing. He pushed the untouched coffee aside. "I'm filling in until Braxas comes back from vacation."

"So you work with the management office?" Nick asked.

The man shook his head. "Nah. The cheap bastards don't want to dish out for a temp substitute. I'm actually doing double duty. My real job is managing their building on Ninth. That's where you guys picked me up this morning."

"Any security cameras in the building?"

Fontineli shook his head and pointed to an area behind and above Nick's head. "Didn't I tell you they're cheap bastards? The only security is in the office, and that's to make sure we don't steal anything."

"You have a schedule?" Nick asked.

The man reached over and took a paper from the printer at the far corner of the desk.

"Thought you might want it," he said and handed over the paper.

Nick thanked him, studying it for a minute or two. The man's presence in the building changed day to day, with no pattern to pin down. Next to the times were notes indicating the jobs he'd done around the building. Nick checked Fontineli's whereabouts there on Monday, when the victims had last been seen alive, but he had come and gone in the early a.m., the hours from six thirty to ten forty-five logged in the system. A note indicated he'd had to cut the visit short to fix a broken pipe in the apartment building he supervised. It would be easy to double-check his alibi.

Nick handed the schedule over to Sacco so he could read it.

"When you came back on Tuesday, did you notice anything strange, unusual garbage dump, or had any complaints from the occupants?"

"You're kidding, right? This place is complaint alley. Don't know how Braxas does it. If it's not someone complaining a pizza box was left on the floor inside the garbage chute instead of chucking it down, it's another who left a trail of garbage juice all over the hallway and messed up the carpeting there. Then there are the roach and rodent complaints from the second and third floors. Broken furniture and discarded junk left next to the elevator here in the basement at all times. Pizza joint complaining their ceiling leak was coming from the apartment right over them, when it turned out it was an old air-conditioner stain. Yesterday some asshole in 2G clogged the toilet by continually flushing paper towels and tampons down it, which backed up everyone's drainage. Nasty smell and dogs barking at all hours on the fourth floor..." He stopped, realized what he had just said, and cringed. "Christ."

"You didn't notice anyone who didn't belong here or anything unusual?"

"Sorry, Detective. I've been covering here for less than a week. It's also an old building. No lobby guard or reception to accept packages for occupants. There's also a lot of deliveries in here, especially for the first floor businesses."

Too many faces and bodies coming in and out would go unnoticed in a place like this. The culprit would have had to stand out for anyone to remember.

"Thank you for your time," Nick said and extended his hand. Fontineli shook it. "If you think of anything, let us know."

After handing the super his card, they left.

"Let's go check out those businesses. Maybe we'll get lucky with security cameras."

CHAPTER SEVENTEEN

AFTER STOPPING HOME for a quick shower, Nick arrived at the precinct a little after eleven. Their last interviews, the managers of the businesses flanking the entrance to the victims' apartment building, had verified security cameras were in place; unfortunately, none had been mounted on the outside. It had not taken long for Nick to realize it would be fruitless to spend more time on them. Most of the images captured were centered in key areas *inside* each business. They'd ended the interviews earlier than they'd thought, with Nick handing cards all around and asking the managers for copies of their videos. Carpenter would pick those up before he left the crime scene later on.

Not that they would find anything helpful anyway, Nick thought, frustrated to the core. Unless evidence to the contrary fell on their laps, the initial assumption still remained true—that the boyfriend (fiancé... husband?) had killed the woman first and then hanged himself afterward. On the surface of things, the case smelled like a suicide pact or murder/suicide. His gut, however, felt there was more to the story.

Nick hated to have so many maybes as possibilities.

He slung his coat over the chair facing his desk and turned on the computer, grabbed an empty three-ring binder from his shelf, dropped it on his desk, and opened the RTCC search engine. He rolled his eyes when the computer showed sixty-five cases of suicides by hanging compiled in Manhattan alone. Currently, it was searching for the same parameters in the Bronx.

Damn.

On the way to the captain's office, he grabbed a soda from the vending machine. He knocked on the open door and stepped inside.

"Small rundown, please," Kravitz said. "Meeting at the PBA."

Nick glanced at the ashtray. The cigar was only mildly chewed.

"The dousing incidents?"

Kravitz nodded. "Strategizing session wrapped up yesterday. Everyone is concerned things may escalate once the weather gets warmer. Need to run the plans with the union lawyers and the membership, just in case."

Nick agreed. This past summer they'd taken a beating, with police officers doused in water and milk. The next liquid thrown at them might not be as harmless. Nick knew the captain's "just in case" had more to do not with how to handle future offenders, but with how to deal with the reprimands and calls for suspensions coming their way if the uniforms took any action. Thugs on the street now had more privileges than law enforcement officers, and to avert serious injuries to those men and women in blue in the future, a plan of action had to be in place. Everyone in the department was disgusted and out of patience with the current resident of Gracie Mansion.

"Just a head's up on a possible issue with the new case," Nick said.

Kravitz stopped shoving papers into his briefcase.

"Explain."

"First glance seems like possible murder-suicide, even a potential suicide pact, with male hanging female first and committing suicide second."

"But?" Kravitz picked up the cigar and began chewing the tip in earnest.

"Something the neighbors mentioned. One of the victims, the female, may have been into some dark web shit. We may need to bring in Cyber Crime to figure things out, if we can't."

"Do Ramos and Carpenter know?"

"No. Not yet," Nick said. "We're getting together for a quick lunch before tackling the case."

Kravitz closed his attaché case with force and put on his coat.

"Brief them and we'll powwow around four."

Nick nodded.

They exited the office together, the captain turning right toward the elevators and Nick toward the conference room.

Once inside, Nick took a swig from his soda and stared at the board. He wrote down the Creasy case bullet points. He stepped back, assessed. Bare bones there, really. Nick wondered if this would be *the case* for him, the cold unsolved one to hound him throughout his career.

He compressed the empty soda can and threw it with more force than necessary into the garbage can. Honestly. He didn't know why on earth the Creasy case had made such an impact on him, nor why seeing this last victim had reminded him of Isabel Creasy.

Nick grabbed the nearest dry erase marker and duplicated all the information he'd written on the board into a tighter space toward the center. Once done, he erased his original notes, drew two separating lines on either side of the Creasy file info, and wrote Victor Hugo's name on the left of it. Next, he wrote down the names of the victims from the First Avenue case on the right.

"Victor Hugo?" Sacco's voice sounded from the entrance. "You've got to be shitting me."

The smell of food triggered Nick's stomach juices. He turned to see his partner dropping a big box from their favorite Mexican restaurant on the table, together with sodas and energy drinks. Sacco had a new change of clothes. He'd also gone home to shower.

"The name's for real," Nick said, opening the food box, and inhaled. Heaven. Nothing like the smell of grilled onions and meat to soothe the hungry heart. The place would stink for hours, but he didn't care.

Sacco pointed. "Two steak quesadillas and one taco are yours. One chimichanga and a burrito for me. Ramos and Carpenter can fight over the rest. By the way, they're on their way in." Sacco gestured with his chin toward the board. "What's that case? I don't recognize it."

"We didn't work it." Nick flattened the wrapper from the quesadilla against the table, grabbed the biggest cut section, and wolfed it down. He picked up the marker once more and jotted down what he knew of the case. "This one is from the RTCC list we were looking at. Talked to Ramos about it yesterday. Something doesn't feel right."

He drank, wrote, and chewed while Sacco did the same, reading the growing information on the board in silence.

"Who's the angel?"

Nick turned to see Ramos beeline it to the food. She looked recently washed and scrubbed. Smelled of lavender, too. He pointed toward Sacco and reached for more of his food.

Ramos rummaged through the box, picked two tacos and two burritos, and left the rest for Carpenter, who came in sniffing and smacking his lips in anticipation of sustenance. He also looked recently scrubbed.

Nick opened a soda while Ramos took a bite and closed her eyes. "God, I was starving." She looked at Sacco. "I owe you one."

Sacco smirked. "Don't think I won't collect."

"Asshole," she said and smiled.

"Tease," Sacco replied.

"Puh-lease," Carpenter said after swallowing a good chunk of what looked like a quesadilla. "Children in the room."

"What they need is to get a room," Nick said, and bit into a taco.

"Like you?" Sacco said and winked.

"At least I'm a man of action and not words," Nick told him.

"Whoa," Carpenter said. "Breaking news. Details, please."

"Sometimes, Carpenter, I forget your perverted side," Nick said. He ignored Sacco's whisper of "I'll fill you in when I get details, kid," and the chuckles around the room. He filled in more information about their recent murder/suicide, suicide/suicide, or whatever the case would turn out to be.

Ramos stood beside Nick a second later, opened an energy drink, and perused the board. "I see you added the Hugo case." She took a healthy swallow and capped the bottle. "I think you're way off there, but..."

Nick reached over and placed a series of question marks after the name.

"That's better," Ramos said and went to sit.

Next, Nick wrote down bullet points about their morning scene with the male victim in the living room.

"Whenever you can, see if you can set up a re-creation of this, Ramos. I have the measurements on the outlying detritus."

"Can I volunteer Sacco for the victim?" Ramos asked. "He's about the man's height."

"Risqué games, Tish?" Sacco asked. Nick turned in time to see Sacco's eyebrows bobbing up and down like a Jeff Dunham puppet.

Ramos blew a kiss Sacco's way, followed by a wink.

"What throws me off is Adnet's manner of death," Nick said. "It's way too complex, almost staged." He looked at Ramos. "Have you seen anything that elaborate before?"

"No. And it was a hell of a production. But, then again, there's always a first time for everything. You know that."

"Has anyone heard from OCME on autopsy time?" Nick asked and turned to write the info he knew about the second victim in the bedroom.

"Nothing yet," Sacco said.

"I don't know, guys," Nick knocked on the board with his knuckle next to the bullet points of the woman's mode of death. "This just doesn't feel right, especially when you put together both victims' MODs. It looks straightforward at first glance..."

"Nothing's ever simple with you," Ramos said, a hint of frustrated humor in her voice.

"What is apparent is that the woman didn't seem to have resisted the hanging. The obvious conclusion is that she was a willing participant, or she was incapacitated, even killed before being placed there." Nick looked at Ramos. "There definitely was no suicide note anywhere in the apartment?"

"Not on our cursory check, no. Not even in the notebooks Carpenter took from their office space." She turned to Carpenter for confirmation, which he gave with a short nod. "Doesn't mean we won't find one when we really get into the evidence."

"Maybe relatives, friends, and co-workers have more info," Sacco added. "Text messages? Social postings? We still have all those to check as well as interviews pending."

"But if there had been any messages to family or friends, someone would have either gone to the apartment to check or filed a missing person's report." Nick turned to Sacco. "Can you have Horowitz check into that?" he asked.

Sacco took out his cell phone and began texting.

"The victims may have left a written suicide note on their computer," Carpenter volunteered the obvious.

"We're still working on the premise of suicide based on what we first saw," Nick said. "Other options need to stay open."

"Mrs. Kyriakou did say Jessica Waitre was depressed," Sacco volunteered. "And there could be another possible scenario. We haven't considered the woman hanging herself, the boyfriend finding her and, not able to deal with her death because of their previous argument, kills himself."

"Hate to agree with Nick on this one, but your 'could be' is an unlikely scenario," Ramos said. "Her feet were eleven point three inches from the floor. And unless she was adept at using that pull-up exercise bar, she would have had to rig the rope in such a way where she would have had to lift her body weight feet from the floor, place her head inside the loop without dislodging it, drape her hair over the rope, and then drop."

Just like the Creasy case, Nick thought. The only hitch to that was that there were two people in the apartment, one of which could have assisted in the woman's killing.

Ramos shook her head. "Nah. There are easier and faster ways to go than what we found."

"Or a longer rope," Sacco said.

"Which the physical evidence doesn't corroborate," Ramos added.

Nick wrote the Tor and Reddit mentions next. Ramos's intake of breath was clear around the room.

"No fucking way," she said. "There's got to be a mistake there. The onion router?"

Nick turned. "According to one of the neighbors, Mrs. Kyriakou, the victims were arguing about it the last day they were seen alive," Nick told them. "She heard them going at each other in the elevator. The man was super pissed the woman had downloaded the Tor browser without his approval."

"She called it a Thor download," Sacco said with a smirk.

"Like the Scandinavian god?" Carpenter asked, incredulous.

"At least she remembered the thing," Nick said. "We need to verify if that and the Reddit info are true. May give a different spin to the case."

"Oh, shit," Carpenter said. "Even I don't surf the Deep Web, not unless it's work related. And I make sure I'm in encryption central here at work. There's some nasty shit out there."

"Well, our witness overheard a very upset Mr. Adnet berate his girlfriend about their online identities being in jeopardy."

"That's the least of their problems if they're surfing dark," Ramos said.

"You have a point," Nick said. "Mr. Kyriakou thought Mr. Adnet was more jealous than worried. But Mrs. K did bring up the fact that Ms. Waitre had been invited to a chat room months back."

"Did she say how far back?" Carpenter asked. "Gives me a narrower window to work with."

"No, just about the invitation. Again, this may or may not change how we approach the case. How much of a priority can you give to this, Carpenter?"

Carpenter shook his head as he finished his food. "I'm still working on three open cases, plus your Creasy case, and after this lovely hurdle you just plastered right on my face, I have to be extra careful. You'll get lucky if I can take out the hard drive and copy it by tomorrow. Analyzing it for password protection will take another good chunk of time, too."

"Hopefully, the victims are typical nontechies who will either write down their password somewhere or won't bother with one," Sacco said.

"That's a lot of maybes," Ramos said.

"You think?" Nick said.

Carpenter pointed to the board with his soda can. "Do you know how deep dark-web shit is encrypted?"

"To the eyeballs?" Sacco quipped.

"What about bringing in someone from Cyber Crime?" Ramos suggested.

Again, the shaking of the head from Carpenter. "They are super backlogged with their own shit," Carpenter said. "And we would still have to give them probable cause of a cyber crime to get them involved. So, guess who has to do the grunge work? And Reddit is a nightmare. There are sub-Reddits of the sub-sub-Reddits of the sub-sub-sub-Reddits. And that doesn't even take into consideration if the victims used a VPN on top of the Tor. Shit."

"Ok. Ok," Nick said. "So you've got your work cut out for you. What else is new for us? Just be aware the victims' online activity may or may not affect how we approach the case. That and what Totes can come up with at autopsy."

Ramos crumpled the empty wrappers of food and threw them into the now-empty food box. "Well, we'd better get our ass in gear and start sifting through the evidence." She turned to Sacco. "Thanks for lunch."

"Captain wants us back here for a briefing around four." Nick said. "Do preliminaries and bring whatever you have. We're off to notify the parents of the male victim."

"Let's hope they can give us good information," Sacco said.

But wishing and getting were two different things, Nick thought, erasing everything on the board. And, sometimes, they weren't that lucky.

CHAPTER EIGHTEEN

THE ODDS OF finding a spot to park in this area of Jackson Heights, known as Little India, were practically zero to nil, especially at this hour. Pedestrian and vehicle traffic competed for space and right of way at all hours of the day in this area of Roosevelt Avenue, with the elevated Flushing Line's steel anchors and cement platforms scarring the air and turning the surroundings claustrophobic. At street level, sidewalks and business fronts were chained in an almost perpetual penumbra, with steel subway brakes screeching in monotonous repetition, vibrating human flesh and cement structures like a constant case of tinnitus. Subway cars disgorged its human cargo every few minutes, adding to the cacophony of different languages, rumblings, and shouts that competed with the ceaseless honking and car traffic reverberations.

Nick thanked the cop gods that the mom-and-pop business, which the male victim's parents owned, was on the backside of Roosevelt and five blocks away from the super busy intersection with Broadway. Nick made a loop up Seventy-Fourth Street, round into Thirty-Seventh Avenue, and down Seventy-Fifth Street in order to access the stores on Thirty-Seventh Road. But by the third time around with no luck at a space to park, Nick's patience evaporated. He stopped at the intersecting corner, ignored the No Parking sign there, placed his "On Police Business" placard on the dash, and they exited the car.

"Good Lord," Sacco said, looking around the area for the business address. "Haven't been here for a while. It's a cultural smorgasbord."

They hadn't walked two yards, and they'd been visually bombarded with a cornucopia of advertising signs: big, small, round, rectangular, triangular, in Hindi, in Spanish, in Sanskrit, in Korean, bilingual, in blues and garish yellows, and all plastered on every conceivable corner of wall, windows, and doorways. Some hit the extreme edge on the gaudy meter; others were so discrete they got lost in the sensory overload.

"More like sorting through a floating refuse pile of advertising," Nick said.

"Can you imagine this place during the summer?"

"You mean barely any space to maneuver on the sidewalk, with street vendors selling wares in your face, or food trucks wafting their aromas into every corner?"

Sacco laughed. "Ah, New York. You've got to love it."

"Or hate it." Nick smiled. "Just keep a sharp one for the Punjab Emporium sign, will you?"

Sacco pointed to something farther down the road.

"I see something with a 'P' there."

The "there" he'd pointed to was a storefront next to a travel agency, which was slightly above a jewelry store by way of a small staircase, and with an Indian grocer on the other side, produce bins outside pressed against the store windows to take advantage of winter's natural refrigeration. The person guarding the foodstuff, however, looked utterly miserable, shuffling right and left to keep warm in the cold air.

Sure enough, the business came into view, its display window full of what was sold within: Indian souvenirs, saris, colorful cloths, incense, jewelry, statuettes, musical instruments, and even Bollywood DVDs. Nick opened the door, grateful for the heat and incense scent that greeted their arrival. Walking around and through the display floor was another matter. Goods were stacked everywhere, with barely any space to slip through. Trying to shuffle sideways, attempting not to bump into anything or crash it to the floor was a feat in itself. Nick felt he was back on the case he'd worked years back of a poor soul who'd been a hoarder. He'd died inside his apartment and one of Totes's people had been injured. Several pillars of newspapers, some seven feet high, had fallen on the tech, practically smothering him underneath the weight. Rescuing him, and then extricating the dead body, had been an exercise in extreme caution.

A petite, older woman emerged out of nowhere, wearing a patterned, colorful blue and gold kurti with a dupatta scarf around her shoulders. She addressed them in what Nick presumed was Hindi and he shook his head in apology, his incomprehension evident.

"Do you speak English?" Nick asked.

The woman turned and directed loud words to the back of the room.

A taller and younger version of the woman, similarly attired, weaved herself toward them.

"Can I help you?"

Nick and Sacco showed their shields simultaneously and identified themselves.

"We need to speak to Mr. and Mrs. Adnet," Nick said. "Are they around?"

"I am their daughter. Can I help you?"

"I'm sorry, but we need to speak to them in private," Nick said.

The woman stared for a second. "My mother isn't here. She's in India, helping one of my sisters-in-law with her new baby. My father should be at the grocery store next door." She called out to the woman, who now stood behind a small table with a cash register on it, and spoke quickly to her. Afterward, she grabbed her coat, draped it across her shoulders, and motioned for the detectives to exit the store.

Nick and Sacco followed her into the grocery store where her visits seemed frequent. Every employee and some customers voiced hellos as she passed by. She stopped for a moment to speak with a young woman behind a table laden with counter bins full of spices in every color, texture, and aromas. On the ground in front of the table lay open burlap sacks, knee-high, bulging with different rice varieties and grains. Getting the answer she sought, she led them to the back of the store where, stepping through the swinging barrier separating the retail space from the warehouse, she knocked on a small door. A voice gave the command to enter.

The narrow office was wallpapered with all types of advertising posters, and samples of foodstuff lay on every flat surface, including the two desk-sized file cabinets against the wall. It gave the small room a claustrophobic feel, further made smaller by an oversized desk. The latter's surface area was full of invoices, receipts, a calculator, and a computer. Behind sat a bearded man, his hair more salt than pepper colored, wearing something that looked to Nick like a longish, Neru-style shirt. When the man looked up at him, Nick saw this could be none other than the father of the deceased. The features were strikingly similar between this man and their victim, except for the gray hair and the beard. This was not going to be a pleasant notification of death.

The young woman went into an incomprehensible diatribe with the older gentleman. When she was done, they both stared back with identical expressions.

Nick and Sacco showed their shields and identified themselves once more.

"Mr. Adnet?" Nick asked in verification.

"How can I help you?" The man spoke in accented tones with surprising Queen's English overtones. "Is this about the theft last week at the shop?"

"No, sir. This is not about a theft. It's about your son, Desha."

Nick pulled a copy of the victim's driver's license he'd printed before leaving the precinct, opened it, and extended it to the father. "Is this your son, sir?"

The woman, who'd been watching their faces intently, suddenly grabbed the nearest chair and sat down, almost as if expecting to hear bad news. Unfortunately, it would be.

"Yes, that's him." He handed the paper back to Nick. "Is there some problem at his work?"

How to begin, Nick thought, disliking this part of the job to his very bones. He stared at the license photograph of this young man who, despite barely smiling back from the usual God-awful picture taken at the DMV, at least had had a future to look forward to two days ago.

"Is Desha okay?" The man stood.

Nowhere near that.

"Mr. Adnet, your son and his girlfriend were involved in an incident recently, and we're very sorry to have to notify you of your son's death."

The wail coming from the young woman raised the hair on the nape of Nick's head. It reminded him of what the Kyriakous had said about their dog, baying earlier that morning. Pain and loss were equal for both animal and human alike.

It didn't take long for all hell to break loose around them. The sister rushed to her father and collapsed in his arms, keening. The father yelled at them in his native language. Store employees opened the office door, their expressions one of shock at witnessing all that was happening inside. Nick and Sacco stood in the middle of the melee with emotions roiling over them.

Nick waited, glancing at Sacco, who had his serious face on, while chaos surrounded them. Death notifications were always a crapshoot, and you never knew how the victim's family would react. Nick had witnessed anger, laughter, silence, and fainting. Hell, he'd been punched in the face once when a victim's cousin had decided Nick's news wasn't to his liking. The man had thought the death notification a joke in very bad taste. Nick had not pressed charges, but his jaw had hurt for a week.

"Sir," Nick interrupted, needing to get the situation back in control. "We have to ask you questions about what happened to your son. I know this is very difficult, but it has to be done. In private." He turned to Sacco.

On cue, Sacco herded the employees out and closed the door. The weeping of the victim's sister echoed loudly in the now-quiet space.

"Please," Nick asked. "Why don't you sit down?"

The father ignored the suggestion.

"What happened? Was he mugged?" He leaned back to stare at his daughter's face. "Didn't I say moving to Manhattan would ruin him?" He cleared his throat as if to rid himself of the anger and pain he was feeling. "Was it an accident?"

"Sir, please," Nick pointed to the chair behind the desk.

Mr. Adnet whispered something soft to his daughter. She nodded in acknowledgment and sat in the chair her father had vacated minutes earlier.

"We're very sorry for your loss, Mr. Adnet, Ma'am," Nick said. "This is always a difficult and painful time for the family and we're grateful for your cooperation."

"When can I see my son?"

"The medical examiner's office will get in touch with you about that," Nick said. "We need to ask you some questions about your son. We'll try not to intrude too much on your grief."

Adnet simply stared, looking as if someone had thrown a bucket of ice water on him without notice.

"Your son was living with a young woman by the name of Jessica Waitre, is that correct?"

"Yes."

By the curt answer, Nick suspected the cohabitation was not a welcome one.

"Did your son, at any time, mention if he was having difficulties with their relationship?"

The simultaneous yes and no answers surprised Nick. And before he could continue his questions, a small spat erupted between parent and child. The words were fast and furious and, surprisingly, in angry whispers.

"Mr. Adnet. Ma'am," Nick interrupted in as loud a voice as he could manage without bringing back the curious. He was sure their employees milled around the door, listening to everything. "What do you mean by yes, Ms. Adnet? Did your brother explain?"

"That is a family matter," the father answered.

"Sir," Nick said, with as much patience as he could muster. "In unexpected death situations, unfortunately, privacy no longer applies." He turned to the sister. "Was he having issues?"

The woman glanced at her father and then at Nick. "Jessie was changing, getting moody more often than not. But when he found out about what she'd done, he was so upset. Threatened that if she didn't get professional help, he'd move out."

"What had she done that upset him?" Nick asked, already suspecting the answer.

"My brother is IT. Sometimes he works from home, and his computer is connected to his work. The company is known to do random checks on their employees' equipment at home. If they found out he had downloaded something illegal or done something he shouldn't be doing, he'd get fired on the spot."

"He was very careful of his work reputation," the father said.

"Desh didn't go into a whole lot of detail," she continued. "Only that she'd been surfing online in places where, if his work did a surprise audit, his job could be at risk."

"Where did he work?" Sacco asked.

"At TeC4M International," the father said.

Nick's hand stilled. *No fucking way. The victim had worked where Isabel Creasy's husband worked?* He felt Sacco stand at attention, too.

"Firm in Wall Street? Does telemarketing on a massive scale?" Nick asked, and rattled the address.

"You know the firm?" Mr. Adnet asked.

Nick's mind was racing.

"When was the last time you spoke to your son? Saw him?"

"He stopped by the store at around closing time on Monday," the woman said. "Then he came to see *baapu* here."

"When would that have been?"

She looked at her father. "At around six, six thirty?"

The father nodded.

"Was he angry or depressed when you saw him?"

"Depressed? Why would Desha be depressed? He's been a happy boy always, full of optimism. Constantly looking to the future, planning."

"He seemed a bit upset on Monday, though," the daughter said.

"Did he give you a reason for that?"

"None?" she said, the question directed more to her father than an affirmation to them.

The father sat down and covered his eyes with trembling hands. "He asked if he could stay with me this weekend. Said he had one or two things to work out and needed time to think without distractions."

"Did he expand on why he needed the time?"

"No. Desha is like that. Wants no help and will work through his issues privately. After he comes to a decision, though, no one can stop him. But a father knows when his son is upset. I suspected the reason and I got on his case with my usual complaints—Jessie was not good for him. He should look for a good Indian girl to marry. He was wasting his talent at that job. He should work here. Carry on the family business." His sigh was shaky, heavy with misery. "We fought."

"But you didn't fight all night, *baapu*," the daughter said. She hugged her father. "We talked about the new baby, about visiting India soon, and about the plans to expand the grocery store. We had a very nice dinner at Kashmir's."

"At what time did he leave?"

"Around nine. He took the number seven back home. Said he'd see us on the weekend."

"Do you know if he was having trouble with anyone at work? With friends? Financially?"

Nick received no answer. He studied the father's face and saw his eyes getting the glazed expression of introspection, of escape into memories and grief. The daughter's attention was also on her father's sorrow and her own. They were imploding. Nick decided to leave them be for the moment. He and Sacco could work with what they'd gotten. If what the father had said was true, the victim had had no thoughts of suicide when he returned to his apartment. What had he found there? Had they had another fight? Had he done something stupid and, in remorse, taken his own life? Nick now had to figure out when and why the dynamics at that apartment had changed. His gut rebelled against the obvious—that Desha Adnet had taken his own life.

Nick dropped his business card on the desk, in front of the father.

"If you remember anything else that may shed light on this case, please give us a call. The medical examiner's office will get in touch soon."

The father stared at Nick. The grief in those eyes slammed him.

"You never told us what happened. How Desha died."

Nick knew the answer would devastate this man, as it did any relative. But he thought about the OCME, the state of the body, and the clinical manner in which they sometimes dealt with death notifications, and thought it might be better if the answer came from him.

"Sometimes the actions loved ones take to escape problems seem incomprehensible to us. Unfortunately, your son and his girlfriend this morning were found victims of those actions." Nick paused, then continued softly. "We're still investigating, but it appears they took their own lives."

Nick nodded to Sacco, and they stepped outside the office. Many of the employees, still congregated around the door, created a small path for them to exit through. Nick felt like Moses parting the waves.

Outside, the cold slammed them. For once Nick was glad for its bracing impact.

"What are the odds?" Sacco said, walking at a brisk clip to the car.

"Infinitesimal," he said, feeling energized. "But it's a crumb, and I'm not letting anyone eat it."

Nick opened the car door but paused when he heard a woman's voice hailing them. The victim's sister rushed in their direction.

"Detectives," she said, a bit winded, the ravages of tears and grief still evident on her face. "There's something you should know."

Nick opened the back passenger door and tossed the car keys to Sacco. "Why don't you get in? It'll be more comfortable inside the car."

Sacco turned on the car and the heater while Nick slid inside next to the woman.

He waited.

"*Baapu* doesn't know about this. Desha asked for my advice the day he came here, you know, getting a woman's perspective?"

Nick nodded.

"He told me Jessie had been very depressed for a while. More overwhelmed than usual at work, too, and he didn't know how to handle it."

"Where did she work?" asked Sacco.

"At Charity for All, a company that helps what they call the underserved. She was the AA to the facility manager." At their puzzled looks, she clarified. "Administrative Assistant."

Nick jotted the information on his pad. He'd do a quick background on this Charity for All once they got back to the precinct. "Did your brother think her depression stemmed from her work there?"

"Sort of. She was not really hands-on with the treatment programs, but I told Desha that didn't matter. Jessie was still exposed to the communications end of things and that company dealt with pretty sad cases."

She glanced at Sacco and Nick. "Mostly, though, my brother thought she was depressed because she was lonely. When they moved in together, he was working at another firm and his hours were normal. But when he started with this company, his work schedule expanded. He loved it because his salary had practically doubled, but Jessie complained all the time that he wasn't there for her. That the time left to them was short."

"She thought he was neglecting her?"

She nodded. "But, then, several months back, she seemed to get back to being herself. Desha was relieved even though he felt things were still a bit off. But he was so busy. The company he worked for was expanding. He usually worked between twelve to fifteen hours daily and, at times, during off hours. When problems sprouted at work, he'd have to fix them immediately, even if it was at dawn. Very stressful."

"He worked from home on those occasions?" Nick asked.

"Sometimes. But lately, because she seemed okay when he got home, he really didn't pay that much attention until last week, when the company called him at two o'clock in the morning to fix something in the computer system."

"That's when he found out about the chat room and the download?" Nick asked.

She nodded. "Jessie had left a window open without realizing it. Desha discovered she'd been involved in this chat room, a real dark one, for weeks. A very depressing place, he said, filled with hopelessness and despair."

She closed her eyes. Rawness was on the surface of the memory. It sucked to be in her shoes right now, Nick thought.

"But?" Nick urged.

"Desha discovered she was using a browser Desha knew would get him fired. When he tried to find out more, he said the site was a jumper, deleting previous sites and opening new ones in order to avoid detection."

"Did your brother give you details?"

"No. He couldn't get into the new site without her password. That's one thing they were arguing about."

"What was the other?"

"He thought she was having an affair with one of the members of the group."

CHAPTER NINETEEN

NICK STOOD AT the head of the conference table. All eyes were on him, expressions reflecting varying degrees of digestion of the facts presented. He knew if he'd proposed this anywhere else, he'd be laughed out of the room or looked at as if he'd grown two heads. But this team had seen some weird shit throughout their investigative years together, had acted on marginal hunches, and hadn't outright dismissed sudden shifts in investigative directions. Sometimes the most insignificant crumb, even a hare-brained idea, had blown an investigation wide open.

"That's a hell of a stretch there," Kravitz told Nick. "Not to mention why that closed case was added on the board."

The connection between the Creasy case and the one from this morning could be labeled a stretch, granted, Nick thought, but it was what he, Sacco, and Ramos had suspected that morning investigating the crime scene. As to the other case, well, he needed to get Totes's input on it before he committed to anything.

However, the more pressing issue at hand was that, if what Nick had suggested a few minutes ago were true, the pressure from the chief, the mayor, the governor, the press, and the good citizens of New York would overpower them and the department like a tsunami.

Then there was the real possibility of nuclear fallout if his theory was a bust. God help them if that happened. The public excoriation would be brutal, with no flesh left on their bones and no place for him and the others to prosper within the NYPD.

"There's a common denominator linking the Creasy case and the one from this morning," Nick insisted, and didn't add his gut had been sending alert signals since they'd learned Desha Adnet had worked at TeC4M.

"The employer," Sacco tossed out into the room.

"That means we can choose from a mutual-acquaintances pool. Witnesses and even suspects to match to both cases."

"And the sister confirmed a possible affair?" Carpenter asked.

"At least a suspicion by her brother. Mr. Kyriakou said he suspected as much as well."

"I'll start digging on that once I'm outta here," Carpenter said, but his tone was not optimistic. "Can't promise quick results."

"We're wading into marshy ground as it is right now," Kravitz said. "The nasties out there are waiting to ambush the department for any stupid or minor slip-ups."

Nick knew who the nasties were and agreed with his boss.

"One miniscule hiccup and there go our careers down the rabbit shit hole," Kravitz finished.

Nick understood. It meant demotion city, with blemishes on their records, or them getting recycled to patrols or desk jobs.

"You've got to give me more than your gut and theories." Kravitz raised his hand, stopping Ramos from speaking. "Simply because one victim was married to a man working for the same company the other victim worked for, is shit on a platter. This is New York. Two cockroaches found within the same territory shared by millions is run-of-the-mill in this town."

"I know that, sir," Nick said. "And I just want the possibility out there. But, honestly, I'm not basing my suspicions on that, but on the method of strangulation of the women. They were too similar."

"What about the male victim," Kravitz asked.

"Not even close," Ramos said. "It was a hell of a production, though. Too much so." She whisked out her sketchpad, opened it, and moved it to where everyone at the table had a clear view of what she'd drawn. She described the crime scene in the living room in detail to the captain.

"Sounds convoluted for a suicide," Kravitz admitted.

"And why do it that way precisely?" Sacco chimed in.

"Why do it at all?" Nick said, shaking his head. "According to the father, the male victim was an optimistic man, with a bright future in sight. He was happy with his work and salary. He was going to spend the weekend with his family to figure out how to deal with his partner's depression and possible infidelity. What changed? What did he find in that apartment that ended his life?"

"Murder on murder?" asked Ramos.

"Possibility. What if Desha Adnet was wrong about a lover? Maybe Jessica Waitre was depressed enough to commit suicide, only she couldn't do it herself. What if she found a proxy in that dark-web chat room to help her? What if Adnet came in at the exact moment when the assist was happening?"

"He'd try to stop it," Sacco added. "I would."

"There was no struggle in the bedroom," Ramos cut in.

"That we know of yet," Nick said.

"Well, if that is the case," Ramos answered, "we should find transference on the evidence."

"Am I the only one here who's thinking there was a struggle in the living room?" Carpenter commented.

"No," Nick said. "But from the evidence, the chaos is limited to a miniscule area."

"Okay, hang on a minute." Ramos pointed to the sketch she'd drawn at the crime scene and tapped the area of the victim's head. "If we're going with the theory of double homicide, the only way the evidence could corroborate it is if Adnet was taken by surprise while sitting on the sofa."

"You're thinking ambush?" Kravitz asked.

Nick stared at the sketch.

"It would make sense only if Jessica Waitre invited this person in before her live-in came home," Carpenter said.

"Shit," Ramos said. "Where the hell would he have hidden himself without Adnet realizing there's a stranger in the apartment? I mean, a dust bunny could not even go unnoticed in that thimble of a place."

Nick glanced up. "What if this new person of interest was both lover and facilitator? What if they were taking a shower when Adnet showed up?"

Everyone stared at Nick.

"You've got to be kidding me," Ramos said. "Washing up before going to the gallows?"

"It's the clean underwear syndrome," Nick said. "Remember that case two years ago, where the victim had cleaned the bathroom to perfection after he'd showered? He then dressed in his best clothes, climbed into the tub, sealed the shower curtain to the walls with masking tape, and created a Picasso out of his head with a gun."

"Yeah, but that man was super OCD, according to his mother," Sacco said.

"Vanity. It's the same mentality," Nick said. "We all know it. It's the psychology of many suicides."

"They want to look their best at their worst moment in life," Carpenter said.

Ramos was shaking her head. "I don't know, Nick. We only found that one used towel under her. The others were neatly folded and untouched on the shelf above the toilet bowl."

"It could have been washed," Sacco suggested.

Ramos shook her head. "No washer and dryer in the apartment. And too risky a move to go get things washed in the basement laundry room. Someone from the building could have been there."

"Or the person could have taken it," Carpenter said.

"That's a possibility, too," Nick said. "But let's keep to what we saw and know of the evidence. What about this possible scenario? Adnet arrives, doesn't know there is someone else in the apartment." He turned to Carpenter. "Where were his wallet, phone, and keys found?"

"Wallet and keys were in a bowl on the kitchen counter next to the door," Carpenter answered. "We found his phone lodged between the backrest and a cushion of the love seat."

"So he didn't go into the bedroom, at least not to leave any personal stuff there. But he'd definitely hear the shower going when he came in."

"The assist hides in the bathroom while Jessica Waitre is showering?" Sacco asked. "That could work, too. Keeps quiet until the boyfriend is out of the bedroom."

"And like most males, the victim doesn't want a confrontation that evening," Nick continued. "He's mellow after visiting the family and only wants peace, at least until his significant other comes out of the shower."

"So what does he do in the meantime?" Carpenter asked.

"He can go into his home office to work."

Carpenter shook his head. "The computer was off, not on sleep mode. Then again, someone could have turned it off, too."

"I'll check for fingerprints," Ramos said, jotting down a quick reminder.

"Let's stick with the possibility he doesn't want to work. It's late. He's tired. So he acts like everyone else does when coming into a silent apartment."

"He turns on the TV," Sacco said.

"Or starts checking his phone," Carpenter added.

"Or both. Now, the person who is hiding has a serious dilemma," Nick said. "He's ready to commit a felony by assisting in a suicide, and he can't let Adnet know he's there. There's also another possibility—if Jessica finds out her boyfriend arrived, she may change her mind and the assist is over."

"But he is still compromised," said Ramos.

"Or in a very awkward situation," Sacco added.

Nick nodded. "Either way, if this person is discovered, he's screwed. He can't allow anyone to identify him. He already has a weapon handy, so he stalks into the living room, sneaks behind Desha Adnet, and strangles him."

Kravitz tapped the open sketch still facing them. "From this position, the victim would have seen the culprit coming, even if he were watching television."

"He could have been lounging a bit," Ramos said. "And if he were like everyone else, he could have been thumbing through his phone for messages, or watching videos, even surfing the net while the television was on."

"And remember, Captain, the perp would have had the element of surprise. Adnet's first reaction would have been to expect Jessica to approach. The response time to finding a stranger in his vicinity would have really delayed his reactions. That would have given anyone time to kill effectively."

"And after dispatching the main threat, the killer waits for Jessica Waitre to come out of the bathroom to finish her off?" Kravitz asked.

"That's my guess," Nick said.

"That's glacial, man," Carpenter said.

"The issue here is how do we prove all this," Sacco said.

"We need to find the link that connects these cases." Ramos slapped the table, grabbed her pad, and made some notes on it.

"Has anyone heard from Totes on the autopsies?" Nick asked.

No one answered. That meant he'd have to visit Totes in his digs. Not a happy thought.

"Let's hope he finds something fast."

"Thanks for the vote of confidence there, GQ," Ramos said, pointing to herself and Carpenter.

"Speak for yourself," Carpenter said, his voice a bit whiny. "This guy was IT. He'd have a password manager and encryption galore."

"You want me to talk to Cyber, kid?" Kravitz asked.

"Let me take a crack at it first," Carpenter said.

"Here's a thought to cheer you up, Carpenter," Nick said. "Jessica Waitre may have left a big trail of evidence in her computer at work."

Carpenter perked up and deflated immediately. "The big trail would be her phone, and we haven't found that yet."

"What do you mean you haven't found it?" Nick's tone was incredulous.

"Her phone and purse were MIA at the apartment. We've only got his," Ramos said.

"Not anywhere?"

"Zilch. And we were thorough. I'm hoping there's something at her workplace tomorrow, but I'm not optimistic," Ramos said. "No one goes anywhere without cell, wallet, or ID."

"Definitely not without a phone," Sacco added.

They all knew what that could mean.

Kravitz rose from his chair. "OK, everyone...scat. Keep me in the loop. And no mention of a serial anything. Once we have concrete evidence, then we'll let loose." He pointed to the board. "And erase everything. You know how nosy everyone here is."

CHAPTER TWENTY

WALKING INTO MILLSAP'S office was always an adventure, even when it was on the third floor over the morgue. Nick squeezed the menthol bottle inside his suit pocket like a talisman. It was always smart to keep it handy when visiting. Depending on how busy or slow the ME's day went, the odor clinging to Totes could be somewhat passable or overwhelming.

Regardless, the place always smelled like a hovering cloud of puke to Nick.

"Stop loitering in the doorway," Totes said. "It's not that bad."

Despite the reassurance, Nick sniffed the air with caution before setting foot inside.

Sacco thumped him on the shoulder.

"Come on," he said. "Be bold. Be macho."

"Not if he's going to vomit all over my pristine office," Millsap said.

And pristine it was, although Nick thought sterile fit it better. Stainless steel battled it out with pressed laminate in shelves, bookcases, file cabinets, and counters. Medical reference books, folders, and binders lay on every surface, whose haphazard arrangement only Totes fathomed. Open desks, joined side by side, created enough surface area to comfortably accommodate a computer, its screen, several copiers, plus other lab equipment.

There wasn't a speck of dust in sight to tickle the allergies.

"Thanks for meeting us on such short notice," Nick said.

Millsap took off his reading glasses and smiled. "Benefit of being the boss. I delegate on the obvious and nonchallenging."

Nick grabbed the nearest chair, rolled it next to Millsap, and sat. Sacco flanked him across the way.

"Will you be performing the autopsies on Desha Adnet and Jessica Waitre?"

"Your victims from this morning?"

Nick nodded.

Totes studied Nick's face a second, dropped his folded glasses on the desk, and leaned back.

"Wasn't planning to. You suspect it's more than suicide?"

"May or may not be. The woman's MO was incredibly similar to the Creasy case. But the man? That's a different story. It smells of foul play, although it could be suicide."

"But you don't think so."

Nick shook his head. "Signs of a possible struggle were evident. Still debatable if staged or last throes."

"Staged? How so?"

It would be like Millsap to seize the important tidbit in the explanation.

"Convoluted, more like," Sacco volunteered. "If I had wanted to commit suicide, I'd choose something simple. Suicides usually do what's fast and expedient."

"It was quite a production," Nick agreed. "Honestly, I'd feel much better if you performed the autopsies. With you at the helm, all bases will be covered."

"Spill."

For the next few minutes, Nick explained everything about the case, including their theories and suspicions about a possible link between cases. By the time he finished, Millsap was no longer relaxed.

"If your gut is right, we're fucked."

"And that's not the best part," Sacco added.

Nick unfolded the case file copy he'd shown Ramos yesterday.

"Do you remember this bag and tag?"

"The farewell and master Post-it dude," Sacco pointed out.

"Ah, yes. The Victor Hugo case." His amusement showed. "Literati he was not."

God help him and medical examiners who thought themselves comedians.

"Why are you asking?"

"I'm interested to see if those marks on the neck, the ones that you couldn't quite identify, were ligature marks."

Millsap stared. Without getting up, he suddenly rolled back his chair and swung left toward a group of binders. He chose one and returned to his desk in the same manner. He flipped the bulky ring binder open to the case he wanted, and began reading his notes.

"He was quite juicy when we got him," Millsap said. "Most of the evidence on dermis was lost. Visible pattern on the epidermis showed chain design tattoo surrounding neck. Impression pattern from the gold chain he wore was evident on the dermis, but random."

"How?"

"Parts of the chain had been caught by the tape when the man was sealing himself in. The pattern was obvious where the tape held the thing in place."

"It was definitely from that chain?"

"Yes. There should be photos of it in the file. The plastic bag around his head was also incredibly tight. It left impression patterns, as well. So did the duct tape. Found evidence of allergic reaction where tape met skin. The patterns I couldn't distinguish were in the back of the neck and really faded. Couldn't match it to the chain or anything else around him." He looked at Nick. "According to the evidence, there was no indication of foul play, forensically, as well. Open-and-shut case of suicide. The team working the case thought so. Nothing to corroborate the contrary." He closed the binder with a snap, not happy at this possible new development.

"Can he be exhumed later on if need be?" Nick asked.

"Smoked and shipped to the family," Millsap said, shaking his head. "Word was they would scatter him to the four winds somewhere in Colorado."

Great.

"Anything new on the Creasy case?"

"Waiting on hair and vitreous. Lab promised results this week. Will you be attending the Creasy memorial?"

Nick nodded. Isabel Creasy's friend, M-Li, was holding a memorial for her friend on Monday. In ambiguous cases, he always liked to study the mourners. Oftentimes, it opened the suspect pool.

"When are the Adnet and Waitre autopsies scheduled?"

"This Friday."

Nick wasn't happy he'd have to wait two more days for something. Anything.

"We'll be there." He'd almost reached the door when Millsap called out.

"I hope, for all our sakes, that your gut is wrong this time."

So do I.

It was close to end of shift when they arrived back at the office. On the way back, Nick had taken advantage of a traffic snarl and secured a meeting with Waitre's employer the next day. Unfortunately, the manager was available only before the cock crowed, so no one was happy when Sacco disseminated that information to the team.

"Hey, Lieutenant," Horowitz greeted Nick. He and Carpenter were talking up a storm next to the elevator. "You saved me the trip. As you suspected," he said and extended phone message slips to him and Sacco. "Charity for All did file a missing person's report on the Waitre woman." He nodded to Nick's desk. "I placed a copy of the report on your desk about an hour ago."

"Thanks, Stan. When was it filed?" Nick asked.

"Logged into the system today." Horowitz pointed to the stack of messages Nick held in his hands. "Death desk is also asking for details on the suicides this morning. Same dissemination?"

"Tell Nat to keep the details of this as under wraps as possible," Nick said, which was code for nothing except two dead bodies found. Natasha Bronson, their Public Information Officer, was a pro at keeping things diluted when necessary.

"Got it. Usual tagline—details, ages, and identities not released pending family notifications, etc."

"That should keep the bottom feeders at bay," Carpenter said.

"Don't insult sturgeons," Horowitz said, angry undercurrents vibrating in his voice.

Nick understood Horowitz's mood. The latest incident with the media had happened that afternoon. Several thugs, riding both motorcycles and ATVs, had ambushed a lone officer while he safeguarded abandoned property at a gas station. The harassment and aggression by those individuals had been dutifully videoed and posted on social media.

It had gone viral.

Local and national news outlets, the new gossip centers, had lapped it up. Anything was worth print and airtime if it embarrassed the NYPD. Media really didn't care about the danger posed to the policeman from the taunting thugs, circling around the officer like sharks. Just the mere presence of law enforcement was insulting, racist, and provocative. Headlines describing the latter had been dutifully splattered across national print and television screens since four o'clock.

If it bleeds, it leads.

Everyone in the department was seriously pissed, not to say worried.

"One day..." Horowitz left the rest unsaid. Escalation lurked.

"FYI," Carpenter said. "Just did a document dump of Isabel Creasy's social media presence. Shared the file with you, Sacco, and Ramos for access."

"What about the Adnet computer?"

"Making a copy of the hard drive as we speak. I'll be going through half the evidence found in their office tonight. Ramos is taking the other half." He looked at Nick. "Still planning on the early interview?" Carpenter asked, his face hopeful he'd receive a negative to his question.

"Sorry. The manager hasn't changed the appointment at cock's crow. Set your alarm for bright and early."

"The captain is not going to be happy with our overtime." And with a colorful expletive, Carpenter turned and headed to the evidence room.

Captain wasn't happy, period, but he'd approved it, grudgingly. After tomorrow? New overtime was a no-go, since the department was fully staffed and back to normal. Budget constraints didn't allow for any more overtime. More's the pity.

"I think I'll go help Ramos scour the evidence," Sacco said, and followed suit.

They scattered in all directions.

Nick reached his desk and discovered Records had brought up the evidence boxes on the closed Hugo case he'd requested. The slosh of paperwork was hitting him in incremental and ever-higher waves, he thought. He texted Laura saying he wouldn't be able to see her tonight as planned.

No good loving for them this evening, unlike what the song said.

For the next three hours, Nick went about creating death books for each victim and filed incident reports on everything. He reached home at the stroke of midnight, dead tired. He glanced at Laura's apartment window overlooking the street, wishing for an excuse. No lights. Shame. Although he would have loved to wake her up bite by sensual bite.

He breathed deeply, letting the cold shock his system, plodded up the entrance stairs to his building, grabbed the mail, and, once inside his apartment, dropped keys and wallet next to his laptop. He headed for the kitchen, took out the Food Emporium's lasagna he'd picked up days ago, nuked it, and went to take a quick shower.

By the time he left the bathroom, he'd reenergized. Too much so. He glanced at his bed, not for the first time wishing that Laura were in it, or he in hers. Wouldn't it be nice if he could spend hours exploring her nooks and crannies, cataloguing and savoring her reactions? Her body was so deliciously new to him. He could spend hours loving and wallowing in the physicality of it all.

Talk about an effective release to his edginess.

Instead, he consoled himself with the piping hot pasta and the beer he'd grabbed on his way to his favorite spot on the couch.

He opened the Hugo file and ate while perusing the photographs of the crime scene.

The victim had been a mess, just as Millsap had told them. What was even freakier were all the colorful Post-it notes scattered and pressed against every conceivable horizontal and vertical surface near and around the victim. Each single piece of paper, in all colors, shapes, and sizes, expressed the dead man's demented final messages—"master" and, especially, "farewell." It was as if the victim's brain had been branded by those solitary words and had needed to regurgitate them in mindless repetition. Every screaming word created in permanent marker ink with sprawling, bold lettering.

What had made this man plummet into such a vortex of insanity? How could the human brain become so dysfunctional as to exhibit this psychosis?

Nick placed his empty plate on the coffee table, got more comfortable, and scrutinized the close-ups of the victim. The man was leaning back in his computer chair, head back, as if exhausted with life, his features indistinguishable inside the translucent bag entombing his head. And, indeed, as Millsap had said, the tape holding the bag in place had been tight. The face and upper neck had remained practically normal, while the lower neck had inflated like a balloon. So much so, the tape had dug into the skin.

He stared at the close-ups of the neck. The gold chain was there, caught under the tape in several places.

Could his suspicions be wrong?

Nick looked at the clock and sighed. He'd been up before dawn and his brain was mush. He needed to decompress, even if for a few hours.

He shut down the computer, crawled into bed, and had barely closed his eyes when the alarm went off.

Thursday, January 16

BY six, everyone was stamping their feet to keep warm, waiting for the manager of Charity for All to open the door. The compound was in the Long Island City neighborhood that boasted the identical name of the Queensbridge Houses only a few blocks away. And, like everything else in the area, this business was surrounded by iron gates guarding the building and a parking area beyond.

"Where the hell is this guy?" Sacco complained for the fourth time. He banged on the entrance door facing the sidewalk with his fist. "Aren't the employees supposed to be here early for interviews?"

"Yes. Manager said he would inform everyone last night. At least, that's what he told me when I set everything up. Said he'd meet us here by six," Nick said.

"This sucks," said Ramos. There was no place where the cold had not already invaded their bodies. "Should have stayed in the van. I'm giving this sucker two more seconds. Where the hell is your car?"

"There," Nick said and pointed to the double-parked car behind him. His gloved thumb hit the redial button on his phone.

The manager's voice came through after the third ring. Straight to voicemail. Shit.

"Your car's closer than the van," Ramos said. Carpenter was so hunched inside his coat he resembled a turtle avoiding predators. "Tag, you're it."

They hustled to the vehicle in record time and practically dove into it. Nick turned the heat full blast.

"I can't feel my nose," Carpenter complained.

"And they say global warming will kill us," Ramos said. "Assholes. All of them."

"What's with this guy?" Sacco asked, his face practically on top of the vent.

Nick redialed. Same answer. "Keeps going to voicemail." He left another message.

"I really want to be done with this. I need to go home at a decent hour today," Carpenter complained. "Stacey is about to brain me. And I'm exhausted."

"Come on, kid," Sacco said. "Your girlfriend is all goo-goo gaga still."

"That's because little Carpenter here is a big tiger in bed," Ramos quipped. "Rumor has it the nights are hot, long, and heavy."

"Good grief, Ramos," Nick said, laughing. "You need to get out of the gutter more often."

"Screw you, baby," Ramos answered. "Although I presume the action at Laura's was spectacular."

"He's keeping details close to the vest still, but, oh boy, look at that smug face." Sacco laughed. "That smile speaks volumes."

Nick wasn't about to fall for it. "How was the evidence hunt last night?"

"Chicken," Ramos accused.

"Most of the stuff I waded through was from college—class notebooks, projects, and lab notes," Carpenter said. "The man was an info hoarder."

"And the notebooks we read through," Ramos added, thumbing to herself and Sacco. "Were also the man's. All kinds of IT shit. Notes, ideas, presentations, logs, problems solved at work, and workshop transcripts. Had a ton of quotes and references from techie magazines, blogs, and websites. I'm sure his web browser will have even more bookmarks on his favorites. No suicide notes anywhere, yet." She turned to Nick. "What about you?"

"Bust, for now."

A sedan turned right in front of Nick's car and stopped at the gate. A man, so bundled up he was barely visible, fumbled with the security code panel on the wall, and the gate creaked its way open.

"Finally."

Everyone, except Nick, scrambled out and scurried to their respective vehicles. Nick followed the sedan into the lot and parked next to the manager's car. The manager dutifully held the back door open until they all hustled inside the facility.

"Sorry I was late," the man apologized to all. "There was an accident on the Verrazano. By the time you called, I was ten blocks away."

He shook hands with all. "Vince Orbe," he said. "I'm the facility's manager. This is quite a shock. Quite a shock. Your heart just goes poof and you're a goner. Can't believe she's gone. Life is so precious, you know?"

Nick didn't disabuse the man of his assumption. He'd only mentioned Ms. Waitre was dead when he'd arranged this meet yesterday.

Orbe guided them through what had once been a cavernous warehouse, now converted into sections to accommodate the functions of this nonprofit outfit.

"I gave everyone the bad news last night and asked if they could come in early, like you asked. They all agreed. Should start filing in soon."

"What services do you exactly provide and to whom, Mr. Orbe?" Ramos asked, genuinely curious. "I've never heard of your outfit."

"We like to operate under the radar. Low profile, you know? In this neighborhood we help the homeless, the poor in the nearby projects, and the addicted," Orbe explained. "Mostly the addicted now. We also offer free services to many low-income families who need basic medical care."

Orbe pointed to the rooms on their right and to their left. "In this section we have basic dentistry, medical, even outpatient minor surgery. We set bones, stitch wounds, vaccinate, even delice. We're blessed that many doctors in the tri-state area donate their time and money to treat these poor souls."

Not unlike Doctors without Borders, but with better digs.

"Do you keep drugs in the facility?"

"No. It's security we can't afford, not on our slim budget. And if word got out we had drugs on the premises? Too risky." Orbe didn't have to explain the consequences to them. "We operate under strict regulated appointments for services needed. Our distributor then delivers what the doctors need on a case-by-case basis, depending on the procedure performed, and removes unused stock daily. Many doctors also bring what they need from their own practices. Any other medications are prescribed, and the client has to fill them at the pharmacy of their choice."

They passed a wide reception area with a desk and several computers, then veered to another section to the right. The hallway was wide, flanked by entrances to rooms on either side. A small rectangle of clear glass, fitted on the wall next to every closed door, afforded a spacious view of the interior.

The manager caught Nick's curious glance as they passed. "The see-through glass is protection for the therapists and social workers," Orbe told him.

"Tamping down possible lawsuits?"

Orbe nodded. "Some addicts sell their toenails and claim abuse in order to get cash and a fix. Others offer quick blow jobs to get money for drugs. And then there are the unhinged, who can attack without cause, especially if they are off their meds. Every room has a closed-circuit security camera and a panic button."

He continued his tour guide spiel on monotone. "This section is reserved for therapy. Most of our homeless and addicts suffer multiple mental health issues, so we have a rotating staff of one psychiatrist, two psychologists, and four social workers. Our goal is a holistic approach to the individual: If you heal the body, you can heal the mind. But, lately, it's a losing battle. The drugs these people ingest are getting scarier by the minute. Incidents with pinky, bath salts, spice, and gray death are rising. We have to be particularly careful."

At that, all of them looked at each other. NYPD was familiar with these latest, deadly blends of designer, synthetic drugs. Want an old run-of-the-mill high? Let's get you some cocaine. Want an atomic blast? Bath salts are your thing. Want to pack a punch that will, literally, down an elephant? Try some pink, pinky if you are fond of cute diminutives, or gray. Pick your color. Nick knew the area around and underground the nearby Queens Plaza, especially during weekends, was a hub of private strip clubs, prostitution dens, and illicit drugs marts, where they sold the really scary shit— pink or gray. Mixed into a deadly cocktail with heroin, small doses ingested sent you on a free ride to the morgue without much effort. Pink's effects, at least, could be countered with Narcan, if caught in time, but the gray death? That shit was lethal and absorbed through the skin in a millisecond. Even using protective gloves offered slim protection. Nick knew of an incident with an officer in Ohio who'd overdosed by touching a bag during an arrest. EMS and doctors treating the addict were also at high risk.

They reached a wide area toward the back, where prefab walls and windows had formed a rectangle smack in the center. An industrial kitchen, similar to some found in schools, stood empty on the left. Round tables and chairs spotted the remaining area, each table with its own napkin holder. On the right, at the very edge of the space, were snack and soda machines pressed against the wall between the bathroom entrances.

Orbe ushered them into the room within the room.

"This is our office," he said, and walked back to a desk at the furthest right-hand corner. "Jessie's desk."

Nick nodded to Ramos, who beelined it to the area.

"I need the password access for your system," Carpenter said.

Orbe jumped at that. "I can't let you do that. We have very sensitive information on our servers, not to mention the tons of HIPAA and other privacy issue violations."

"The warrant is specific," Nick said, and handed the document to the manager. "We're only interested in personal emails or anything of that nature that's there. We'd prefer to make copies here rather than have to lug the computer with us."

Carpenter simply stood there, waiting.

"I'll sign you in."

After Carpenter got his wish, Nick gestured for the manager to follow him outside. "Why don't we sit down until my people are done? We have a few questions about Ms. Waitre."

Orbe nodded, but kept a watchful eye on Ramos and Carpenter through the windows, his expression worried. He sat at the nearest table.

"This sucks. Really sucks." He looked at Nick. "Never in a million would I have guessed. Thought maybe she was playing hooky. But that didn't jibe, either. If she'd skipped, it would have been for a sick day, and she would have called."

"That's why the missing person's report?"

Orbe nodded. "She loved work. Barely took any time off. Our clients loved her. Yesterday was the baby shower for Irma, our receptionist? Jessie would not have missed it."

"What were her responsibilities here?" Nick asked.

"She does, I mean, did, I...shit." Orbe took a deep breath. "She did all the administrative assistant work dealing with our homeless and drug treatment programs. Whatever our program director or I needed, she'd do. That could be assist purchasing, inventory control, deliveries, appointments, and coordination of services. She also tended phones, mail, and faxes."

"Did she seem upset or depressed to you lately?"

"A bit. Always took things too much to heart sometimes. But it happens to all of us. This type of job gets to you, you know? Dealing with the sick of society can do that. But we get over it. Family support is our greatest ally, and Jessie had Desh. The other thing is," Orbe continued, glancing at both of them. "Once we clock in here, we're so busy we don't get much time to mull over our own emotions. But you should talk to Daine Lunney, one of our rotating social workers. Those two used to hang around at lunch a lot. Jessie looked at her as a mother figure, sometimes even helped with Daine's cases. She'd be your best barometer. Should be here soon."

"Other than her boyfriend..."

"Poor Desh. How's he taking all this?"

Neither Nick nor Sacco volunteered the boyfriend had bought the farm, too.

"Did Jessie hang out with anyone else here? Outside?"

"Listen. I mind my own business, although, I once overheard Daine and her talking by the soda machines. She was warning Jessie about something dangerous and Jessie dismissed it. I didn't hear the rest. Daine would be the best one to know."

Personnel began to peek every so often into the area where they were. Nick looked at the manager. "I see your people are filing in. Let's schedule two at a time for interviews. Could you start sending in those who knew Jessie best, first? That way we can get the interviews done without much interruption to your needs."

Orbe nodded and strode toward reception. True to his word, two people appeared, one a very pregnant Irma, eyes swollen from tears.

Nick identified himself and Sacco, and the interviews began. They spent the next two hours talking to every employee and volunteer who filed in. By the time they were done, hunger was making Nick's stomach embarrassingly active. Through the window he saw Carpenter closing his evidence kit, and Ramos explaining the evidence sheet to the manager. They were having a very energetic conversation.

He turned to Sacco. "Anything that juts out?" he asked.

His partner shook his head. "Nothing outstanding, except she was nice...she died so young...her poor fiancé, boyfriend, whatever..."

"Yeah." Nick rubbed the back of his head. He was itching for some breakfast. "Same here. We'll compare notes when..."

"You Detective Larson?" a woman's voice interrupted.

Nick turned. The belligerence in the tone surprised him. Petite, dressed in a conservative black pantsuit, the woman's posture and expression were aggressive, made more so when she flattened a hand on top of the table and leaned forward, her body language an in-your-face, better-pay-attention-now attitude.

"I don't give a shit how you take this, but I say Jessie was *murdered*. I'm sure of it."

"And you are?" Nick asked, his voice calm.

"Daine Lunney," she said.

He pointed to the chair next to her. "Please, Miss Lunney. Have a seat."

She ignored the request. "And it's Mrs. Lunney."

Sacco dragged his chair and placed it beside Nick's, while Nick introduced him.

"Murder is a strong accusation, Mrs. Lunney. Why would you say that?"

"I told her," she stressed each syllable, and every time after each *told her*, she rammed her finger into the tabletop. "Told her that meeting was dangerous. Told her to stop texting him. Told her the online site was not only depressing, but also creepy and manipulating its members." Her eyes glazed. "Especially for someone in her frame of mind."

"Which was?"

"The world sucks, people suck even more, apocalypse is the new black, we have no future, nothing is worth living for, people hate me, and Desh despises me. Can't do anything right. I'm worthless. Don't have a life. Gloom and doom to the max. Last time I talked to her..."

"When was that?" Nick interrupted.

"Monday. Here, at work. I told her to stop what she was doing, go to therapy and talk to Desh, even if Desh wasn't in a very forgiving mood at the moment."

"Why not?"

"She'd downloaded something from the net that may have compromised his work computer at home. To an IT man like Desh, that's like poisoning your own child. I tried calling him yesterday, again, but he's not answering his cell. He must be devastated."

Nick glanced at Sacco. Second time someone assumed Jessie was the only victim. He'd leave it that way for now.

"I'm still confused why you'd bring up foul play."

"Tell me this, because I don't believe this bullshit she died of a heart attack. Did she ingest pills, or was it drugs? Suicide, right?"

"I'm not at liberty to say the method used, but yes, it was suicide."

"I knew it. Here." She dove a hand into her pocket and dragged out her phone. "Let me show you." She flicked it on, scrawled a convoluted pattern on the display screen with her finger, and scrolled through to the information she wanted. She amplified what was there and extended the phone toward Nick. It was a text message. Sacco leaned forward to see it better.

_____Mon, 1/13/..._____

Desh going to leave me. Fed up. Stormed out. U said not 2, but I'm seeing UNoWho 2nite again. Understands my pain. Knows how to help. Has just the thing to make me feel better.

6:28 P.M.

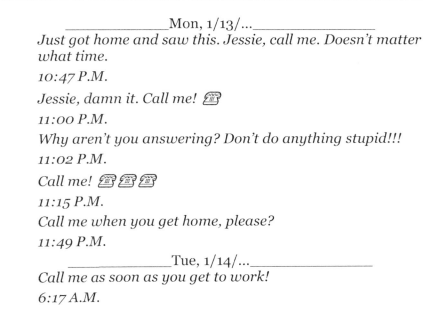

_____Mon, 1/13/..._____

Just got home and saw this. Jessie, call me. Doesn't matter what time.

10:47 P.M.

Jessie, damn it. Call me! ☎

11:00 P.M.

Why aren't you answering? Don't do anything stupid!!!

11:02 P.M.

Call me! ☎ ☎ ☎

11:15 P.M.

Call me when you get home, please?

11:49 P.M.

_____Tue, 1/14/..._____

Call me as soon as you get to work!

6:17 A.M.

Nick saw Lunney had kept the barrage of "Call me!!!" texts going until last night, when he knew the manager had contacted all employees about Jessica's death.

"Monday is date night with my husband," she filled in as Nick pointed to the times on the screen with his pinkie. Sacco nodded. Lunney had just corroborated a time frame of death that matched that of the Adnets'. "I was on the subway on my way to Canal, so I didn't feel the vibration when the notification came in. And we don't look at our phones when we're having time together."

"May I?" he asked, extending his hand for permission.

"Sure." She placed the phone in his cupped hand.

Nick minimized the window and pulled up the recent phone log history. Jessica's name and number popped up daily, practically hourly, Nick saw, until last night.

"Mind if we copy this?" Nick asked.

"Be my guest."

Nick strode to the office, opened it, and called out to Carpenter, who stood next to Ramos. She was asking questions of the manager.

"What's up?"

"Listen. Mrs. Lunney gave us permission to copy this." Nick maximized the text message window, then brought up the call log. "And this."

Carpenter, no slouch at capturing visuals quickly, whistled under his breath.

"Anything of value in the office?" Nick asked.

"Not much, yet. Dragon fire there," Carpenter's head twitched in the direction of the facility's manager, "didn't give me much privacy to check." His fingers flew confidently over the screen, dropping down menus, typing, and forwarding things at the speed of sound. Nick envied the young who zipped through the landscape of technology with the ease of navigating a familiar neighborhood. "Kept hovering and riding my ass at everything. I spent my time duplicating all Jessica's files on the thumb. I'll check later, in peace and quiet."

A couple more maneuvers on the phone and Nick had it back.

Carpenter turned, but Nick stopped him. "Still no sign of Jessica Waitre's phone?"

"Nada."

Nick returned to a now-sitting Daine Lunney. He handed back the phone and pointed to it.

"Do you know who this 'UNoWho' Ms. Waitre was referring to is?"

"No."

"She also wrote 'again' on that text. Had she met this person before?"

"For coffee and God knows what else. Two months ago. I told her it was dangerous." She swallowed. "Here we are."

"From all you've told us, she was depressed..."

"Clinically depressed, yes."

"Why didn't she seek help?" Nick asked. "You have therapy services here. Why didn't she take advantage of them?"

"Embarrassment, pure and simple. Didn't want anyone here to know. Told her if not here, then there, or anywhere." She cleared her throat, tears threatening. "She didn't."

"Were you close?"

"As close as anyone can be to a co-worker. She was a sweet soul. Achingly young." At Nick's look, she sniffed. "Listen, I may not look it, but I'm close to the big six oh. Hell, my kids are older than her by more than a decade."

Nick's lip twitched upward.

"She was also a dichotomy—street smart and yet incredibly naïve. Too gullible and easily hurt on the personal level, if you ask me. I don't know what's with this younger generation, but there's a lack of resilience to some of them. No armor. Almost stunted in some areas of emotional growth. Self-absorbed to the point of narcissism and when things don't go their way, they disintegrate emotionally. No resistance against brutal reality."

"Immature, then."

"No. And yes. Not quite." She shook her head. "Shit. Can't believe I'm screwing this up. Been at my job for twenty years, and I can't find the freaking words to adequately describe her."

"Why don't you take a calming breath and try again," Nick urged. "This has been upsetting."

"To say the least," she admitted. She closed her eyes and breathed deeply. Canyon deeply.

"Okay. Jessica lived in a sort of artificial bubble, wallpapered in a Disneyesque view of life. She was the Princess protagonist in her own fairy-tale script, who searched and hungered for approval constantly. She defined herself through others."

"Unlike some of us tough-skinned New Yorkers," Nick said. Case in point...him. He didn't give a rat's ass what others thought of him.

Lunney smiled a bit, appreciating the momentary lightness.

"Unfortunately. Coping became an issue for Jessica. Her perfect world was fraying at the edges. The more Desh worked, the more needy she became, and that plunged her deeper into the morass of social media." She ended the last statement with a heavy sigh. "There's some really unhealthy shit out there."

Nick agreed. Social media was a never-ending voracious cesspool of want to the vulnerable. Nick didn't know why the selfie on Isabel Creasy's phone came to mind, the one where she seemed to be entreating the universe for acceptance. Nick knew that anyone who didn't have the proper emotional filters in place could easily be brutalized at the slightest rejection. He'd seen the results.

"And, despite your warnings, Ms. Waitre kept at it?"

"Yes. Her world was small and growing smaller. Not many friends here, just acquaintances."

"She's not from New York?" Sacco asked.

"No. Grew up somewhere in New Hampshire. Came to the city as a teacher for one of those teach-the-US outfits that sells idealism to lure in desperate graduates needing a job but which, instead, rounds them up tight into a miserly two-year stint at the worst schools in the area."

"I've heard of those," Nick said. "You're roped in like a bad cell phone contract."

"She met Desh at the Bronx high school she taught in during the last months of her tenure there. He was a temporary replacement for someone in the computer lab." Memories brought a fond smile to her face. "The way she described it, it was love at first sight. What I really think is she thought of Desh as her savior. He's funny, ambitious, and smart. He offered reprieve from ugly reality, which left her free to step back into her fairyland. So she poured all of herself into his life, his friends, which is also a mistake, especially taking in the cultural differences. You can't erase your personality that fully without consequences.

"Unfortunately, when your self-esteem meter predicates on everyone else's acceptance, well, that's not a good place to be at. Jessica was constantly checking for likes, for comments, for support. Her time outside of work was consumed and subsumed in those postings."

"Faux reality in small sound bites and photographs," Nick said.

"You got that pegged right. To a depressed individual, however, everyone seems to be having more fun, living a happier life, a fuller and richer life. Depressed people experience all that and only see their void, which seems to be the size of the Marianas Trench. They forget things in social media are basically snapshots of life smaller than a Band-Aid, but it expands the emptiness they inhabit. Add to that the constant negativity and issues here at work, well, it makes the emotional abyss a tad darker and harder to overcome. Without therapy, faith, family, hobbies, or a good support group to anchor you, the exposure to the void leads to drugs, or worse, suicide. And we have an epidemic of that in the young."

"And Jessica was in that rut," Nick stated.

She nodded.

"I'm sure working here, with the clients you deal with on a daily basis, wasn't helpful," Sacco stated.

Lunney leaned forward. "Working in a place like this may satisfy some people's sense of good karma, but, emotionally, it's a vacuum cleaner to dust. Don't get me wrong, it helps the clients...well, some of them, anyway."

"Not all?" Nick asked.

"A high percentage are so far gone from drug abuse and mental illness that there is no turning back, except institutionalizing them. We, unfortunately, have to send them back into the streets, where they just walk one click to Queens Plaza and pick their favorite drug flavor." She took a calming breath. "Let's not go there."

"Tell us about the chat room, if you can," Nick said, veering the conversation back.

"Horrible place."

"Can you give us information on that?"

"Not a lot. We talked about it several times over lunch, but after the creep got hold of her, she became more secretive," Lunney said. "Spent hours on it at home, though. Desh should know. Have him show you."

"Do you know, more or less, why this..."

"Creep got in touch?" she interrupted. "Somewhere around October, Jessie discovered an online forum of depressed people who were toying around with the idea of suicide. I told her to get the hell away from them after she showed me some of the conversations."

"But she ignored you," Nick said.

She nodded. "A couple of weeks after, someone contacted her through the forum's messaging board. She showed me the text. There wasn't much to it, except the snide remark that the people in her group were all liars and that, if her intentions about suicide were really serious, he'd help." She huffed in deprecation. "Guy was in serious need of a spell check, too. Anyway, when she told me she was considering his suggestion, I went ballistic. A mistake on my part. Never confront depression with anger. But I was so frustrated with her, and also scared for her. Despite my warnings, Jessie turned a deaf ear to my advice. She made contact with the guy and avoided me afterward. She only opened up last week, but only after Desh found out about what she'd been doing."

"She finally asked for advice?"

"More like wanted a sounding board to validate her misdeed. That's when I found out she had previously met the creep for coffee. According to her, he was a nice man, who understood her pain because he was suffering, too." She breathed in as if she needed oxygen and looked at Nick with sorrow. "What bull. This guy is a stalker. Knew the exact buttons to press. He may not have done the actual deed, but he pushed her to do it, I'm positive. Maybe even supplied the drugs for an overdose. Ultimately he's responsible for her death. You need to find that internet site and get his ass before someone else dies."

"We'll do our best to figure things out," Nick said, his tone reassuring. "You've given us a good deal of information we didn't have before." He took out his card and slid it over to her. "If you remember anything else, even if you think it's stupid, please call me, or Detective Sacco. Every bit of information is important."

"When you see Desh," she said, tapping the card on the table in an impatient gesture. "Can you ask him to call me?"

"Mrs. Lunney," Nick said, getting up. "I'm sorry to be the bearer of worse news, but Mr. Adnet is also deceased."

The shock evaporated all thought, all reaction, Nick saw. By the time he left with Sacco, Daine Lunney still sat immobile, frozen like Lot's wife the instant she'd turned to watch the conflagration.

CHAPTER TWENTY-ONE

"HERE WE GO...again," Nick whispered, entering the elevator that would take them to TeC4M's floor.

Breakfast had not settled well. He'd had to wash down the dry, all-natural muffin from the miniscule joint down at Water Street with tasteless coffee. Worse had been the constant complaints from Sacco about the new-fangled plant-based bull advertising that meant absolutely nothing, except as a means to guilt people into buying overpriced goods. Didn't flour and sugar come from plants, Sacco had grumbled?

Nick hadn't disagreed. Organic... plant-based... natural... regular... it was all a marketing con. He simply wanted to have had time for a hearty breakfast of eggs, bacon, pancakes, and potatoes. He was still hungry.

His stomach echoed the sentiment.

They arrived to find the same receptionist at the welcome desk, concentrating on a computer screen to her right and speaking simultaneously into her wireless phone headset. She turned and gave a little start of surprise.

"Guess she recognized us," Nick said to Sacco.

She mumbled something quickly and tapped her ear for silence as they approached.

"Detectives." Her voice reflected not only surprise, but also a ton of curiosity. "How can I help you today?" She paused. "Here to see David again?"

People can't help but be nosy.

"Actually, we'd like to speak to..." Nick took out his flip notebook and searched. "An M. Jeffries, your IoT manager."

She tapped the gadget in her ear and quickly pressed some numbers on the phone pad. "Yeah, hi, Maressa. Two NYPD detectives want to speak to you." After the briefest pause, she asked, "She'd like to know what this is about and if it can wait. She has a meeting in five."

Nick smiled. "Police business. And no, she'll have to skip that meeting."

She relayed the message and, once more, tapped her ear. She gestured to a small space facing her desk that served as a reception area. "She'll be right out. You can wait for her there."

Nick thanked her, moved away, but didn't sit.

Sacco leaned into Nick, his voice low and his back toward the receptionist. "What the hell is an IoT?"

Nick looked at his open pad. "Internet of Things. And don't ask. Haven't the foggiest. Had to find out from Carpenter what the hell that acronym meant."

"Damn jargon for everything."

Nick agreed. Technology changed faster than warp speed. A great aid, as investigative tools went, but only if you could differentiate the newest binary Dick from gigabyte Adam. A learning curve every six months.

He felt his phone ping, and read the message.

"Ramos and Carpenter are on their way. ETA in ten minutes," he said and turned at clicks on the floor. Maressa Jeffries was approaching at a fast clip. She was short and compact. Preppie looking, with an angular face framed in a short, professionally cut and maintained bob of jet-black hair with azure highlights. The latter covered her ears and neck in chic layers. She compensated for her stature with incredibly high heels, and her silk blouse, as blue as her hair, was tucked inside gray pants that screamed dressed for management.

"Gentlemen, we're really busy here today. How can I help you?"

Nick and Sacco flashed their shields and identified themselves. "Ma'am, can we speak in private?"

"What is this about?"

"Ma'am. We need to speak in private," Nick repeated in his best, somber cop voice.

After a small pause, she gestured to a door a few feet to the right of the receptionist and ushered them into a windowless, rectangular conference room with an elliptical table and corresponding ergonomic swivel seats occupying most of the space within. It reminded Nick of their interrogation rooms in that it was claustrophobic. The only plus here was the better decoration and comfy chairs.

Jeffries automatically went for the head of the table and sat, placing her cell phone within finger reach.

He and Sacco remained standing.

"I'm really rushed, gentlemen. I can give you ten minutes, tops."

"We're here about one of your IT employees, a Mr. Desha Adnet."

"Desh?" Her confusion showed in her next question. "I thought this was about David and the death of his wife."

"No, ma'am. Can you tell us about Mr. Adnet and his work here?" Nick unfolded the DMV copy he'd shown the father. "This is said employee, correct, Ms. Jeffries?"

A quick glance, with an even quicker nod confirmed the answer.

"What can you tell us about him?"

"He's one of our best IT persons. Recognizes the issue faster than most. Responsible. Prioritizes his jobs well and there's no job he won't tackle. Logs on time when working off-site, is goal oriented, and very professional. If you want to speak to him, though, he's not here. Took some PTO due him starting Tuesday. Should be back tomorrow." She stared at them. "Is there a problem?"

When neither Nick nor Sacco answered fast enough, she turned cautious.

"Do I need to get my supervisor or legal involved?"

"No, ma'am." *At least, not yet.* "Unfortunately, we're here to notify you of Mr. Adnet's death."

She stared, struck speechless, her eyes rounding wider with every second.

"What?"

"Mr. Adnet and his partner were found dead yesterday morning at their apartment."

"Oh my god." Her breathing escalated. "Oh my god, oh my god, oh my god. This is going to screw up so many schedules, projects..." She grabbed her phone. "I have to notify HR, our supervisor..."

"Ma'am..." Nick began, but she wasn't listening, looking at her phone calendar and vocally ticking off bullet points in her brain.

Nick placed his hand over the phone screen and gently lowered her hands to the table.

"Ms. Jeffries, we need to ask you questions about Mr. Adnet. I know this is difficult, but we need you to focus."

Her eyes calmed. Nick sat next to her and Sacco took the chair opposite, flanking her.

"What can you tell us about him? Were you friends?"

"Friendly co-workers," she said quickly. "Nothing outside, except at company-sponsored events and employee celebrations. But you couldn't help but be extra friendly with him. He was always upbeat. Mega optimistic. It was infectious."

"So there were no issues here?" Sacco asked.

"Minor ones and all work related, but...don't we all? Our work is high stress, so is our frustration when things don't work, or when someone screws up the system."

"Was he upset or dejected lately?" Nick asked, but quickly clarified. "That you noticed, as far as his interactions here at work."

"No, not at all," she said. "Just super quiet and focused." She paused. "More than usual, now that I think about it. But everyone's overworked in the department. The cyberattacks to our system have been vicious lately, and we've been going crazy deflecting them and fortifying our firewall. We have a shitload of data on our customers that hackers would drool over to either sell or ransom. Desh was working on a new security solution for our verticals to avoid future breaches. Inventing new shit. Mega advanced."

That last statement agitated her. "Shit, shit, shit." She sprung up, her priorities slamming her. "How the hell are we going to finish that project? This is a disaster."

Nick stood, ready in case she bolted. Sacco did the same. They weren't finished here.

"Miss Jeffries, please." Nick gestured to the chair. "That you know of, did Mr. Adnet have any personal friends here? Enemies?"

"Enemies? What? Didn't you hear me before?" At his expression, she added, "No. No." She looked around the room as if it could give her clues. "I mean, there's always a dash of healthy competitiveness in IT, but nothing noticeable or reportable to HR. The only people I know Desh socialized with here were David and his wife. They seemed to have hit it off. "

"David Creasy?" Nick asked.

"Yes." She stared at Nick. "Oh." She sat very slowly. "Oh."

Nick didn't know how she was putting her two and twos together, but was certain rumors would fly as soon as they stepped out of this room. Rough days ahead for Mr. Creasy.

"We need to see Mr. Adnet's office..."

"Cubicle," she interrupted. "No one here has an office, except the CEO."

Employees blended into a homogeneous heap, Nick thought, unwittingly surveilling each other for the company's benefit. Very *Animal Farm.*

"If you could show us his work space, we'll be as unobtrusive as possible."

"I have to run this by HR and legal..."

"Ms. Jeffries, Fourth Amendment rights here are no longer applicable. We need to check his workspace for any evidence that could clue us as to why the victim died in such a manner. We'll need to check his computer, as well, for personal communications linked to the case."

"Definitely not," she said, outraged. "Our computer has proprietary information in it and you'll need a warrant to get anywhere near it. Of that I'm certain." She grabbed her cell, made some fancy maneuver to open the screen, and began to text at manic speed. "I'm getting in touch with legal right this minute."

Nick didn't respond. He simply opened the door and glanced out. Carpenter and Ramos, together with two other FID techs, were waiting in the lobby area. As if on cue, both turned at the sound of the opening door, saw Nick's head movement in invitation to get up close and personal, and approached.

"Can I have the warrant?" Nick asked Ramos.

Ramos stared at Jeffries, who had stopped her furious texting at the sound of the word "warrant." She handed the document to Nick, who handed it to Ms. Jeffries.

"This covers anything inside, or on, Mr. Adnet's desk, as well as any personal communications in the computer that can be of evidentiary value." Nick stood by the open door. "Now, if you could please lead us to his desk, we would appreciate it."

Nick stepped out, not giving Jeffries much choice but to follow.

By now, several employees were loitering around the receptionist's desk, all curious, all speculating in hushed voices. Nick and the team ignored them, waiting for Jeffries to lead them.

"Hold all my calls," she snapped at the receptionist. "And get legal to IT as soon as possible."

The woman, continuing in a staccato huff, bypassed the glass doors on their left, which led to the main hive of workers Nick had visited before. Instead, she guided them through another set of doors, this time solid wood, at the opposite end from the conference room they'd exited.

A small hallway, heavily carpeted, muffled their footsteps.

It was incredible, Nick thought, how corporations differentiated employee strata with subtle, but effective subliminal codes. The drone area, where Isabel Creasy's husband labored, huffed and puffed like a well-oiled machine. No one, not even those in the company's reception area, could evade the constant humming and buzzing of human activity and noise.

This space, however, felt almost meditative, where words should be hushed, whispered. No sacrilegious vocalizations. Definitely entering a higher plane, where the real merit and distinction existed. And, definitely, the higher pay grade.

Well, we'll disrupt that peace soon.

He was wrong.

The sounds of chaos blasted them. Startled, they pivoted in unison, Nick in an almost crouch, hand on gun, expecting a frontal assault.

"Detectives, please." The receptionist sped walked in nervous hiccups to them, her voice a bit distorted in its volume and anxiety. "Please, please come. They're going to kill each other. I called 911, but you're nearer."

Nick turned to Jeffries. "We'll handle this. Ramos?"

She nodded in understanding, placed a hand on Jeffries's back, steering her toward their original destination.

Nick and Sacco hurried the opposite way, following the receptionist, who was already at the connecting door.

Angry words blasted the air when she opened it. Above the din, Nick identified the higher pitches of a woman, screaming at the top of the decibel scale, and a man's voice, equally angry, trying to overpower the woman's. In between, other voices rose and fell attempting to calm the offended parties.

Nick and Sacco stepped into the lobby and scanned the room, assessing the situation, but paused at the sight greeting them.

"No fucking way," Sacco said next to him.

In the middle of the fray stood none other than M-Li Watson, Isabel Creasy's best friend, scarlet faced, straining against the restraining hands of EriK Wexler, the massage therapist from the New Age spa. Facing the virago, and equally restrained by co-workers, was none other than David Creasy, spewing verbal jabs at his ex-wife's best friend.

"You are a fucking bastard," Watson spat the words at Creasy. "A screwing, opportunistic dick of major-league proportions."

"And you are a conniving bitch," Creasy shouted back.

"M-Li, please," Wexler said. "You've got to control yourself."

"Yeah, asshole," Creasy turned on the massage therapist, derisive contempt on his face. "Control your leash handler before I brain her."

Nick saw Wexler's jaw clench, knew that underneath the coat, the muscles were gathering and tensing. The situation would deteriorate into a free-for-all in less than ten seconds.

"Shit," he said under his breath. "You take Creasy," he told Sacco. "I'll take Watson and friend."

But before he and Sacco could reach them, Wexler smiled in the nastiest way possible and released M-Li Watson, who went after Creasy's face with perfectly manicured claws. Nails raked flesh, real hatred fueling her actions. Creasy roared, as blood pooled around the visible welts.

"You bitch." He swung at her and missed. "I'll sue you for this."

"You already did," she spat back, trying to get another piece of him.

"NYPD," Nick's voice boomed. "Enough."

The authoritative bellow froze everyone. It gave Nick and Sacco enough time to reach the melee and bodily divide and conquer. He faced M-Li Watson and Wexler, his back to Sacco, their bodies a solid barrier between the two who wanted a piece of each other.

"Don't make this worse than it already is," Nick warned her.

Watson wouldn't have it. Wexler, less riled, understood the message on Nick's face and grabbed her arm, holding her in place. Despite the restraint, she leaned to Nick's left, staring daggers at David Creasy, and wagging an angry finger at him with her free hand.

"That bastard has no scruples. No humanity."

"Get off your saintly melodrama," Creasy's voice came from behind Nick. "You two were going to screw me over." There was a pause. Nick turned to face Creasy, saw his palm blot his face.

"Fuck. I'm bleeding," he said.

"Should have gone for your balls, you son of a bitch," Watson said, still incensed.

"Bitch," Creasy yelled and made a move toward M-Li Watson.

The guy was really going for her, Nick thought, flabbergasted. *What an idiot.*

Creasy, however, had forgotten Sacco. His partner shifted, blocked, body language Morse coding he'd tackle Creasy's sorry ass to the floor.

"You want to be forcibly restrained?" Sacco warned and dangled his cuffs in front of Creasy's face.

"That goes for you as well, Mrs. Watson," Nick warned. "And I strongly suggest you not move or say another word."

"M-Li," Wexler said, grabbing her shoulders this time. "Listen to the detective."

"I'm pressing charges," shouted Creasy. "I have witnesses. You all saw what she did to me, right? Right?"

"Settle down," Nick said, emphasizing each word. "As it is, you've both given me enough reason to cuff and charge."

It was as if a dam had burst open. M-Li Watson turned to Wexler and collapsed against his chest, sobbing. The man patted her back with hesitant taps, clearly awkward with giving comfort.

Nick turned to the growing number of people surrounding them. He figured most were there to ogle in morbid curiosity rather than help. The area needed to be cleared.

"OK," Nick said, turning around three-sixty in order to catch everyone's eye. "I want everyone out, except these three. Get back to work."

The area emptied out quickly, with one or two co-workers patting Creasy on the shoulder, offering support.

"Why aren't you arresting her?" Creasy pointed at her. "She started it."

That got M-Li Watson riled up once more. She turned around with ferocity. This time, however, Wexler kept a good grip on her.

"Me?" she huffed. "You're suing me for something that doesn't belong to you. Opportunistic bastard. And Isabel not in the ground yet."

The elevator banks dinged and two patrol officers stepped off and approached. Nick quickly identified himself and Sacco.

"Need one of you to call in another unit over here," he said. "Then please escort this gentleman to the Sixteenth. Have Sergeant Horowitz there put him in an interview room."

The officers nodded, one calling dispatch from his shoulder unit, while the other went for Creasy.

"What?" Creasy was outraged. "I'm not going anywhere." He began to back away.

Sacco, who wasn't too pleased, jiggled the cuffs. "Your choice. Go quietly, or get these slapped on."

"This is police brutality," Creasy complained, but stayed still.

"What I've got is plenty of probable cause," Nick said in disgust. "Disorderly persons, assault."

"Not to mention dispute in a public place," Sacco added.

"I want my lawyer."

God, Nick thought, this was turning into a shit day. He hoped Laura was having a better one.

"WHERE the hell are you taking me?"

It was close to eleven o'clock and their cab was heading uptown, nowhere near Laura's apartment. Minutes ago, she and Erin had left the lawyer's office near Midtown. Contracts had been finalized, read, signed, and filed. Money transferred.

She no longer had a business in NYC. Her original dream was snuffed.

Very depressing.

On a lighter note, she had a future venture in another state and a healthy paycheck from this buyout.

The best, however? Nick. Hands down.

"It's a surprise," her friend said. "I knew you'd be down in the dumps after the lawyers. So I made arrangements for a treat."

"Please, not food," Laura said. She didn't think she could enjoy a meal at this moment. Besides, what she really wanted was to find Nick and get lost in his lovemaking, a definite plus in generating endorphins. He was a meal she could indulge in for hours.

The cab stopped. When she got out onto the sidewalk, a trendy day spa boutique franchise business faced her.

"I booked us two hours of decadent pampering," Erin said and grabbed her hand. She pulled Laura inside before she could protest or back out.

To most, the place was nirvana to the senses: muted New Age music, invigorating scents, infused waters, and restrained, identically attired employees, whose only goal was to serve and please.

Laura felt she was in a *Westworld* movie set.

"I don't know..."

"Oh, shush," said Erin and gave their names to the smiling receptionist.

"You're all checked in," the woman said within seconds, her voice soft so as not to create jarring noise ripples in the atmosphere. "Your massage therapists will be out shortly."

Erin grabbed Laura again and dragged her to the small waiting area, the air filled with the soothing echoes of running water.

"Listen, I'm not going to run away."

Erin dropped her arm and filled two cups from a water glass container with slices of cucumbers floating on top. She handed the water to Laura.

"You're going to love this place. One of our clients recommended it, and it's got raves on Yelp." She took a sip of the water and sighed. "I came to sample the goods two weeks ago. Divine."

Laura sipped her water. Erin gulped the rest of hers down and grabbed some more.

"And you know we need this," her friend said and plopped into a cottony chair. "We've been under a ton of stress."

"There's that," Laura agreed.

"And my winter skin needs a ton of pampering."

Laura grinned.

"Ms. Devraux? Ms. Howard?"

A male and a female staff member, megawatt smiles creasing their faces, searched the waiting room. Within a millisecond, Erin had planted herself in front of them, eager to start.

Amid light, polite banter, they were guided into a couple's room with soft lights, soft music, two massage tables, and an array of Crock-Pots on top of a counter at the edge of the room that held black and pink rocks separately. The soft hum of a whirring fan added the closing period to the ambiance statement.

"We really, really need to relax," Erin answered the query of the male massage therapist, whom she'd selected when given the choice. "We've been under megaton stress."

The woman turned to Laura. "We'll definitely pamper your muscles and get all that tightness out in a jiff. Once the session is over, we'll escort you to your facials."

They were given directions to lie face down under the covers and given a few moments of privacy to disrobe to comfortable level.

"What the hell is comfortable level?" Laura asked.

Erin stopped stripping to stare. "Please tell me you've had a massage before?"

"Well, ah, no."

"You never fail to amaze me," Erin said and continued disrobing. "No bra. Panties are an option. I leave on my thong."

Laura disrobed, leaving her panties on. She was about to scoot under the warm blanket when her phone pinged.

"You're supposed to mute that," Erin scolded in a soft tone.

"It's from Aaniyah," she said and read. The message was short.

Appeals deliberated. We lost. Negotiating details and filing appeal.

Laura scooted under the blanket and placed her face down on the headrest. Her tears dropped silently onto the carpeted floor.

"SANDRA." The correction officer's voice reached her from somewhere in the vicinity, outside the doorway of the prison's beauty salon. "You have a visitor."

"That would be my lawyer," Sandra said and retrieved her hand from the inmate. She was today's guinea pig for the manicure. Many of the women holed in this dump took advantage of this stupid recidivist program the incarceration system do-gooders provided for prisoners. A chance to become model, productive citizens once they shook off their puke-green jumpers.

Tax dollars hardly at work.

"Don't give away my spot," she said and caressed the woman's face. "I'll be back in a snap, sweetie."

Sandra smiled. She always played nice when convenient. This trainee had talent, unlike the other inmate who'd royally bungled the manicure job months back. That bitch had made Sandra's hands ugly, with bleeding cuticles and messy nail-polish edges. But she'd thanked the woman as though she weren't seething inside, knowing opportunities to get even always abounded. Sure enough, kitchen duty several weeks ago bumped her into the manicure butcher. So, as one who always took advantage of a situation, Sandra had snatched the eye drops she'd pilfered a while back from an inmate who suffered from chronic allergies, had dropped a few squirts into the soup the butcher was preparing, and had continued with her duties.

The results had been delicious.

She nodded to the waiting corrections officer and followed her. As they approached the meeting rooms, Sandra did a quick inventory of herself while brushing her hair with her hands.

"Prepping for your act?" the officer asked.

"What act?"

The laugh came out more like a snort.

"Curtain's up," the guard whispered cynically, ushering her inside.

Sandra ignored the comment and concentrated on her lost-waif persona. She waited by the door, seemingly afraid to move forward.

Sure enough, her new lawyer rushed to her side and carefully guided her to a chair.

She wanted to snicker, but simply smiled.

Strike a pose. Isn't that what the Madonna song said? Hands between her legs, shoulders hunched, eyes on the edge of the table, Sandra became the picture of docility, signaling with her posture and expression a tad of dejection sprinkled with a dash of hope for a positive answer, while expecting none. She'd perfected the move since the age of thirteen, where she could work up the sympathy factor on some of the johns her mother pimped her out to. Usually, the ones who fell for her act were family men, or professional career men, who already felt guilty enough about their need to whore. When they found out she was a minor, they were more than happy to dish out more money than the job cost and, mostly, went home content with the minimal, sloppy blow job. The extra money given, she pocketed and saved.

"I'm afraid to ask," she said low.

"The court ruled in our favor, Sandra," her lawyer said, a pleased note in his voice. "You'll be evaluated by a team here..."

Her head snapped up and her eyes narrowed. She caught herself in seconds. *Shit.* She'd almost blown her charade. And she needed to keep him in the dark as long as possible. Fortunately for her, Mr. Lawyer was reading a text on his phone and had not seen her reaction.

Back into pose.

"Here?" She looked up, rested her arms on the table, hands clutched. "I thought maybe I'd be transferred first."

Mr. Lawyer shook his head. "That was the only nonnegotiable for the prosecutor, and the court agreed."

She generated a trembling sigh and made sure tears welled in her eyes.

"But, how could you say we won? I'll still be here..." She scanned around in quick, furtive movements, and leaned forward. Her next words were whispered, only for him. Mr. Lawyer leaned in, exactly as she wanted.

"...with the murderers," she whispered, tingeing her last words with sufficient horror.

Sandra watched the lawyer's eyes fill with compassion. *What a patsy.* He often forgot *she* was a murderer. It was just unfortunate she'd gotten caught at it...this time.

"It's a delay, yes. But it works in our favor," he said and clasped her hands. "Be patient. The court wanted to establish preliminary evaluation before transfer. It will demonstrate the necessity for treatment, which was blatantly dismissed previously. Egregious conduct, and constitutional rights trampled, like I've said before. You belong in the psychiatric facility. Not here."

She squeezed his hands hard.

"You are my savior." She made certain her voice cracked with emotion. "The only person who believed me and fought for justice. I want... No. I deserve punishment for what I've done, and the loss of freedom is the cost, I know. But I deserve to get well and have my mental condition treated with a little humanity."

She brought his hands up and caressed them with her cheek, like a puppy begging for tenderness.

"Thank you." Under her eyelids, she kept an eye on Mr. Lawyer's reaction. "Thank you."

What she saw made her want to laugh.

What a patsy.

CHAPTER TWENTY-TWO

NICK, HAND ON doorknob, stopped. Took a calming breath. Angry didn't define his mood at the moment. Creasy and company had cost them two hours of investigation into the Adnet case. Two hours down the tubes. Not to mention the waste-generating reports because of this bull incident. If he could have his way, he would dump them in holding for the next forty-eight hours as a cool-off period. Instead, he'd have to waste valuable time on interviews and pussyfoot around his favorite, lawyers.

Ramos, Carpenter, and the FID techs had come back pissed from TeC4M as well. They'd had to deal with constant interruptions and lack of cooperation from the IT people while gathering evidence. Usually, Nick and Sacco would field any distractions so Ramos and her team could do their work effectively. Instead, they'd been handling the bozos now waiting in the precinct's interview rooms.

"Where's my lawyer?" David Creasy's voice boomed as soon as Nick opened the door. "I'm not talking without him. And I need a doctor. Look at my face."

So much for finding out what the brouhaha had been all about in a cooperative and civilized manner. That pissed Nick more. He slammed a legal pad in front of Creasy and deposited a pen next to it.

"What the fuck is this for?"

"I need your statement of this morning's events," Nick said, sorry he couldn't throw the pad at the man's face. A pain in the ass couldn't describe Creasy's attitude ever since Horowitz placed him in this room. "That should keep you entertained until your lawyer arrives."

Nick turned to leave.

"Hey. Where are you going?" Creasy pushed the writing pad away. "I can say what happened faster than I can write it down. Don't you have a recorder or something? And I'm thirsty."

Asshole, Nick thought and felt a whole lot better. "You invoked. Legally, I can't hear or ask a single question until your legal representative is present, even if this is only an informal interview." *Asshole.* "As a matter of fact, I shouldn't even be in the same room with you." Nick pointed to the pad. "Write...please."

"This is bullshit," Creasy grumbled, but he drew the pad closer and picked up the pen.

Nick left before he actually blurted the asshole chant in tune with his thoughts.

He joined the others gathered round the screen monitoring the interview rooms on this level. He sat on the corner of the nearest desk and watched with the others. M-Li, head bowed, was still crying, ignoring the pad in front of her and creating a little pile of used, crinkled tissues next to it. EriK, with the capital K, was writing profusely, as if an open faucet was linked to his hand and brain, the words flowing without pause onto the paper.

"Were you able to reach Mrs. Watson's husband?" Nick asked at large. He felt sorry for the poor woman, whose heart seemed to be breaking with every sob.

Sacco nodded. "Should be here any minute."

Ramos leaned forward and shook her head. "That guy is writing a freaking Bible," she said, pointing at the massage therapist. "Hasn't paused for breath. Unbelievable."

Sacco shrugged. "Maybe he's feeling verbose."

Ramos chuckled. "Going SAT on me, Sacco? I'm impressed."

"What can I say?" Sacco said. "You're rubbing off on me."

"You are what he'd like to be rubbing off on," Carpenter said.

"Jee-sus," Nick said and made as if to cover his ears. "Crudeness abounds. Let's concentrate here, please. Anything of value in Adnet's cubicle?"

"Nothing, except I did find a small diary-like journal that doesn't quite seem to fit the profile of the man," Ramos said. She looked around, a smirk on her face. "Pink with little curlicues on the cover."

"Probably swiped it from his girlfriend," Nick said.

"My bet is a definite yes. I would have, if I'd discovered my significant other had been downloading shit from the dark net. I'll check it as soon as I get to the lab. It may have personal info...maybe even passwords in it."

"What about you, Josh?"

Carpenter shook his head. "Nothing except work related. From what they allowed me to see, the guy was good. He was inventing his own version of code to create a stronger firewall for their system. Impressive."

"They ride your ass too much about getting his personal emails?" Nick asked.

"Still have the burn marks," Carpenter said, a smile hovering on his lips. "But I'm nothing but persistent. As far as this Adnet guy, the man was either really professional, ethical, or paranoid. I suspect a bit of all. Every email and computer file was clearly catalogued and work related. I'll dig later for any hidden files."

"If the man was that good in all things IT, I wouldn't put it past him he'd hide things," Nick said and scanned the monitors. He saw Wexler had stopped writing.

"Let's get this show going," he told Sacco and stood. "Let me know if you get anything new on the evidence you gathered today."

Ramos nodded. "Powwow and Thai food in the conference room at two?"

"You know what I like," Nick said and walked the few steps into the room holding the massage therapist.

"Thank you for your cooperation, Mr. Wexler," he said by way of preamble. "You remember my partner, Detective Sacco?"

Wexler nodded.

Nick sat opposite him, while Sacco lounged on the chair at the corner of the room, behind the man.

"Where is M-Li? I want to see her."

"Mr. Wexler, we'd like to go over what happened at TeC4M this morning." Nick patted the pad, which he'd taken and placed near his left hand. "And thank you for your statement." Nick would read it later to compare notes.

"I'm worried about M-Li. She can't be alone at this moment."

"We've notified her husband," Nick said. "In the meantime, why don't you run down the scene for us at Mr. Creasy's employer, please?"

Wexler's expression hardened. "What a bastard. Do you know he had the gall, the freaking gall, to sue us?"

Nick gave a noncommittal hum. Wexler took it as his cue to continue.

"She called me early this morning. I thought she wanted to hash out more details about the memorial service. But, no. God, I've never heard her that angry."

"She told you Creasy had sued?"

Wexler shook his head. "Not when she called. She simply told me to meet her at TeC4M. Honestly, I thought David was being an asshole about the memorial. She'd asked him...hell, more like begged him...to contribute to the cost of the flowers, but he'd brushed her off."

"What happened when you did meet her?"

"When I got to the lobby, she filled in the details. Explained what he'd done and that he was claiming community property or some such bullshit to get ahold of the patent and profits. I couldn't believe it. And yet, I could. I just don't know how he found out about the product trials. He always thought Isabel was tinkering with her creams and chemicals as a hobby that kept her amused and away from him. By the time she told me what happened, M-Li had worked herself into a lather."

"And upstairs?"

"I tried to calm her down. Hell, I was trying to calm *me* down. While on the elevator, we came up with a stupid strategy to be reasonable, to ask him nicely."

"But that went to hell when you requested to see him?" Sacco asked.

Wexler glanced at Sacco and back at Nick. "Exactly. We asked nicely the first two times. But when he told the secretary to call security to throw us out, that got M-Li going. She walked over to the connecting door, opened it, and screamed at the top of her lungs for David. And *that* got *him* riled. He came at us, furious. The receptionist was beside herself."

Nick eyed Sacco for a second. That corroborated the receptionist's earlier recounting of the event, although her version was more colorful. According to the woman, M-Li had marched to the glass doors, ripped them wide, and had yelled at the top of her lungs, "David. You bastard. If you don't come out here this minute, I'll drag you out of your synthetic cubicle and wipe the floor with your deceitful face, you scum." The receptionist had stared wide-eyed at both Nick and Sacco as she continued, "She would have, too. Went totally nuts. That's when I rushed to get you."

Nick leaned back and studied the man facing him. Today he was wearing jeans and a sweatshirt, his hair still frizzed and up in a disheveled man bun. His earlobes were sans grommets, deformed, as if ballistic missiles had bored through, permanently scarring the lobule and leaving them exposed and deflated like misshapen balloons. Why on earth people self-mutilated was beyond him.

"You deliberately let go of Mrs. Watson when you knew she was so out of control. Care to elaborate?"

Something ineffable flitted across his eyes and was gone in a second.

"I'm human, so sue me. Oh, wait. He did sue me." He shrugged, but leaned forward. "I evened the score. Lying scumbag. And I don't care if he's disfigured for life. Shame he won't be."

So much for love of neighbor, thought Nick. Strange, though. It had also left Wexler's hands clean. He wasn't the one facing possible charges.

A low vibration sounded. Wexler reached into his jeans' pocket, dragged out his phone, and checked the message there. "Listen. Am I under arrest or something? I've got work to do."

Nick shook his head. "No. You're free to go for now. We'll contact you if anything else is necessary."

Wexler stood.

"Before you leave...did you know a Desha Adnet or a Jessica Waitre?"

The man closed his eyes as if he were in deep thought. "Nah. Doesn't ring a bell. I can do a quick check of client names, if you want, but if they're not regulars, I wouldn't know." He walked past Nick but paused. "What about M-Li?"

"I'm afraid she'll be our guest a bit longer." Nick signaled Horowitz from the doorway to escort their guest out of the building.

"Please go easy on her," Wexler said. "She really didn't mean it."

Nick said nothing, watching Horowitz lead the massage therapist to the elevators. Runaway emotions always had consequences. As it stood, things could go two ways for Wexler's friend. One: charges would be lodged, parties booked and released on bail or, two: they'd make nice after Nick explained a few things, then leave with a small slap on the hand, and a hefty fine for disturbing the peace.

More lawyers. More paperwork.

Lovely.

Nick went to his desk, dropped the pad with Wexler's statement upside down on top.

"Husband and lawyer are here," Sacco said and pointed to the monitors of the interview rooms.

All parties accounted for and present, Nick saw.

"Who do you want to tackle first?"

"Let's go for Watson," Nick said. He went to the small fridge pressed against the wall and took out two water bottles. "The asshole can wait."

M-Li, her head pressed against her husband's shoulder, was quiet now, Nick saw. Mr. Watson, a lawyer for a multinational firm on Park (or so Nick had been informed), had calmed her, his hand a monotonous up and down her arm in a soothing motion. Nick sized him up.

Watson was as tall as his wife, brown hair and eyes to match, dressed to dazzle in a silk Armani suit, tie and shirt to match, a handkerchief peeking tastefully from the front jacket pocket. The comforting hand sported an impressive Rolex anyone in the precinct would mug for, and the entire "Hey, I'm rich, influential, and powerful" look was tastefully finished with a pair of gold, initialed cufflinks.

Freaking A. Who the hell wore cufflinks nowadays?

Sacco placed the extra chair he carried across the table where man and wife sat. Nick deposited the water bottles in front of them.

M-Li Watson reached for hers with shaky hands, opened it, and took a good gulp.

"Thank you."

Nick only nodded and focused on her husband.

"Mr. Watson, has your wife..."

"Yes," he interrupted. "She should have called me, or our lawyer, instead of that idiot friend of hers."

"You had an important meeting this morning," she said on a small hiccup, and took another swig of water.

"And interrupting me for this is better?" The sarcasm slammed heavy. M-Li winced. "Has the creep pressed charges?"

"He's my next interview. Let's see what happens after I'm done. However, I would like to understand what went down this morning at that office." Nick stared at the husband. "We," he thumbed himself and Sacco, "witnessed the assault."

"Assault?" The man looked at his wife. "M-Li? Please to God tell me you did not touch that man."

"She scratched his face," Nick supplied.

"After he threatened and insulted me," she spat out in anger. "He tried to hit me, but he missed."

"Are you freaking nuts?" The voice decibel increased tenfold. "One thing is to throw insults at each other, but this? This?"

"I'm sorry. I'm so sorry." She began to cry.

"Shit." He enfolded her in his arms and began rocking her. Nick could read the concern, the love, and the exasperation there. "It's okay, honey. It's okay. We'll sort this out."

Nick waited for about twenty seconds.

"Your friend, Mr. Wexler, said that Mr. Creasy sued you both. Could you expand on that?"

M-Li grabbed a tissue and blew her nose. She spoke from the shelter of her husband's arms.

"That SOB served papers this morning, suing us for half of any and all research, trademarks, and sales rights for any and all products that come out of Isabel's research. He somehow found out that this product line may have huge profit projections and wants a piece of it. Claims he has rights, since he was married to her while she invented the thing. Oh, and he demanded negotiating rights for any future deals with any marketing firm who may want to carry and promote the product, the bastard." She turned to her husband. "Can he do that?"

"Depends on whether he's claiming commingled versus community property," her husband replied. "If it's the latter, he can kiss his lawsuit goodbye. In any case, his claim is flimsy at best since he didn't contest anything in the divorce. That is, unless he can find a sympathetic judge who'll want to skewer you. Highly unlikely, though."

Nick thought of Angie, his ex-wife, and his messy divorce. He knew about the differences M-Li's husband referred to, including one term he didn't mention, equitable distribution. Either way, you usually were fucked if the person suing had a good lawyer and an endless supply of money to fill the lawyer's retirement fund with. Or a woman who played the judge like a fine-tuned melody to get what she wanted. Or the scumbag who didn't want to work for a living and milked the woman for all she had because she earned more money. Or the couple more intent on destroying one another than safeguarding the welfare of their own kids. Or the drug addict. The drunk.

Nick had seen it all...and more.

The couple facing him, however, looked well equipped to hold off any predatory practices *ad infinitum.*

"You're referring to the product line you mentioned Ms. Creasy was working on for you and Mr. Wexler?"

M-Li nodded. "Yes. The moisturizer, the peel, and the new nail polish. I'm surprised you remember. Other products are pending, until we can fill Isabel's shoes." Her voice hitched as she fought new tears. "No one can replace her."

"What happened once you got there?"

"I waited until EriK met me in the lobby. He didn't understand the insistence to face David. Why all the fuss? He thought it was about getting a flower donation for Isabel's memorial." She scoffed. "It was a different story after I told him what David was up to."

"I can't believe you didn't call me to discuss this before you went gallivanting into the sunset to face David," her husband admonished. "I would have called an Uber to bring you to the office. Or I would have gone home."

Nick wasn't about to allow this interview to degrade into a marital airing of grievances. They could do that on their own time.

"Why didn't you leave after the second denial to meet?"

"I wasn't about to let him get away with it."

Mr. Watson's expression said it all.

"Mrs. Watson, do you know a Mr. Desha Adnet or a Ms. Jessica Waitre?"

The question seemed to throw her off.

"No," she began, and then her eyes snapped alive. "Wait. Isabel knew a Desh. Are we talking about the same person?"

Nick made a note on his open file and circled it. Connect the dots.

"Isn't he the one who was designing the website for Isabel?" her husband asked.

"Yes, but we transferred the domain and contents to my server and webmaster a few days before Isabel...when Isabel..." She swallowed some water. "She used him..."

"Only her?" Nick interrupted.

"Until two weeks ago, at least, this Desh had administrative permission to work on the website, but only because Isabel had paid for some design changes in advance." She looked at her husband. "Didn't want to pay for the same services twice."

"Did you ever meet him, or socialize with him in any way within these past two weeks?" Nick asked.

"Why ever would I?" she asked, bewildered. "He finished about a week ago and turned everything over to my webmaster, who deleted the man's access to the server then. Everything was done online. I did talk to this Desh on the phone after Isabel's death to explain what I wanted to do, but that was the extent of it. Very nice young man and he did create a beautiful website. EriK raved about the site, too."

"Why didn't you keep his services?" Sacco asked.

"No need to retain two different web architects on the payroll when one will do. I used mine. Gives me more control of changes and additions."

"Do you know if Isabel Creasy socialized with Mr. Adnet and Ms. Waitre?" Nick asked.

"She may have," she said. "But Isabel hung around a lot of different people with David that I wasn't aware of or wasn't friends with."

"Other than today, have you, at any time, visited TeC4M in the past week?"

Her husband leaned forward. "I'm not sure I like where this is going, Detective. Why the deviation with your questioning? I can attest to the fact we didn't socialize with this Desh person. Any and all business interactions and transactions were done by phone or online, as my wife stated. What is this really about?"

"We're looking into the recent deaths of Mr. Adnet and Ms. Waitre. Since he worked at TeC4M, we're questioning anyone who may have had a connection to them."

The shock was clear.

"He worked with David?" she whispered, horror behind it.

Nick nodded. "Same company, different department."

She grabbed her husband's hand and turned to face him. "That's how David knew. I've been wracking my brain, trying to figure out how on earth he discovered what we were planning. This Desh person must have said something about the changes and the transfer of the website." She faced Nick. "A bit before the divorce was final, Isabel made sure everything, and I mean everything, was switched back to her maiden name. I helped her. She didn't want to receive a cease-and-desist order later when the business was up, running, and profitable."

"David is, and always has been, an avaricious son of a bitch," her husband supplied.

M-Li nodded in agreement. "He's mercenary when it comes to money. He didn't appreciate it when Isabel took her measly salary and reinvested it into her research," she added.

"And now, he wants a piece of the pie," her husband said. "And you, my dear, did not help matters with your actions today." He stood. "Has David pressed charges?"

"Not at the moment," Nick supplied. "As I said, he's my next interview."

"If he does press charges, we are looking at a possible misdemeanor, correct?"

M-Li covered her face as a shudder wracked her body.

"Yes."

"In that case, Detective Larson, I'm taking my wife out of here. If David does press charges, his lawyer can contact my office. The lawyers can duke things out. We will be at your disposal through our lawyer as well."

Nick and Sacco stared after the couple, as Horowitz, pressed into escort duty once more, led them to the elevators.

"Think the asshole will press charges?" Sacco asked.

"He's pissed enough," Nick said, thoughtful. "Greed might intervene, though, if there's enough money in the horizon from the lawsuit. If that's the case, he'll settle for some scabs on his face."

"What are the odds?" Sacco asked, but more as a rhetorical question.

"Let's find out."

"It's about fucking time" hit them the moment Nick opened the door.

Nick ignored Creasy and introduced himself and Sacco to the lawyer, a Mr. John J. Fitzgerald, lawyer at large, according to his card. Nick wondered if Creasy had chosen him because of his reputation or the inference of power from the name. Hard to decide.

"Have you had time to confer with your client, counselor?"

"Yes." From the lawyer's look, it seemed he was having second thoughts about representing the man sitting next to him. His expression was sour and dour all at once. "I've looked over the written statement." He ripped two pages from the pad and handed them over.

Nick thanked him and sat.

"Mr. Creasy, can you, in your own words, run through what happened this morning?"

The lawyer nodded to go ahead.

"That bitch came to my work and created a scene I won't be able to put down. God knows what HR will log in as a reprimand on my file. It'll affect my scores. And look at what she did to me." He pointed to his face. The welts had diminished to nothing and intermittent scabs decorated his cheek. He'd be right as rain in a few days.

"Will you be pressing charges?" Nick asked, his manner mild and questioning.

"I understand you witnessed the, ahem, altercation?" the lawyer asked.

Nick nodded. "He went for her, she for him. She got him first."

Creasy stiffened and opened his mouth, but the lawyer squeezed his arm.

"After *conferring* with my client," he said in a very clear warning for said client to shut up. "He realizes his ex-wife's friend is under a tremendous emotional strain. He will let this slide, in deference to his ex-wife's memory. Mr. Creasy is a reasonable man. He doesn't hold any grudges."

What a Samaritan, Nick thought and glanced at Sacco. A smirk flashed and was gone. There was more money to be had with a lawsuit than a misdemeanor.

"That is extremely magnanimous of you, Mr. Creasy. I'm sure Mrs. Watson will be very grateful. Unlike you, however, where you can let bygones be bygones, I need a few questions answered to complement my incident report. Paperwork. Can't be helped." Nick shrugged. "At what time were you aware of Mrs. Watson's visit?"

The lawyer's eyes narrowed, but he gave another nod to his client.

"I had just clinched a three-hundred-dollar-deal package when Liz buzzed."

"Liz being the receptionist?"

Creasy nodded.

"Whereabouts where you when Liz buzzed you?"

"At my desk. I had a ten-minute break coming. Had an urge for Starbucks. Get some fresh air. Re-energize."

Imagine that. If he'd gotten more energized before facing Watson, maybe *she* would have pressed charges on *him*.

"Just out of curiosity, why did you refuse to see her?"

He shrugged. "Didn't want to deal with her. That's part of my past that's over and done with. I've moved on."

"Understandable," Nick commiserated. "Yet, Mr. Creasy, you are still suing Mrs. Watson for a past you've moved on from." Nick focused on his lawyer. "You representing him on that?"

Mr. Fitzgerald, lawyer at large, looked as though he had a bad taste in his mouth.

"Yes."

"Heard the lawsuit has something to do with your ex-wife's research. Can you expand on that?"

Creasy fidgeted. "I only want what is due me from the years I put up with Isabel's hobby."

"Really? You've been divorced, how long?"

"Four months give or take."

"You waited that long to file a lawsuit, especially when I hear the divorce was uncontested?"

"That's a lot of hearsay, Lieutenant," the lawyer interrupted. "And it's not to the point of this interview."

"But it is, as well as to the altercation we witnessed," Nick said. "How did you hear about the plans Mrs. Watson and Mr. Wexler had?"

Now Creasy was getting uncomfortable.

"Would it, by any chance, have to do with a Mr. Desha Adnet and/or a Ms. Jessica Waitre?"

The man visibly jumped. "How did you..."

But the lawyer clamped a hand over his client's arm and squeezed.

"Lieutenant, really," Mr. Fitzgerald interrupted. "Fishing? Again, that information is not relevant to this interview."

"Humor me, counselor. You see, Mr. Adnet was in charge of creating a website for Mr. Creasy's ex-wife. Said Desha Adnet was in control of design and maintenance of Isabel Creasy's website until about a week ago, when he transferred administrative control to Mrs. Watson's webmaster. Mr. Creasy was not merely a co-worker with Mr. Adnet, but may have socialized with him and his girlfriend. According to Ms. Jeffries from IT, Adnet and Creasy were friends. And now, Mr. Adnet, together with his girlfriend, Ms. Jessica Waitre, are dead."

"Is this a fucking joke?" Creasy asked.

"Death, Mr. Creasy, is never a joke."

Shock replaced pissiness.

"But, but, that is impossible. I saw him on Monday. He was fine on Monday."

"So that was the last time you saw Mr. Adnet?"

"I need to confer with my client...in private, Lieutenant."

"Counselor, this is a friendly interview. We're simply adding information about our victims from co-workers and friends. His insight may give us the answers we need."

"Give us a few minutes," the lawyer insisted.

"Very well."

Nick and Sacco stepped out.

"That took him by surprise," Sacco said.

"Yeah. I don't think he faked that one." Nick's eyes unfocused for a moment. "Did you catch the hiccup with the first two interviews?"

"You mean the fact Mr. Adnet's name didn't ring a bell to our massage therapist with the capital K?"

Nick smiled. You could always count on Sacco to catch on.

"Maybe he wasn't aware, or informed about who created the website for Isabel Creasy. Maybe he was only interested in the results, not the details. We'll have to ask."

"We certainly ambushed him with the info, too," Sacco said. "Could be an honest oversight."

"Adnet's name is too distinctive to have been forgotten. But, you never know. If everything was done by phone, and Mrs. Watson was in charge of that exclusively, it could be labeled a mistake. Anyways, something needing more follow-up," Nick said and turned when Mr. Fitzgerald opened the door.

"We're ready."

They settled in the same positions as before.

"My client is completely shocked, Lieutenant, but he will answer any questions you may have, if those answers don't interfere with the current litigation."

Nick opened his pad. "Tell me about Mr. Adnet. When you met, became friendly."

"Can I have some water, please?" Creasy asked.

The man was rattled and his voice shook. Still in some shock, Nick saw.

Without being asked, Sacco stepped out. Within seconds, he placed an unopened, sweaty bottle of water in front of Creasy, from the interview room next door no doubt.

"Met Desh at a company gathering to welcome new employees," he said, while opening the bottle. He guzzled long and deep. "He'd just come onboard a month before the bash."

"And when was that?" Nick said, jotting notes.

"Close to two years ago."

The dots were starting to connect.

"Were you friendly at work?"

"The occasional what's up at the lounge, hallway, or elevator. Inane conversations. Met his girlfriend at the company's picnic about a year and a half ago. Shy thing. My ex-wife hit it off with Jessie right away, though. Then Isabel discovered Desh was IT and got him involved in creating a website for her creams and shit. Desh obliged in his spare time. Isabel was delighted. I thought it was all a waste of time and money. Wouldn't go anywhere."

Nick didn't comment. The lawyer's hand had slowly moved toward his client. Creasy hadn't realized he'd just undermined his own lawsuit.

"Did you stay friendly with them after your divorce?"

"Went out a couple of times, but not as often, especially after I hooked up with Leah. Jessie didn't want to deal with her. Almost looked insulted. My girlfriend doesn't like her either. Claims those nonprofit charity types are hypocritical do-gooders and faux bleeding hearts."

"We'll need to speak to your girlfriend. Where can we reach her at?"

Creasy reluctantly gave the phone numbers. "At least let me warn..."

"We'll be discreet," Nick said. "When was the last time you saw Jessica Waitre?"

Creasy grabbed his phone and scanned through his calendar.

"Week after Thanksgiving. Went to Acqua for an early dinner and then hopped over to see *Knives Out*. Man, embarrassment all around."

"How so?"

"Can bet my next sales goal they'd been fighting before we got together. Recognized the signs. Told Desh the next day he could have canceled. I would have understood. Nobody's good company when there is trouble on the horizon. Shit, I know the signs. Been there, done that."

"Can you give us more detail on Ms. Waitre's state of mind that day?"

"Glum. Rude. Obvious she didn't want to be there. Behaved more like a wife of Beverly Hills bitch than the norm. Desh told me later Jessie was under a lot of strain at work because of the holidays and all. Apologized."

Nick added a note: *Jives with what Daine Lunney told us.* He'd need to get a timeline set up.

"Did you meet socially afterward?"

"Not really. December is our worst month. We got slammed with work. And Desh was working night and day writing a program to block all the bastard hackers who attack the system daily."

"You mentioned you saw Mr. Adnet on Monday, right?"

"Went with him to Starbucks for a caffeine pick-me-up. Asked him how the firewall was going. But he was distracted. Had to ask him twice about it before he focused."

"Is that when he told you about the transfer of your ex-wife's website?"

"Now, Lieutenant," the lawyer interrupted. "You know better."

Nick almost shrugged. He didn't give a shit about the lawsuit. He had bigger fish to fry.

"What else did he say?"

"That's about it. Told me he'd see me next week. He was taking some PT days to work from home. See his family. Had some decisions to make."

"Did he expand on those decisions?"

"Nah. But his father is a pain in the ass and has been pressuring him to get back into the family business. They were planning expansions, I think he said."

"Apart from being distracted, did he seem upset, angry, or depressed?"

Creasy laughed. "Desh, depressed? Shit. Negative emotions slid off him like food on Teflon."

"But he was distracted," Nick added.

"We heard through the grapevine at work that the hacker attacks were getting vicious. Like all IT, he dove into his cyber world and didn't surface until he had a solution. Didn't think much about it."

"Did he mention any problems with Ms. Waitre?"

"Like I said, very brief conversation. He got his coffee served first and that was the last I saw of him." He shuddered. "Oh, shit."

"Was there anybody else in the office Mr. Adnet may have been friends with?"

"Maressa Jeffries would be able to help you more on that than me. Don't know many in IT, except as acquaintances."

Nick nodded and closed his notebook. "Mr. Creasy, please stay available." He looked at the lawyer, who'd stood up at the evident dismissal. "I have your card if anything changes."

Nick watched them go from the doorway. Dots were hovering around Isabel Creasy's case, but none he could really sink his teeth into and draw a picture. Still, it was better than nothing. At least they had a connection to this last case. Now the real work started. Nick needed to dig into that.

He and Sacco went to their respective desks and began filling out incident reports for the morning debacle at TeC4M.

Thirty minutes later, they were all huddled around the conference room table.

Nick opened his chicken Massaman curry and inhaled. He was starving. Dumped some rice on it and began eating.

"Recap," he said between mouthfuls. "Some of today's players knew, in one capacity or another, Isabel Creasy, Desha Adnet, and Jessica Waitre."

Carpenter's fork paused before he could shovel more chicken larb into his mouth. "Really?"

"A thread," Ramos said, reaching for a crab angel. "Finally."

"Very thin one, at the moment," Nick said. "But it's a direction to follow, which we didn't have previously."

"How exactly are these people connected?" Carpenter asked.

Sacco went for the last crab angel but Ramos slapped his hand away and snatched it.

"The Creasys were linked to Adnet and Waitre, first through the workplace and then socially," Nick said.

"That is," Sacco added, "until David Creasy dumped his first wife and got himself a new girlfriend." He opened his notebook. "A Leah Santori. Seems Waitre and Santori didn't quite gel after a few couples' night out."

"Still doesn't tell me jack shit about a possible clue, or direction we can take to solve this," said Ramos.

"Desha Adnet had created a website for Isabel Creasy's products, which her best friend now has possession of. So that links Watson to Adnet."

Sacco swallowed the Thai fried rice he was wolfing down at an impressive speed. "The massage therapist did not recollect knowing Mr. Adnet. That is debatable, especially after speaking with Mrs. Watson. Either it was a simple oversight or he's truthfully ignorant of the fact."

"We'll double-check on that later. Right now, the question is are these two cases a matter of simple coincidence..."

Ramos scoffed. "Not the way I'm seeing it and you are presenting them."

"Ramos, you're suspicious down to your beautiful pinkie toes," Sacco said.

"Look around the table, bud," she smiled, "and tell me your beautiful pinkies aren't, too."

"Somehow all of them caught the killer's attention. The question is how and what set things off. There has to be some sort of clue or connection somewhere in the ether, Carpenter. You've got to find me something. We know Jessica Waitre was being stalked through the dark web. Maybe that's the connection."

Carpenter hummed. "I'll check for malware, any targets on Creasy's computer. If there is a link, that may be the source. Adnet was too IT savvy not to know someone was trying to hack his computer."

"Dig long and deep," Nick told him. "We need something."

"But what if there is no connection?" Carpenter asked. "What if they were picked at random?"

Now that was a thought Nick didn't want to explore. A crime where the killer had a connection to the victims was solvable. A killer who didn't...

"Let's hope that's not the case, kid," Nick said. "If not, we're screwed. That means a random psycho is out there selecting victims on a whim."

"You know," Ramos said. "Carpenter here does have a point, Nick. What if there is no connection? There's still the possibility one or both women wanted to commit suicide, even by proxy, whether we like it or not."

"Not Isabel Creasy, Tish. The more I think about it, the more convinced I am Creasy's case doesn't fit what we've seen with Waitre's case. That one feels...different. And that's what throwing me off here. But we'll keep all our options open for now. And Totes hasn't done the autopsies yet, either. He may have something to say about this."

"Is our computer still compiling cases with similar MOs?" Ramos asked.

Nick nodded and grabbed a fried donut. "What about the women's personal cell phones?" he asked.

"Zip. Disappeared." Ramos said.

"Have you gotten that data for cross-check from the phone carriers?" Nick asked Carpenter.

"Have Creasy's cell phone logs. Waiting for Waitre's to compare." He sighed. "If there is anything matchable."

"We need to sift through the pile of evidence we found in Adnet's apartment," Nick said. "That is if there are no more surprises or interruptions." Nick stretched. "Thanks for the lunch, Ramos. Let me know how much I owe you."

"Lieutenant..."

Everyone turned to look at Horowitz at the doorway.

"There's been another one."

CHAPTER TWENTY-THREE

THE AREA AROUND the crime scene was one of the nicer places in this part of town. The address Horowitz had given them was nearby Sutton Place, the building planted on the north side of a quiet, tree-lined street between First and Beekman. It was an older structure braced tastefully by even older, white-brick properties.

The lobby Nick entered was small and under renovation, with warning cones and taped-off sections dotting the area in warning to the residents. Nick knew those notices were more to avoid future damages from litigious renters than the accident-prone ones.

A uniform greeted them, his face tinged with a rather suspicious pasty hue.

"Sir," he swallowed. "Victim is..." He paused and swallowed once more.

"Are you okay?" Nick asked, a bit concerned.

The officer swallowed. "It's bad in there, sir."

"You first on scene?"

"And my partner," he stated, opened his notebook and pointed to a civilian sitting in the corner of the reception desk. The man was bent over, hands on head, and elbows on knees. "Mr. Julian Toro, there, was present when the victim was discovered. He's the manager."

"And the other is?"

"Mr. Omiata Iwu."

Nick glanced at Mr. Iwu. In his late forties, he was listening to someone on his phone, his horrified eyes bulged, one hand covering his mouth. Even this far apart, the man's pallor was evident.

"Where's the scene, officer?" Ramos interrupted.

"Second floor, apartment 2B," he answered.

Ramos, Carpenter, and their group headed for the elevators.

"Victim's name?" Nick asked.

"Micaela Latimer, according to Mr. Iwu. She was subletting the apartment from him. When she didn't pay her rent and hadn't answered any of the gentleman's phone calls, texts, or emails for over a week, he came to deliver a notice of eviction."

"He has a key to the place?" Nick asked, nodding in the general direction where the two men sat next to each other now.

"Affirmative. They both do. Mr. Iwu wanted the manager with him when he served the eviction notice. According to him, after they received no answer to their ringing, they entered the premises to ascertain the place was not trashed or abandoned. That's when they found her."

"Did they touch anything?"

"They didn't have to," the officer said. "Well...you'll see." He swallowed.

Nick nodded and turned to Sacco. "Let's see what those two have to say."

"Gentlemen," Nick greeted them, studying the men's clammy skin, pallor, and overall expressions of distress. Shock vibrated from their eyes. It did not bode well about what they'd witnessed at the crime scene. He introduced himself and Sacco.

"I know this is difficult, but we need your statements over what happened this afternoon."

The man, who had been pointed out to Nick as Omiata Iwu, spoke as if in a trance.

"I only wanted to warn her," he said. "Never gave me trouble. Never would have..."

What the hell? Nick looked at Sacco. His partner was thinking the same thing.

The manager visibly jumped. "It's not what it sounds like," he said, his nervousness evident. "We never expected... I mean we've been burned before. But this? This is too much like *Dawn of the Dead* shit."

"At the moment, I'm not thinking anything except trying to find out what happened," Nick said. "Mr. Iwu, before you say anything else, can I ask when was the last time you saw the victim?"

"I think I'm going to be sick," was all the man muttered.

Nick glanced around the area and spotted a plastic garbage pail half-hidden by the crescent-moon reception desk. "Here," he said, placing it below the man's chin. Iwu hugged it, bending the plastic out of shape. He dry-heaved several times.

"My officer tells me you were subletting the apartment to Ms. Latimer, is that correct?"

Iwu nodded and dry-heaved once more.

Nick turned to the manager, hoping for better luck. "Were you aware of the sublease?"

Julian Toro huffed. "It's legal. The owners of the building allow it."

"Owners?"

"This is a condoplex," Toro said, as if that explained everything. "It's been that way since the early '90s."

"How long have you been managing the place?" Sacco asked.

"Nearly thirteen years," he said, a tinge of pride in his voice.

"Do you reside on the premises?" Nick asked.

The man scoffed. "I live in Elmhurst, man. Can't afford a place like this, even if I sublet the sublet."

"Office?"

"In the basement."

"We'll need all documentation you have on Ms. Latimer." Nick turned to the other man, who'd finally gotten hold of his need to puke. "Mr. Iwu. Are you the owner of the apartment?"

The man shook his head and swallowed. "No. I sublet it for my cousin. He's in and out of the country too often to use it. Diplomatic attaché."

"Works at the UN?"

"Used to, a while back. The reason he bought the place. Didn't want to sell it when he was transferred back to Abuja." Before Nick could ask, he added. "Nigeria."

"Can you go through what happened this afternoon?"

The man visibly blanched, but kept his composure.

"Miss Latimer's rent was due last week. Occasionally, she may be a day late in payment, especially if she's traveling, but she usually would leave a message or send an email letting me know she was out of state. Dependable renter, for the most part. But last week, she didn't pay rent. I let it go for a day or two, sending her reminders. When she didn't answer any of my calls, texts, or emails, I knew something was going on. Usually that means the apartment has been vacated without notice or the tenant is avoiding me due to lack of funds." He swallowed. "It was neither."

"Do you usually show up with an eviction notice this early?"

"I've been burned before. One renter thought himself a squatter and skipped paying the rental for two months. It took me six to get rid of him. Trashed the place in protest before he disappeared. We had to replace everything, from furniture to kitchen cabinetry. So now, I keep blank copies of eviction notices and fill in names to show I'm serious."

"More as a threat?" Sacco asked.

"More like I'm in earnest about taking legal action. Once the renter is confronted, I leave with renter's check in hand." He glanced at both Nick and Sacco. "But it's first strike you're out. I break the lease immediately, giving the renter two weeks' notice to vacate. It's worked, up till now."

"When did you arrive here to let Miss Latimer know she'd be evicted?" Nick asked.

The man looked at the manager. "Around two, two fifteen?"

Toro nodded. "I'd just gotten delivery of the marble floor we're installing."

"Why didn't you stop by earlier in the week?" Nick asked Iwu.

"I was at Disney World with my kids," the man answered. "Vacation. Returned yesterday."

Nick turned to the manager. "Did you go check if she was in?"

"We've been busy renovating the lobby, as you can see," he said. "But I'm not a babysitter. Placed the reminders under the door on behalf of Mr. Iwu, but didn't keep track of her goings. And, legally, I'm not allowed to enter the premises unless there is an issue inside the apartment. I go in only when invited, and the owner or tenant has to be on the premises. Keeps me out of trouble or blame if something goes missing."

"When did you last see Miss Latimer?"

"I don't remember. She usually leaves before I arrive to man the lobby. Oftentimes, she works late and I don't see her return at all. I leave at six. After that time, the owners use their key fobs to come and go. If visitors arrive after hours, tenants have to come downstairs to allow them in. They're serious about their security, especially since we don't man the desk in the evening."

That may change, Nick thought, once the owners learned about this incident.

"So you both went to the apartment around two-ish," Nick said. "What happened next?"

"We knocked, and knocked," Iwu said, wiping his upper lip. "Then we noticed that the last reminder notice Mr. Toro had pushed halfway through under the door was still there."

"And you suspected she'd bailed on you," Nick said.

"Who goes inside their apartment and leaves notices or mail on the floor?" Toro asked. "So, yes. And it wouldn't have been difficult to scram. She already knew my routine."

"Any security cameras around the building?" Nick asked.

"No."

"Okay. Let's go back to this afternoon. You knocked, saw the notices under the door. What next?"

Both men swallowed, hard.

"We called out we were coming in," said Iwu.

"So we opened the door," continued Toro.

Both men closed their eyes, trying to block the image. But Nick knew once seen, never unseen. The mind always supplied every single grisly detail. A snapshot forever engraved.

"She was just there, under the fan," Iwu said. "Just hanging." Softer. "Just there."

"Did you go in? Touch anything?"

"Fuck, no," Toro said. "We closed the door and got the hell out. Called 911."

"How can something like this happen?" Iwu asked of no one. His chin wobbled, fell to his chest, and he began to cry.

Nick didn't say anything, simply walked to the elevator with Sacco as Toro placed a comforting arm around the weeping man.

As soon as the elevator door opened, Nick was greeted by one of Ramos's techs, who thrust a plastic zip bag his way.

"What the hell?"

"Sir, Ramos ordered I give it to you on pain of death. My death. Just in case. You'll need your masks before you get in there." With the warning and bag given, he turned and left.

It was never a good thing to go to a crime scene with a full stomach, Nick thought. He unearthed the menthol vial from his coat pocket, rubbed a bit of the paste under his nose, handed the vial to Sacco, and put his mask on, following the tech. Maybe if he were an optimist, he'd be able to survive the afternoon with his stomach contents intact.

The small hallway in front of the crime scene was too narrow to hold the many lab people and uniforms recording the scene. Everyone was in beehive mode.

"You think we can fit in there?" Sacco asked.

They managed to avoid the human throng around the doorway.

"Is it me, or is it getting colder?" Nick said as soon as they crossed the threshold.

"Welcome to the Arctic," said Ramos, seeing their approach. She was next to the body, bagging the victim's right hand. "All windows in the apartment are wide open." She pointed up to the ceiling fan where a rope was anchored. "Nice of him to refrigerate the premises, although she's a mess. Poor thing."

Nick stared. Micaela Latimer hung like some grotesque puppet on a string underneath the ceiling fan in the middle of the living room. The entire area was freezing, but that hadn't stopped the decomposition process from taking hold. Bloated, her body swayed to the breeze that sliced through the apartment. She was wearing Christmas-red silk pajama bottoms with a white t-shirt, imprinted with the "I love New York" slogan, now stretched taut because of the expanding body. The clothing was now stained with fluids Nick didn't even want to think about, and her exposed skin had an almost shiny complexion in places.

"Guess?" he asked Ramos. He swallowed, hard, more in pity for the victim than from his stomach roiling.

"By lividity and lack of rigor," Ramos said, lifting up the bagged hand in a very gentle move. There was no resistance. "I'd approximate she's been hooked there for over three days." She leaned in a bit to stare at the victim's arm. "By amount of bloat, and the fact she's been refrigerated, maybe five days, although the skin shows some red peeking through the green. Eight to ten days. Maybe. Totes will be able to give a better timeline. And I hope he gets here soon. Don't know how long she'll stay up there. Rope cutting through."

Nick turned from the body to study the living room, taking very shallow breaths. The menthol and the low temperature in the apartment helped keep his stomach at ease. He scanned the area around the victim and saw it was immaculate. A sofa with classic lines, covered in an exotic, neutral material, was pushed close to the wall to the right of the victim. Matching club chairs and end tables bracketed it. A metallic-and-glass coffee table stood within arm's reach, a mixture of magazines, crystal bowls, and a small leather box resting on top. Nothing looked out of place. Opposite the sofa, a cream-colored accent cabinet hosted the twin of the lamp on the left end table across the way, with a tall, bulbous-shaped planter positioned in the middle. Someone had dumped inside it white, twisted twigs that looked more freakish to Nick than decorative. The rest of the area had other knick-knacks placed strategically around. Regular upholstered chairs created the end points to the cabinet, except the nearer one was now under the victim's feet, the fabric soiled from what the body had already expelled.

The scene looked remarkably similar to the Creasy case.

"Shit," was all Nick said.

"You got that right," Ramos answered. She took out her ruler and measured. "Limp toes two inches from the top of the cushion. Same."

"The captain is not going to be happy about this," Sacco added.

"Are you?" Nick said, knowing they had a serial on their hands and still wishing he was wrong.

She studied Nick. "How's the stomach holding up?"

"Manageable." He stared at the open window, where the cold afternoon air sliced through. "All the windows open?"

"Yep. Whoever did this screwed us. Totes is going to have a hell of a time giving us TOD."

If it was true the victim had been hanging there for more than seventy-two hours, with windows open to the elements, the messed-up fluctuations in temperatures this past week would throw off body decomposition by slowing and accelerating it randomly.

At least the cold inside the apartment kept the smell to a minimum.

"Anything under the chair legs?" Nick asked.

Ramos smiled, but shook her head. "No need." She tried to rock the chair, but it stood solid against the floor. "Level. I checked the freezer, just in case. No silicone mold."

"Any note?" Nick asked.

She pointed to a piece of paper inside a plastic sheet protector. "But I don't buy it. You'll see."

Life is worth shit.

People say they care, but they really don't.

What they are is hateful monsters.

Liers. All of them. Time to sleep.

"Ah, hell," was all Nick said.

Sacco pointed with his pinkie. "Same misspelled word. Same phrase." He looked at Nick. "I know kids nowadays can't spell shit, but what are the odds?"

"None." He turned to Ramos. "Purse?"

"In the excuse for a foyer. On the chair next to the decorative table."

Nick walked where Ramos had directed while Sacco inspected the inside of the accent cabinet in the living room.

The purse, more like a gigantic disposable sack, had been negligently tossed on top of the chair. It was laying like a drunkard, half on, half off. He lifted it and walked directly into the dining area across the way, depositing it on the rectangular table. He started the process of relieving the purse of its contents, placing each item meticulously beside each other.

A cursory inspection of the wallet showed it had the usual credit cards, NY driver's license—identifying the victim as one Micaela Latimer, twenty-seven, resident of same address—membership cards, folded receipts that swelled the wallet to double its size, and money. Nothing taken that he could see. Next was the makeup bag, which bulged with the usual, make-yourself-pretty stuff women always carried around. Nothing out of the ordinary. Next came a hairbrush. A small can of pepper spray. Mints. Tissues. Notepad with a pen slipped inside the spiral spine. A rolled-up fashion magazine. Pantyhose. *Pantyhose? What the hell?* Eyeglass case. Eye lubricant for contact wearers. Tampons. More receipts. Loose change. Lip balm. Matches, but no cigarettes. Deodorant. A small can of air freshener.

That was it.

No phone.

"Okay. Listen up," he said loudly enough for all of them to stop. "I want every single person, right now, to search for a cell phone. Search every cushion, every cabinet, every closet. Check the floor, behind furniture, under furniture, anywhere where a phone could fall."

Nick shouted for Carpenter.

"Yo," he answered from the other side of the apartment.

Nick followed the voice into a small rectangular room converted into a media/reading room in soft tones of green and wood. The window to the street was also wide open and the ambient temperature felt even colder than outside.

"Have you found a laptop or any personal files, bills?"

"An iPad. Haven't gotten to the bedroom to check for laptop or files yet."

"Shit." Without a code, there would be no way to open the thing. Not even with a warrant. "Go to the bedroom. Check to see if she has a laptop there. I need a phone number."

Nick went to the wall-to-wall shelving unit and opened the cabinet doors below the TV screen. Inside, on the first shelf, was a DVR box, a Blu-ray player. On the bottom shelf a heap of DVDs was neatly stacked, according to title and size. Nothing else. Inside the cabinet on the left, he found a gaming console, game cartridges, multiple controllers for the gaming system, one gaming headset, and some eyeglass wear. Everything neatly arranged. The woman liked order. Turning to the cabinet doors on the right, he found a CD player with an impressive number of audio CDs around it, on top, as well as on the bottom.

He straightened from his search and studied the room. Everything organized. Minimal decorative elements. Very few personal photos. Actually, there were only two. He picked one up. It was a graduation photo, with the victim shaking the hand of a robed professor. Rather pretty, with youngish features, a much better take than the license picture. Blond hair peeking out from her graduation cap. He picked up the other photo. Seemed to be an office event. Everyone smiling, with the victim holding up some sort of plaque. Maybe a group work award of some kind, he thought.

Carpenter arrived, tapping the keyboard of a small laptop with one hand while holding the thing in the crook of his arm.

"Can you get in?"

"Already in. No login password. Must use this here exclusively." He tapped a few more keys and smiled. "And she even has a password organizer. How kind." He wiggled his finger around the mouse pad a few times. "Jot this down."

Nick took out his phone and dialed. The phone rang and rang, but not a peep from inside the apartment. The voicemail server spit out the usual at the tone, leave a message. Nick waited. A peppy, very young voice gave a short greeting.

"Hi, peeps. Mica here and not here." A bubbly laugh. "Leave one."

Nick disconnected.

"Like the others," Carpenter said.

Nick nodded. "Like the others," he agreed and gave the cease-and-desist order to everyone.

Sacco walked in. "There's not a dust mote out of place. Talk about OCD."

"And nothing too personal either," Nick added and scanned around. "Doesn't feel home to me. More like a place to sleep and keep your stuff in. Only two photos here."

"You're showing your age," Carpenter said, closing the computer and slipping it into a plastic evidence bag. "The woke generation does everything virtual."

"Well, your Wokeness," Nick said. "When you find them, make sure you send me those photo files ASAP."

The next search, this time of the bedroom, didn't yield anything valuable or a clue. Clothes and intimates were arranged neatly in their respective places. Jewelry was organized in the same manner inside several see-through plastic boxes in the closet. Another jewelry case, on top of a small vanity table, was full of the victim's often-used, cherished, and more expensive pieces.

Nothing was out of place. Nothing ransacked or riffled through. A quick search of the bedside tables told Nick the victim was sexually active, cautious, and very fond of the DIY sexual-release-type toys. The bathroom didn't offer any further clues, either.

When they walked back to the living room, Totes and his people were getting ready to leave. They had already removed the victim from her death perch and had tucked and zipped her inside a carrier body bag.

"You and your fucking intuition," Totes said as soon as Nick came into view. Ramos smiled.

"Hope I'm wrong, you know." He breathed in shallow spurts. "Evidence is flimsy at best and invisible at worst. At the moment, we're at worst."

"Well," Totes said in a cheerful voice, giving his people the okay to leave with the body. "That's three autopsies tomorrow for me, and you. A fun day together."

"May be worth my stomach contents to get answers."

"If I find any."

Joy, was all Nick thought.

Following the ME and the body to the lobby, they parted ways to seek the manager, who was nearby as if directing traffic, barking orders to the laborers who were grouting and laying the floor.

"We need a copy of the sublease application and any other document you have on the victim," Nick said, during a pause in Toro's diatribe.

The manager pointed to the reception desk. "Made a copy of my files. They are inside that envelope."

Nick thanked him and retrieved the manila envelope. Once in the car, he gave it to Sacco.

"She subleased the place a year and a half ago," Sacco said, skimming through the rental agreement. "Puts an out-of-state emergency contact number there."

"What's the area code?" Nick asked, avoiding a Grubhub delivery cyclist who'd veered in front of him trying to steer clear of a bus leaving its stop.

"Have no clue." Sacco did a quick search on his phone. "Here we go. Area code 402...Omaha. So she's not local."

Great, Nick thought. Another one from out of state, with no familial ties or safety net close by.

Like the others.

"Employer listed anywhere?"

"Yeah. Brooklyn." Sacco did another brief search. "It's an outfit which, according to their website, is located in the Digital DUMBO area."

Nick grimaced. They would have to deal with nightmare traffic to get there. DUMBO was short for Down Under Manhattan Bridge Overpass, an area which had been an old, run-down industrial district revamped now as an artsy, trendy place. Many start-ups, including digital advertising and marketing firms, had jumped on the lower-rent bandwagons the then practically deserted, turn-of-the-century factories offered, and the advantage of escaping strangling regulatory nightmares brought on by doing business in the city. The transformation began around the '90s. And with so many firms attracted to the area, so began the boom in shops, restaurants, and other service-oriented businesses. It also brought in builders. Expensive apartment complexes and office buildings now dotted the area.

Sacco kept reading. "Duncani Studios. Say's here it's an advertising agency. Multiplatform. Mixes digital and traditional. Serves clientele worldwide."

"Call and tell them we're on our way."

It was after 4:30 p.m. when they reached the victim's work address. The building, an older, six-stories brick building, surrounded by more modern glass-and-steel ones, hosted Latimer's employer near the intersection of Front and Main Streets, and the surrounding hub of restaurants and shops. They rode the elevator to the fourth floor where a peppy receptionist, à la TeC4M, greeted them and announced that a Mr. Gordian from HR would be with them shortly. Within seconds, a young man Nick would gauge at about his early thirties came to lead them to his office.

"Gentlemen," he said, offering them a seat after introductions. He closed the door. The office had a decent-sized workspace, with expensive, new ergonomic furniture, even more expensive electronics, and a view to a beat-up old bank building that resembled more a gas station from the '50s. Unlike the other buildings in the area, which were practically on top of each other, the man had sky and space for a view, with Pebble Beach and Main Street Park across the way, the East River beyond, and the FDR intersecting the Manhattan Bridge landscape at midhorizon.

"Your phone call was a bit cryptic, Detectives. What can I do to help?"

"Do you have a Micaela Latimer working for the firm?" Nick asked.

"Had."

"Did she quit?" Sacco asked.

"Actually, no. We had to dismiss her."

"The reason?" Nick asked.

"Sorry, gentlemen, but that information is confidential."

"Unfortunately, Mr. Gordian," Nick said. "Confidentiality went to hell this afternoon. Ms. Latimer was found dead in her apartment."

The shock made him lean too far back in his chair, almost toppling him. He quickly recovered his physical and mental balance. Unexpected news, Nick saw. But he also caught the wariness, the masking. There was a story here, something Mr. HR did not want revealed.

"I'm sorry. I need to bring management in on this," Gordian said, dialing an extension, and requesting management's presence.

Nick and Sacco waited.

"What's so urgent?" came the voice from behind them.

Nick turned. A man in his late forties stood in the doorway. Receding hairline, with silver-framed eyeglasses that spotlit manicured eyebrows and sharp eyes. He was about Nick's height, a bit heavyset, the plumpness of his body camouflaged by a dark sports jacket over a soft green tieless shirt. Khaki pants. If this was management, that meant dress code casual was the norm around this workplace.

"We have a problem, Ian."

Both he and Sacco stood, as Gordian introduced his boss, Ian Duncan, the owner of the firm.

"These are Detectives Larson and Sacco," Gordian continued. "They're here..." The expression on his face was pained.

Nick took over. "We're investigating the death of a former employee of yours, a Micaela Latimer."

"What?" The man turned with impressive speed and closed the door to the office.

"Ms. Latimer was found this afternoon in her apartment. Our medical examiner places her death at about a week or so ago. Apparent suicide."

The stillness and furtive glance to Gordian would have been missed by many, except Nick.

There it is, the tell. Something is up.

"We were told," Nick continued, "that she was fired. When exactly did that occur? And also," he glanced at both men, "we'd like to know why."

"Detectives, this is a rather delicate situation and, frankly, we would prefer to keep it in-house."

"A death by suspicious means is never a private affair, Mr. Duncan. All we can offer is discretion in our investigation. However, we need to know context in order to solve it. We owe it to the victim."

Nick waited.

Duncan sat down in one of the chairs they'd vacated.

"There was an incident with Ms. Latimer at our annual Christmas office party," Duncan said. "Complaints were filed. HR investigated the claims and we concluded that Ms. Latimer's behavior and that of one of her co-workers was a blatant violation of our rules and policies on conduct. Image is everything in our industry, our bread and butter so to speak. Any whiff of impropriety, especially flagrant public impropriety that can reach our clients' ears, is grounds for dismissal. Both Chet and Micaela disregarded that one sacrosanct rule, and were terminated as of last week."

What was so egregious that it would terminate employment almost immediately? Nick looked at the men. A lot had been said and, yet, nothing. That meant they were dealing with serious shit, like sexual harassment, discrimination, retaliation of some sort, or physical/verbal threats.

"What exactly went down?" Nick asked again.

No reply.

"Gentlemen. We will need the terminated co-worker's name and contact information." The men visibly cringed. "We also have Ms. Latimer's personal laptop. Our IT department will investigate every social platform out on the internet, every email, every comment. We have face recognition algorithms. If there is anything out there, we'll find it. What happened?"

Ian Duncan sighed. "Show them, Henry."

With obvious reluctance, Gordian turned to his filing cabinet and retrieved a USB flash drive from within a file there. A few maneuvers later, the video came to life on the computer screen.

Nick and Sacco watched as a lively party, inside what seemed a private room in a restaurant somewhere, was in full swing. The festively decorated room, with music blaring in the background, had a small dance area devoid of tables and chairs. That dance patch was the focus of the video they were now watching. Several employees were there, including the victim who, by the way she was behaving, Nick saw, was plastered with enough booze to fuel her to the nearest galaxy.

That surprised him. From the evidence at the apartment, the woman was super OCD, the neatness and organization within suggested someone who needed to be in control at all times. The behavior he was seeing right now was out of character.

"Look at the drunken slut."

The maliciousness of the tone coming from the video surprised Nick.

"Chet, stop it."

A woman's voice.

"Oh, it's going to get even better. Wait for it."

It seemed to Nick that the man Chet knew the script, almost as if he had planned the subsequent scene.

Whoever had ordered Chet to stop, moved into view and out the door on the far left side.

A new song started, one of those current, popular rap songs constantly blasting from the radio airways. The victim, already in a dancing, drunken frenzy, veered toward another employee, a pretty woman in her twenties, and began dancing around her. Latimer's invitation to dance was aggressive and oftentimes lewd, with occasional touching. Interspersed with the action visible on the video, spurts of low, spiteful chuckles filtered through from the videographer. Some people around the dance floor started egging the victim on, others fidgeted awkwardly, and others seemed quite uncomfortable. The target of Latimer's focus first chuckled nervously, followed by shock when, a few seconds later, Latimer began humping near the other woman's crotch. The camera zoomed into Latimer's sexually suggestive movements and then panned up to capture the disgust registered on the other woman's face.

More satisfied laughter rumbled from the Chet person videotaping the scene.

"This is going to go viral."

The camera zoomed in and out a couple of times.

The harassed woman pushed Latimer away and left the room, holding a hand to her mouth.

Probably went to the bathroom to throw up after that, Nick thought.

The video ended.

Silence.

"A complaint was filed the very next day," Gordian said.

"And upon my suggestion, we placed Ms. Latimer on administrative leave," continued Duncan. "It was a first infraction, drink related, and off-site, although it was a company event. However, we warned Ms. Latimer, advised her about the complaint, and suggested she spend some time working from home. She was a very valuable member of our team and, frankly, I didn't want to lose her. She was creative, competitive, resourceful, and had great rapport with her clients."

Gordian picked up the tale from there.

"We resolved the complaint in-house. Ms. Latimer apologized, and both parties went back to their routines, satisfied with the outcome."

Nick doubted it. From that moment on, the woman from the video, the focus of Ms. Latimer's attention, would probably skirt around their victim, polite but distant, and be skittish whenever the other woman was around. She wouldn't ever be caught alone anywhere with Ms. Latimer, not ever again. No. Things would not be normal around this office again.

Gordian nodded to the monitor and continued. "Unfortunately, this video surfaced about eight days ago. True to Chet's word, it went viral."

"It hadn't been posted before?" Nick asked.

"No."

"Was it sent to the woman's boyfriend or husband?"

"Yes." Duncan looked aggrieved. "Her fiancé."

"Let me take a stab at this now," Nick continued. "The release of this video was due to some unresolved rivalry issues between Ms. Latimer and this Chet person?"

"We all are extremely competitive, Detective Larson," said Duncan. "If we're not, we fail. Sharks and piranhas are sweet kittens in comparison to the competition out there in our field of work. It's part of what we do here. Keeps creativity and productivity to the max. What I didn't know was that the rivalry was acrimonious and more personal than anyone suspected. If not..." His chin pointed to the black computer monitor. "If not, I would not have suggested she take on Chet's client on a last-minute, urgent project while he was on vacation."

"The client liked her work better," Sacco stated.

Duncan nodded.

"I would have replaced Chet's loss with one of my client accounts, if the idiot had not gotten so spiteful as to lose all reason and post the video. No one knows yet, but I'm reducing my own workload as accounts director to concentrate more on my CEO duties."

Nick and Sacco stood. "Thank you, gentlemen. We need to interview your staff," Nick said.

Duncan looked at his watch. "It's after five. Everyone scrambles out when the bell rings, so to speak."

"I can compile a list of our employees with their phone numbers," Gordian volunteered. "If you care to wait a bit more."

"Could you email those to me?" Nick asked. They needed to get out of here and begin sifting through the evidence. Nick was getting antsy. He and Sacco took out cards. "I'd appreciate though the contact information of this Chet, the victim of Ms. Latimer's harassment, and the woman whose voice berated Chet. We also need a copy of the video."

At the look on their faces, Nick added, "As I stated before, we will try to be as discreet as possible. But that is evidence that may shed light in our investigation."

Nick and Sacco waited until Gordian compiled the information requested on a sheet of paper and copied the video on a USB flash drive.

With list and video copy in hand, they left.

CHAPTER TWENTY-FOUR

BY THE TIME Nick and Sacco returned to the precinct, they were cranky, it was late, and they'd gone two hours over shift.

"Oh, oh," whispered Sacco.

Nick looked up. If the floor under Kravitz's shoes had been alive, it'd be bitching all the way across the Hudson about the captain's crushing steps. He pointed at them as he neared.

"Conference room. Now."

Ah, shit.

"Am I going to have to muzzle you both? Put you back on domestic duty?" Kravitz said, closing the conference room door with more force than necessary. "I thought I was clear on this."

"What the hell did we do?" Nick complained.

"Didn't I tell you NOT to mention that 'S' word? Today, I've been asked five times, by different people, if it's true there might be a serial on the loose."

"Captain, we haven't said shit," Nick burst out, anger simmering. "We haven't even had time to pee since before the sun was up."

"Then who the hell is revving the rumor mill?"

"You got us," Sacco said. "We just got in."

"You didn't get it from Ramos or Carpenter, of that I'm sure," Nick added.

"So who the hell has a loose mouth?" Kravitz almost shouted it.

"Bet my next overtime it's coming from within FID," Nick said.

"Can't afford your overtime, not anytime soon."

"Ah, Captain," groaned Sacco.

The captain sat on the nearest chair. Nick noticed Kravitz's cigar had given up the battle. It was mush.

"I know suicides by hanging have been increasing," Nick said. "But the techs at FID are not stupid. In less than two weeks, they've had to process three incidents that are questionable and nearly identical. The only wrench in the pie is Desha Adnet's death. Speculation by now must be rampant."

"They're not allowed to speculate out loud," Kravitz said in a not so pleasant tone. "Imagine if this gets out to the press."

"Then you'd better gather the flock and give them explicit orders," Nick said. "And soon. You know the rumor mill takes a life of its own if left unchecked."

"Roundup already set for nine in the a.m."

"Hope you're not expecting us to be there. We've got autopsies tomorrow. Three."

"Totes expediting this last victim?"

Nick nodded. "Three for one sale."

Kravitz threw his cigar into the nearest trash can. "Ok. So what's the story on this latest one."

Nick, with Sacco filling in when Nick paused, briefed Kravitz about the crime scene, the interview with the victim's employer, and the agenda for the following day.

"Have you set up interviews yet?"

"Sacco set up one tomorrow afternoon with the complainant. Waiting on a call back from the other woman in the video. We haven't gotten through to this Chet individual yet."

"I'm taking you both out of the new cases roster for now. You've got your hands full with these three."

Nick was relieved. "We haven't gone through much of the evidence yet," he agreed.

"Heard Carpenter has a ton of IT shit to sift through, and Ramos's lab is getting crowded. She's getting cranky."

"What if another questionable suicide pops up?" Nick asked his boss, hoping Providence gave them a small break.

"We'll tackle that as it comes," Kravitz said. "Any theories?"

"Not much, but I put in a call to Dr. Kilcrease to come on over. Maybe he can give us some insight. I want to run by him what Ms. Lunney told us about Jessica Waitre, and have him see the video from this last victim. Maybe he can see a correlation...or something. I'll take anything at this point."

"Am I interrupting?"

The medical examiner's voice surprised them. He usually did not grace these halls, if he could avoid it.

Nick stared, hard. Something was wrong. Millsap's expression seemed strained.

"Horowitz said I'd find you here," he said and closed the door quickly. He breathed. "We have a problem."

He handed some papers to Nick. "For your Creasy files."

"What are these?"

"Lab results. The additional testing I requested." Millsap chose the chair nearest the captain. "Ramos is fit to be tied." He glanced at each. "To put it bluntly, gentlemen, Mrs. Creasy was drugged first and left to suffocate to death later. The ligature or the respiratory depression would have been the final cause of death. Either way, a very unpleasant way to die. The only plus in this macabre scenario is that the victim may not have been aware she was dying by the time she was hanged."

"What?" Nick asked, doing a quick scan of the lab results in his hand.

"We're dealing with U4, gentlemen. Pink or pinky, as druggies so euphemistically call it. Worse, though, is that it's been spiked with DMSO."

"What the hell is that?" Kravitz asked. "I don't speak your geek."

"Dimethyl sulfoxide. It has many applications, although currently, it's used more as an anti-inflammatory agent or an absorption mechanism to increase other medications' penetration through the skin. Hormone and nicotine patches have it. However, by mixing DMSO with the pink, it facilitates and accelerates percutaneous absorption of the drug. Highly toxic." Millsap glanced at everyone. "And the chances of ODing become exponential. Bottom line, gentlemen, the victim was rubbed with the stuff like a piece of meat and left to OD while being prepped to hang."

"God," blurted Nick.

"That's a nasty visual, Millsap," said Sacco.

"If it hadn't been for Nick questioning the apparent cause of death, Horowitz's and Ramos's keen eyes, and my own dissatisfaction with cause of death, we wouldn't be talking."

"A user?" Sacco asked.

"Doubtful," Millsap answered. "Users go for the cocktail with heroin or fentanyl. Not that that is any better."

"How the hell was she exposed, then?" Nick asked.

"That is where I'm stumped and your challenge. Was it a user she knew? Someone convincing her she should try it out? Hair analysis has her clean before time of death."

"Why didn't the original tox screen flag this?" Kravitz asked.

"It's not included in regular screening. But with drug users ODing and dropping like fleas from this stuff, we may have to consider including the test into our protocol from now on. Fat chance, I say. It's unlikely I'll get the budget to add GC-MS testing, unless absolutely necessary." Millsap grimaced. "If the serial rumors are true..."

Kravitz's expletive vibrated within the room. "I don't want anyone speculating unless I give the OK on this. We've still got jack shit on these cases. We need something solid to present to the DA before we go blabbing all over the precinct about the S word."

Millsap's expression told Nick their ME believed it was already too late to quench the whispers. "Like I was saying, if the latest victims have been exposed to this shit, I have to be extra careful tomorrow in the autopsies." He turned to Nick. "Make sure you double glove tomorrow. I'll have disposable protective gear for both of you, as well."

"More importantly," Nick said, "we need to find out how the victims were exposed. That could lead to a suspect."

"If," Kravitz countered. "To be determined, yet."

"Ramos, bless her, swabbed every orifice in sight on the last four victims," Millsap said. "Especially the women. I'll be doing the same. I don't like unknowns."

"Don't we all." Nick said.

Millsap slapped his hands on the table. "Well, gentlemen. I'm off. I need a good dinner and a very, very big glass of wine."

"You, two, off," Kravitz told Nick and Sacco. "Heavy day tomorrow for all."

Nick nodded and followed everyone out the door. Being sent home might be nice only if you wouldn't have to work late into the evening, with no overtime pay.

At his desk, Nick grabbed Creasy's death file and added the lab report to it. Checked his email and found Mr. Gordian had sent him a contact list of employees. *Efficient.* He printed that out.

He grabbed an empty binder and started the Micaela Latimer death book.

"We may have hit pay dirt with Latimer's laptop," Carpenter's loud voice reached Nick from the vicinity of Horowitz's desk.

"Hold on, kid." Nick hotfooted it to the elevator before Carpenter could disappear into it.

Carpenter froze as if someone had hit the Pause button, with only his head and eyes still moving with impatience.

"Spill."

"Latimer's laptop was not password protected," Carpenter said, swiveling to face Nick. His body began swaying side to side, as if electricity were running through a live wire. He was on to something, Nick could tell.

"I know. You said that at the apartment."

Sacco joined them. "What's going on?"

"Kid says we hit pay dirt with the Latimer laptop."

"Remember I said she had a password organizer, too?"

Nick nodded. So did Sacco.

"Someone who doesn't know shit about computers tried to delete stuff from the Messenger account. And it wasn't her."

"How the hell did you come up with that jewel?" Nick asked.

"The attempt was done five hours after her last login. And there hasn't been any more logins since. The good part for us was that it was done quickly, maybe from a phone. My guess the person was in a rush. Didn't realize that by deleting the conversation from his or her end, that action doesn't delete it from Latimer's."

"Have you read any?"

"The last one. Man, Nick, she invited the fucker to her apartment. She let her killer in."

Crap, Nick thought. What a moment for the victim's building not to have security cameras.

"Can you track who this person is?"

"I have an IP address, but I have a feeling it's going to be the road to nowhere."

"Send me everything you've got and copy Sacco on it."

"I'm already compiling. Soon as I'm done, you've got them. And, by the way, I should have the phone records from Adnet and Waitre tomorrow. The phone company sent confirmation it's complying with the warrant."

"Get those to me as soon as you get them."

Since no more questions came his way, Carpenter pivoted and hurried down the hall to take the stairs to his office floor.

"I'm cross-eyed," Sacco said. "Like the good doctor said, I need food and a massive drink. But more than that, I need a shower and some Zs. I'm exhausted."

"Yeah." Nick rubbed his neck. "As soon as I'm done with the incident report, I think I'll go home, too."

"Laura waiting?"

"No."

Sacco slapped him on the shoulder. "Go home, man. Grab your beauty. Get laid. That's the best way to relax. I'd do the same if Ramos were more cooperative."

"You are seriously fucked, my friend."

"Hey. If I had a beauty like Laura waiting for me..."

"Shut up and go home. Go get Ramos and treat her to a nice meal. Maybe she'll accept your one hundredth invitation."

"Maybe I will." Sacco smiled, saluted, and was gone.

Nick's computer pinged. *Well, that was fast.* He checked his email and, sure enough, Carpenter had already sent the info to them. He copied the file to his Dropbox account and sat down to finish the report. He'd print everything for the binder tomorrow.

The office floor around him settled into its nightly hums. Writing to its rhythm, his mind tuned out and settled. Thoughts of Laura undulated in playful whiffs in between the clicks from his keyboard. Images of when they'd made love teased. Concentration ebbed. His want and craving for Laura increased. He hadn't seen her, talked to her, or touched her since the night before he'd been called out to the Adnet and Waitre crime scene yesterday. Had it only been yesterday? It seemed like that had happened months ago.

Nick stopped. What the hell was he still doing here? It was already nine. Tomorrow would be a crap day with the autopsies first thing in the morning. Laura was his chance at a new beginning, a fuller life. He would be an idiot if he began a relationship letting the cases consume him to the point of working at all hours. With his ex-wife, he'd had an excuse. Plunging into the crime puzzle and solving victims' deaths was preferable to facing Angela, the living vampire waiting for him at home, who reveled in sucking away his joys, his life.

He stared at the incident report. Nothing could be done about the victims now, except trudge through the evidence. He'd be the better cop, focused and tenacious, if he stopped and picked up the leads tomorrow. A couple of hours of personal downtime would not make a difference to these poor souls.

He saved what he'd written and shut the computer off. Traffic to the apartment was light for this time of night and he enjoyed for once the biting cold, the crisp, invigorating air. He stopped by Mama Grimaldi's on Third, grabbed the carry-out he'd ordered, and was opening his door by nine forty-five.

He stepped into his apartment at the same time his neighbor, Lorena, stepped out of hers. Curious to see the last client of the day, Nick paused. A family of five walked out—mother, daughter, grandmother, and two smaller children. Lorena followed the entourage, dressed in a flowing white dress, a white scarf around her head in imitation of Rosie the Riveter, the look complemented with white bangles, bracelets, and earrings. She resembled a dressed-up white dove on its way to a party.

"*Muñeco!*" she greeted him and waved fingers at him. A barrage of quick Spanish suddenly filled the hallway. Quick cheek pecks. Farewells by all.

"So glad you're here," she said as she was escorting the family out the vestibule. She waved one last enthusiastic goodbye. Once the clients were out of sight, she took the scarf off and vigorously rubbed her hair. At Nick's sardonic look, she smiled. "Itchy."

"I bet."

She started taking off all her bangles and jangles, laughing softly. "Gotta dress the part. I am what they need, but they need to expect the part."

Nick laughed. "That's rather convoluted, and yet, I understood it."

"Listen, *muñeco*. I'm glad you're home early. Your love has been by several times today. She's very sad. I sense a shadow lurking."

Leaving his apartment door open, Nick walked quickly to the kitchen counter and dropped the food there. "When was she here?" he asked, coming back to Lorena.

"Saw her from the window while I was doing my sessions. Today is my busiest day, so I couldn't go and find out. Last I saw her was when my clients the Dominguez brothers were here. Around six o'clock."

She went to her door and paused. "Go to her. She needs you."

"Is that a reading?"

"Not even a guess. An observation." Her eyes traveled up and down Nick's figure. "And you need her tonight, too." She closed her door softly.

Nick went back to his apartment and showered in record time. He was toweling his hair dry when a soft knock echoed around the apartment. He threw the towel on the floor and hopped into his sweats on the way to the door. He knew who it would be.

Laura's back was to his door when he looked through the peephole. He opened the door.

"Hi."

When she turned, the joy in her chocolate eyes was breathtaking.

"Hi," she said, and the next thing Nick knew, she was buried in his arms, weeping.

"Well, that is a fine hello," he said, trying to keep the situation light. He stepped back, her body still clamped around his. He closed the door.

"I'm sorry, I'm sorry," she repeated into his chest. "It's just been a crap day."

Hadn't it been for all?

"My business...Erin," She cried a little harder. "The appeal... not fair."

From the disjointed snippets she threw in between sobs, he filled in the blanks to her day. It sucked to be Laura at this moment. No more business. No more sister locked up where she belonged. He rocked her, soothing her silently with his motion, his hand pressing her head to his chest in comfort. After a few minutes, he drew her back, cradled her face, ducked his head and leaned into a kiss. Her hands slipped from around his waist to around his wrists, almost as if she were anchoring herself to him, or making sure he would not pull back.

"I'm sorry," she said when they both came up for air. His thumbs wiped away the tears.

"It's okay," he said.

"I do so love you," she confessed, framing his face, and, this time, she plunged into a carnal kiss to end all kisses.

He didn't need further invitation. He lifted her as she stood and carried her, feet dangling, to the bedroom.

Five hours later, Nick sat in front of his computer, reading through the Messenger posts Carpenter had retrieved from Latimer's computer.

Unlike Laura, who lay asleep in a satisfied heap on his bed, sex, reheated food, and more wonderful sex had energized him. Thirty minutes ago, after staring up at his bedroom ceiling for that long, he'd given up, had closed the door, and charged up his laptop.

He scanned the list and chose the last message from Latimer.

What Nick read there made the back of his neck crawl. Their IT guru had been spot on. Latimer had gratefully invited her killer into her home.

Nick leaned back and rubbed his face. The video, which Carpenter had not seen yet, put the conversation he'd just read into brilliant context. The woman had had some serious issues. Lonely, confused, sexually conflicted, and guilty about her feelings, she'd been easy prey. Add to that an attack on her pride and joy, her work, where her achievements and accomplishments were linked to her self-worth, and you had a recipe for disaster...definitely self-destruction. Nick knew it took only a second for a depressed individual to make an irreversible decision. Add to the mix some pathologically screwed individual who wanted to lead you to your eternal resting place quicker than God intended and, well, that was a recipe for disaster.

He reached for pad and pencil. Made three columns, each headed with one woman's name. Created some rows underneath, wide enough to add information into them. Ok. What did the three victims have in common? He wrote "not local" under each. No family support. Creasy was from Montana. Latimer was from

Omaha. Waitre was from New Hampshire. All three were transplants to the city that doesn't forgive. Both Waitre and Latimer had been targeted by what Nick would, from now on, label as the FUP, the fucked-up perp. He riffled quickly through his flip notebook. No. He didn't have a screen name in the Waitre case as yet. He'd hound Carpenter tomorrow for that info. The phone records should display it. He squinted at the computer screen and at Carpenter's anorexic message. No ID on this either. He printed "SCREEN NAME" to the side of the table and circled it several times as a reminder. Would they match, he wondered?

If only they were that lucky.

In the "friend" categories, only Creasy had a support system here. The other two, well, Waitre had had only Desh and his family, and that had been going down the toilet the week before her death. You could count Lunney as a friend, but from what he'd gleaned at the interview, the relationship was more like mother-daughter, with Waitre the more skittish in that relationship. Mrs. Kyriakou? Same as Lunney, Nick thought. Lastly, as far as Latimer was concerned, it didn't seem as if she'd had any friends aside from her co-workers...maybe. He and Sacco would have to delve into that after the autopsies tomorrow. The woman who'd dissed Chet in the video, a Sofi Guldur from the information given to them by Gordian, could be a sympathetic acquaintance. That didn't mean Latimer would confide in her. Best buds they probably weren't. As to the other woman? Even Latimer's heartfelt apology would not endear her to Oriana Tamone, the victim of the sexual harassment at the Christmas party, especially after the video had been released.

Nick wrote M-Li's name inside Creasy's column and underlined "friend" several times underneath. Squiggled a question mark next to Lunney's and Kyriakous' names in the Waitre column. With Latimer, he simply planted a question mark. He'd assume there were no friends to be had there, as yet.

Now for the suicide notes.

Unlike what people thought, many suicides did not leave notes. But Creasy and Latimer had supposedly left one. Waitre hadn't. As Sacco had pointed out, and everyone had caught on to, the short notes had one misspelling. Ok, so that fault was normal and could be found in the eight million plus population of NYC. But for both missives to have the same word, spelled the same way, and the rest close in phraseology? Well, the odds were definitely in their favor. The victims couldn't have written them. They didn't know each other. Or...wait... There was a connection between Creasy and Waitre. Isabel's husband had worked with Desha, and he, in turn, had worked for Isabel. The couples knew each other. The women, according to David Creasy had hit it off. Nick quickly scribbled that information under the women's names. Doodled another question mark under Latimer's.

His mind retreated back to the suicide notes. What was up with "liers" and "sleep"? Was the FUP pissed off at the world because he was an insomniac? Did his need, or fetish, have to do with putting people to sleep by hanging them? Or did he get some sort of pleasure watching as they suffocated, his prey vulnerable, at his mercy, unable to fight for their lives? Were the victims surrogates for someone he wanted to kill, but couldn't because, deep down, the man was a coward?

Boy, wasn't Kilcrease going to have fun with this one.

Nick stared at his chart. A pattern was crystallizing. He just wished the evidence would emerge faster and point to a specific suspect, or at least a person of interest. At this point, anything would satisfy Nick.

He stretched and popped a few bones as he wrote U4 under Creasy's name. He grimaced. The abbreviated version of the drug's name sounded like an unexploded ordinance designation. And maybe it was, in some morbid sense. You used, you imploded. Death in powder form.

How on earth had Isabel Creasy been exposed or gotten hold of that nasty, toxic shit? None of the people surrounding her were users. There would be signs, and there were none. A quick thought flashed through Nick's mind. The lab where Creasy experimented on her future products? He made a quick note on top of the page to call the lab tomorrow. Dealing with so many chemicals, maybe that was where she'd been exposed. Could it have been an inadvertent touch by someone who had been using it? Faulty safety protocols followed by someone else at the lab? Contamination of some surface there? Nick shook his head, as if to convince someone who might be watching. No. The effects of that shit were immediate and gruesome, if left untreated. Creasy would not have had time to go home and eat that wonderful last meal Totes had mentioned. Double checking didn't hurt, but after meeting the director of the lab, he sincerely doubted it. The other two victims—would their drug panel show U4 as well? The autopsy was tomorrow, but the results of the trace evidence would not be back any time soon, unless Totes placed firecrackers under everyone's ass at FID and did the impossible.

What else? Nick sensed he was missing something. Overlooking something. Felt it. He checked the chart again and thought of the women. After a bit, he wrote "vulnerable" under two names. Needy came to mind and he wrote that as well. Dysfunctional relationships? Maybe with Creasy and Waitre. He didn't know about Latimer. Depressed? Lunney had definitely labeled Waitre as such. Latimer, by her words, fell into that category as well. The wrench in the shop was Creasy. Yes, she'd been depressed before and during her divorce. But according to M-Li Watson, she'd been liberated the moment she had signed on the dotted line. New life. New apartment. Freedom to pursue her dreams. Out of the three victims, she was, well, normal, the one whose future didn't look bleak or disastrous, not like the other two victims.

Her death, if Nick followed what evidence they had, didn't make any sense at all, especially by suicide. His gut had been sending alert signals ever since he'd viewed the first crime scene. And, right now, it was churning even faster.

Nick slashed several lines under the chart he'd created and wrote FUP in bold, encasing the acronym in a thick rectangle of lead from his pencil.

This person, whoever he was, was a stalker par excellence, grooming his victims, filling an emotional void, and then leading them, unknowing or maybe even willing, to their gory deaths. Lambs to the slaughter, as the saying went. This man, he'd have to have gargantuan muscles à la WWE, AEW, or MMA to do this type of kill. Any policeman or fireman who'd dealt with the human body understood the amount of strength required to hold a limp, almost dead weight upright, let alone holding it in place while pulling on a rope. Once the tautening took place, the rope would take care of keeping the victim upright, but it still wouldn't be an easy pull. Unless he was using a tool they were unaware of.

Lots of stuff to nibble on, but nothing chewy or tangible enough to bite and keep hold. The good news, at least, was that the man might have a family, if taken at face value. That was a new avenue of investigation to pursue...if true. From the virtual conversation Carpenter had sent him, there seemed to be a sick mother somewhere, and a sister who had died. How recently?

Anyone's guess. But the mother was an angle to look into. He wrote down sick mother and then hospital, nursing home, hospice? Or, they could be chasing chimeras. The killer could have invented a family to earn sympathy votes from his victims.

Nick sighed. Nothing was ever easy. True or false, they would have to follow this lead. In Manhattan alone, they had twenty-three hospitals, not counting nursing homes and hospice care. Then there were the other boroughs to check. And this clue didn't even take into account when the woman had been admitted. Could have been the date of the conversation with Latimer, or a year ago. Plainly speaking, it was going to take a shit load of man-hours.

Worse yet, the killer might be taking care of his mother at home. That meant going through thousands of home-care-worker lists.

The bedroom door opened. Seconds later, soft arms slid down his torso and lips nibbled at his neck.

"You should go back to bed," Nick said, stretching back and holding her in place. He kissed her with renewed hunger.

"Not without you." She rested her chin on top of his shoulder. "What are you working on?" She kissed his neck.

"Three women who were killed in the same manner."

"By the same person? Is that what you have?"

"Evidence points that way, but we won't know for sure until we can prove it."

She kissed his shoulder. "If there is anyone who can solve this, it's you."

Nick knew Laura's experience with her own case had colored her perspective. His insistence that she didn't fit the profile of a killer, despite the overwhelming evidence against her, had, in the end, proved her innocence. And he wouldn't have been able to prove it without his team, and the faith they had in him, despite the obvious. Nick knew Laura would be forever grateful to all of them.

"You, my sweet, are prejudiced."

"With cause," Laura admitted. She glanced at the pad resting on top of his leg, scrutinizing some of the information there. "That is so sad. Were they young?"

Now *there* was another thing in common that he should write down, he thought. "Range between late twenties and early thirties."

"What is this?" Laura pointed to the U4 reference. "Is that a band, like U2?"

Nick's laughter bubbled from deep within his stomach and rumbled around the apartment. He turned suddenly, grabbed her, and flipped her over the sofa on top of him. Pad and pencil fell on the floor. Still laughing, he kissed her, tasting and exploring in deep satisfaction.

"You're good for me, you know?" He speared his fingers through her hair and framed her face. "And, no. It's not a band. It's a street drug."

"Sorry."

"Is that your favorite word now?"

"No. Then again, saying it leads to very satisfactory activities. You are a very creative and understanding man," she said with a sexy smile. "You made me forget all my woes very efficiently." She kissed his eyelids. "Very thoroughly." She kissed his lips. "Very enjoyably." She bit his chin. "Are you up for another round?"

He pressed her against him.

"What do you think?"

Their combined laughter echoed around the room, but was quickly muffled into silence.

CHAPTER TWENTY-FIVE

Friday, January 17

THE AUTOPSY THAT morning had been a harrowing experience. Nothing beat examining three dead bodies in the early morning, especially one that was in a healthy state of decomposition. Add to that an autopsy room full of techs and assistant MEs, and assistants to the assistants, all dressed in PPEs, face shields, double gloves, and masks, and roiling the smells around into every cranny of the room the moment they moved. The only thing Nick had wished was to have worn a hazmat suit with its own filtration system. That would have alleviated the smells. In any case, the entire thing had seemed surreal. Everyone looked like they'd beamed onto a scene from the movie *Outbreak* or the television show *The Hot Zone*. And all because of possible exposure to a synthetic drug created and discarded years ago by an American lab and currently produced and exported to the US for distribution by a Chinese pharmaceutical.

Enhanced for optimum osmotic assimilation.

Surreal didn't cut it.

Later, at the precinct, he'd taken a shower, but he still could not quite get rid of the clinging smell of the dead in his nostrils. The only good thing was that, despite not getting much sleep during the previous night and early morning hours, and the sad affair of dissecting the dead for clues, Nick was refreshed, mind clear and focused.

He owed that to Laura.

Nick approached Ramos, where she was bent over a microscope.

"You look ready to chew the world into pulp and spit it out as paper," Ramos said after a cursory glance. She slipped a new slide under the microscope. "Good night with Laura?"

"Perv. I have pervs for co-workers," Nick said, but the smile was wide and satisfied. "Did you accept Sacco's invitation?"

"Nah. And he didn't even try hard. In all honesty, we were both pooped. Got some well-deserved Zs for a change, unlike you, I'm sure." She studied Nick and gave a knowing nod. "How's Laura doing, by the way?"

"Not so well." Nick put up a hand. "And before you start ragging on me about possible lack of male prowess or ability to satisfy a woman, I do have to mention she finalized the transfer of Les Gâteaux to Erin yesterday."

"That sucks."

"Aaniyah also dropped on her the results of the appeal. Overall, a bad day."

"Last I heard, Ward was asking for a retrial and transfer to a psych ward." Ramos said. "Did she get it?"

Nick nodded. "Yeah. And what Sandra Ward wants, she seems to obtain."

"She's a manipulative psycho. Bet if a rock had organs, she could make it pee." She took another slide and replaced the one under the microscope.

"What did Millsap have to say?" she asked.

"He's looking at internal organs quite differently now, let me tell you. Highly suspects the two women were marinated with U4 before they were strung up. He won't commit until he has examined all tissues minutely and everything tested."

"What about the male victim?"

"That was a different story. Ligature strangulation. Not self-inflicted."

"So we're dealing with murder all around."

"Safe bet," said Nick. "What's up? You called."

"I have something for you," Ramos said, pointing to the slides. "Rope material on the three cases is identical. Will test further for rope composition and trace evidence on the last two cases. This man was prepared, and probably wore gloves."

"That makes sense, though," Nick said, disgust in his voice. "What you may not know is that the victims issued invitations to the FUP to enter their homes."

Ramos turned. "What?"

"My new acronym for the person of interest."

Ramos digested the information. In a matter of seconds, she started laughing. "Fucked-up perp?"

Nick nodded. She knew him so well.

"Priceless." Ramos turned her attention back to the microscope.

"And, yeah, he would have come prepared," he said and outlined for her the last communication from Latimer. "So, instead of wine or flowers," Nick finished, "the man arrives at their doorstep with a dose of U4 and a rope."

"Nasty romantic."

"I'm curious," Nick said, checking his phone for new messages or emails. Nothing. "Do you have any other trace results?"

"In the Creasy case," said Ramos. "Some lavender, lanolin, and other chemicals. Won't bore you with the list."

"Her creams?"

"Only the jar she was using and based on the reports given to us by the lab she rented."

"What about the other victims?"

"Haven't gotten the swab results back."

"What about trace on the Creasy rope?" Nick asked. "Any trace of U4?"

Ramos paused. The loud F-bomb startled a tech two tables away.

"Shoo, shoo." Her arms reinforced word with action. "Go do more detecting. I have work to do."

Nick went back to his desk and found Sacco studying Nick's scribbles and chart from the previous evening.

"Have you run this by Kilcrease yet?"

"Not yet. He should be here soon." Nick took the sheet of paper from his partner, wrote age, a question mark, and circled it. He added a fourth column, labeled it Desha Adnet, and scribbled murder under it.

"I'm going to scout around Latimer's neighborhood and see if there is any Ring security system, or anything pointing a camera at the doorway of the victim's building."

Divide and conquer worked for Nick. "Do you know if Carpenter is in? I want to see if we're dealing with the same FUP."

Sacco chuckled. Nick had explained the acronym in autopsy. Sacco liked it so much he swore he'd call every person of interest in the future that way. Brevity had its perks.

"Hoping for similar screen names?"

"Yes," Nick said. "And while you're hunting, I'll track down the elusive Chet Emberson."

"Remember we have a p.m. interview with Oriana Tamone," Sacco said.

"Has Sofi Guldur called back?"

"Horowitz hasn't left any messages on our desks," Sacco said.

Nick nodded and waved to Kilcrease, who had stepped out of the elevator. "I'll check voicemail later."

"Hey, boys," Kilcrease greeted. "Heard you may have a...you know what...about which your boss doesn't want anyone to whisper."

"And hands were lovingly slapped at roll call this morning," Nick added.

Kilcrease's smile was pure amusement. "I'm sure someone will find a way to pay back for the muzzle. How can I help?"

Nick pointed to the conference room. While Sacco and Kilcrease got comfortable, he dialed Carpenter's extension.

"See if there is a screen handle for the suspect on both the Waitre and Latimer conversations," Nick told Carpenter when he answered. "That goes for Creasy's, too." He could only hope. "Get back to me as soon as you can. I'm in the conference room for now."

Nick sat.

For the next twenty minutes, both he and Sacco went over each crime scene, possible victimology, and witness reports. They went over impressions, hunches, and observations. Played the Latimer video. Nick then handed over his brainstorming sheet to the doctor and waited.

Kilcrease pored over the information there. After a while, he leaned back in his chair.

"What are we dealing with here?" Nick asked. "Apart from the obvious."

"Two possibilities. It could very well be a troll, one who picks a random victim from a search on internet sites like Facebook, Snapchat, Reddit, Omegle, TikTok, even Instagram."

Sacco groaned. "Man, Doc, just in Manhattan alone it could be one suspect in one and a half million inhabitants."

"It happens. Remember Markoff, the Craigslist killer?"

Nick remembered. That situation had been what he called murder by stranger. Those cases were a bitch to solve. If the cops had not gotten an email address from his last kill, they'd never have found him. Markoff had chosen his victims at random by checking and answering exotic ads placed on that platform.

"The second possibility is that your suspect knew them."

"We already know Waitre and Latimer met the guy before their deaths," Nick said.

"What I meant was that their paths intersected somehow before he actually contacted them. Maybe he saw them at a neighborhood supermarket, or a coffee shop. Definitely online. My bet is he trolls through Facebook first. Photos in particular. It's really mind-blowing what intimate things people post there about their feelings, lives, family...vulnerabilities."

"A smorgasbord for predators," Nick said. "We know."

"This person preys on his victims' weaknesses, which seem to revolve around their lack of self-worth. They somehow crave to be recognized, celebrated, loved above all things."

"Acceptance," Nick stated. He rose and held up a finger. "Hold that thought."

He sprinted to his computer, quickly scanned for the photo he wanted, printed it, and brought it back to show Kilcrease.

The psychiatrist studied the photograph. He glanced at Nick. "I see what you mean. It's there in the eyes."

"Mrs. Lunney said similar things about our second victim, Jessica Waitre," Nick said.

"Vulnerable people believe in a vision of self that doesn't jibe with reality. It clashes with the world. I call it the sitcom syndrome. These people conform to what they watch and hear on TV, movies, and videos. They gravitate to people who emulate that specific behavior and speak that lingo. Life, to them, is not complex, and issues can be resolved in a short span of time, or by posting a profound quote. Unfortunately, when issues persist, when behaviors around them deviate from their expectations, and truth and reality win out, some minds can't cope. They haven't been honed or tempered by adversity and failure, which reverses those into successes."

Kilcrease paused, deep in thought.

"This person," Kilcrease tapped the sheet of paper. "He probably sees himself as a benevolent angel, understanding his victims' pain and, therefore, facilitating the means to the end, literally. From what you said, he waits to be invited. He's not pushy. Manipulates until his victims think it's their idea to commit the last act of all acts. He's there to fulfill a purpose: take them out of their misery by rendering a service that is compassionate and humane."

"Like putting a dog down," Sacco said. His expression reflected his disgust.

"So what type of psychopathy are we dealing with?" Nick asked.

"Difficult to diagnose without an actual patient in front of me," Kilcrease answered. "But, again, it can go two ways. One: you have a true psychopath, between thirty and forty on the Hare Checklist scale. Two: you could have a person who has severe APD."

"That's antisocial personality disorder, right?" Sacco asked.

Kilcrease nodded.

"What makes you think that?" Nick asked.

"Sick mother. The fact he uses nonviolent methods to kill."

"Come on, Doc," Sacco scoffed. "Nonviolent?"

"No. Wait," Nick countered. "He does have a point. This FUP..."

"What?" Kilcrease was at a loss.

"His acronym for fucked-up person," Sacco said.

"Larson," Kilcrease chided, despite his low laughter. "Really."

"Sue me," said Nick. "This *unknown perp* drugs his victims with his own lotion of U4 before hanging them. By the time the suspect stages them to his satisfaction, the victims are half-dead already." And as Millsap had said a while back, the victims slowly asphyxiated and didn't even twitch with discomfort.

"He probably defines his actions as magnanimous," Kilcrease finished.

"I'm going to have to change that acronym," Nick said. "This person is seriously fucked up."

"The reason why I'm leaning more towards APD than the prototypical psychopathy of a serial. This unknown person may have been abused as a child, or have gone through a traumatic event in his formative years that viciously scarred him for life. From what you told me and I saw of the conversation between him and the last victim, the mother might be the key. Could her sickness have triggered this behavior? Hard to say, again, without analyzing him in person. My educated guess is the mother's heartlessness was what sent him over the edge—the dismissal, the fact she doesn't acknowledge he exists. Maybe he resents the fact the sister is not there to take care of the mother, or that the sibling was better loved by the parent. There's transference here of some sort somewhere. That's the reason he can sympathize with his victims."

"Up to this moment, we don't have anyone who fits that profile," Nick said.

"Once you have a suspect," Kilcrease said, "everything will click into place. However, you have another issue here."

"And what is that?"

"This is not the same template, unless your man breaks it," Kilcrease said.

"Template?" Sacco asked.

"This individual's behavior does not follow the norm."

"You mean for a serial," Nick said.

"Indeed. He doesn't follow prototypical psychopathy in the sense where the kill fulfills the hunger. It's the others' needs that demands fulfillment."

"I'm sorry, Doc," said Sacco. "But I don't follow you."

"I'm afraid I do."

Kilcrease studied Nick.

"Well," said Sacco. "I don't."

"Correct me if I'm wrong," Nick said, looking at Kilcrease. "Serials kill because it's a compulsion. They have a void to fill and feed constantly, something they cannot achieve living their normal lives. This person we're dealing with, however, executes the will of others. Only that gratifies his need. So, until he gets permission to be *humane,* he does not make a move. Isn't that right, Kilcrease?"

"Afraid so. He's still searching, still stalking and grooming. But he lives a normal life until one of his targets asks for help. That holding pattern can go for weeks, if not months, unless something triggers him, or he feels threatened."

Nick rubbed his face. Up to now, from what evidence they'd gathered, the suspect had no worries. He was still anonymous online, no one had seen him with their victims, and there was no security video giving them a hint as to who he was. He, Sacco, and Carpenter had thousands of photographs to go over. That didn't include any other social media platforms the victims may have used. And facial recognition software would take time to compile and would probably be useless if the person was a stranger. Nick wouldn't know whom to choose in the background. The only break they'd get would be if they got lucky...very lucky. In the meantime, the police posed no threat. As Kilcrease had said, it could take days, weeks, even years before his services were needed.

Leave it to the universe to give them a different type of sociopath.

"So basically, we're screwed," Nick said.

"Afraid so."

Shit. Shit. Shit.

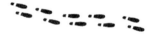

Saturday, January 18

ARJEN had skipped his part-time job today earlier than usual, claiming he had the runs. After stocking shelves for two hours this morning, and dealing with assholes for more, he'd had enough. So by eleven, he'd skedaddled out of there. He didn't give a shit if he got canned, he didn't want the job anyway.

He huddled into his down jacket, cursing everyone he knew. As of yesterday, his stepfather and mother had not relented about the car confiscation. The two choices given, which were neither to his liking, remained: either he walked or he hitched a ride with his mom. He cursed. Screw the last choice. He wouldn't be caught dead with his mom driving him around like he was a six-year-old. He'd hear no end to the ridicule, if seen by his friends. So he'd opted for the bus and was walking the rest of the way home.

He kicked a neighborhood garden ornament and quickened his pace. The wind was brutal, the cold—insane. Fitting, he thought. Life basically sucked—at least, life as of today. Yesterday had sucked at school, too. Someone had blabbed he was smoking weed and he'd been kicked from the soccer team after testing positive in a pee cup. His social studies teacher had given him a D on his last paper, and his friend Russ had told him to fuck off. Arjen was not looking forward to his mom's reaction to these latest debacles.

It didn't help, either, that his mother's personal sex boy-toy had not played ball, either. Arjen had waited until the man had finished servicing his mother that day and had caught up with him two blocks away from the house. The creep's initial shock at Arjen's sophomoric attempt at coercion had waned quickly. He'd first had the gall to laugh in his face. Then he'd told him to grow up and get a life. That had brought reality crashing down on Arjen's head in a rather effective manner. The creep stated that if he posted any pictures on Snapchat, as Arjen had threatened to do, or rat on his mother about her extracurricular activities, only *Arjen* would suffer. He'd not only be kicked out of his home, but also jeopardize his mother's cushy and respected life, one she valued and protected at all costs. As for himself, the man had said he would simply move on to the next needy housewife. No skin off his nose. The blackmail Arjen had undertaken would actually be a résumé enhancer for him.

He hated to admit it, but the creep had been right, even when he'd resented the man for making him feel like a silly, selfish two-year-old brat. The reality was stark: he couldn't piss his mother off. She was the only one who was working for and with him on the sidelines, a wall between him and his stepfather. If she found out what he'd done, and was doing, like skipping school and work, she'd be registering him in military school faster than he could light his next joint.

It wouldn't do to have mom as your enemy.

That day, deflated, but not defeated, Arjen had still persisted by using a bit of deception. He'd pulled up a still shot from the video he'd taken of his mother and the man going at it, showing and threatening to send it to her as an attachment in a message. The creep, the gall of him, had laughed *again* and countered with a threat of his own—the photo would be the focal point of their sexual activities next time around. He'd get her naked as soon as he walked in, and would make sure she climaxed while he showed her the photo. Orgasms, he'd told Arjen, were doubly intense when someone knew they were being watched. The creep had also invited him to witness and enjoy the ride. After all, being a perv voyeur such as Arjen was, he'd probably masturbate as he observed the action between the creep and his mom.

Needless to say, Arjen had given up his blackmail scheme and gone back home like a dog with its tail between his legs.

He rammed his cold hands into his jacket pockets. The screwup on his part just showed how sad the state of affairs the world was in when blackmail could no longer manipulate people. How the hell was he going to solve his problem? Arjen was still pissed, not getting his way, and had no one who'd help him play the game. He needed to come up with a new plan. A more successful one. It was the only way to get his mother and stepfather to toe *his* line.

But all was not lost. Skipping work today could prove to be a stroke of genius. He needed to think things through and come up with a new scheme. Maybe his cousin in Jersey would put him up, incognito, for a couple of days. Nah, he thought, kicking at another neighborhood fence. His aunt would call his mother as soon as he showed up. What about his uncle in Chicago? He mulled that idea around for a bit. He could hitch a ride to the Huntington Station of the LIRR and get off at Penn. There he could catch an Amtrak to Chicago. How many days was a train ride anyway? He hadn't a clue. But even if it was twelve hours or twenty-four, it was enough of a span where he'd be incommunicado. He could even stay at a motel somewhere in between for a day or so, catch some Zs, some porn, and call his uncle once he arrived at his destination. Everyone by then would be worried. Looking for him in all the wrong places.

Once he surfaced for air like a dolphin, they'd be relieved. Ecstatic to know he was safe and to get him back. His mother would do anything if he came home safe.

Now, that could work.

He shook his head. Logistics first. He had very little money, just the allowance he was given at the moment, and no debit card. But he knew where his mother stashed cash for rainy days, as she said. Arjen sneered. The stash was more to indulge in extracurricular activities...secret extracurricular activities. His mom couldn't afford for his stepdad to see suspicious credit-card-purchase trails. By doing what she did, she kept his stepfather blind to all that moved. Case in point, he was still blissfully in the dark his dick didn't have exclusivity rights to his wife's vagina. He had competition.

Arjen was almost to the door when he noticed his mom's car was there. Shit. Why was she here so early? Today she volunteered at the Y, supervising preschoolers who were learning how to swim. Never got home before four o'clock. Maybe too few had showed up? Didn't matter. There would be too many questions to answer if she saw him, and he hated to feign sickness when he felt fine. His mother would be ramming all kinds of remedies down his throat and he would be obliged to swallow them.

Disgusting.

He grabbed the mail and scooted around the house, heading for the basement door and opening it as stealthily as he could. He would hang out in here until it was time to show his face at home, as if he'd been at work. He could strategize in peace for a couple of hours and improve on this new germ of an idea. His mother never came down here, unless she had to wash clothes. And today was not laundry day, so he was safe. Even if she came down, he'd scoot to the bathroom and hide there before she could catch him.

Listening to the occasional creak of the floor as his mother moved around upstairs, he started to work out all the kinks in his plan. He realized, after searching for schedules and train itineraries, he'd have to leave today. Otherwise, he'd be stuck here for another week. He needed clothes, but he scrapped that idea. His mother could catch him sneaking up to his room. The better plan was, once in the city, he'd drop by the Target near Penn, on Thirth-Fourth, and buy what he needed. Getting the cash was no issue, either, because the stash was in the kitchen, in plain sight, in a cutesy cookie jar made to resemble a 1950s stove. They never kept cookies in it. It was only decorative.

The bell upstairs rang. He heard his mother's footsteps, but ignored the activity upstairs.

What if he ran out of cash? Arjen couldn't count exclusively on the money left inside the jar. Let's face it, he didn't know how much was in there. If only he had a debit card. He tapped the mail envelopes against his hand in impatience as he tried to figure that one out. His mother always left her purse and car keys on the small alcove near the back door of the kitchen, next to the phone, answering machine, and her laptop. The cookie jar was right there, too. She stored her grocery and store receipts inside and threw them out once she balanced the checkbook. If, and it was a big if, his mother was nowhere near the kitchen (he crossed mental fingers, hoping she was in her bedroom, way upstairs), he could pilfer her ATM card from the wallet and use that. Arjen muffled his laugh. His mother didn't realize he knew all her passwords and codes. With card and cash in hand, he'd sneak out the way he came in, hop on the bus to Huntington Station, and buy the train tickets with the cash. He'd use the ATM inside the train station to get more cash, and he'd be on his way.

No one would be the wiser, until he arrived in Chicago.

He got into stealth mode and climbed the stairs.

CHAPTER TWENTY-SIX

Monday, January 20

NICK HAD TAKEN over the conference table, all the binders and his brainstorming notes spread out in front of him. An empty pad and a pencil lay next to his laptop for additional annotations. There had to be something they were missing. So, today, he'd decided to pore through all the evidence, interviews, statements, and reports once more. Maybe creating a chart of businesses each woman sponsored would give him a pattern. Maybe they frequented the same stores, or a coffee shop, or a restaurant—something that would put these women in the same place, even if they didn't do it at the same time. But first, as soon as Sacco returned with his own favorite protein drink, they'd concentrate on the security video obtained from a neighbor across the way from the Latimer crime scene, which he'd cued on the laptop and was set to go.

They were drowning in paper and leads to nowhere.

The entire team had spent hours scouring phone records during the past two days. Leading up to time of death, each victim had called one particular number. There were three telephone numbers of interest in total, but no crossovers. That meant they were dealing with burner phones, untraceable incoming and outgoing calls, stopping abruptly on date of death. Carpenter had verified they no longer pinged anywhere in the metro area and beyond. Everything else on the victims' personal cell phone logs had been the usual—calls to family, friends, co-workers, online inquiries, music, videos, orders for both food and goods, messages, etc., etc.

More trace evidence results from the autopsies of Waitre, Adnet, and Latimer three days ago, were forthcoming...but not any time soon. Usual delay culprit? Backlog. Too many cases citywide to muddle through. Ramos was waiting on chemical analysis of all skin swabs to distinguish items regularly used by each victim, such as soaps, perfumes, moisturizers, and other normal substances, from the cocktail used for the drug's transmission. They were running a DNA panel as well in the hope they'd get lucky with the killer's own DNA mixed in with his victims'. But those results would take longer.

The captain was pushing for priority processing.

Carpenter had not cracked Adnet's password to his personal emails and computer files yet and had asked for help from Cyber. Ramos had finished reading Waitre's journal, the one Adnet had confiscated and taken to work, and had handed it over yesterday, with a *have fun* heavy on the cynicism and glumness. After ten pages, Nick had understood. He had almost thrown the thing against the office wall in frustration. Yes, he felt sorry for the victim, was even more sympathetic that she'd died in such manner, but the thing read more like a teenager's pubescent angst than a mature woman's concerns. Nick definitely couldn't relate to the constant pity fest and complaints about everything in the world and everyone inhabiting it. Jessica Waitre had not stopped for a moment of introspection, or paused to seek a solution to counteract her issues. She hadn't taken any action against her perceived wrongs, just complained and complained, angry twenty-four seven, and thinking the world at large was against her. Life was so unfair to her, exclusively.

No wonder the woman had been depressed. She had created her own emotional black hole and had been teetering at the border of her event horizon, oblivious to the fact she captained her ship and could blast away to safety at any moment.

On the interview front, nothing new had cropped up. He and Sacco had spoken to the two women from Duncani Studios. As Nick had suspected, they had not been on friendly terms with the victim, both on and off work. Assurances were issued about their respect for the deceased, her work ethic, imagination, and creativity. What was not said, and what Nick had inferred from body language and attitude, was that both women had been a bit envious of the victim. The mutual criticism? Latimer's drive. Pushy had been the restrained adjective Ms. Tamone had used. Charitable on her part, thought Nick, especially when the woman had had an ax to grind with the victim. After all, Ms. Tamone had been the target of unwanted sexual overtures at that Christmas party.

Chet Emberson, on the other hand, was MIA. Not in the true sense of the word, but in that, according to his family, he'd taken off on an Asian spiritual trip in the hope of finding balance and himself. In other words, Nick thought, the man had left Dodge in a hurry, hoping that out of sight might result in out of mind and he could start fresh...in another company, of course.

He was due back today.

On the maybe good news front, heavy on the maybe, Nick and Sacco, after ringing every doorbell, every business, and speaking to the majority of renters around Latimer's apartment that weekend, had found a tenant across the way, whose windows faced the street and the building, and who had a wireless home security system. He'd been very cooperative, giving them a copy of the security video of the night in question. Nick had reviewed it in a cursory manner last night. He had been tired, anxious to get to Laura and relax, make love, and get some sleep. Besides, the images hadn't been that sharp. So much for digitized video.

On the personal front, Nick had never been happier. He and Laura had settled into a routine of sorts this past weekend. She had spent one night in his apartment. Yesterday, he'd spent it in hers. Today was up for grabs. Her new business was taking off, and she was progressively busier, video chatting with her new partners, inventing new recipes, and new decorative looks for her cakes, from which Nick had profited greatly. Everyone in this new venture was very pleased, especially Laura. A trip down south was coalescing, set to happen around two weeks from now. Nick hoped that, by then, these cases would be solved. He'd love to take a few PT days and accompany Laura, meet her new team. Hell, he could wish, couldn't he? But...that was for further down the line. What was important was that this morning, before she'd left at the crack of dawn to help Erin at the bakery, they had agreed on an intimate dinner at Les Garçons on Eighth.

"Hey, gorgeous." Sacco's usual greeting for Mandy Penzik came from just outside the open conference door.

Nick looked up. Sure enough, Mandy Penzik, their resident ASL interpreter and ten-year veteran of the force, was giving Sacco a hug in the doorway. Nick waved her in.

"What brings you to our neck of the woods today," Nick asked, giving her a hug. She worked out of their precinct. Steve Penzik, her husband, a detective for the Suffolk County Police Department, worked near Babylon. After their marriage ten years ago, his first and her second, they'd settled in Floral Park so neither could complain one was closer to work than the other.

"Video recording an alert for Nixle," she said. "A Wyandanch kid's missing. Possible person of interest in his mother's suicide." She opened the folder, slipped a sheet of paper out, and handed it to Nick.

"Families," Sacco said. "Got to love them."

"Screwed-up human relations, my first husband would counter," Penzik said, and made the sign of the cross. She always did that when mentioning her late husband. A sign of prayer and respect, she affirmed.

"What happened?" Sacco asked.

She pointed to the sheet in Nick's hand.

"The incident report gives a bit of the details. Mother committed suicide. Stepdad found her and assumed son and mother had argued. Must have been a doozy."

Nick glanced at the kid's horrid photo, possibly taken at the DMV, and skimmed the report, his attention half on what Mandy Penzik and Sacco were discussing.

"Anything unusual pop up?" Sacco asked.

Nick read. The victim, a Mrs. Clara Mulder, had been found by her husband, Aron Mulder, on Saturday at about 6:00 p.m., after he'd arrived home from work.

"Possible issue with the son," she said. "Steve mentioned cash and an ATM card were missing from the wife's purse. No sign of the kid."

The man, Nick kept on reading, had taken his wife down and had tried to revive her, but it had been too late. EMS, when they arrived, had declared her dead on scene. Husband, so hysterical about her death, had gotten sick. Sedated and taken to the hospital for observation.

"They put out a BOLO and Steve gave me that to share here, just in case someone spots the kid in the city."

Nick suddenly did a double take. Took her down? Down? His eyes darted from beginning to end of the report until he found what he wanted.

"The Nixle alert is being posted and disseminated as we speak," Penzik said. "I have a presser..."

"Shit, shit, SHIT."

Nick's explosion caught them by surprise.

"Trying to give me a heart attack, Larson?" Penzik said. "What the hell is wrong with you?"

Nick dropped the report on the table and took out his cell. "What's Steve's cell number?" When she didn't respond fast enough, he pressed with more emphasis. "Give me Steve's cell number, Mandy. Now. Better yet, speed-dial it on yours and put it on speaker."

Sacco picked up the report Nick had dropped and started scanning the information there.

"Have you seen the kid? Is that it?" Penzik asked, speed-dialing.

Nick shook his head.

"Hey, sexy," her husband's voice came over the speaker. Before he could say anything more personal or private, Penzik interrupted. "Hey, back. And you're on speaker..."

Nick interrupted without preamble, "Steve, it's Nick. Get your ass over here to the precinct. Now."

"Is something wrong? Mandy, are you all right?"

"Mandy is fine," Nick cut in. "It's your alleged suicide that's the issue."

Sacco's "Aw, shit" alarmed Penzik. "What the hell is wrong with you guys?"

"Fuck you, Larson," Steve Penzik said. "I'm busy. And there is no alleged nothing. The woman killed herself. Evidence corroborates it."

"I don't give a crap what you think your evidence proves, Steve. Get your ass over here now. You've got a murder by hanging."

"You're fucking nuts. This was no homicide. Shit, Nick, we've already processed close to fifty suicides in Suffolk alone since the start of the year. This is no different. Trust me."

"I bet my next paycheck your victim left a suicide note that says it's time to sleep and everyone is a liar, which, by the way, is misspelled."

There was dead silence at the other end of the phone. After a while, Steve Penzik's voice came through. "No one knows that except us."

"And your victim's phone is missing, right?" Nick continued.

"How do you fucking know all this?" Steve Penzik's curse echoed around the quiet conference room.

"How do I fucking know?"

Nick stopped. Breathed deep to gather oxygen and patience. Counted to ten. "Listen, Steve. I'm not being a hard ass, but we have a situation here. Your suicide hits all my crime scene MO bullet points. Three times, to be exact. We already have four victims gracing Millsap's slab. We need to compare notes ASAP. My bet and gut says our serial did your suicide."

There. He'd said it.

"We'll be right over."

"Oh, crap," was all that Mandy Penzik said, retrieving her phone. She'd been at the meeting Friday where a few butts had been skinned by the captain concerning the spread of unsubstantiated, unverifiable rumors about a possible serial.

"Sorry about that." Nick handed the phone back.

She shrugged. "What can I do to help?"

"When is your presser?" Nick asked.

She glanced at the wall clock. "In about three hours. I'll need one to prep for it."

"Would appreciate another pair of eyes with this video." Nick pointed to the laptop on the desk.

"No problem." She took a seat to the right of the screen.

Nick tapped a key to wake up the computer. He sat facing it. Sacco took the chair on his left.

"Give me a minute." Nick dialed OCME on his phone. He punched Millsap's extension before the recorded, cheery robotic voice could waste his time with a multiplicity of options. He turned to Sacco while waiting.

"The report mentioned the stepfather was taken to the hospital," he said. "Call Ramos to let her know. She needs to contact her counterpart in Suffolk to warn her, warn the hospital. They need to test before it's completely metabolized."

Nick lifted a finger for silence and spoke to Millsap almost in code, short phrases significant only to them. After Millsap, he briefed Kravitz. Hung up and briefed Carpenter.

"Shit, Nick," Penzik said.

"More like scary shit," he said. "How old is this kid?"

"Seventeen."

Nick entered the DMV site and tapped in the young man's name, address, and date of birth. Driver's license popped up. He sent a copy off to the printer.

"Let's see if we can compare notes."

He hit the Play button on the screen and they huddled forward.

The tenant who'd supplied the security video had set his wireless alarm-system security camera on the window facing the street. The man's residence was on the fourth floor, two stories higher than Latimer's apartment across the way. According to the tenant, he'd angled the camera to capture the two sides of the street so he could keep an eye out for his parked car. There had been too many incidents lately of vandals, homeless, druggies, and thieves prowling the neighborhood and breaking into cars for loose change or anything inside that could be sold.

The entrance to Latimer's building was visible, but from the higher angle. Nick knew it would be difficult to get a good look at who went in and out of the building, even when zooming in. The windows of the victim's living room were a better bet, but still at an angle that didn't hold much promise for them.

"There should be a law," Penzik mumbled.

Nick understood, thinking this was a déjà vu moment from the movie *Rear Window*. It reminded him that, to this day, normal people lived their lives blissfully unaware of their surroundings, particularly when at home. With today's technology, anyone could catalogue and record their doings, with them not being the wiser. Sometimes it sucked to be a cop. They knew too much about the dirty flip side of life.

"Image is not very sharp," Sacco said.

"I think it's the window," Penzik answered. "Smudged from outside."

Nick thought it was useless to have a security camera when the target and its surroundings were blurry. He checked his records and fast-forwarded close to the posted time when Latimer had invited the killer into her home.

The street traffic and pedestrians came and went. Crosstown buses occasionally blocked the view of the entrance. Neighbors would, every so often, stop with their dogs and block the view.

It was tedious work. Nick fast-forwarded a few times, until he caught someone standing in the entrance doorway. Only thing visible was the man's back. Nick grimaced. The man resembled a shadow figure in the night with his black sweatshirt, its hoodie pulled up, black sweatpants, and black sneakers. A large bag, like a gym bag, hung from his left shoulder. No identifiable marks on it, not even a logo. He was ringing the bell and waiting, looking neither left nor right, almost huddled within himself. Was the posture from the cold, or from the fact he didn't want to be identified? Nick stopped the video.

"Here." Nick wrote down the timestamp. "Could be our perp."

"Look at the bag." Sacco touched the screen. "Big enough to hold the tools needed to assist."

Penzik leaned back. "Did you notice he's looking straight down? What New Yorker does that at that hour? You shuffle, shift, and turn around to see what's going on behind you. The man shows no impatience to enter, either."

"Let's see who let him inside," Nick said and hit Play.

If it hadn't been for the memory of the colorful silk pajama pants Latimer had been wearing when they'd seen her at the crime scene, Nick would not have recognized the slim woman who opened the door and flung herself at the man. He stopped the video, grabbed Latimer's binder and flipped through the photos there until he found what he was looking for. He brought the open binder closer.

"Same pants," he pointed. He zoomed in, but the picture almost pixelated. "Can't tell if that's the shirt she was wearing."

"Maybe Carpenter can clean that up with his Visual Editor," Sacco said.

Nick started the video again, rewound, and replayed the scene several times.

"That hug caught him by surprise," Penzik stated.

Nick looked at her. "Why do you say that?"

"Come on," she said with a smile. "If you're a man you lean into your woman's embrace. He just stands there and pats her. Awkward."

Nick forwarded the footage slowly, focusing his attention on Latimer's apartment windows. You could see shadows inside the place moving here and there. After a bit, the lights inside the apartment went out. Minutes passed. Nick kept staring, waiting.

"Look at the window," Sacco said and pointed.

Sure enough, the apartment window on the left of screen lifted, then the one beside it. Same thing happened a few seconds later, on the bedroom side. They could all see the silhouette of the person behind each window, but there was not enough ambient light coming from the street to illuminate any features or details of the killer. At least, not in this security footage. Maybe Carpenter could enhance it somehow to capture more details. Much later, the hooded man left the building, head down, a spring to his step. He turned toward Second Avenue and disappeared from view.

Nick logged all the additional timestamps on the pad to give to Carpenter. He jotted those in the death folder, as well.

"Damn," was all Penzik said.

Nick stared at the timestamps. "The man either lives close by or works around the area. It didn't take him more than forty minutes to arrive at the apartment."

"Could have been already in the vicinity, doing things, you know." Penzik said. "I check my emails on the phone while I'm running around. Messages, too. Answer everything with it."

"You think the mother could be at Presbyterian Medical nearby?"

"If we'd be so lucky," Nick said, but at the same time, was also shaking his head. "The questions remain, though: does he really have a sick mother? That could be a lie to get the sympathy meter going. Who the hell are we looking for? We know it's a man, but nothing else. Without a name and a warrant, if there is a sick mother, the hospital will give us shit."

"Millsap could pull some strings," Sacco said.

"We don't have a name, Vic." Nick's frustration frayed the edges of his voice. "But at least we have a time and a direction. Maybe Carpenter can get security video from the CCTVs from the area and backtrack the perp's steps. Give us a better view of his face and where he'd been, where he's going."

"Suffolk knows," Ramos said as she walked inside, burdened with her own files. She dropped everything on the table. "Everyone from the Chief ME, to the Deputy Chief ME, to the Assistant of the Chief ME, to the supervisor of Forensic Investigation. They were not happy." She veered to Mandy Penzik and gave her a hug.

Kravitz arrived with Millsap in tow. A cigar, chewed and unlit, hung from his lip.

"Get more chairs," Kravitz told Carpenter, who was a few steps behind. "Full house coming." He nodded a greeting to Penzik. "Your husband and his partner are here."

A few moments later, Horowitz escorted Steve Penzik and his partner, Amarita Shapel, into the conference room.

Millsap opened the floor discussion. "As soon as Nick called, I contacted SCME and warned them about exposure to U-47700 from the victim."

"Pink," Shapel said. "We're dealing with pink?"

"Pink on steroids, I'm afraid," finished Millsap. "The drug's been spiked with DMSO. That makes it easily absorbable through the skin. It's the MO, too, apart from the hanging. If your lab and the hospital verify, it's the same killer."

Steve Penzik's curse was heartfelt. His wife rounded the table and gave him a kiss. "Sorry. Have to get ready for the presser," she said, and with a wave for everyone, left.

"What do you know about this kid?" Nick asked.

"Arjen Pender is seventeen. Caucasian. Blond hair, brown eyes. Around five-eleven, one hundred fifty pounds. Lives with his mother and stepfather in Wyandanch. Resentful of stepfather."

"Hates his guts according to his best friend," chimed in Shapel.

"Biological dad out of the picture and life since about ten years ago. Used to be on the soccer team at his high school, but was kicked out last Friday after testing positive for weed. Last anyone saw him was at work, Saturday morning. The manager at the grocery store said he left early. Claimed he was sick."

Penzik opened a file folder, turned it around so everyone at the table could see the photograph there. He tapped the face. "Found this photo at the house. It was taken at some school activity about two months ago, according to his friend."

The boy was exactly as he'd been described. Nick studied the physique. He had lean and strong muscles, but the kid was not their killer.

"You can scrap him out of your suspect list." Conviction colored Nick's voice.

"Well, he's still a person of interest," Penzik said. "Until we can confirm the victim was indeed drugged with U4, the boy is still a suspect. You've worked Domestic. You know arguments escalate to the point of physical abuse and worse. In a fit of rage, Pender could have strangled her and staged it as suicide."

"Get real, Penzik," Ramos scoffed. She tapped the photo. "That kid doesn't have the upper body strength to lift a cat, let alone his mom. And how the hell did he know what to write on that suicide note? We've kept that bit of evidence under wraps. Hell, it's subterranean."

"Deeper than the subway tunnels," chimed in Sacco.

"No one outside this precinct knows we have three suspicious suicides by a possible serial," Nick said. "And not a soul has mentioned the pink connection, either."

"As a matter of fact," Kravitz interrupted. "On pain of dismissal, rumors that had been floating around the office last Thursday were squelched...by me."

"Captain was very specific about it at Friday's meeting," Carpenter agreed.

"No, Steve. This," Nick tapped the crime scene photo he'd taken out of Penzik's file. "This is our killer's MO."

"Maybe the boy is on the run," Sacco suggested. "Could have witnessed his mother's murder."

"He did take cash and his mom's debit card," Penzik admitted.

"And disappeared." Nick glanced at everyone. "The thing is, is he a runaway because he's pissed at his parents or because he witnessed a murder? Does he have family in the area?"

"Cousin and aunt in Jersey. An uncle in Chicago," Shapel said. "They've been notified to call the precinct immediately if the boy appears."

Kilcrease's comment about things changing if their killer felt threatened suddenly came to mind. Had this kid jeopardized the killer's safety net somehow? Had he seen his mother's murder? Nick's sense of urgency increased.

"We have to find this kid," Nick said to no one in particular. "I assume he's not answering his phone."

"No pings since Saturday," Penzik said.

"Any other friends he could crash with?"

"Only one. Russ Acker," Shapel said, looking at her notes. "But Pender is not there. We checked. The friend, at first, was pissed. They'd had a falling out. But after learning what had happened, he got scared. Told us about the plans Pender had to emulate a dangerous 48-hour Facebook challenge he'd seen on the net. Arjen had wanted to get even with his stepdad and mom for grounding him. Make them anxious."

"I've heard of that game," Sacco said. "My niece was yapping about it a couple of months back. Told her it was bogus. And if she ever got it into her head to do something so stupid with her friends, I'd drag her butt to Juvie, and leave her there for a week. That was the end of it."

"She was probably more scared about the possibility you'd tell your sister," Nick said.

"There is that," Sacco agreed.

"What about train stations out your way?" Ramos asked Penzik and Shapel.

"We have two detectives working on train rosters and security footage. They should get back to me soon."

Nick yelled for Horowitz.

"Yes, Lieutenant?"

"Get somebody over to Penn Station. Find out if an Arjen Pender bought a ticket to Chicago or to Jersey. He's a minor. Probably paid cash. Check for possible ATM transaction, just in case, under the mother's name, Clara Mulder."

"If he was there and bought a ticket at the Quik-Trak kiosk, instead of the ticket agent, we won't know about it any time soon," Carpenter said.

"But there is a waiting area until train departs, and I'm positive it's image wired," Nick said. "We'll check that ourselves." He turned back to Horowitz. "Send another uniform to Port Authority and to Grand Central. He may have decided on the aunt, instead of the uncle. Closer to home. Same routine. I have a copy of the kid's DMV photo at the printer. Disseminate that. Tell the terminals to get surveillance footage ready for us around the time of departures." He turned to Carpenter. "Get your IT cap on. If the kid is stereotypical of his age group, he'd have done everything by phone on Saturday." Nick turned to Penzik. "Do you have his cell number?"

Penzik rattled it off for Carpenter.

"On it." Carpenter stood.

"Check our Domain Awareness System, too," Nick told Carpenter before he stepped outside the room. "Maybe we'll catch the kid on the CCTVs and shadow him to wherever he went."

During the next half hour, Nick briefed Penzik and his partner about what they knew about their killer and the MO. Ramos promised to set up a video chat with her counterparts to brief them as well. It was decided Nick and Sacco would work Manhattan in search of the young man, and Penzik and Shapel would work Suffolk, since those were their territories.

"Suggest to your superiors to contact Chicago PD to search for the kid," Kravitz told Penzik.

"I'm not sure Chicago will be very cooperative," Penzik said. "They've had thirty-four murders just in January and that doesn't count the injured by these rampant shootings. Those take a higher manpower precedence than a kid who's running to his uncle because he's pissed at his parents."

"Suggest it anyway," Kravitz said. "Maybe they can give you access to their surveillance."

Penzik nodded.

Kravitz slapped the desk and got up. "Ok, everyone, let's go find this kid."

Which was easier said than done.

Four hours later, after interviewing security at Grand Central and Port Authority, and not catching hide nor hair of the young man during the departure times of the trains, Nick and Sacco had ended up in Penn Station. There, they'd found the kid. It took a bit of persuasion and discussion with security personnel there to hand over what they wanted without a warrant, but Nick and Sacco had returned to the precinct with copies of the surveillance footage from the train station. They'd caught sight of the young man eating a sandwich and waiting for his ride to Chicago. From his leisurely behavior, the kid had been unaware of the tragedy transpiring at his home. Nick had notified Penzik and had informed him Carpenter would send them a copy of what they had as soon as Nick returned to the precinct.

"Penzik called," Carpenter turned from his computer to face Nick. "Do you have the thumb?"

Nick gave Carpenter a sealed evidence bag.

"I've got some footage of the kid on Thirty-Fourth Street," Carpenter said, signing for the evidence. "He went into a Target and bought some things. Wanna see?"

Nick nodded and waited. Carpenter brought up the footage and pointed. "Here he is."

Arjen Pender came into view as he entered the automatic sliding doors of the Target at Herald Square.

"I compiled all the moments when he's in view. Better than having to scan the entire store over and over again."

Nick nodded and watched as the kid casually strode around the store. This one was no runaway due to abuse or mistreatment at home. Neither was he running for his life after witnessing a crime. What Nick saw was a spoiled kid who didn't think about anything much, except himself, and needing payback for a grounding.

"Did you send this to Penzik?" Nick saw Arjen Pender ride the escalator down to the basement without any rush. There the kid bought a backpack, sweatpants, a sweatshirt, and some underwear. Travel-size toiletries were in order as well. Nick guessed Pender had decided expediency ruled the day and spending his mom's money more convenient than packing a bag with his own stuff.

"Already in their hands," Carpenter said. "Waiting only for the Penn Station surveillance you got."

Another shot came into view, which showed Pender riding the escalator up. There he bought some grab-and-go food and drinks for the trip. He paid for everything with a card, rejected plastic bags for his purchases, and dumped everything inside his new backpack. He left the store at the same leisurely pace as he'd entered.

"That kid has no woes," Carpenter said. "Wouldn't want to be him when his uncle nabs him."

"The shock of his mother's demise and the fact half the cops along the Eastern Seaboard are looking for him as a person of interest, may put the fear of God in him." Nick shook his head. "Maybe."

"Cocky little fellow," Carpenter said. "I've got to give him that."

"Yeah. Listen..."

"Give me a sec."

Nick waited until Carpenter had uploaded the surveillance from Penn Station and sent it on its merry way.

"Okay, shoot."

Nick gave Carpenter a CD this time, the one he'd entered into evidence the night before, and had seen earlier with Sacco and Mandy Penzik.

"This is security camera footage from a tenant across the way from Latimer's," he said. "I need you to give me as clear a still of the suspect as you can. He had to wait to be let inside the building." Nick handed over the timestamp log he'd created. "You'll find him at the times I highlighted. He worked in complete darkness inside the apartment, and there's a small chance you may catch a glimpse of him at the window. With the naked eye, we couldn't see much."

"I'll work with the infrareds and other filters. Changing contrast sometimes helps. See if I can enhance it."

"I also need a search of the DAS." Nick's forefinger tapped the last timestamp. "He left in the direction of Second Avenue at that precise time. See if you can find him anywhere in the area with the CCTV system. Show me a face, a profile, a direction. Something tangible I can follow."

"On it."

"Another thing, can you get for me any appointment records the victims may have entered into their calendars in the last three months?"

"If they were logged into their accounts, I can pull those off the cloud."

"Send those to me as soon as you can," Nick said. "I want to check if the women frequented the same places, or doctors, or anything. There has to be a common thread somewhere."

Nick felt he was attempting to create a genealogy tree with blinders on.

"What if it is victim by stranger?" Carpenter voiced everyone's worst fear.

"Even those can have one thing in common. The issue is finding it. This one, however... I don't know, Josh. It has a personal feel to it. I'm missing something, or the piece to solve the puzzle has not fallen on our laps yet."

"Hope you're right. Anyways, I'll send you the info as soon as I have it."

"Thanks, kid." Nick slapped the doorway frame on his way out.

Let's see if we can get lucky on this.

Horowitz stopped him on his way to his desk. "There's a Chet Emberson here to see you."

"Show him to Interview 1," he said. "I'll get Sacco."

Five minutes later, they entered to greet a man in his thirties, chestnut eyes and hair, the latter professionally styled at shoulder length, with a scraggly beard growing in patches on his thin face.

"I know why I'm here," Emberson said without preamble. "And I don't know how I can help. I wasn't anywhere near the US when she died."

"We know," Nick stated and introduced himself and Sacco. "Regardless, we're interviewing anyone who knew Ms. Latimer personally or worked with her."

"I had nothing to do with her outside of work."

"But you did have, may I say, an animus toward her at work," Nick told him.

The man groaned. "They showed you the video?"

"Indeed."

"Bastards," Emberson said under his breath. "They'll never let me live that down."

"The internet is not known for its forgiveness, and neither are victims of malicious postings," Nick said with no pity. "And we have laws..."

"You arresting me?" The man was incredulous.

"No, Mr. Emberson. What we are interested in is your version of things, to start with. Impressions. Knowledge of the woman."

The man leaned forward, aggressive. "Listen, we were all hammered at that party. And yes, I had a bone to pick with that bitch after she took over my account."

"Mr. Duncan said it was his decision, not her doing."

"I don't give a shit what Mr. Duncan said. He hasn't been in the trenches for a while, being more intent on the company's image and bottom line than in the shark lines. Latimer was an aggressive bitch. She'd been after that account, my account, for ages. Crowed about already being a customer and enjoying their excellent services. Kept harping on the fact she was perfect to take the company's branding to higher levels. I outmaneuvered her at every turn, until I went on vacation."

"Mr. Duncan mentioned an emergency came up?"

Emberson nodded. "A class action lawsuit was slapped on my client's most fierce competitor, one of the many casualties of the latest #MeToo movement. It broke all over the news within hours. My client needed a campaign to counter perception of complicity based simply on similarity of service. Needed to demonstrate care, professionalism, and inclusivity. Right up Latimer's alley."

"Any truth to the lawsuit?" Sacco asked.

"Actually, yes. Rumors had been going around the industry for a while about sexual misconduct. Not all franchises, and not all employees within those, but it takes one or two to dirty the water for all. My client didn't want the stain of the shit pile to blotch their business through mere association. It always can."

"What is your client's name?" Nick would check them out later.

"Scandinavian Therapy Industry Franchisees, LLC. STIF for short."

Nick almost sniggered. His partner did.

"Can you tell us about the party?"

Emberson pulled on his anorexic beard. Nick couldn't decide whether it was sparse vacation growth or simple lack of facial hair. If Nick didn't shave daily, he'd have a beard thicker than Santa Claus.

"Like I said, some of us were more plastered than others. Booze ran freely that night, and we didn't eat much. Dinner consisted of appetizers. Plenty of them, but not enough to absorb all the alcohol we were consuming. Someone, I forget who, told me to watch Latimer, who was showing her true colors on the dance floor, revealing she had the hots for Oriana. I checked out the action and, sure enough, Ms. Control Freak Latimer was making overt sexual moves to none other than Oriana Tamone, Born Again and Midwestern Values girl." He shrugged. "I made a video. Thought it was funny. Actually forgot about it until the bitch came to me all apologetic that she was going to be the new account manager for my ex-client."

"Do you know if Ms. Latimer had any enemies, or did she ever bring friends over to work?"

"Enemies? No. Not unless you count every single person in the office. We're the take-out-the-knife-and-slice competitive, and trample each other over revenue streams or new accounts. But it's normal. Micaela was all work and no play. Came early, left late. Never spoke about her family. Never saw her with anyone but, then again, we didn't socialize. Don't even know if she had family."

Nick glanced at Sacco. There was nothing to be had from this interview any longer.

"Thank you for coming, Mr. Emberson." Nick handed him a card. "If you can think of anything about Ms. Latimer that we could use, let us know."

Nick watched as Horowitz escorted the man to the elevators.

"What do you think?" Sacco asked.

"Rivalry was intense, it seems, and I can't picture them growing any sort of bond of any kind."

"Probably avoided each other like the plague, and threw barbed darts at each other's back."

"You got that right."

A small knock preceded the entrance of Carpenter into the conference room.

"I have the handle you wanted," Carpenter said. He didn't look pleased.

"What is it?"

"HighMaster212. Got it from Latimer's computer and from the document dump the phone company sent me of Waitre's phone. Still working on Creasy's."

Nick wrote it down in his notebook. Without thinking, he underlined "master" several times. He checked his action. Stared.

He studied Carpenter, who was looking a bit disturbed.

"Something on your mind, Josh?"

"Did you catch it?"

"I'm at a loss here," Nick told Carpenter. "That, or my brain isn't functioning fast enough after the workout we've been through today."

Carpenter pointed. "You underlined it." He looked at Nick. "The Victor Hugo case."

Both Nick and Sacco straightened to attention.

"When I saw it, it rang a bell, especially after you'd dredged up the case recently," Carpenter said. "The man made an impression on all of us with his wall-to-wall 'Farewell' and 'Master' Post-its. Out of curiosity, I went back and rechecked my notes. Sure enough, the screen name HighMaster212 popped up multiple times, among a dozen others. But we dismissed it due to the victim's truly bizarro behavior."

"Lead detective had no reason to suspect anything other than suicide," Nick said. "Even Millsap agreed."

"But you know what struck me now as bizarre?" Carpenter glanced at both men. "We never found a cell phone in his apartment, although he had service and bills for one. Everyone assumed he'd lost it."

"Keep digging, Carpenter," Nick said. "And don't forget to send me any appointment records."

Carpenter nodded and left.

Lucky or cursed, Nick thought. They'd never had so many possible leads dumped on their laps so quickly. And still, they had no one.

Zip-a-Dee-Doo-Dah.

Horowitz poked his head into the room. "Lieutenant, you've got a call on two."

Nick went to his desk and picked up the receiver. "Larson."

"Nick," Steve Penzik's voice sounded relieved and excited. "We've got the kid. His uncle is flying back with him tomorrow. Plane arrives in Islip at one thirty."

"We'll be there." He turned to Sacco. "The kid's in our hands."

"Maybe our luck is changing," his partner said.

"We can only hope."

CHAPTER TWENTY-SEVEN

Tuesday, January 21

MANHATTAN WOKE UP to a rainy, windy, and miserable day. Sleet was announced to pelt them later, and plunging temperatures during evening rush hour could transform the tri-state area streets into ice rinks. Warnings flashed across all TV channels, each urging residents to stay off glossy, dangerous roads.

Nick couldn't stop pacing. They'd arrived at the Suffolk County police precinct with time to spare, despite the Long Island Expressway doing its best to block their way or keep traffic to a crawl. Steve Penzik and his partner had left to pick up the uncle and the kid at the airport, and were due to arrive soon. In the meantime, Sacco was munching on one of his favorite protein bars while sitting in the interview area set up for the coming meeting. Nick had turned down sustenance from the vending machine when Sacco offered to get him something. He wasn't hungry, despite leaving their precinct two hours earlier and missing lunch altogether.

Nick heard Steve Penzik's voice before he came into the room.

"Finally." Nick and Sacco stood.

The young man from the photo stepped inside, followed closely by a man similar in features, but taller, older, at around forty Nick would place him, with chestnut hair to his shoulders and slanted sad eyes.

Steve Penzik and Amarita Shapel made the brief introductions. As everyone sat, Nick studied the victim's son, who was wearing the clothing he'd bought at the Target a few days previously. His eyes reflected fear more than grief, although they were red rimmed, probably from intermittent crying.

Life sucked for this kid at the moment, Nick thought. It had been a hard life lesson learned. The young man's spiteful goal to frighten his parents into submission had turned on him instead with a vengeance, not to mention lifelong, not temporal, consequences. The best-laid plans...

"Thank you for coming, Mr. Bogarde," Penzik said as his opening salvo. "We're very sorry for your loss. This is really a trying time for your family."

Stefan Bogarde's eyes were etched with deeper sorrow. "It doesn't sink in. I can't understand. She was a strong woman. Was happy. Why would she do something so horrible?"

"Can you tell us a little about your sister?" Amarita Shapel said softly. "Do you know if she was having any issues with Mr. Mulder?"

"Good God, no," Bogarde said. "The man was a saint and worshipped the ground she walked on. As far as I know, they were happy. She was happy. She loved her life."

"Was she still in touch with her first husband?" Shapel paused to look at her notes. "A Geric Pender?"

They waited, although everyone here knew the answer, Nick thought.

"We haven't seen hide nor hair of that bastard since he skipped out on my sister ten years ago. Hasn't even paid alimony. Went back to the Netherlands to abuse someone else after we slapped him with a restraining order."

"What do you mean abuse?" Penzik asked.

Bogarde glanced at his nephew. Nick realized by the uncle's expression that the forthcoming details of a prior marriage, gone bad, had never been divulged to the young man next to him.

"Beat the crap out of her for years," he said softly.

The kid flinched. Shock replaced fear.

"The last beating was so severe, she lost the child, a baby girl. And from the complications of that miscarriage, my sister could no longer have any children. That destroyed her. Always overshadowed whatever happiness she enjoyed. The family helped her as much as we could and she moved in with our other sister until she was able to finalize the divorce and start a new life."

Another broken soul, Nick thought. A magnet for their killer. The issue now was how on earth had he targeted this woman. Nick didn't believe it was because the son had somehow threatened the killer's safety net anymore. Maybe Clara Mulder had been programmed for extinction months ago, especially since Nick knew mother and son had been arguing, and the kid was getting into drugs.

"When did she marry Aron Mulder?" Shapel asked.

"Seven years ago; they met at a church social. My other sister's husband loves to organize those. They have them as often as they can. Clara didn't know why she accepted that invitation. She had been refusing every single one for years. Later, she always joked at the memory."

"Yeah," the kid spoke for the first time. Resentment colored his words. "The hand of Fate. She only went because she was climbing the walls after a week of taking care of an itchy kid with chicken pox...me."

Silence followed. All eyes focused on him. The young man blushed as he shrank into himself. Arjen Pender somehow didn't want to be the center of attention now, even when, three days ago, that was all he'd wanted.

"I'm sorry to have to ask," Detective Penzik started, "but did your sister have any trouble with people at work?"

"She didn't have a job. She volunteered," Bogarde said. "We spoke often, despite the fact that I live in Chicago. One thing I am positive of: she delighted in being a housewife and taking care of Arjen and Aron. Her social life revolved around her husband, their friends, church, and her son. She relished their position in the community. Was very proud of it."

"So, no real issues with anyone, that you know of. Did she have any other close friends we could contact?"

The snicker caught all of them by surprise. Nick stared at Arjen Pender, who had realized what he'd done and was trying to retreat back into the protective shell he'd created. He was nervously rubbing his smartphone and trying not to look at his uncle.

The kid knew something and he was embarrassed.

"Is there something you aren't telling us, Mr. Pender?" Nick asked the boy in a casual manner before Penzik or Shapel could ask another question. When the kid didn't answer, Nick became a bit more confrontational. "Mr. Pender. If you know something, we need to know."

"Does my uncle have to be here?" the kid asked.

"Why the hell don't you want me here?" the uncle said, vexed. Bogarde's eyes narrowed in sudden suspicion. "What the hell have you done?"

"Does he?" was all the young man asked.

Nick stared at his counterparts. Their expressions reflected his own thoughts: Arjen Pender wanted to divulge information that was either embarrassing to his mother or to his uncle, maybe both. Or maybe he was covering his own ass. Either way, the uncle needed to leave.

"Would you mind giving us a moment alone with your nephew?" Shapel asked, and stood, placing a hand at Bogarde's back and showing the way to the door. The motion left the uncle no choice but to follow. Nick was certain she would reassure the man, placing him in front of the window where he could see what went on with his nephew. Whether he would be privy to what was said inside was a point to be determined.

"Well, Mr. Pender," Steve Penzik started. "What is it that you don't want your uncle to know?"

"Listen." His Adam's apple jiggled up and down from excessive, nervous swallowing. "I know what I did sucked, but I was so angry at them for grounding me. Shit. It was only a little weed." He stopped, realizing he was speaking to cops inside a precinct. "I only wanted to scare them a little." His breath hitched. "If I hadn't left..."

The kid broke down.

Nick understood. Regret would forever gnaw at this young man's conscience, compounded with a ton of guilt he hadn't been there to protect his mom. That pain could never be erased, and only years of therapy would show he might not have been able to defend her. The killer was strong, cunning. The kid might have wound up dead as well, and they'd have two victims instead of one to deal with.

They all waited until the grief, shame, and recrimination spent itself. Sacco pushed the Kleenex box close. Pender took a tissue, blew his nose, took another, and dried his eyes.

"I can't believe... my mom..." Another bout of weeping seized him.

They waited.

"Why don't we do this?" Detective Penzik said. "Why don't you tell me, Detective Larson, and the rest of us here what happened the day you went to Chicago."

"Got home earlier than I should've," the kid said between hiccups.

"We know," Penzik said. "Your employer said you weren't feeling well."

"I lied," he admitted. "Didn't want to deal with customers' bullshit. When I got home, though, her car was in the driveway."

"You mother was home? Was that normal?"

"Not for a Saturday. She usually volunteers at the Y, helps the swimming instructors there with the toddlers learning to swim. She loved that job."

Guess the kid understood why now, Nick thought.

"Did your mom know you were home?" Penzik asked.

"Are you shitting me? If she knew I had skipped work, she would have been super pissed. So I snuck in through the basement where I could think about the Facebook game. That's when I figured visiting my uncle in Chicago would be perfect. I'd stay at a motel on Sunday, tourist the city. Chill. I gelled my plans. Looked some stuff up. Then the doorbell rang and my mom went upstairs a few minutes later. I took my chance, snuck into the kitchen, got the stash cash and her ATM card. I wouldn't need Russ."

"Your friend told us he refused to join in the game," Penzik said.

"Russ is a wuss. Afraid of his own shadow and especially his mom."

"He told us he was not against your plan, just that you had absolutely no plan—doing things in a rush."

"Well," the kid blew his nose. "When Russ left me solo, I tried to coerce the creep to play along, but he laughed in my face."

"The creep?" Nick asked.

Arjen Pender looked to where his uncle stood on the other side of the glass. He leaned forward.

"Can he hear me?" he whispered.

"No," Penzik assured him.

Nick studied the kid's body language once more. This kid was uneasy about something. And he hadn't stopped fidgeting with his smartphone since he'd snickered at an earlier comment. A light bulb went off in Nick's mind, uprooting the memory of another video taken on the sly.

"You have a video," Nick stated.

The kid's body jerked. Nick had nailed it.

"A sneak video of your mom?"

The kid nodded.

"And this creep?" Nick continued.

Another nod.

Holy shit. The mom had been having an affair. And the kid knew.

"How long had this," Nick cleared his throat, trying to find the right word, "activity been going on?"

"Six months," he said. "They had a steady appointment every fourteenth of the month. He came, did his thing, and left. My mom called their meets her relaxing sessions, as if they were yoga or some such bullshit."

Everyone was staring at the kid. *No wonder Pender had been pissed at the parental units.* This wasn't exclusively about being busted for smoking weed and being grounded.

"Did you post the video?" Nick asked.

"I threatened to, but the creep said to go ahead. It would be a résumé enhancer."

So the creep had laughed at the boy's blackmail attempt.

"Does this creep have a name?" Penzik asked.

The kid shrugged. "Don't know."

"Do you have the video?" Nick asked.

An affirmative nod of the head, a wary and miserable expression on his face.

Pender fidgeted with the phone, opening apps and setting things up. He flipped it so the screen would show what was there in landscape mode. With one finger, he slid the phone over to their side of the table.

The kid didn't want to see the show.

Nick hit Play.

They heard the sounds first, animalistic grunting that had the videographer, in this case, the son, giggling nervously and softly. The hallway, where Pender was taking the video, was a bit dim, but that didn't really matter. His goal was the open doorway into which, what Nick presumed, was the master bedroom. Once at the entrance, instead of turning into the doorway to video the action happening on the bed, the kid zoomed to the images reflected in a sizeable mirror above a dresser across the way from the action. It was a neat trick to capture everything that was going on inside and keeping his presence hidden.

What they saw next was appalling, made more so because it had been taped by the son. Witnessed by him. Captured by him.

As Nick watched the figures humping and groaning, he thought this went beyond sex in the raw. There was a current of desperation, of brutality, in the act. Nick's sense of disgust reared up. He'd seen a similar play a year ago when Sandra Ward had recorded her sex session with Laura's ex-husband, just before she'd butchered him on camera.

Nick hit Pause. It was hard to watch and he'd had enough. The kid didn't need to hear this any longer—didn't need a reminder of the images he'd so carelessly taken.

Nick exchanged glances with Sacco. "Brings back memories, doesn't it?" Sacco whispered in his ear.

Nick nodded.

Silence reigned in the room. After a few seconds, Steve Penzik went to the young man, who had been weeping silently, and helped him up by the arm.

"I think you've had enough," he said, sympathy brimming in his voice. He looked at Nick and Sacco. "I'll have a word with his uncle. They're staying with the aunt. Be right back."

"My phone?" the kid asked.

"We have to keep it for a bit, as evidence," Penzik told him. "We'll get it back to you as soon as we can."

Nick watched as Penzik spoke to the uncle, whose anxiety increased as Penzik spoke. When the conversation ended, Stefan Bogarde nodded and went with the uniform Shapel had called over to escort him to his sister's, his nephew held tightly inside the crook of his arm.

"That was ugly," Penzik said. "Wait till you see, Amarita. Homemade porn." He rubbed his face. "God, I'm getting too old for this shit."

"The kid took the video?" There was incredulity in Shapel's question.

Everyone nodded.

"Did the creep look familiar to any of you?" Penzik asked, rewinding the video.

"Was a bit hard to stomach," Nick answered. "Wasn't looking for details."

"Ready for Round Two?"

Not really.

They watched the performance once more, this time to the end. The kid had taken about thirty seconds more of video than what they'd seen. The camera phone recorded his sneakers for a bit as he retreated down the hallway. The video stopped.

Shapel whistled. No words necessary.

"Can you go back and pause it where he zoomed into the figures on the bed?" Nick asked.

Penzik obliged.

With his fingers, Nick expanded the image. Stared.

"No identifying tattoos that I can see," he said, but one arm was hidden from the camera.

Sacco pointed to the man's face, his bushy hair frozen. "Can you expand the view of the face?"

Nick obliged and, again, studied the image. "The hair is in the way. I can only see the tip of his nose."

He rewound and they watched. The hair was indeed hanging over the man's face, and moved to his heaving motion, but never enough to give them a clear view of his profile.

"The angle doesn't help," Penzik said.

"He's not that tall," Shapel noticed. "About one or two inches taller than our victim. That would make him five-ten, five-eleven?"

"We need to get this to IT," Penzik said. "Maybe they can spot something we haven't."

"Email it to Carpenter as well," Nick said. "The more eyes the better." He slid the phone over the table to Penzik, who placed it inside an evidence bag.

"Any news about the husband?" Nick asked.

"Stable condition. Heavily sedated, though," Shapel said. "They'll notify us when he's awake."

"Did you catch what the kid said? About someone ringing the bell?"

Penzik stared at Nick. "With our luck, it may have been the UPS guy leaving a package at the door. We'll check with the neighbors, see if someone saw something or has security footage."

Nick nodded. It was useless to stay there any longer. After brief goodbyes, they returned to the precinct, with the rain pelting and the temperatures dropping.

When Kravitz saw them, he waved them into his office.

"What's the rundown," he asked.

Nick closed the door. He quickly briefed the captain about Penzik's case.

"I'm glad my children and grandchildren are grown," Kravitz said. "Even more happy those grandkids don't have any children yet. What a mess."

"Captain, maybe it's time we bring Crime Stoppers in on this," Nick said. "Have them coordinate with the media."

"Do we have a clearer picture of the suspect in question, one that is not a shadow, or a naked ass humping in a video?"

"No."

Sacco jumped into the conversation. "We could hit the sick-mother angle."

"That's an idea," Nick said. "In either case, it will be out in the airways. Someone is bound to hear, wonder, even know."

"And show your hand to the suspect," Kravitz added. "The man would realize we are no longer dealing with his staged suicides, but with actual murder. He may go underground."

"There is that," Nick admitted.

"Let me mull this one over. If Penzik and Shapel don't have any footage, a photo, or a witness for the visitor to their victim, then we'll disseminate, let Crime Stoppers have a go at it." He glanced at both. "The barrage will be nonstop, and you'll be spending the next millennia following leads up your butt."

"Yeah." Nick slapped the chair arms and got up. So did Sacco. "But it's better than being dead in the water, like now."

"Heard Ramos was looking for you guys," Kravitz said to their backs.

Minutes later, Ramos waved them into her office.

"Got a confirmation about U4/DMSO toxicity from Suffolk," she said by way of greeting. "Same turd as ours. Asked their lab to expedite all trace analysis."

"They'll have results faster than ours?" Sacco commented.

"Hey, they have an itty-bitty county to deal with, and a state-of-the-art facility. Their wait lines are much, much shorter." She glanced back from studying some results on her computer screen. "Heard you saw another salacious video à la Sandra Ward this p.m. Is it true the son filmed it?"

"Yep."

"Sick."

"Do you have anything else for me?" Nick asked.

Ramos tapped her laptop screen. "This. Puzzling to say the least."

"What is it?" Sacco leaned forward to see better.

Ramos laughed and pushed Sacco back. "As if you could read analytical chemistry." She glanced back. "That, my boys, is DMSO. Traces of it all over every ligature, in all skin swabs, but nowhere else. Not in victim's moisturizers, creams, or makeup. Nowhere. And it is stumping me. I would blame MASPEC, but then it'd get mad at me. Temperamental machine."

"Is the DMSO prescribed?" Nick asked.

"I wish. It'd be traceable that way."

"So it's an over-the-counter thing," Sacco stated.

"Yes. Its benefits vary from the treatment of osteoarthritis to shingles. Usually bought at your friendly neighborhood health store either as a gel, cream, or even pill form."

"Or by mail, or the internet, I'm sure," Nick added. "I'll tell Carpenter. He can check if the victims bought that crap for personal use. Check Creasy's lab work. She may have used it in her work."

Ramos got up to get a report being spit out from the printer. She patted Nick's face on her way. "Done already. But, you're a man after my own heart."

"Brilliant minds do think alike," Nick joked, but turned serious. "Any speculations, Ramos?"

"Hell, Nick, plenty. But those don't count in my department."

"What about Creasy's product creams?"

"That's what's stumping me. Creasy's creams don't have a single atom of pink or DMSO. I've tested every single jar she made and had in her apartment. Only found Laurocapram. That applies to the other product from the lab, as well."

"We may need to contact M-Li Watson and Wexler to test their samples."

Ramos shook her head. "I think you're driving to a dead end there. You said they'd been experimenting with her cream already. DMSO wouldn't hurt them, but mixed with pink? They'd have wound up at the hospital, or dead. Besides, neither Watson nor Wexler showed symptoms of drug exposure during their interviews. And, trust me, they'd be symptomatic."

"Doesn't hurt to ask," Nick said.

"You heard about the date change of the memorial, again, right?" Sacco said.

"Yeah. Poor people." M-Li and the Isabel Creasy family had postponed the memorial yesterday. They had planned a small ceremony at St. Malachy's on Forty-Ninth and Eighth, planning to transport Isabel Creasy's ashes to Montana for burial. Unfortunately for them, Millsap had still not released Isabel Creasy's body for cremation. M-Li had decided to go ahead with the memorial sans ashes. She would not postpone it again, she said. She needed closure. So did the family. They, however, were very displeased and had let Nick know on Saturday when he'd had the misfortune to pass on the news.

"By the way, Nick, Carpenter was looking for you. Something about calendar appointments and sicko videos."

Nick smiled and left those two to their own devices. Things could be heating up between them and he wasn't about to become the third wheel.

He stopped by the elevators, checked his notes, and dialed M-Li's number.

"Mrs. Watson, this is Detective Larson."

"Hello, Detective." There was a small pause. "Is this official or unofficial business?"

"An inquiry."

"So I don't need to get my husband involved?" she asked, half-relieved. "David hasn't filed charges?"

Not yet.

"Mrs. Watson, how many jars of cream did Isabel Creasy give you as trial?"

"One. She gave another to EriK. Hold on." Her voice became muffled, as if she had placed a hand over the mic and was asking someone a question. She came back on. "Yes. EriK's here and he said one, also. We were supposed to use it daily for a month and fill out a questionnaire she had prepared for us after we finished the jar."

"Have you had any type of reaction to the cream?" he asked.

"None. Actually, it's extremely hydrating. Perfect for what we plan."

"Could you ask Mr. Wexler the same question, please?"

Same routine as a few seconds ago. "No. EriK says he hasn't experienced any problems with it, either. Is there an issue?"

"Not that I know of. But our lab supervisor has asked we get samples to verify a few discrepancies. Is it possible for you and Mr. Wexler to bring in those jars for testing? I promise we'll return them immediately."

"Not a problem. We can do that tomorrow, after the memorial." There was a pause. "Or you can come to the memorial and get them there."

"Can't promise anything. We're juggling simultaneous cases."

"Well, I'll remind EriK to bring his from home tomorrow. We can deliver them to you afterward."

"Thank you, Mrs. Watson. Appreciate the help."

Three minutes later, he walked inside Carpenter's IT cave. As usual, Carpenter was at his computer, typing furiously.

"You rang?" Nick said, staring at the monitor and the gibberish Carpenter input there at supersonic speed. He'd have a better chance of deciphering hieroglyphs than what was currently scrolling down the screen.

Without surfacing for breath, Carpenter tapped a very short stack of papers with his elbow. "The calendar timelines you wanted."

Nick reached over and took the sheets of paper. He held up a sealed evidence bag. "Is this what I think it is?"

Carpenter's glance was even quicker than the nod. "Man, talk about screwups. That kid is a sicko. His mom, well, I was horrified for the son. Some people don't get it."

"What's that?"

"That your selfish actions will stain someone else's life to the point of eternal, pathological dysfunction."

And that, Nick thought, was how you created some serial killers.

CHAPTER TWENTY-EIGHT

Wednesday, January 22

"YOU LOOK LIKE *The Thinker* of Rodin."

Nick glanced up. He had been spread out in the conference room since about eight in the a.m. with all his notes, the binders, and his laptop in a semicircle about him. It was now eight thirty. For about that long, he had been staring at the paused video with the naked figure of Clara Mulder's lover, not understanding why the need or the persistence. There was something about the man that had caught his attention, and he was almost certain it was the guy's hair. Now, why was that? He simply could not figure out exactly.

He pointed to a box at the other end of the table when his partner came inside.

"Compliments of Laura," he told Sacco.

At the mention of Laura's name, Ramos, who was not far behind Sacco, pushed him out of the way and beelined it to the box.

"Is this what I think it is?" She opened the lid, leaned in, and breathed. "OMG. I've died and gone to heaven."

Nick smirked.

"Are those flowers?" At Nick's nod, she turned back to the box. After a brief hesitation, Ramos picked a pink cupcake.

"Candied lavender and rose petals," Nick informed them. "Laura gave me a whole description about the frosting and the batter, but I honestly couldn't retain the jargon. I just enjoy the results."

"That is new," Sacco said, simply dipping his hand and grabbing the first cupcake he made contact with.

"New designs and flavors for her new venture," Nick answered.

He rewound and played the video. He'd muted the sound for everyone's benefit, especially his own. Concentrated on the image. There, a flash of something. Color. Or was it the woman's nail polish that peeked through the gaps of undulating, frizzy hair?

Nick rubbed his eyes. He'd been at this for the past half hour and hadn't gotten anywhere. He paused the video, leaned back in the chair, and took up the thinking pose once more.

"Don't stare, Ramos," he said. "It's rude."

She finished chewing. "You have the look."

"What?"

"The Look," she said, and grabbed another cupcake, a rose petal one this time. "The look that says your gut is churning. The look that says something is wrong. The look that will get us into trouble or solve the case."

"What's bothering you?" Sacco asked, sitting next to Nick.

Nick tapped his computer screen. "This guy."

"What about him?"

"There's something about the hair that is bothering me."

Ramos guffawed. "You're paying attention to guys' hairdos now, Larson?" She licked her lips and fingers daintily. "Never would have thought."

"Shut up, Ramos," he said. He played the tape for a few seconds, then tapped and paused. "There."

An infinitesimal flash of color.

"Looks like purple," Sacco said.

Ramos came around and squinted at the screen. "Nice ass," she said.

"Good grief, Ramos."

"Hey, it's true." After a few seconds she pointed. "Could be her nails showing. Safe bet is if her toes are painted purple..." She tapped the screen. "And they are, the fingernails probably match the color." She squinted some more. "Hard to tell. Her hands are obscured by the hair." She leaned back. "Love that gel color, though. Prismatic Fan is my favorite of the purples."

Nick stared some more. Vague rumblings in his subconscious fought their way toward the light. Where had he seen similar color and in the hair?

"Is this your attempt at a Venn diagram?" Ramos asked, pointing to his notepad.

"Failed attempt," Nick said. "Tried to place the women's appointments in order, see if some matched. Nada. The victims frequented establishments offering similar services, but unless you count the occasional Starbucks, those were not even on the same street, let alone the same borough. Some I couldn't even recognize, our victims kept using some sort of shorthand to identify their appointments."

Ramos picked up the list Carpenter had compiled and ran quickly through it.

"I recognize the name of a beauty salon here in the city. Very foo-foo, fee-fee. This store sells brand name makeup and perfumes at wholesale prices. Let's see..." She flipped to another page. "Food, restaurant, grocery..." She looked at Nick. "Someone liked their massages."

"That would be Creasy," Nick said. "Never missed her Friday, according to her friend and the spa's manager."

"Wasn't that Deep Tissue and Hot Stones?" Ramos asked.

"Yep."

"This isn't it." Ramos flicked the paper and scanned the top. "It's Latimer's list, and a different franchise."

A thought struggled and scrambled its way up Nick's brain. He stared at his notes.

"Son of a bitch."

He minimized the window with the paused video and opened a new one.

"Give me that list." He reached out, shaking his hand in impatience when Ramos didn't comply fast enough.

"Nick's on the hunt," she said, slapping the papers in his hand. "Fess up."

Nick shook his head and typed Scandinavian Therapy Industries Franchisees, LLC in the search window. Sure enough, bless Wikipedia, there it was, right smack at the top of the list."

Sacco, who had been watching Nick's frantic typing, whistled under his breath. "Chet Emberson's ex-client?"

Nick raised a finger as if to say, hold that thought, clicked on the link and scrolled down through the information quickly. The details about the corporation were long, from a general description of services, to history of founding, to expansion of new markets and products, to corporate governance. He scrolled down some more. There. There it was: a thorough list of the company's franchisees, their names, date of founding, and corporate information, nicely divided by continents, countries, and states.

"Which one?" Nick asked Ramos.

She pointed with her nail. "This one. Scandinavian Delight on Park."

"You know it?" Sacco asked.

"I go there, as a treat, when I can afford it. Great service."

Nick searched and, yes, there it was. Scandinavian Delight LLC, a franchise offered by the parent company STIF. He searched for Deep Tissue and, again, a franchise offered by STIF.

That was the link.

Son of a bitch.

No wonder something about the hair had bothered him. The color and the frizz.

In almost frenetic spasms, Nick opened Creasy's binder and flipped sections until he came upon the written statements from the incident at TeC4M. He had not read them, but had placed them in the to-do pile after they'd been interrupted by the Latimer case. He began skimming. *Let me be correct on this.* And there it was, bold as ever. He took his pencil and circled the misspelled word several times. He pointed.

"Suffolk sent me these," Carpenter interrupted, strolling in and waving several photos. "Thought you'd want to see them right away. They're from Mulder's next door neighbor's security camera." He saw the box and the empty discarded cupcake cups on the table. "Hey, are those from Laura?"

Nick reached over, snatched the photos, and splayed them in front of him.

The first showed a man, dressed in similar gear as the one from the Latimer's footage, carrying a similar black gym bag. No identifiable features, even when the image was better and closer up. The face was still half hidden by a hoodie, the latter puffed up on the top, as if the head were malformed. Reminded Nick of the Coneheads from SNL.

The second photo showed the woman greeting the man, a smile on her face, arms outstretched, as if expecting to give and receive a hug.

The third showed the woman closing the door, still having a conversation with the man. This time, however, the hoodie was down. And even though the man had his back turned to the camera, his head was slanted slightly to the right, listening to what Clara Mulder had to say.

Nick saw the man bun. The grotesque earlobes. But, above all, he recognized the grommets.

"It's EriK with-the-fucking-capital-letter-K Wexler," Nick said, everything coalescing in his brain. "Our common denominator and possible killer."

Nick grabbed Carpenter by the arm and forced sat him in front of the laptop.

"Get me everything and anything on EriK Wexler—birth certificate, driver's license, certificates, or professional licenses. Family members." He took a cupcake from the box and placed it next to the laptop. "Here, some sustenance while you dig around. I need an address for a warrant. All phone accounts, screen names, social media. We've got to tell the captain."

"Tell me what," Kravitz said from the doorway. "Why is everybody crammed in here and not working?" He saw the cupcake next to Carpenter, then zeroed in on the box. "Laura sent these?"

"Captain, we may have our killer."

Kravitz's hand stilled above a lavender cupcake. "May? Not definitely have?"

"A definite person of interest," Nick said and went through everything, showed him everything. "We have probable cause for a warrant to search his premises and we need to bring him in for questioning."

"Suffolk has probable cause," Kravitz said. "These are their photos, their case."

"Suffolk wouldn't have smelled the shit if we had not shown them the turd," Sacco said, a bit exasperated. "They were closing it as a suicide."

"Captain," Nick cut in. "All our cases predate the Long Island one. Wexler is the common denominator in all. He's the one who was friends with Creasy, who possibly knew Waitre through the

Creasy connection, who worked at Latimer's client's franchise. He's the one who shows up on the same day that Clara Mulder dies. The only thing we need is for the victim's son to corroborate if the man in this photo is the creep he mentioned. We need to grill Wexler. Check that gym bag."

"Bring him in," Kravitz said and grabbed two cupcakes. "I'll discuss probable with Aaniyah."

Armed with sustenance, Kravitz left.

Nick grabbed his files, notes, and binders and exited the conference room. After leaving everything on his desk, he retrieved his gun, and met Sacco in the hallway.

"We'd better get going," Nick said. "The memorial starts in forty minutes."

"Before, during, or after?" Sacco asked.

"Before, preferably, if we get there in time. Don't want to mess things during the memorial service. Mrs. Watson's life has been messed up enough already."

Nick paused at the threshold of the conference room. "Carpenter, show me the goods as soon as you have them. We'll be back soon."

"Ah, Lieutenant? We have a problem."

What now?

"Make it quick."

"There's no DMV record for an EriK Wexler. Even if he doesn't drive, he'd need the ID to get a job, a professional license."

"Call Deep Tissue. Better yet, go there. Get Wexler's W-4 and job application from the manager, or a copy of his certificate or license, a social security number, or whatever he used in order to work there."

"Without a warrant?"

"Take Ramos. She won't leave without the info."

Sacco chuckled all the way to the car.

The day was turning out much better than the so-called meteorological experts had predicted the day before. As Nick headed west on Forty-Ninth, he was glad the rain had stopped around midnight, and temperatures had hovered above the freezing mark just enough so that the promised ice-rink streets had not materialized. Sunrise had also brought with it temperate weather, if you could call forty degrees balmy, but it made the day more pleasant than yesterday. If they had to wait outside for Wexler to arrive for the memorial service, it was nicer than having to huddle in the cold rain.

He parked opposite the church, sprinted across, and opened the thick, solid, street level wooden door, sprinted up the staircase to the church door, and into the church proper.

St. Malachy's Roman Catholic Church, where M-Li Watson was holding the memorial service for her friend, was a beautiful little church, built in Gothic Revival architectural style, and had stood between Broadway and Eighth Avenue since the early 1900s. Better known as The Actors' Chapel, its proximity to the theater district allowed it to cater to the needs of both theater and community residents in the surrounding area; its Encore Community Center was also well known for serving the needs of the elderly by providing healthy meals, shopping escorts, and social events in the basement. Meeting space was provided during the week to other groups, including the "salon" gatherings of the St. Genesius Society, where actors, writers, directors, and comics met for talkbacks.

Nick remembered attending the occasional concert there, as well, where he'd been awed by the best musicians and choral voices in the city.

"Wow," Sacco whispered. "Very Gothic."

"Teleports you across the pond, doesn't it?" Nick said, equally soft. He inhaled the smell of incense, candles, and beeswax.

On the transept, nearby the first pew, a blown-up photograph of Isabel Creasy, who was forever captured young in death, had been placed on an artist's easel stand. M-Li Watson and her husband stood by the photograph, quietly speaking to one another. About a dozen people were in attendance, scattered around the front pews, reading what Nick saw were memorial booklets. Of EriK Wexler, there was no sign.

Almost as a final farewell, M-Li caressed the face of the woman with trembling fingers. Her husband squeezed her shoulder, and led her to the front pew.

She froze at sight of them. "Detectives?"

"What are you doing here?" Mr. Watson asked, a bit more irritated.

"We wouldn't have interrupted unless it was urgent," Nick said.

"Couldn't this have waited until later?" M-Li asked.

Not for what we need to do. How to tell this woman a friend and possible future business partner was a potential suspect in her best friend's murder? That Mr. Wexler would not be attending the memorial because Nick was taking him in for questioning?

"Where is Mr. Wexler?" Nick asked as blandly as possible.

"He's bringing in the flowers," M-Li said. "Is there a problem?"

The elevator announced its arrival with a slight whirr and a ping. M-Li's attention shifted and she pointed. "There he is." She breathed in, her intake quivery, almost weepy. "Oh, they are beautiful."

Nick turned to see EriK Wexler holding the elevator door with one foot and dragging out two ornamental funeral flower arrangements. He placed them out of the way next to the pew nearest the elevator, released the door, and straightened. He waved to M-Li to join him and noticed Nick was there with Sacco, waiting.

He locked eyes with Nick's hard ones. The smile that was forming froze. And, without warning, he bolted for the exit before Nick had taken one step in his direction.

"Shit."

Nick ran down the nave and bounded down the exit steps two at a time, with Sacco inches behind. He slammed open the chapel's door, not caring who he rammed it against, and caught a glimpse of Wexler's pelting figure to his right, in a mad dash toward Eighth.

He flew after him.

"Call it in," he shouted at Sacco, not waiting to see if he followed. If the man reached Eighth Avenue, the chase would be a nightmare, giving Wexler a perfect avenue to disappear. Nick couldn't afford to lose him.

Not for the first time in his stint as a New York cop, Nick cursed the streets, the traffic, the mob of pedestrians, and the dolt tourists that got in the way. A few yards ahead, Wexler rounded the corner, heading uptown. Nick, with shield high in the air for everyone to see, kept running and shouting, "Freeze, Wexler. NYPD. Damn it. Freeze."

He rounded the corner himself, and almost crashed into a shopper coming out of the Food Emporium. He had to do some fancy maneuvering not to fall flat on his face. The man with the groceries flipped him the bird and shouted the typical New York niceties after him. But, damn it, in those few seconds, Wexler had gained distance. Nick ran faster, cursing.

"NYPD. Stop, damn it."

Wexler glanced back and plunged into the waiting crowd of tourists standing by to get into a double-decker sightseeing bus, the ones that usually snarled traffic all around Midtown. He then pelted across Fiftieth street, regardless of cars, taxis, pedestrians, and buses, with Nick a few seconds behind.

The sidewalk after Fiftieth became narrower, so much so that people had to perform quick maneuvers to avoid pedestrians, tchotchke shop stands displaying postcards and cheap tourist souvenirs, and floral shop buckets holding colorful daily bargains. Nick lost Wexler for a few seconds until he dashed left, aiming for the west side of the avenue.

That was when Nick realized the man was shooting for the subway station across the way.

"Oh, hell, no."

Desperate, he glanced at the traffic signal back on Fiftieth and saw it was green heading east. Pushing aside people crossing Eighth, and leapfrogging over a dolly full of boxes for delivery which a UPS delivery man was carting across the street, Nick ran in an intercepting course toward Wexler until a taxi pulled up to the curb, effectively blocking his way.

With a ferocity he hadn't felt in a while, Nick punched the hood of the cab, twirled around the fender, and ran to the subway entrance. Wexler was nowhere in sight.

Nick scrambled down the steps to platform level and fare control, but he couldn't see Wexler. He slammed his shield against the Plexiglas barrier. "Did someone jump the turnstile?"

The token operator pointed. "Went one level down to the E train."

Nick had heard the rumbling and screeching of the train in its approach or departure echoing around the area. He leapt over the turnstile with the words "Hope you get the bastard" coming from inside the token booth. He practically skipped three steps at a time going down sideways, but by the number of people disgorged and crowding the steps and escalators at the bottom, he knew the subway had just spit everyone out.

When he hit the platform, the train was clunking merrily away down the tunnel.

Winded, spitting mad, and not believing their bad luck, he dialed Sacco to find out where he was and to come pick him up.

By the time they arrived back at the precinct, Nick had marshaled the troops to scour the city, had officers surveilling Wexler's employer and Watson's nail spa, another officer ordered to escort M-Li Watson back to the precinct after the memorial service, and had gotten hold of Aaniyah Foster to set up a meeting with a judge as soon as one was available. Nick would fill out the affidavit to search Wexler's home as soon as he stepped inside the office, but there was a little hitch. He could not fill out the statement of purpose without a freaking address. And Carpenter was having issues. Nick didn't understand what the hiccup was.

It was like Wexler did not exist except in a mysterious, invisible ether.

Nick stamped all the way to Carpenter's office, where Horowitz had directed him. Oh, and Horowitz wanted Nick to thank Laura for the cupcakes. They were delicious.

"Here, try this," Ramos said, ignoring the men as they stepped inside. She recited some numbers while leaning over Carpenter, who was still working on his computer.

"Talk to me," Nick said, when what he really wanted was to shout until the windows imploded. How was it effing possible not to find someone in today's super connectivity highway?

"No quips, Ramos," Sacco warned behind Nick. "He's sweaty and in a foul mood."

"So are we." She slipped a sheet of paper across the table to Nick. It was the W-4. "The spa faxed this over. States that EriK Wexler resides at this address in Astoria. But when we tried to verify the address, so we don't get screwed, public records show it's a home, the owner listed as a Ms. E. W. Ormond."

"Did you try the Social?"

"That's what we're inputting right now."

"Any luck with DMV?" Sacco asked.

"Nothing under Wexler."

"What the hell kind of ID did he present when applying for a job at the spa?" Nick said.

"Look for yourself. Right face, right name, wrong address, and wrong driver's license number. I think it's a fake. Fill in the blanks from a stolen one."

"What about therapist licenses?"

"Those have his name on it," Carpenter said. "Legit. Online and trade school courses. Certified five years ago as a therapist."

"Where the hell did this guy come from?" Nick was ready to pull his hair out.

The computer pinged and Carpenter went back to it, typed a few lines of code.

"Ah, Nick?"

"What?"

"Did a search on anything with EriK Wexler, E. Wexler, and the social security number. Got this."

Nick stared. Last year's tax returns. Same address in Astoria. But the name was wrong. At least not what he expected. The social security had spit out, not EriK, but an Erica W. Ormond.

"The dead sister?" Sacco asked.

Nick shook his head. It felt like his brain was encased in a huge, constricting spiderweb. "Something is not right. Maybe the sister is not dead, if he has a sister. Mother? Carpenter, do a nationwide search for Erica W. Ormond, E. W. Ormond for birth certificates. Also DMV searches nationwide for that name."

Horowitz came in to advise the uniform had brought in Mr. and Mrs. Watson, and he'd placed them in the conference room.

"Thanks, Stan," Nick said. "I'll be right there." He turned to Carpenter. "Where's my laptop?"

"On top of your desk," he said.

Good God, the way they were striking out they'd need a reverse genealogy expert to figure out this veritable who's who labyrinth of names and misdirection.

As soon as they stepped inside the conference room, Mr. Watson went on the attack.

"This is outrageous," he said. His wife was in tears, again. "Aren't you satisfied with the commotion you caused at the memorial? Wasn't that enough? Now we're brought here as though we're criminals?"

"Mr. Watson, please." Nick gestured for him to take a seat. "You can file a complaint afterward, but right now, I need to ask your wife a few questions. EriK Wexler has to be found."

"I don't understand," she said, wiping at her tears.

"Mrs. Watson, do you know an Erica Ormond?"

"No." She looked at her husband. "Does that name ring a bell to you?"

He shook his head.

"Do you know if EriK has or had a sister? A mother?"

"Never mentioned a sister. But Isabel said his mom was sick, and he was taking care of her. Ovarian cancer. Last stages."

"Did you ever visit Mr. Wexler's home?"

"I didn't. But Isabel did. Went there several times, although, when we all met, it was usually either in Isabel's brownstone or my nail salon. More convenient, since we all worked in the city. I know he lived somewhere in Astoria."

"Did Isabel say anything else about him?"

M-Li Watson was thoughtful for a while. "He never really talked about his personal life. Very shy about it. Lived for the moment and his work. Only once did he mention where he was from. Isabel and EriK were having a friendly exchange about whose small town was more Podunk than the other's."

"Where was that?" Nick asked.

"Somewhere in Connecticut. Oh, and he did say his parents had divorced when he was young."

"Is that all?"

She shrugged. "Pretty much. I got together with them to discuss the new venture, more often than not. Isabel was the one who was really close to him."

Her husband chimed in. "But didn't she say she was really pissed at him when you saw her on that Friday? That she was going to confront him about an issue that had cropped up?"

"That's right," she said. "Goodness, with everything that was happening at the time with her move, the product testing, and everything else, I completely forgot." Her eyes teared. "And then, she died."

"Did she say why she was upset?" The conversation with M-Li's employee, the wax expert, bubbled up, about Isabel being angry and her "not with my stuff" remark.

"No. We were excited about her move, her new apartment, her new life." She swallowed. "No."

"Can you at least tell us what is going on?" asked Mr. Watson.

Nick didn't want to say the man M-Li had been friendly with was probably her best friend's killer. That news would have to come later.

"I'm sorry, but I can't," was all Nick divulged.

"In that case, Detectives." Mr. Watson stood. "Our guests are waiting for us. And no offense, we would like to see the last of this place. We are free to leave, correct?"

Nick nodded. "I'm sorry your memorial was disturbed."

"Everything around Isabel's death has been disturbing," M-Li said, following her husband out of the conference room.

As soon as Horowitz took over escorting the Watsons out of the precinct, Nick turned to his office, phone to his ear.

"Yo," Carpenter said.

"Anything?"

"Computer still searching."

"Concentrate around Connecticut. That's where Mrs. Watson said he was born. Also check hospitals and hospice care on a Wexler or an Ormond admitted with terminal ovarian cancer."

"It'll take time."

Wasn't that what they didn't have?

"I'll be at my desk filling out the affidavit. Just get me the right name and the right address. I don't need any screwups so that a clever lawyer can get the warrant tossed out of evidence at trial."

After twenty minutes of crossing his t's and dotting his i's, and leaving an address and possible aka's blank, Nick searched for Sacco.

"Let's go," he said. "Carpenter got the parents' names on Ormond's birth certificate, found the marriage certificate, and gave us a shitload of numbers we need to call."

But hunting down Wexler's parents was turning out to be exhausting work. From Carpenter's list, broken down by surnames within town, county, and state, they'd spoken to many, but had struck out as much.

They'd been working the phones for hours, leaving messages to call back for those not home, dealing with callers who were either nice, or rude, or simply uncooperative. Not many appreciated having the NYPD calling them at home.

Nick crossed out another Wexler name off the list. Sacco was working half the Ormonds, while Ramos had the other half. However, at the rate they were going, Wexler had no worries. A leisurely cruise to Argentina would sail faster.

He scrubbed his face with his hands. His eyes were gritty and he was running out of spit. "Anyone want a soda, or water, or anything?"

Headshakes as they continued to speak softly into the phones.

Nick stretched, went to the door, and asked Horowitz to bring in some water bottles from the refrigerator. He sat back, picked up the phone, and dialed the next number.

When the phone was answered, Nick went into his spiel. "Good afternoon, Ma'am. I'm Detective Nick Larson from the NYPD. I'm looking for a Mr. Mathis Wexler, who was married to a Miss Jill Ormond in Washington, Litchfield County, Connecticut in 1989."

"That's my brother-in-law, Detective."

Nick was shocked into pausing. "Your brother-in-law is Mathis Wexler."

"Yes, but he doesn't live in the area anymore. Moved to Kansas a while back."

Nick covered the mouthpiece and waved for Sacco and Ramos to stop and pay attention.

"We need to speak to him, Ma'am. It's rather urgent. Do you have a phone number where we can reach him?"

"I'm sorry, Detective Larson. I don't give out phone numbers. I can have him call you at your work."

Nick rattled off the precinct number and his extension.

"Please, Ma'am. It's urgent we speak to him."

"I'll relay the message." And she hung up.

"Think we got a break?" Sacco asked.

"Let's hope so."

Twenty minutes later, the call was patched through. He put it on speaker so everyone could hear.

"Detective Larson, this is Mathis Wexler. My sister-in-law said it was urgent I call. What is this about?"

"Sir, we are working four cases where your son, EriK Wexler, is a person of interest. But we can't find his name in any legal records or documentation. It does show, however, the name of Erica W. Ormond. Is that your daughter, sir?"

The silence was such that Nick thought he had lost the connection.

"Sir?"

"I never had a daughter, Detective Larson. Just a son." There was pain in the voice. "His name is Nathan, and I haven't seen him in years."

"I'm sorry, sir. But I am a bit confused. Did your ex-wife remarry? Is this EriK her son?"

More silence, then a pained sigh.

"What I am saying, Detective Larson, is that Nathan and Erica are the same person. It was my ex-wife who filled out the birth certificate. Erica Wexler Ormond is my son. Jill simply fulfilled her fantasies... she had always wanted a baby girl, and my son paid for her delusions."

Understanding reared its ugly head. Nick looked at Sacco and Ramos, and both had a sick expression on their faces. They finally had all the pieces, and the picture they formed was horrifying.

They now had a legal name to place on the affidavit for the warrant: one Erica Wexler Ormond, resident of Astoria, also known as EriK Wexler, massage therapist and executioner extraordinaire.

One for Kilcrease's case studies.

CHAPTER TWENTY-NINE

Wednesday, February 5

TWO WEEKS LATER, Nick watched as EriK Wexler was brought into interrogation, hale and whole.

Two weeks ago, the same EriK Wexler had been an inch away from greeting the Devil.

That, to Wexler's displeasure, had been thwarted.

And it had been all Nick's fault.

Two weeks ago, after descending onto a simple two-story home in Astoria near the Steinway Street subway station, Nick and Sacco, with warrant in hand, had found documentation, health insurance bills and statements of the facility caring for Wexler's mother. And, true to Nick's gut, they'd found EriK Wexler sitting by his dead mother's bedside when they arrived, gym bag open at his feet.

"I should have done this a long time ago," he'd told Nick, unmoving. No emotion. No regret. No guilt. Later, Totes would report that Wexler had slathered his mother with Isabel's Creasy's aromatic cream, laced with a lethal dose of DMSO and pink combined, and had watched as his mother had basically suffocated to death. Hypoventilation, Totes had reported, caused by substance-induced respiratory suppression. Wexler's mother had not received the mercy of the ligature, and had clawed for breath and oxygen until her carbon dioxide levels stopped her heart.

Two weeks ago, Wexler had also smeared his arms with the same substance he'd spread over his victims so carefully, counting on following his mother to the afterlife. It would have been a happy day in hell had that happened, if it were not for Nick. He simply had refused to allow Wexler to exit this world so effortlessly and without consequences.

Oh, hell, no.

He'd moved heaven and earth to have the doctors counteract the effects of the drug. For a week, doctors and nurses fought to bring him back. And now he was here, face to face with the piper, so to speak, with a full house of spectators on the other side of the two-way mirror.

Kilcrease was there. He'd spoken to the father multiple times since that initial phone call. He'd learned Mathis Wexler had fought the courts for years, trying to save his son, while his ex-wife pumped the child with female hormones to convert a delusion into a reality. Nathan Wexler, throughout all his formative years, had lived a life half as a girl and half as a boy, until the courts had revoked visiting rights to the father, under the guise it would be too traumatic for the child to have his identity changed so fecklessly every weekend. Kilcrease had also learned EriK Wexler, emphasis on the K, had attempted suicide several times, especially after puberty. The last attempt had altered him in such a manner he'd left home for parts unknown, only coming back when his mother fell ill with cancer.

Ramos was also there. She had discovered jars of DMSO and pink in an impromptu lab in Wexler's kitchen, where the man had mixed his lethal lotion. She'd also found, at the bottom of Wexler's gym bag, rock fragments from a broken basalt rock that matched the one she'd found in the ice. Wexler had used those for hot/cold stone massages with his private clients—the reason the silicone mold was kept in Creasy's freezer. Wexler had admitted Isabel Creasy loved her cold stone therapy. He'd performed this service many times at her house, as a service to a friend.

Carpenter wouldn't have missed this even if they'd given him a VIP invitational tour to the Apple corporate headquarters. He'd found the victims' phones in a drawer by Wexler's bed, as well as the burner phones he'd used to contact each woman. Carpenter discovered Wexler had been using different handles, including the elusive one of HighMaster212, via his computer.

Waste not, want not, Nick thought.

Sacco and Kravitz were there to hear the confession.

Hell of a party.

"How are you feeling today, Mr. Wexler?" Nick asked, as the man was cuffed to the table.

"Fine, thank you."

"You understand why you are here, correct?"

Wexler nodded.

Nick took the photo of Micaela Latimer and placed it in front of Wexler.

"I'm just curious, Mr. Wexler. Why did you choose her?" Nick asked.

Wexler studied the face. "She needed me." He looked at Nick. "Do you know how many people spill out their lives and sorrows on a massage table? I listened and relieved her. But it was a physical relief. I knew her pain, her division. I had struggled with it for years, so I understood her. What she didn't realize was that she would never be happy. But she wasn't strong enough to change, or to end her misery. So I helped." he said simply. "She was grateful, at the end."

Nick slid Jessica Waitre's photo next to Latimer's.

"Why her?" Nick asked.

"Fragile soul. Didn't understand the world, and couldn't cope with the world's cruel indifference and apathy." He chuckled. "Thought the world was ending, too. Ridiculous. It didn't matter, though. I helped end the world for her."

Nick stared, burying his revulsion as best he could. He placed the photo of Desha Adnet next to that of Jessica.

"What about him?"

"It was only fitting that he should keep her company in death. She so loved him." He leaned forward, his eyes earnest. "Jessica was convinced Desh was leaving her. Told me she'd do anything to prevent that. When he came in, I was prepping her. I locked the bathroom, turned on the shower, and waited. Never saw me coming. Struggled some, but I'm way stronger." He shrugged.

"Why, you're the very image of mercy aren't you?"

Wexler nodded in almost childlike agreement. "That is my purpose in life, Detective. I couldn't understand why my suicide attempts were always unsuccessful, although I tried to end my life many times. Then it came to me. My path was clear—to help those who needed to die but couldn't. To fulfill their wishes. I only helped those, who were lost and hurt, to attain peace. To find their final sleep. Forever apart from the lies of the world, which had made their lives loathsome."

Nick controlled his reactions. Lifted the photograph of Clara Mulder from the file and placed it beside the others.

"Why her?"

"What a screwup," Wexler said and laughed. Actually laughed in amusement. "Had a husband who adored her, and yet she felt the need for punishment. Sex and pain were one for her." He shrugged. "So I gave her what she needed."

"Forgive me if I'm a bit confused," Nick said. "She didn't want to die, and I'm sure she didn't request your help. So, why?"

"Her dick son," he answered. "Threatened to expose me. Can't have my clients cancel on me because of bad press." Wexler's face turned serious. "I take my career very seriously. Have never touched anyone improperly while at my jobs. Clara was no longer a client."

In your mind, perhaps, Nick thought.

"I was going to wring the neck of the sick little voyeur of the son," Wexler said, without prompting. "I waited for him to come home, but he never showed. So I left."

That kid would never know how lucky he'd been.

Lastly, Nick took the photo of Isabel Creasy and placed it on top of the others.

"Why her, EriK?" Nick asked. "She was your friend. She had a world of opportunities ahead of her. She was finally happy. I'm certain she didn't ask for your help." He leaned back to study him better. "So, why?"

Wexler's forefinger traced the image of the woman.

"Do you know you can buy pink on the internet as a research chemical? For thirty dollars a gram you can even have it delivered to your home. I wasn't calming my clients enough before they suffocated. Victor's violent struggles, when I strangled him, taught me to find a better, more gentle way." He sighed.

"You mean Victor Hugo?"

He nodded. "The idea came to me while I was taping the bag around Victor's head. I'd heard murmurs about U4 on the streets and had seen some of the effects from the druggies hanging out around the city. Researched it. Discovered I could mix it with topical creams, add DMSO for even better skin absorption, and massage it in. Perfect relaxation. So I ordered it, using Isabel's tax id. Unfortunately, she discovered what I'd done and confronted me. Said she'd report me. I had no choice."

Nick couldn't believe his ears. "Wait. So you're telling me you killed Isabel Creasy because she got in your way?" he asked, incredulously.

"Yes."

Well, hell.

CHAPTER THIRTY

Wednesday, February 12

THE NIGHT WAS crisp. Promefheus, carrying fire and bound in all its golden glory, benevolently oversaw the skaters before him at Rockefeller Plaza. After weeks from hell, this afternoon Nick and the gang had left the precinct on the dot, as if they were students playing hooky. They'd gathered their significant others to celebrate a successful release at end of shift and had spent the afternoon and early evening at El Torero's Happy Hour, downing drinks and tapas. Dinner at Pasta & Pesto followed. Now, well wined and dined, they'd walked to Rockefeller Center. Laura, pressed against Nick's side, was chuckling softly at the antics of Carpenter and his girlfriend, who'd decided to skate in The Rink. Sacco and Ramos were shouting inanities at them and laughing uproariously.

Life tonight was good.

More than good.

Perfect.

The stress was fading. After seven intense days of crossing all their t's and dotting all their i's in the Wexler killings, the captain had given them a day off tomorrow. A well-deserved day off, since more hard work awaited when they returned. Nick's interviews with Wexler had pointed to other murders disguised as suicides. They would need to slog through all the case files regurgitated from the RTCC and figure out which ones had Wexler's fingerprints all over them.

The media, when the killings were revealed, had not been kind either throughout this past week. They had bitched, nonstop, about how irresponsible NYPD's behavior had been. How reckless for not alerting the public about this serial killer. "Cover-up",

"Conspiracy" shouted the print headlines. Transparency and accountability were other choice nouns spit out through the airwaves. The mayor and the governor had latched on, echoing the media's sentiment in every news outlet, grandstanding as usual. The police commissioner, the chief, the PBA, Nick's captain, and the rest of the Sixteenth Precinct hadn't given a crap about what they'd thought.

They'd gotten their killer. End of story.

Nick nuzzled Laura's neck, nipping and soothing, delighting in the soft tremors his touch generated.

"Oh, ho," Laura whispered and nudged him.

"What?" Nick's head came up. Laura pointed to the skating ring.

"OMG, he's lost his mind," Sacco blurted in between chuckles.

"Don't mess things up, PC," encouraged Ramos.

Nick concentrated on the skaters, saw Carpenter on one knee, hands extended toward his girlfriend.

"The kid's proposing?" Nick asked and guffawed. *So that was the surprise Carpenter had mentioned at dinner.* "About damn time."

"Don't you dare refuse him, Stacey," Ramos scolded.

Carpenter waved them to shut up.

Every person in and around the rink clapped, the volume getting louder when Carpenter placed the ring on his fiancée's finger...roared when they kissed.

"This is our cue to exit, stage left," Nick said.

"Damn right," said Sacco. "My gonads are starting to shrink."

"Want me to warm them?" Ramos asked.

Nick stared at them. No comeback from Sacco, which said a lot, and his partner's eyes had turned serious, questioning.

In answer, Ramos slid her arm around Sacco's waist. Sacco didn't think twice. Like a weathervane changing direction, he turned and headed toward Fifth Avenue, Ramos pressed to his side.

Nick whistled.

"You think? Finally?" Laura said. They watched Sacco and Ramos disappear left at the end of the esplanade of the Channel Gardens.

"If they don't, I'll be severely pissed and out twenty bucks."

Laura laughed.

"Cab or walk?" he asked Laura.

"Walk."

Hand in hand, they strolled south down Fifth Avenue, toward their apartments. Nick breathed deeply. The city had been merciful this night, with temperatures in the high forties. Every New Yorker had gushed out in celebration of the fact, mingling with tourists, filling the streets, enjoying the town, the night, and life in general.

Rare moments for Nick. Moments he keenly delighted in when they happened.

"I've made an executive decision," Laura said.

"And what's that?"

"I'm taking tomorrow off, too."

Nick stopped. Enfolded her. Tasted her. Ignored the whistles and the "get a room" comments surrounding them.

He took her hand once more and ambled across Forty-Ninth.

"Tonight's perfect, isn't it?" Laura said, a tone of wonder in her voice.

"Yeah. Something to always remember."

"Think it'll last?"

Nick thought for a moment.

"For a little while."

"Yeah." She let go of his hand and wrapped her arm around Nick's waist.

"It doesn't mean we won't get on each other's nerves," Nick said.

"I'm counting on it."

Nick laughed. A few seconds later, however, he turned serious. "Just promise me one thing. Don't give up on me."

She framed his face with her gloved hands.

"Never."

The complete trust and love he saw there disarmed and scared him.

"Laura, I'm serious. Things have a habit of turning to shit when I least expect them. The job always takes a toll."

"Have you forgotten the bane of my existence? A leech has better table manners than her after sucking their fill of blood."

Nick closed his eyes. Kilcrease had texted him today that Sandra Ward would be released three weeks from now. Hopefully that would be the end of the sister saga. Medicated and incarcerated, never to bother them again.

The best-laid plans of mice and men...

"Let's not spoil this night with work and psychos." He grabbed her hand and pulled her at a quick clip to the corner of Forty-Eighth and Fifth. He raised his hand and whistled for a cab.

"In a rush?" She was breathless and laughing.

"Damn right. Haven't gotten to dessert yet. And I'm planning on seconds."

The End

Acknowledgments

When the idea of a Detective Nick Larson germinated in my devious mind, I knew I was in for a ride. What I didn't expect was for it to be a space launch.

And what a ride it's been.

The seed's germination was in 2004, when I wrote a short story for a critique group at FIU, led by the incredible John Dufresne. That story turned out to be the first chapter of the novel. The tillering stage came in 2014, but after the death of my beautiful mother, depression set in and there was no way I could write. I planted another seed, which launched my first short story collection in 2016: The Fish Tank: And Other Short Stories. Within the covers of that collection, my prequel short story "Mirror, Mirror," was born.

I really did not dive into the writing of this novel until late 2018. First came the research. Then, the sifting of all the information. Then, the characters' list. Finally, the calendar of events.

Arduous to say the least. Don't know the times I was completely cross-eyed with the elements of the novel, making sure there were enough hints, and red herrings...that the characters were well-developed, and that the crime and the plot was unique.

I think I passed the test.

Above all, I'd like to extend my most grateful and heartfelt thanks to Detective III Jorge Luis Ramos (Ret.) of the Los Angeles Police Department for his insight, his patience, and his guidance during the creation of this novel. Any, and every single mistake in police procedure is mine, and mine alone.

I want to thank my wonderful BETA reader Margarita Torres, a true mystery/detective aficionado, for her comments. She was a true weathervane for direction on a true course, or a complete bust.

To Anita Mumm, from Mumm's the Word Editorial Services: thank you for your wonderful developmental editing. You steered the ship into harbor.

Toni Lee: thanks, thanks, thanks. Without your eagle-eyed proofreading, the novel would not be the best it could be for publication.

To Scott Carpenter, as always, my gratitude for an incredible cover. If we lived closer, I'd bring chocolate chip cookies and tacos in celebration.

To Meredith Bond, for incredible formatting.

Lastly, to my husband and family...I love you. Thank you for your patience and love.